B

ANDREW TAYLOR and University in widely and worked London, but gave up his work to concentrate on his writing. He now lives in Gloucestershire, near the Forest of Dean, with his wife Caroline and their children.

'Another cracking yarn, well conceived and totally riveting. Andrew Taylor paints a fascinating picture of a corrupt world turned inside out and feeding on its own poisons – and he enhances his growing reputation as one of Britain's most accomplished young thriller writers'
The Citizen

'Mr Taylor is a sophisticated writer. He handles dialogue smoothly and naturally, his characters are believable' *New York Times Book Review*

THE SECOND MIDNIGHT

'An ingenious idea . . . echoes of Le Carré'
Christopher Pym, *Punch*

'First-class adventure' *The Irish Times*

'An intriguing story told in sharp, vivid prose . . . an excellent novel' *Yorkshire Post*

ANDREW TAYLOR

BLACKLIST

FONTANA/Collins

First published in Great Britain by
William Collins Sons & Co. Ltd 1988

First published in Fontana Paperbacks 1989

Copyright © Andrew Taylor 1988

Printed and bound in Great Britain by
William Collins Sons & Co. Ltd, Glasgow

For Caroline again
with love and thanks

PROLOGUE

'Beautiful?' the fat man said in English. He waved across the oil-stained water towards the coastline of Asia.

It wasn't beautiful at all.

'Yes,' Claybrook said.

The Turk slithered along the rail until his arm touched Claybrook's. Claybrook edged away.

'In the fall,' the fat man continued, 'the nights grow longer.'

Claybrook tightened his grip on the rail. Out of the corner of his eye he could see a pinstriped sleeve next to his. The cuff was frayed. One of the buttons was missing.

'No?' the man prompted.

For the first time Claybrook looked directly at him. The Turk wasn't fat at all. He was a thin man inside a fat man's clothes.

'The fall?' Claybrook said reluctantly. This was happening in the wrong place and at the wrong time. 'The English call it autumn.'

He would have liked to glance over his shoulder to see if anyone was in earshot. He heard and felt the throb of the ferry's engines. Seagulls screamed. Behind him people were having conversations he didn't understand. A baby cried.

The Turk had a black plastic briefcase in his free

hand. He lifted it on to the rail. He changed his mind and hugged it to his chest. His green eyes were fixed on Haydarpasha Station. They were watering.

'Eleven o'clock tonight,' the Turk whispered. He was having trouble breathing. His breath came in waves towards Claybrook's nostrils. 'The Red Dahlia on Siraselviler Caddesi. You know? In Taksim? It is a nightclub with a disco.'

Claybrook nodded.

'Good.' The Turk shot out his wrist and looked at his digital watch as though remembering he had another appointment. He smiled unexpectedly, exposing yellow teeth.

'Have a good day,' he whispered.

He backed away from the rail. He waddled into the crowd at the head of the nearest companionway and vanished down the steps. He was a thin man but he waddled.

Claybrook dined at the hotel.

It was fortunate that no one at the Consulate had offered to put him up. He didn't need to make excuses. The meal was no better than the hotel.

Afterwards Claybrook went up to his room and finished the letter to Patricia. Writing to her was a form of torture. It reminded him that they weren't together. When he was away from her she was reduced to a memory. She became no more real to him than she would be if she were dead. In his bad moments he sometimes wondered if the years they had had together would be worth the wrench when death separated them.

He had finished by ten o'clock. He took a light overcoat with him because the nights were beginning to get chilly. The clerk at reception sold him a stamp for the letter. Claybrook let the man overcharge him. He dropped the letter in the mailbox on the counter.

He was tempted to take a taxi but doubted whether they would let him charge it to his expense account. In the end he waited for a *dolmus*. When it came, it was crowded with adolescents smoking American cigarettes.

The minibus dropped him in Taksim Square. It would be better to walk from there. If nothing else, he needed the exercise. When he retired, he promised himself, he would get fit again. Anything would be possible once he had retired.

The Red Dahlia was in the basement of a modern hotel. The entrance was down an alley. As he walked over the pockmarked asphalt, cats skidded for cover. He guessed that the hotel's kitchen was somewhere down here. Istanbul was a city of cats with long, rakish lines; starvation made them elegant.

Over the door was a sign advertising Coca-Cola. Inside was a small vestibule crowded with potential customers. Most of them seemed to be middle-aged German tourists, talking loudly to make themselves heard over the thud of the music.

The entrance charge made Claybrook wince. The attendant gave him a numbered ticket in exchange for his overcoat.

A flight of stairs led downwards. Claybrook followed a group of Germans who seemed to know where they were going. The music became louder. He wondered if it was what they called heavy metal. Jess would know.

The stairs came out at one end of a long, low room.

Multicoloured lights flashed in time with the beat of the music. Claybrook had a confused impression of a mass of people swaying to and fro like a many-headed organism animated by a single heart. The air was heavy with tobacco.

For an instant he came absurdly close to panic. He wanted to run up the stairs and join the stray cats in the alley.

A woman coming down the stairs jostled against him. In broken English she apologized prettily in a way that was also an invitation. Turkish, Claybrook thought, but pretending to be French. His head cleared.

'*Il n'y a pas de mal, mademoiselle.*' He smiled at her and moved away.

There was a bar along one of the shorter walls. Claybrook struggled through the crowd. It took him five minutes to catch the bartender's eye.

The lager tasted of nothing in particular but it was blessedly cold. Claybrook leant against a wall and hoped that he wouldn't have to wait long. From where he stood he had a view of both the bar and the stairs though the people, and the lighting, made continuous observation difficult. It was already five past eleven.

'Are you lonely?'

The man was Turkish and hardly out of his teens. His shirt was unbuttoned to his waist, presumably to display the silver chain he wore round his neck.

Claybrook shook his head.

The man did not give up easily. He asked the same question in German, French and Turkish. Claybrook gave him the same reply each time. At last the youth shrugged and wandered off in search of easier prey.

'Playing hard to get?'

Claybrook swung round, spilling his drink. The voice was familiar but the dark glasses, the tight jeans and the leather jacket were not.

'You're late,' he snapped.

'Only ten minutes.'

'You look ridiculous,' Claybrook said.

'No. You do. You must be the only man wearing a tie in the whole place. Here, have a proper drink.'

It was whisky. Claybrook sipped it and wondered what it cost in a place like this. The other man leant against the wall; his shoulder touched Claybrook's. The dark glasses had mirrored lenses. The twin reflections of yourself distracted your attention from the face behind the glasses.

'Why here?' Claybrook said. 'I thought we'd settled on Lahore. Or even Hong Kong–'

'Careful now. How's the office?'

'The same as ever. They could've sent an eighteen-year-old instead of me. Or even a bloody memo.' Claybrook laughed. 'But it really doesn't matter any more, does it?'

They drank in silence for a moment; the music insulated them from the rest of the room. A woman tried to climb on to a table. She slipped and fell. Her friends laughed.

'Well?' Claybrook said.

The glasses flashed. 'Opportunity knocks. I heard something which could be useful. Not just for us but for you personally.' The lips twisted. 'It's a chance to serve your country. And if all goes well you'll retire in a blaze of glory. You'd be a hero. Just think of it.'

11

'I don't want to be a hero. What d'you mean?'

'You remember Tonanyev?'

Claybrook frowned. 'I thought he was dead.'

'He will be if someone doesn't give him a safe home.'

'He's left his old home? I don't believe it.'

'He's getting on a bit. Age puts things in a different perspective. They say he's difficult - quirky. I think he'd fall for a low-key, personal approach. Needs the human touch, you might say. And you could define human as being the polar opposite to Maddox-Brown.'

'What makes you think I could do it?' Claybrook resisted an urge to tear the glasses off. 'Or even that I want to?'

'Ah, come on. Of course you want to. Just to show them how wrong they've been for all these years. But that would just be the icing on the cake. It's the cake that counts.'

Claybrook nodded slowly. It was a fair point. 'And if I fail?'

'You've lost nothing. Tell Maddox-Brown: that way you'll salvage some kudos. Though I don't think he'd succeed where you've failed.' The voice acquired a hint of mockery. 'And at least you'll know that you've done your best to serve your country. A comforting thought for the long winter evenings of your retirement.'

'Oh for God's sake,' Claybrook said. 'Anyway, it's too dangerous.'

'Not if you move fast. My information is that they think he's in Austria still. He's a wily old man. Hasn't lost his touch.'

'Still . . .'

'Think it over while I get another drink.'

The bar was even more crowded now. Claybrook was glad of the respite. He felt oddly excited by the possibility of trying to do a deal with Tonanyev. The cake was attractive. The real surprise was finding that after all these years he wanted the icing as well. He knew it was self-indulgent, even foolish. But there was no harm in it.

The whisky glass was back in his hand. He swallowed half of its contents in one go. His head felt as if it was less tightly attached to his neck than usual. 'Tell me more,' Claybrook said. He bent closer.

'I'm not sure where Tonanyev is living. Knowing him, he's probably got more than one place. But he goes to the same teahouse nearly every day. Regular as clockwork. It's down below the Blue Mosque, next door to a barber's. But don't get there before him. He won't go in if he sees a Westerner there.'

'Where?' Claybrook demanded. 'Which street?'

The glasses swung towards him. The light brightened. Claybrook saw his face distorted in duplicate: his open mouth bisected each frame.

'It's near another mosque. Little place with one minaret called Kücük Ayasofya; I don't know the street name. A lane goes down from it towards the railway. The teahouse is on the left-hand side. It's got a courtyard with a sort of garden. You can't miss it.'

'When does he get there?'

'Eleven-thirty usually. Sits there and reads the papers. If you time it for about midday.'

Sweat trickled down Claybrook's neck and lodged between his neck and his collar. It itched and he would have liked to scratch.

'How do you know all this?' he said.

'News gets around, especially to people like me. I won't be more specific. All you need do is tell Maddox-Brown that you saw Tonanyev on the street and acted on impulse. He'll swallow it because he'll share the glory. He believes what he wants to believe.'

'Yes,' Claybrook said. 'We all do that.'

'Would you put me through to Mr Maddox-Brown?'

The woman at the Consulate switchboard grunted. Claybrook heard clicks on the line. He wondered who was listening.

He swung his feet on to the bed and rubbed the spine of the book that lay face downwards on the coverlet. It was Trollope's *Doctor Thorne*. When they sent him abroad he always packed Trollope.

'Maddox-Brown.'

The voice was fast and nasal. Maddox-Brown spoke as if both words and time were rationed.

'David? Chas Claybrook here. Look, I'm afraid I won't be in this morning, and maybe not this afternoon, either.' Claybrook tried to inject a note of feebleness into the conversation; he was sounding too vigorous. 'I've been up all night. Must have been something I ate.'

'Gippy tummy, eh? Oh well. The work won't run away.'

'No,' Claybrook agreed.

In his mind's eye he saw the ten grey cabinets in the Consulate's basement, each stuffed with files that needed to be standardized. The Office Services memo called it a Compatibilization Programme. The memo called Claybrook a Co-ordinator.

'All right?' Maddox-Brown said. 'Goodbye.'

It was a place for old men.

Claybrook would have missed it if he hadn't had such precise directions. The street entrance was a narrow archway squeezed between the barber's and a hardware shop.

Before he went in he glanced quickly up and down the street. The single minaret of Kücük Ayasofya was a stone finger raised to the blue sky. People were shopping, smoking, talking, walking and riding mopeds; none of them looked suspicious though several were watching him. You expected to be watched in Turkey, even in Istanbul. Strangers were public property.

The archway gave on to a yard which might once have been a garden. Now it was a patch of earth, parched by the summer. Short lengths of rusting iron pipes lay in a confused heap just inside the archway. In the centre was a square pavement of cracked black and white slabs. As Claybrook went in, dusty chickens scuttled away from him.

A raised verandah ran round three sides of the yard. Old men were scattered among the tables in ones and twos. Some were playing backgammon; others had newspapers. All of them were looking at Claybrook.

He felt as though he was a spectator who had wandered by chance through the gladiators' entrance of an arena. He wanted to protest that this was a case of mistaken identity.

Tonanyev had the corner table on the right of the archway. Claybrook had never seen him in the flesh but he recognized him at once from the photographs. The face had aged, of course; but the thin, high-bridged nose was the same and the eyes still slanted downwards at

15

their outer edges. As a consequence Tonanyev's expression was a permanent blend of surprise and distress.

Claybrook stood there for a moment, looking round as though for a table. Then he sauntered towards Tonanyev's corner. He climbed up the wooden steps of the verandah. His shadow slid across the table and touched the newspaper that Tonanyev was reading. The old man did not look up.

'Excuse me,' Claybrook said in English. 'Mind if I join you?'

Tonanyev nodded ambiguously. He kept his eyes on the newspaper. He was reading yesterday's *Herald Tribune*.

Claybrook dropped the tourist map of Istanbul on the table and sat down. His hands were trembling so he clasped them on his lap.

An elderly waiter with hennaed hair and a dirty apron shuffled down the verandah and took Claybrook's order for tea. Claybrook began to relax. At this time of day the October sun could have belonged to a fine June day in England. He angled his chair so his head and shoulders were in the sun.

The tea came. It was lukewarm and heavily sugared.

'You're a tourist?' Claybrook asked.

Tonanyev sighed. He raised his head and stared across the table.

'Your subtlety,' he said quietly, 'amazes me.'

'I'm sorry.' Claybrook tried the effect of a smile. 'I didn't know how to begin.'

'How did you find me?'

'By chance. I saw you outside. We've never met but I recognized your face. You haven't changed much since London.'

'By chance? We are taught not to believe in chance. Sometimes I think that is a weakness.

Tonanyev's English was fluent but the words came slowly and with obvious effort. It was as if he had lost the habit of speaking in any language.

'You think I'm lying?' Claybrook said.

Tonanyev shrugged. 'Yes, no, maybe. It matters less than you think.' His eyes moved away from Claybrook's face and stared into the yard. 'Did you know they used to play chess here? On the paving stones over there. It was ... what's the word? A gimmick? Something to bring the tourists in. Those pipes were the pieces. But the tourists didn't come. No one wanted to play.'

Oh God, Claybrook thought. *Bloody Russian melancholy*. Aloud he said: 'You can't stay here.'

'Why not?'

'Because sooner or later they'll find you. You know that.'

'Perhaps.'

'You don't want that,' Claybrook said without conviction. 'And I can help you avoid it.'

'Of course you can,' Tonanyev agreed. 'Are you married?'

Claybrook blinked. 'I beg your pardon?'

'You have a wife? Children maybe?'

'Yes, but–'

'I was married for forty-three years,' Tonanyev said. 'Then my wife died. Not from old age or from sickness. She was knocked down by an automobile. A big black Zil. They said the driver had been drinking. He was severely disciplined.'

'I'm sorry.' Claybrook thought of Patricia. 'Truly I am.'

17

'It was an accident,' Tonanyev went on. 'It happened by chance, just as you happened to catch sight of me. It was something that the rules didn't cover. You understand?'

'Not really.'

'At least you are honest.'

Tonanyev rubbed his chin. He hadn't shaved for some days and his face was covered with silver bristles. His eyelids drooped.

Claybrook liked him. He knew the meeting was pointless. Tonanyev wasn't coming anywhere of his own free will. Claybrook wondered what he would say to Maddox-Brown. He was tempted to say nothing.

The sun warmed him. In the end the simple things were important. It was better to sit here in the sun than to pore over old reports in the Consulate's basement. Something had been gained.

The noise from the street outside had a soporific quality. Claybrook didn't look round when the two men came through the archway.

Tonanyev's eyelids flickered open. He looked like a tired hawk, Claybrook thought; Pat would have liked to photograph him.

Then the guns opened fire.

1

'Do you never stop eating?'

Frank's hand was buried in the crisp packet between his legs. His eyes were on the road and his other hand was on the wheel. When Blaines spoke, the rustling stopped. Frank's eyes met Blaines's in the rearview mirror.

'Sorry, sir.'

'So am I, sonny, so am I,' Blaines said. 'Just give it a rest, will you?'

He lit a cigar and stared out of the window. It was a bright October afternoon. The sun made the car uncomfortably warm. It wouldn't last. There were black clouds massing on the western horizon. The wind came in gusts that sliced across the lanes. Still, from the other side of a pane of glass the Cotswolds looked like a picture postcard.

Wish you were here. Wish I was anywhere but here. Having a bloody awful time.

Usually Blaines sat in front with the driver. But not today. He didn't want to talk to anyone on this journey. Come to that, he didn't want the journey to end. It was typical that on today of all days the Pool should have sent Frank to drive him. Frank was a nasty little man with a smug little smile. The superior sort. Probably had a degree in applied theology.

The Ford Granada slowed for a roundabout. Halcombe was only seven miles away.

'Not long now, sir,' Frank said.

Blaines belched smoke at him. 'So you can read signposts too? Well, well. So can I.'

Frank popped a piece of chewing gum into his mouth. 'The Claybrooks' place is on the outskirts, isn't it? Do you know where?'

'Drive right through the town. There's a right-hand turn just past the derestriction signs.'

Blaines had never been there but he had memorized the route years ago. Chas had asked him down for a weekend just after he and Pat bought the place. Blaines chickened out of going at the last moment. He wished he could chicken out now. He wondered if Chas knew why he'd postponed the weekend indefinitely. Pat did, of course; so probably Chas did too.

The familiar pain snaked through Blaines' chest. Indigestion of the heart.

'Pretty place,' Frank said.

Most of Halcombe was built in stone the colour of pale honey. The town glowed in the sunlight. Every other shop sold antiques. The streets were crowded with new cars and sleek pedestrians.

'Shut up,' Blaines said.

A few minutes later Frank said: 'Here we are.'

It sounded like a personal triumph. He swung the car across the road, cutting in front of an oncoming bus. The bus hooted.

Blaines' head bounced off the window. 'For Christ's sake.'

'Sorry, sir.' Frank smiled. 'I thought you were in a hurry.'

20

Blaines ignored him. Frank's behaviour niggled him a little. He filed it away for later. The sun ducked behind a cloud.

On one side of the road was a new housing estate. Dozens of little red boxes huddled together for protection. On the right, the houses were older – brick-built semi-detached cottages, probably built for agricultural labourers round the turn of the century.

It was all wrong. The Claybrooks deserved the honey-coloured stone and the sunshine, not downtown Halcombe.

'Number twenty-three,' Frank said. 'Rosevilla. You want me to stay in the car?'

Blaines nodded. He edged along the seat and clambered out. Chas made a joke of the name Rosevilla. A previous owner had tacked it on to the cottage. It wasn't a villa and when the Claybrooks moved in there had been no roses.

The driver's window was slightly open. Blaines heard the rustle of the crisp packet. The boy must have worms or something. The possibility cheered him. He dropped the remains of his cigar and ground it into the pavement.

A concrete path crossed the little front garden. There were roses now in the centre bed. The lawn was trimly mown and there wasn't a weed in sight.

He rang the doorbell. The front door needed a new coat of paint. His stomach felt empty as though he hadn't eaten for days. He strained to hear footsteps inside but there was too much heavy traffic on the road behind him.

They said time was a healer. How long was it? Fourteen or fifteen years? Jess and Nell were still at

21

school when the Claybrooks moved from London.

Suddenly Patricia was standing in the open doorway. For an instant he couldn't reconcile his memory with this tall, grey-haired stranger. She was wearing yellow rubber gloves and a long plastic pinafore with an old Guinness advertisement splashed across the chest. The pinafore was stiff and angular; it masked her figure. *Protective clothing*, Blaines thought; *she doesn't want to be contaminated*.

'Yes?' she said. 'What is it?'

The voice hadn't changed. It was low-pitched and gentle. The corners of the American accent had been smoothed away but it was still there. As she spoke, past and present slid together in Blaines's mind. Time was overrated as a healer. And she hadn't even recognized him.

'It's me, Pat.' He realized the sun was behind him. 'Eric.'

'Eric . . .?'

'You know,' he said with a hint of exasperation. 'Eric Blaines. From the office. Remember?'

'Of course.' Pat held open the door. She stripped off the gloves and held out her hand.

'Forgive me, I'm still not thinking straight. In any case, I wasn't expecting anyone to come so soon. And I didn't expect one of the chiefs. Maybe an Indian First Class if I was lucky.'

Blaines barely touched the hand. *Expecting*? He looked over her shoulder to avoid looking at her face.

The hall was a mess. Someone had scattered newspapers and books on the oatmeal carpet. The framed photographs were hanging askew.

'Well, come in,' Pat said.

He edged past her. The hall was narrow and the sleeve of his coat brushed her arm. His feet crunched on blue and gold shards of china.

'What happened?'

Pat slipped ahead. 'Come in the kitchen. I've got that reasonably straight. Didn't they tell you?'

Tell me what? 'Not much,' he said. From the back you could see her legs and her waist. They belonged to a far younger woman.

'It happened this morning. In broad daylight. I was out shopping.'

Blaines seized the cue: 'Was much taken?'

'Very little. A portable TV, an old cassette player of Jess's – stuff like that. They missed what's left of my jewellery. Either that or they didn't want to take it. Rather an insult, I thought.'

'But they did quite a bit of damage. Is the rest of the house like this?'

Patricia nodded. 'Let me take your raincoat. You want some tea?'

'All right.'

He sat at the table and watched her moving around the kitchen. Her movements were quick and deft; she didn't have to think what she was doing. She was on home territory. He had never seen her in a kitchen before.

'So I called the police.' She gave a little snort of laughter. 'They went all coy and polite when I gave them your phone number. Stopped calling me "love" and started calling me "madam".'

The back door was half-glazed. On the top part there

23

should have been eight panes of glass. Now there were seven. Someone had tacked a square of hardboard over the place where the eighth had been.

'That how they came in?' Blaines said.

Patricia nodded. She poured boiling water into the teapot. The tip of her tongue protruded between her lips.

'Any witnesses?'

'No such luck.' She sat down on the other side of the table.

'You can get into the back garden from a lane that runs parallel with the road. No one uses it much. The people next door are away. There's an old lady on the other side but she's half blind.'

'What about beforehand? Any phone calls with no one on the other end? Notice any parked cars outside?'

'Nothing like that. I'm wasting your time, aren't I? But Charles, said there was a standing order about contacting the department. Sugar?'

'Three. Not much milk. What do the police say?'

'They figure it must have been kids. Probably looking for cash.' She gave him a brief smile. 'Some hope.'

'So they settled for kicks instead?'

'It could have been worse. A few things were broken but mostly they just dumped things on the floor. Charles'll be furious. All the books need sorting again.'

She poured the tea into the mugs. Her hands were clean but rough-skinned. with the nails cut back to the fingertips. In the old days she let them grow and put paint on them.

'The worst thing,' she went on, 'was having them here in the first place. It's like a violation. Your privacy's raped. You think it only happens to other people.'

24

'You think the police are right? Just kids?'

She looked at him for an instant. There were lines around the grey eyes. She wore no make-up. He looked away and wondered if he dared light a cigar.

'Who else could it have been?' Her voice hardened. 'Eric, what is this? I told the police about two hours ago. You turn up on the doorstep . . . why you? You don't even work in the same department now. And how d'you get here so fast? Helicopter? Magic carpet?'

Blaines sighed. The air wheezed out of his lungs.

'I didn't come about the burglary.'

'Then why are you here?' She put down the mug very carefully on the table. Her eyes met his. He looked away. 'It's Charles, isn't it?'

He nodded. 'I'm afraid it's bad news, Pat–'

'I can do without the build-up, okay? Just tell me.'

'He's dead.'

Her expression didn't change. They sat in silence for two or three seconds. Blaines wished it hadn't happened. He wished he wasn't fat and old. He wished he could put his arms around her. He wished he wasn't here.

'No,' she said at last, 'it's not true.'

'We heard from Istanbul. It happened this morning.

'An accident? A car–?'

Blaines shook his head. 'He was shot. It was an accident in a way. I don't think he was the target. He was in a café or something. A couple of men turned up and opened fire on the customers. We don't know why, not yet. Terrorists, maybe, or a gang killing.'

It was growing darker in the kitchen. Suddenly a burst of rain sprayed against the window. Blaines jumped. Patricia sat rigidly in her chair.

'It must have happened very fast,' Blaines said awkwardly. 'I doubt if he even realized.'

The coincidence of the timing nagged him: Chas Claybrook died at roughly the same moment as his home was burgled fifteen hundred miles away.

'He . . . he was taking early retirement in January.'

'I know,' Blaines said. 'I'm sorry.'

'And it was such a damn silly job. They could have sent anyone out there.'

Blaines cleared his throat. 'Can I get you something? A drink?'

Patricia pushed back her chair. She switched on the striplight. Blaines didn't know whether to be relieved or worried by the absence of tears. She opened the cupboard over the refrigerator and brought out a half-bottle of brandy and two glasses.

'You pour.' She sat down again. 'Brandy's traditional, I suppose. Do you have to do a lot of this? I'd've thought you're too important now.'

Blaines gave them an inch of brandy apiece. He pushed Patricia's glass across the table.

'This is unofficial,' he mumbled. 'I imagine someone from the department will be in touch in an hour or two. Probably a personal visit. Sometimes they phone first.'

The brandy tasted harsh. Patricia stared at her glass but didn't touch it. She had locked herself away out of his reach.

'Would you like me to fetch someone? Jess? Nell? Or a friend?'

'Friend?' she said. 'Charles and I didn't need friends.'

The words were like a slap. Patricia touched his arm.

'I'm sorry. It's the shock, I guess. I'm glad it was you not someone else who came.'

Blaines, acutely embarrassed, choked on the brandy.

She waited until he had finished coughing. 'Jess'll take this badly. She quarrelled with Charles just before he left.'

'I thought they were very close.'

'They are–*were*. Boyfriend trouble. It wouldn't have lasted. Charles tended to be overprotective.'

'They'll question you,' Blaines said in a rush. 'They'll want to see any letters or postcards. They'll ask you about phone calls. Standard practice, I'm afraid.'

'That's okay.' She took a sip of her brandy and made a face. 'Eric – would you mind if I asked you to go? Don't get me wrong but I'd be better alone. I need some time to get used to it.'

Blaines was on his feet before she had finished speaking. He was trespassing, he thought. That was nothing new: the Claybrooks always made other people feel like trespassers in their private domain.

'But you'll keep in touch?' Patricia said. 'Please, Eric.'

'Course I will.'

He picked up his raincoat and shrugged himself into it. His shirt parted company with the waistband of his trousers. He was uneasily aware that a roll of fat was on public display. But to tuck in the shirt would be to draw attention to the flesh it was meant to conceal. He wrapped the raincoat tightly round him, noticing that it had lost another button.

Patricia followed him into the hall.

He grabbed the door-handle almost with relief. 'I'll give you a ring tomorrow if you want. And if there's anything I can do–'

'Eric?' Patricia was standing very close to him. 'Now

27

Charles is dead there's really no reason why I shouldn't see Greg. Is there?'

Blaines felt the blush begin. These days, thank God, he blushed rarely. But when he did, the red stain crawled up his neck, over his face and into his hair.

'Better not,' he said gruffly. He turned away from her and hoped she hadn't noticed what was happening to his face. Had Chas known about Greg too?

'Why?'

'We'll talk about it later.' He opened the door. The cold air rushed in. He shivered. 'Imagine what the press would make of it. They'd drag out the whole story.'

He broke away from her and walked quickly down the path. Neither of them said goodbye. The door closed behind him. Frank started the Granada's engine.

Blaines got in the back. His weight made the car rock.

Frank stuffed the remains of a bar of chocolate in the glove compartment. 'Home, James?'

'The office,' Blaines snarled. 'But find me a call-box first. And if you say another word, or eat another mouthful, I swear I'll bloody murder you.'

'Leave it.'

The doorbell rang again.

Jessica pulled her mouth away. 'I'd better go. It might be Simon.

'Sod Simon.'

Jack slid his hand from her waist and squeezed one breast. He recaptured her mouth. His tongue was like a warm, frisky snake which had recently bathed in beer. He must have had a drink on the train. Or two. She nuzzled closer, wondering why she found him so exciting.

Dear slob.

The doorbell rang again. This time it was a long burst which undermined the excitement. She wriggled in Jack's grip, dislodging the hand that was fumbling at her waistband.

'For Christ's sake! Ignore it, won't you?'

'It won't take a moment. He said he'd bring round the prints. He knows I'm in.'

'He can put them in the letter box.'

'They're too big.'

She pushed him away and escaped to the hall. Her hair was a mess and her breathing was anything but regular. Her skin tingled from the stubble on his face.

Behind her Jack swore.

The bell rang again.

Jessica stabbed the button below the little black grill. 'Yes?'

'Jess, it's Nell.'

Nell? In London?

She pushed the buzzer that operated the lock on the door downstairs. Jack retreated to the kitchen. Soon he would be in an even worse mood. She had forgotten to buy the lager. Jack in a rage and Nell on one of her rare visits: it was a recipe for catastrophe.

Jessica opened the flat door and went on to the little landing. She had the top flat in a large terraced house. Jack called it the servants' quarters and said he felt at home here. He advertised the fact that his grandmother had been a kitchen-maid the way other people were proud that their cousin had married a baronet.

What the hell was her sister doing in London? Nell disliked the city. Nor did she have much time or money

29

to spend. She never dropped in. Nell lived her life by the timetable: she planned her movements months in advance.

Jessica wondered if she should warn Jack. She had tried to keep him away from her family: they belonged to separate worlds and she wanted to keep it that way. Her father had met Jack by accident and that had been disastrous enough. Her mind shied away from the memory.

'What's wrong, Dad? You don't like the thought of your daughter—'

'Of course I don't. But Jess – it's not just that. He's dangerous . . .'

The stairs were uncarpeted. Nell's footsteps were slow and deliberate. She paused on each landing. That wasn't surprising with only two months to go. It must be like carrying a suitcase around with you and never being able to put it down.

Jessica bent over the banisters. Nell plodded upwards as if she was climbing the side of a mountain. Her hair was as black as Jessica's but cut short. The style looked neat, sober, practical and above all inexpensive.

Why did Nell always make her feel guilty?

Her sister rounded the last turn of the stairs. She was wearing her good coat – a Jaeger she had bought in a sale because it would last for ever.

'Nell—'

Jessica started forwards, her hands outstretched. She always found herself gushing when she greeted Nell. It masked the irritation and the affection.

They kissed each other on the cheek.

'How are you? How's Tum-Tum? The stairs must

have been the last thing you wanted. But you look blooming...'

Nell didn't look blooming; she was wilting. Jessica was talking too much and too fast. But it was easier to go on than to stop.

'How's Matthew? And John? It's been ages. Let me take your coat.

By now they had reached the tiny hall of the flat. Nell put down her handbag. Jessica helped her out of the coat and found a hanger in the closet. Most people's coats would have been flung on a chair; but not Nell's.

Jack's motorbike leathers were on the floor of the closet. Jessica quickly closed the door.

'Come and sit down. Would you like a drink? There's some gin, I think; or sherry?'

Now that was tactless: pregnant women with consciences weren't supposed to drink.

'But I expect you're off alcohol.'

Nell's shoulders twitched in what was almost a shrug. Translated to words, the movement meant that she was never exactly on alcohol. She glanced quickly round the living room. No doubt she was cataloguing the rumpled cushions, the unemptied ashtray and the layer of dust on the table.

'Or some tea? Fruit juice?'

Nell shook her head. She was paler than usual and there were bags under her eyes.

'If I could use the loo...?'

'Of course.' Jessica led the way into the sitting room. That was another thing she should have remembered about pregnancy – the undignified need to empty your bladder every two minutes. 'You know where it is? In the bathroom next to the bedroom.'

Jack's razor was on the basin. His pants and socks were drying over the bath. It couldn't be helped.

Jack himself appeared in the kitchen doorway. She knew he was still angry. He ran his eyes over Nell, taking in the bulging pinafore dress and the sensible shoes.

'I'm going out,' he said abruptly.

'This is Jack Jedborough,' Jessica said to Nell. 'Jack, this is my sister Nell Dallow.'

'How do you do?' Nell said carefully. Her face was blank with disapproval. Their parents must have told her about Jack.

'Uh huh,' Jack said. He was already halfway across the room. He ignored Nell's outstretched hand.

'When will you be back?' Jessica said.

'Not sure.'

The flat door slammed behind him.

'Sorry.' Jessica realized she was fingering one of the buttons on her shirt. Jack had undone it and she had forgotten to do it up.

'I'll just go to the loo,' Nell said brightly. She used her vicar's wife's voice, the one that meant that she knew better than to judge people on their outward appearances, however unpleasant they might seem.

'He's a bit upset today.'

'It's quite all right, dear. Shan't be a moment.'

When Nell had gone, Jessica did up the button and sat down. She hated herself for making excuses about Jack. She hated her sister for making them necessary.

Nell came back. She paused by the big dormer

window that looked east over the rooftops to the trees of Holland Park.

'I love your view,' she said unexpectedly. 'It makes London look like a foreign city.' She sat down carefully with a sigh of relief.

'Are you sure I can't get you something?'

'No, thank you.' Nell stared down at her feet. There was a frown on her square, plain face. 'In a way it's a good thing that Jack went out.'

Oh God. She's going to give me a lecture about hurting the parents and falling into evil ways.

'I've got some bad news, I'm afraid,' Nell went on. 'Mother thought one of us should tell you and I was nearer. I'm sorry about the lack of warning.' Without warning the face crumpled. 'Oh Jess. It's Daddy. He's dead.'

Jessica thought: *Daddy – she hasn't called him that since we were children.*

Nell was crying silently and that was wrong too. Nell never cried; she was sensible instead; she was the older sister who always knew what to do, who never kicked against the inevitable because God would think it bad manners.

'She heard this afternoon.' Nell gulped. She fished out a neatly-folded bundle of paper handkerchiefs from the pocket of her dress. She selected one of them and blew her nose. 'A man came down from the department, an old friend of Daddy's.'

The last time I saw you we quarrelled over Jack. You had no right to say what you said and nor did I. But I was going to meet you at the airport next month and it would have been all right …

'It was some sort of accident in Istanbul. Mother doesn't know the details yet.'

Jessica wondered why she couldn't cry herself. She was an unnatural daughter. Outside the light was fading; the sky darkened; street lamps glowed; the rush-hour traffic grumbled through the intestines of the city. Everything was normal. So bloody normal.

'It's so unfair,' Nell wailed. 'He was so near retirement.' She clasped her hands across her swollen belly and looked at Jessica. 'I keep thinking of how he was when we were young. So – *solid*. D'you know what I mean?'

Jessica nodded. She got up and knelt down by Nell's chair. Her sister was trembling. The handkerchief was a sodden mess.

'The baby knows,' Nell said between sobs. 'He's kicking me.'

Jessica put her arms around her sister. Nell clung to her.

This is wrong too. She's the older sister. She should be comforting me.

'Bishops aren't allowed to top themselves,' Blaines said. 'Didn't you know?'

The Superintendent sighed. 'There's a note, sir.'

He picked up a transparent folder from the desk and handed it to Blaines. Inside was a single sheet of notepaper. *From the Bishop of Rosington, The Bishop's House, Rosington, Cambridgeshire.* There was a ragged red stain on the top left-hand corner.

Brundish had scrawled a few lines underneath the letterhead.

'It's as bad as a doctor's,' Blaines said. 'I mean, sod it, what's the point of writing something that no one else can read?'

The Superintendent hung on to what was left of his temper. 'Would you like me to read it, sir?'

Blaines shook his head.

There was a knock on the door.

'Come in,' the Superintendent shouted.

A young detective-sergeant put his head into the room. His hair and his complexion made Blaines think of carrots. He had never liked carrots.

'Sorry to interrupt, sir. The ambulance is here. And Mrs Brundish would like a word.'

Blaines looked up. 'That's the Bishop's wife?'

'Yes, sir.'

'Tell her to wait five minutes.' Blaines went back to the letter. 'And tell the ambulance to wait too.'

'Sir, she says it's urgent. She's in a bit of a state. The secretary's trying to calm her down but –'

'Shut up,' Blaines said without looking up. 'Just keep her out of here.'

The DS glanced at the Superintendent, who shrugged. Both of them knew the folly of offending Mrs Brundish. For one thing, her brother was on the Police Committee.

When the door closed, Blaines turned back to the Superintendent.

'Do themselves proud, these bishops. I thought the Church of England went in for radical politics and the simple life.'

He waved dismissively at the room. Privately the Superintendent thought it was just the right setting for a senior bishop with a national reputation. A Venetian window framed a view of the cloister garth and the central tower of the cathedral; at least a thousand books – fat, sombre hardbacks in the main – were marshalled along one wall; the furniture looked early Victorian, the sort you inherited from your grandparents. There was an ivory and ebony crucifix on the wall over the desk, directly above a silver-framed photograph of Mrs Brundish.

Blaines picked up the photograph. Mrs Brundish stood by a rose bush; she was waving a pair of secateurs at the camera.

'No wonder he decided he couldn't go on.'

The Superintendent compressed his lips. He had had this sort of interference before but had never grown used to it. Usually they sent well-groomed types who spoke with Oxbridge accents and disguised their ruthlessness by saying please and thank you. Blaines – Colonel Blaines – was a surprise. Uncouth, that was the word. Surely that was egg on his trousers?

Blaines tapped the letter. 'Who knows about this?'

'My DS – he found it: it was underneath the body. Me. The Chief Constable. And you.'

'No one else? You're sure?'

The Superintendent nodded.

'Then that's the way it'll stay. Okay?'

'No, sir. I can't do that.'

Blaines stuck a small cigar in his mouth. He took his time looking for matches. The Superintendent opened a window. Mrs Brundish's views on smoking were well known.

'No such word as can't, sunshine.' Blaines inhaled deeply and coughed. 'Your Chief Constable agrees with me. Or he will when he's heard from London. Your DS will do whatever you tell him to; that's what sergeants are for.'

'In cases like this there's a well-established procedure laid down by the Home Office–'

'And even you agree with me in your heart of hearts, don't you, my lad?' Blaines paused. He looked for an ashtray and, finding none, flicked ash on the carpet. 'You're due for promotion next year, they tell me,' he went on. 'Might have got it this year if you hadn't had that little dust-up with a Councillor. What was his name? Vosper, that's it. Left a bit of a question mark hanging over you. Eh?'

The Superintendent's hand was in his jacket pocket. It balled into a fist. He felt a stitch or two in the lining give way.

Blaines came closer. Cigar smoke eddied around the policeman's face.

'There's a political angle, see? Brundish wasn't just any old bishop. Every time you turned on the TV he seemed to be yapping away about something. Point is, the PM liked what he said. All that guff about traditional values. No point in upsetting the apple cart, is there?'

The fat man moved away. The Superintendent stared at him. Blaines separated the letter from the folder.

The Superintendent sucked in his breath. 'Fingerprints–?'

Blaines dropped the folder on the desk and stuffed the letter into his pocket.

'If you do upset the apple cart,' he said gently, 'I'll see you fucking buried in the apples.'

*

'Dear God,' Wreningham said. '*Suicide*? Surely there's some mistake? The PM would hate that.'

'Drank half a pint of Glenmorangie and stuck a twelve-bore in his mouth.' Blaines belched. 'What a way to go.'

'He owned a twelve-bore?' Wreningham had elocution-class vowels; they were well-adapted for expressing outrage. 'A bishop?'

'He only shot clays. Not a bad shot. It was good PR: everyone likes a sportsman. The idea was that shooting things made him human. Don't quite get it myself.'

'It'll have to be an accident,' Wreningham said firmly. 'Brundish was going to chair the Select Committee on Public Decency.' His voice rose in pitch. 'Is there any reason why it shouldn't be an accident?'

Blaines let a silence develop. He enjoyed watching Wreningham squirm behind the big desk. It was one of those pleasures that were all too rare.

'There was a letter,' he said at last. 'Three people know about it: the Chief Constable and a Superintendent and a Sergeant from the local C I D. No problem with the Chief Constable or the Sergeant. The Superintendent needs watching.'

'And the letter? I must have all the details, Eric.'

Blaines fumbled in his pocket, produced the sheet of paper and tossed it on the desk.

Wreningham reached for it. His hand stopped a few inches away. It was shaking. He lowered it to the desk. He looked at Blaines and swallowed twice.

'Is that . . . blood?'

Blaines nodded. 'O Rhesus Positive to be precise.' If Wreningham wanted all the details, he could have them.

'I see.' Wreningham hunched forward so he could see the letter without touching it. 'What appalling handwriting,' he said with relief. 'Would you decode it for me?'

Blaines scraped it towards him. 'It's addressed to Mrs B, by the way. She hasn't seen it. "My darling Mary, Forgive me but I can't go on. The JCC business. It's simple blackmail. This is the only way out. My love to you, James." Short and to the point. Unlike his public speeches.'

'JCC?'

'We've known about that for years. Jerusalem College, Cambridge. Brundish was there in the late thirties. He wasn't very godly in those days. Knew a load of Commie pooftahs.'

Wreningham raised his eyebrows. Blaines thought he plucked them.

'He was homosexual? Are you sure?'

Blaines grinned. Wreningham would shy away from 'pooftah' because the word implied a degree of sexual discrimination; 'gay' was ruled out because it hinted at sympathy, if not approval; but 'homosexual' was a perfect politician's word – accurate but neutral.

'I wouldn't have said it otherwise,' Blaines said. 'Look, nothing was proved but it is just possible he was recruited. He was screened in '63 and again in '67: all very discreet. And he passed with flying colours. But a tiny little doubt remained. In these cases it always does.'

Wreningham smoothed his hair back over his ears. 'Blackmail?' he said slowly. 'Brundish can't have been a rich man.'

'His wife has a little money of her own. He got a

reasonable salary. And he must've earned a certain amount from his books and TV appearances. We'll check all that, of course.'

'I just hope we've heard the last of it.' Wreningham grew more cheerful. 'Still, we must count our blessings. At least he's dead, that's the main thing. The blackmail dies with him. Even if the media do get hold of the story –'

'There's another possibility,' Blaines pointed out. 'The letter doesn't actually mention money. We don't know what the blackmailer wanted.'

The cheerfulness oozed away from Wreningham's face. 'You mean – they might have been trying to reactivate him? After all these years?'

Blaines grinned. 'Not a bad moment, with the Select Committee coming up.'

Wreningham stood up. He was a neat, slight man with delicate features; they called him 'Beau' behind his back because his clothes always fitted so well. It was known that Wreningham did not dislike the nickname.

He crossed the room and opened a small cupboard in the panelling.

'We're running late. A glass of sherry?'

Blaines grunted. A glass of cat's-piss. But at least it was alcoholic. Wreningham gave him a drink about once a month. The tactic reminded Blaines of his grammar school headmaster who would occasionally offer his prefects a cigarette in the privacy of his study after school hours. In both cases the manoeuvre was designed to create an atmosphere of relaxed equality; the manoeuvre failed now as it had in the past.

Wreningham handed him a glass. He strolled across

the room to the fireplace and leaned on the mantel. Above the fireplace was a full-length portrait of a bewigged eighteenth-century gentleman in a similar pose; the gentleman was propping up an urn but the principle was the same.

'I shall have to refer this one, Eric,' Wreningham said. 'What exactly do you advise? Tragic accident while cleaning his gun? That sort of thing?'

Blaines swallowed the sherry in a single gulp. So Wreningham wanted to sit on the fence: if anything went wrong he would just be a middleman who had passed on Blaines' advice.

'Well, you're the best judge of that,' Blaines said. As an afterthought he added, 'Sir.'

Wreningham looked sharply at him. 'Perhaps you should hang on to that letter for the time being. Just in case.'

He returned to his desk. As usual it was a gleaming expanse of leather broken only by a blotter, a telephone and the statutory photograph of his wife and children. Someone must have told him once that an uncluttered desk was the mark of an orderly mind.

He opened a drawer and pulled out a shorthand pad. 'Ah yes. There was something else. The business in Istanbul. Any news on that?'

'Five dead,' Blaines said. 'A right-wing group claimed responsibility.'

'The Grey Wolves?'

Blaines shook his head. 'Nowhere in that league. Call themselves the Sons of Ataturk. There may be some overlap in membership; Koslove isn't sure.'

'Koslove?' Wreningham wrinkled his nose. 'What's he

got to do with it? What does Maddox-Brown say?'

'Much the same. He's working very closely with the Americans. Hasn't got much choice.'

'The target was Tonanyev?'

'That's what the sons of Ataturk said.' Blaines put his empty glass on the desk. The base was sticky with sherry. He hoped it would leave a ring on the leather. 'They phoned Reuters and spun the usual line: in the name of humanity they had executed the KGB criminal Tonanyev. No mention of three old Turks and one British citizen.

'It would be better if the link with the Consulate didn't come out.'

'No problem there. Claybrook's billed as a British tourist. There's no mention that he was at the same table. He's like the three old Turks: just happened to get in the way of the bullets.'

'I don't like it,' Wreningham said. His eyes were fixed on Blaines' glass. 'What on earth was he doing there?'

'That's what Koslove would like to know. So would Maddox-Brown. Claybrook phoned in sick yesterday morning. The Americans had been keeping an eye on Tonanyev for days. They nearly had a fit when they found out who Claybrook was. Thought Maddox-Brown was trying to poach.'

'Maybe he was. The ambitious sort, isn't he?'

'If he was, I doubt he'd've used Claybrook.'

'Not the best of friends, eh? I wonder.' Wreningham aligned his pad with the edge of the blotter. 'You heard the rumour, I imagine? That Claybrook was going to try his hand at writing after he retired? Not a popular activity but then he always was a trouble-maker. Perhaps this solves a lot of problems.' His eyes slid upwards and met Blaines's. 'You must have known him in your old job.'

Blaines nodded. 'I saw the widow yesterday.'

'Really? Was that necessary, Eric? There are proper channels.'

'I know, sir.' Blaines said. 'But I thought you'd like the department to be directly involved. In view of the Sandridge connection.'

Wreningham glanced at his watch. 'I must be off in a moment,' he said quickly. 'Claybrook can wait.'

Blaines stood up, interested to note that Wreningham was still sensitive about Sandridge. 'Don't let me keep you.'

'We meet again on Monday,' Wreningham said without much enthusiasm. 'Have a good weekend.'

He picked up his briefcase and ushered Blaines across the carpet. For a moment Blaines thought he was going to get his back patted.

'Oh, by the by,' Wreningham paused at the door. 'I was talking to Dublin today. You remember they're sending us a liaison officer?'

Blaines nodded.

'I've decided to attach him to you.'

'Oh Christ. Is that a good idea?'

'You're so good with these oddballs, Eric. Shouldn't be a problem.' Wreningham showed his perfect teeth. 'After all, we've nothing to hide, have we?'

'Full cooperation?'

'Oh yes.' Wreningham smiled up at Blaines. 'Within limits, Eric, within limits. You're the best judge of that. He'll be coming on Monday week. Chap named Liam Caragh.'

43

2

Major Aughrim stared affectionately at the elk's antlers. They measured ten feet across.

'His name's Blaines,' he said. 'Colonel Blaines.' He shook his head sadly at the enormous skeleton.

Liam Caragh glanced up at the Irish elk. The movement allowed him to check that no one was within earshot.

'Bit of a dinosaur,' Aughrim continued. 'Always expecting him to get the chop. Comes across as being about as subtle as a charging bull but don't let that fool you.' He rubbed his plump little hands together and smiled at Liam. 'What about a cup of coffee?'

'I'd like that, sir.'

Liam hoped his relief wasn't too obvious. Aughrim's habit of using the Natural History Museum as an extension of his office had always struck him as startlingly indiscreet.

Upper Merrion Street glistened with rain. A light drizzle was still falling. Liam put up the umbrella. Aughrim sidled closer to him.

'The Shelbourne, do you think? Bewley's? Or shall we try the Westbury Centre?'

It was a difficult decision because Aughrim took his coffee seriously. He was said to have sacked a secretary who had tried to convert him to the ergonomic advantages of having instant coffee in the office.

'Perhaps the Westbury?' Liam suggested. 'We went to the Shelbourne last time. And Fitzpatrick mentioned you went to Bewley's yesterday.'

'A good point. Variety is so important. Blaines is very close to Koslove.'

'Koslove?'

'Ah, I was forgetting. You wouldn't know. George Koslove. He works for the National Security Council. At present he represents their interests in London.'

They walked along the north side of Stephen's Green and turned into Grafton Street. Aughrim said nothing; no doubt his mind was occupied with the taxing decision of whether to choose Tanzanian or Kenya Peaberry. Liam knew better than to interrupt.

He was grateful for the silence. The liaison job excited and terrified him; he needed time to work out the right questions. He had known it was in the offing for over a month but had tried to persuade himself that he didn't stand a chance of getting it. It would go to someone like Fitzpatrick – one of the army boys, from a respectable military family where the parents got married in a Catholic church before they thought of producing children. Seventy per cent of the service intake still came from that sort of background.

They weren't bastards who were never quite sure if they counted as Catholic or Protestant; and they weren't ex-coppers, either.

Aughrim upset Liam's calculations by ordering Mocha for both of them.

'They're trying to soothe us,' he said while they waited for the coffee to arrive. 'Every now and then they wonder

46

if it might not be a good idea to cooperate with us in deed as well as word. They feel guilty – the English often feel guilty, have you noticed that? We found out they'd been eavesdropping on the London Embassy again, and that upset them. They behave as if they still own us; we all know that but they don't want to admit it. You're a sop to their consciences.'

The waitress brought their coffee. When she had gone, Liam said: 'Isn't there a risk that they'll stuff me in a corner and leave me to vegetate?'

'Of course there is.'

Aughrim dribbled cream over his spoon on to the surface of the coffee. Gradually the white layer entirely masked the black. He sighed with pleasure.

'That's what you have to prevent,' he went on. 'Poke your nose into everything. Make yourself indispensable to people like Blaines and Koslove. Get to know the names and faces. You've got one thing in your favour: they'll all want to pump you just as much as you want to pump them.'

'When do I start?'

'Monday week. Sorry about the lack of notice.' Aughrim's tone meant: *You're lucky to have been chosen at all*. 'Three-month posting to start with. The Embassy will give you any facilities you need. Then we all review progress.'

Aughrim sipped his coffee. It left a rim of cream on his upper lip. He dabbed at it with his napkin. He smiled at Liam.

'If any,' he added softly.

There was no need to spell it out, Liam thought: he would be on probation. If it all worked out, he could hope for accelerated promotion; if it didn't, he'd be moved sideways to Monaghan or Dundalk and spend the rest of his career gazing fruitlessly across the border. Or, worse still, they'd send him back to Special Branch with a label round his neck saying 'Defective Goods. Return to Sender.'

'What are you doing at present?'

'There's the Connolly case,' Liam said. 'Otherwise just routine.'

'Connolly? Nasty business. Still, the damn fool was asking for it.' Aughrim sniffed. 'If you ask me, most blackmail victims have only got themselves to thank.'

'It was Mrs Connolly really,' Liam pointed out. 'The video was taken long before their marriage.'

'Same difference. He shouldn't have married her in the first place. We've got better things to do than mollycoddle sex-starved generals. Know where they met?'

'Las Vegas.'

'Well, there you are,' Aughrim said with the air of one who has clinched his case. 'I ask you. You'd better brief Fitzpatrick.'

Liam nearly smiled. *A smutty little police case*, Fitzpatrick had called the Connolly investigation when he thought Liam was out of the room. *Just right for a smutty little Garda.*

'May I tell Emma, sir?' Liam asked. 'Emma Lazonby?'

He had always hated the regulation that the department should be informed of all relationships, whether marital or not.

Aughrim inflated his cheeks. His face looked like a small pink balloon. He expelled the air gently.

'Of course,' he said. 'I imagine you'll want to thank her.'

*

48

'I need my head examined, don't I, Ma?'

The white face was motionless on the white pillow. Lines radiated from the eye sockets and from the corners of the mouth.

'So much for merit,' Liam said. 'There was me thinking that at last it was what you knew that counted; not who you knew.'

The freshly-laundered sheet was drawn up to her neck and tightly tucked in at the sides. One arm had been allowed to lie on the bedspread. A colour television flickered in one corner; the sound was off.

'Emma put in a good word, you see. She worked in the department once – have I told you that? Aughrim plays golf with her dad. At the Royal Dublin, of course. Where else?'

His mother's eyelids twitched. The breathing changed note like a car changing gear.

'Victor Lazonby, he is. You'll've heard of him. A TD, of course. An ornament of the Dáil. A personal friend of the Taoiseach no less, or that's what he likes you to believe.'

The door opened behind him. Liam let go of his mother's hand.

Sister Elizabeth smiled down at him. 'I brought you some tea.'

He took it with a word of thanks.

'Mrs Caragh's always the better for seeing you, you know,' the nun said. 'The doctor won't believe me, but she is.'

'I have to go to London,' Liam said. 'For at least three months. I won't be able to come so often. I was just telling her.'

The nun frowned. 'Is there someone else who could come?'

Liam shook his head. 'I should get home on some weekends. I'll let you know.'

Sister Elizabeth left them alone.

'Ma, it's good news really. You know me – I'd have been miserable if they'd chosen someone else. And if it works out, it'll be great.'

Liam sipped the tea. There was too much milk for his taste. He poured the rest of it into the tradescantia that trailed over the window-sill.

'It's just . . . I wish it hadn't been Emma. But never mind. It's my problem.'

He put down the empty cup and took his mother's hand. She was fifty-six, but she looked twenty years older. He remembered how she had sat with him as a child, night after night, until he fell asleep. Now it was his turn to protect her from the dark. Darkness everlasting.

The sheet rose and fell, regularly but almost imperceptibly.

The Krug was cooling in the refrigerator; the claret was breathing on the kitchen table; and Liam was dying for a drink.

He had a small, purpose-built flat off Upper Leeson Street. He had been proud of it until Emma saw it. *A bit poky, darling. Fine for a bachelor who's out all day but* . . . He owned it – or, to be precise, at least half of it; and the proportion he owned increased as time went by and the overall value rose against the fixed amount of the mortgage.

He glanced round the living room. A Chopin prelude was pouring gently out of the speakers. Damn it, he was still proud of the place. It was something achieved, something they couldn't take away. He had come a long way from two rooms in a terraced house near the docks in Cork City. He didn't mean to go back.

The casserole was making his mouth water. He had chosen the recipe carefully – a mixture of pork fillet, prunes, mushrooms and almonds. The great advantage of a casserole was that you didn't have to plan to eat at a set time. The jacket potatoes were in the oven. The salad was made. He had even mixed the dressing.

Suddenly there was time on his hands. He had done everything that could be done. He parted the curtains and peered down through the rain at the parking spaces at the side of the flats.

A few minutes later a white VW Golf Convertible pulled off the road. He picked up the umbrella and left the flat. Emma appreciated chivalrous touches. She said they made her feel wanted.

He reached the car just as she opened the door.

There was enough light to see her smile. 'Oh darling. how nice.'

She kissed him quickly under the umbrella. He had a brief and tantalizing impression of warmth and perfume before she dived back into the car. She re-emerged with a bottle in her hand.

'Champagne,' she said.

Liam thought of the Krug and wished that one of them hadn't bothered. She gave him the bottle and took his arm. He noticed that she hadn't brought an overnight bag.

51

'So nice not to go out,' she said on the stairs. 'On a night like this it's much more comfortable to stay in. Something smells good.'

In the living room Liam helped her out of her coat. She stood there for a moment, taking in the Chopin, the table laid for two and the shaded lights. She was wearing a black dress of some soft, clinging material. Her legs were astonishing. The flaming red hair looked freshly cut and washed.

'I'm sorry I'm late. It was chaos at the Castle. You know what it's like just before a State Visit.'

'It doesn't matter.'

He put an arm round her and tilted her head towards him. To his surprise she responded easily, even eagerly. He stroked the nape of her neck. Slowly he began to move his hand down her spine.

'Darling.' She pushed him away. 'You're still holding the champagne. It'll never get cold enough to drink.'

He smiled at her. 'There's a bottle in the fridge already. I'll open it.'

She followed him into the kitchen and watched with flattering interest as he stripped the foil from the neck of the bottle. She had the knack of making you feel large and masculine.

'I tried to ring you before I left work. About six-thirty – I thought you'd be back.'

'I went to see my mother,' Liam said. 'Could you pass me the glasses?'

She set them on the work surface beside him with two sharp clicks. He knew Emma disapproved of his mother and for several reasons. Usually they avoided talking about her.

He poured the wine and gave a glass to her. She took his hand and led him back to the living-room.

'Cheers,' she said. 'Liam, I'm so proud of you.'

'You know about London?'

'Daddy phoned Major Aughrim about something else. Aughrim mentioned it. Darling, it's wonderful news.'

'And I gather it's at least partly your doing?'

Emma smiled up at him. 'Well, it never hurts to have friends.'

She sat down on the sofa, edging along to the corner so there was room for him to sit beside her. 'If it all goes well,' she went on, 'you could end up replacing McCall when he retires. He's only got about a year to go. You'd be the youngest section-head there.'

Liam put his arm round her. 'I thought of that. But–'

'You could do it, I'm sure. And then the sky's the limit.' She snuggled closer to him and slipped a hand inside his shirt. 'Anything could happen.'

Anything?

'We could buy a house,' she went on. 'Settle down.'

She means get married.

He put his hand on her leg.

'Oh darling,' she said. 'I forgot. I left my suitcase in the car. Would you get it for me?'

The memorial service commemorated a stranger.

Afterwards the Claybrook family clustered in the porch of St Stephen's. It was the first Monday in November and the weather had changed abruptly from Indian summer to English winter. Everyone was muffled against the cold. The wind combed through the monuments in the churchyard. The gravestones were streaked with bird droppings and lichen; there were cherubs with sightless eyes and angels with broken wings.

The air was fresher in the porch. In the church it tasted of dry rot and stale devotions. It was no colder here than it had been inside where the mourners huddled together in two pews with room to spare. Around them the empty church had made silent statements about the decay of faith and the quality of Charles Claybrook's friendships.

'I thought it went very well,' the Reverend John Dallow said. 'Do you want to go on ahead, Mother? Nell and I promised we'd give the Rector a lift.'

Jessica sensed rather than saw her mother stiffen. Her long black coat and her pale face made her seem like someone else. She had once told Jessica that she hated the way John called her Mother: *It makes me feel about ninety-four. I should be sitting by a hob with a cat on my knee.*

John ran his eye round the little group; he was expert at sorting sheep from goats. 'Jess, if you take Mother with Auntie Sylvia and Jean, we should be able to manage the rest.'

Jessica nodded. Her mother looked blankly at her. The group divided into two.

The latch on the church door went up with a crack. The Rector beamed at them. None of them knew him well.

'Not kept you waiting, have I?'

No one talked on the drive back. The church was on the other side of Halcombe. Jessica thought of the gin waiting on the dining-room table. The two bottles were

54

her contribution to the funeral feast. Not that they had a body to mourn. Her mother had agreed to allow them to inter what was left of Charles Claybrook in the Anglican cemetery in Istanbul. They told her it was administratively simpler. The memorial service was Nell's idea.

He was a genuinely good man, John had said in the address, *who did many kindnesses by stealth. He was tolerant of other people's views and had a gift for friendship.*

Jessica thought: *He was a bad-tempered atheist, who hadn't much time for anyone except his immediate family. He was a disappointed man though I don't know why. I loved him. And the last time I saw him I said I never wanted to see him again.*

The little house was welcoming after the church. The central heating was on and there was a fire in the sitting room. Best of all, Jessica had plenty to do. She dispensed sandwiches and plates; she poured drinks; she hung coats and she found ashtrays.

'Such a sad occasion,' Auntie Sylvia said as she helped herself to her third vol-au-vent. 'When was the last time we saw you?'

'I think it was Uncle Cyril's funeral,' Jessica said.

'Now that was a do.' Auntie Sylvia cackled. 'A real funeral.'

She looked sharply at Jessica. 'I never think it's quite the same without a body and a choir.'

Jessica laughed.

'I hear you've got a new boyfriend,' the old lady went on. 'He's not come with you?'

'He's working,' Jessica lied. 'Couldn't get away.'

She had told Jack about the service. He hadn't

bothered to say he wasn't coming. There was no need. He didn't approve of God and he hadn't approved of Charles Claybrook.

'None of your mother's relatives are here, I see. Not grand enough for them?' She popped the rest of the vol-au-vent in her mouth. 'But I can't say I'm surprised. Some folk have got long memories.'

'We've never seen anything of them.'

The old woman sniffed. 'If you ask me, it's downright unnatural. Oh, I know there was a lot of trouble at the time, and I daresay a lot of heartache too; but it all happened thirty years ago. Forgive and forget, that's my motto. When all's said and done, family's family.'

'Jean's looking well.'

'You want to talk about something else?' Auntie Sylvia patted Jessica's hand. 'That's all right by me, dear. Jean's forty-five and still unwed. I don't know where we went wrong. Are there any ham sandwiches left?'

Jessica put the plate beside her great-aunt's chair. They had started on the second bottle of gin. She would have to hurry if she wanted a refill. A hand on her arm prevented her from moving away.

'We had eighty-six for your Uncle Cyril.' Auntie Sylvia glanced round the room in a rapid mental calculation. 'But never you mind, dear. Cyril came from a big family. His mother had eleven and eight of them lived. Did you know that?'

Jessica shook her head.

'But your father was an only child, of course, like Jean. And in my generation there was only your grandfather and me. Let's face it, the Claybrooks don't multiply.'

'Apart from Nell.'

56

Auntie Sylvia accepted the change of subject. 'And how's little Matthew?'

'He wasn't well enough to come. Nell and John are very worried.'

'I wonder if they're wise, having another. It'll mean a lot of extra expense.'

The Rector's glass was empty. Jessica used it as an excuse to escape. There were no secrets as far as Auntie Sylvia was concerned, only interesting topics of conversation.

The buffet lunch crawled on until the middle of the afternoon. Her father's cousin, Jean, a plain woman who managed a baker's shop with grim competence, became tipsy. She drank as she did everything else: with deliberation and without unnecessary words.

The Rector was the first to leave. He was the only person, Jessica noticed, whose condolences were both unembarrassed and seemingly sincere; he was a truly professional mourner. The handful of Halcombe acquaintances trailed away in his wake.

At four o'clock the taxi came for Auntie Sylvia and Jean. They were going back to Sheffield by train. As the taxi drew away, Auntie Sylvia leant out of the window, urging everyone to come to stay with her. Jean sat back in the seat, breathing heavily. She waved her fat white hand very slowly in farewell.

'Thank God for that,' Mrs Claybrook said as she closed the front door.

'Why don't you put your feet up?' Nell suggested. 'We'll clear away.'

Patricia smiled down at her; she was taller than her daughters and her son-in-law. 'You look as if you need to sit down yourself.'

'Jess and I will wash up.' John interrupted. 'You two sit down. We'll bring you some tea in a moment.'

The washing up took much more than a moment. John was a slow, inexpert drier-up who had to be told where everything went. He managed to break two glasses. He talked relentlessly, first about what a wonderful couple the Claybrooks had been and how well Mother was bearing up.

'We wonder about how she'll manage,' he went on. 'I hope she doesn't have to sell the house.'

'Why should she? There'll be a pension, won't there? I thought that's why people joined the Civil Service.'

'Didn't Mother tell you? She had a letter; she mentioned it to Nell before you arrived. There's a difficulty about pension credits or something. It won't be as much as she thought.'

'That's absurd.' Jessica emptied the washing-up bowl and wondered why her mother had told Nell and John about this but not her. Her mother always favoured Nell. 'Dad worked there nearly all his life. Must have been at least thirty years.'

'Yes. But I gather that originally he wasn't on the permanent strength; that's the problem.'

'It's just bureaucratic nonsense. Surely she can appeal?'

John shrugged. For a few moments they worked in silence. Her brother-in-law knocked over the rubbish bin.

'And how's the writing going?' he asked as he crawled across the floor. 'Nell said you had something in the *Sunday Telegraph* the other week.'

'A pithy little piece on winter hemlines,' Jessica said as

lightly as she could manage. 'All of two hundred words.'

'How fascinating. It must be wonderful–'

'It's not. It's called trying to make a living.'

According to Jack it was called churning out crap.

She realized she had been rude. 'Any news about Matthew?'

John stood up, dusting his knees. His round face had lost its habitual cheerfulness. Matthew had chronic glomerulo-nephritis which would eventually lead to kidney failure.

'I'm afraid not. In the end it comes down to money. There's a clinic near Boston. They might be able to help.' He polished the plate as though he was trying to scour away the pattern. 'But it's out of the question.'

'I wish I could do something,' Jessica said.

John shrugged. 'I know. Thank you.' The plate came apart in his hands. 'Oh dear, I am sorry.'

'It doesn't matter.' Jessica took the two pieces from him, wrapped them in newspaper and threw them in the bin.

The phone rang in the hall. Both of them rushed to answer it. They collided in the doorway. Jessica reached it first. Against reason she hoped it was Jack.

'Is that the Claybrooks'?' a man's voice demanded.

'Yes. This is Jessica Claybrook.'

A burst of coughing came down the line. 'Can you tell your mum I'm sorry I couldn't get to the service? Something came up.'

'Yes, of course. Would you like to speak to her?'

'No. Don't bother.'

'Who shall I say called?'

'Just tell her it's Eric. She'll know.'

59

Jessica put down the phone and went to look for her mother. She was in the sitting room with Nell. It was obvious from their absorbed faces that they were talking about Nell's pregnancy. For an instant Jessica felt excluded from the secret society of mothers.

'If it's a boy,' Nell was saying, 'we were thinking of Gregory Charles.'

'Not Gregory, dear,' her mother said. The animation faded from her face. 'It's . . . such a solemn name, I always think.'

'Maybe you're right. David?'

Jessica told her mother about the call.

'Eric?' she said. 'He was a colleague of your father's. You must have met him before we moved. Fat man with a head like a turnip.'

'I thought it was odd that no one came down to the service,' Nell said. 'Did they send a wreath?'

Patricia Claybrook nodded. 'To tell the truth, I told them not to come. Except for Eric. I suppose he counts as a friend.'

'You Caragh?' Blaines said. 'You're five hours late. Sit down.'

'I'm sorry, sir. The Embassy must have got it wrong.'

Bog-trotter accent with fake-posh overlay; poodle haircut; poofy little suit with – Jesus Christ! – a bow tie; five foot nine or ten, and light with it, not much more than a hundred and fifty pounds at a guess; and a swarthy little monkey face that looks too clever by half.

'There's a cubby-hole next door,' Blaines said. 'You can have that as an office. Got yourself somewhere to stay?'

'Yes, the Embassy had–'

'Tea trolley comes round at eleven and three-thirty. You missed it today. Ten pee a cup and believe me, sunshine, that comes expensive. Biscuits extra. You got your pass downstairs?'

'Yes, sir. But it's only a temporary one.'

BIaines smiled through the cigar smoke, 'Then you'll have to have it renewed, when and if necessary. Typing pool's on the floor below, Room 203; junior officers, for the use of. Don't screw any of the girls: some have got influential dads and the rest have AIDS. Anyway, most of them are as ugly as sin. Okay?'

'I'm not quite sure what I'll be doing. Major Aughrim thought–'

'Old Terry Aughrim! Dear God, I haven't seen him since Belfast in '76. Still drinking that coffee?' Blaines blew out his cheeks in a preposterous imitation of Aughrim's face. 'In one hole, out the other, that's the ticket. You come with me, young Caragh. There's plenty of work for you. You know what they say about idle hands? Or don't they say that in the Emerald Isle?'

Caragh smiled but said nothing. For a moment Blaines almost felt a spurt of liking for the boy. Fortunately the telephone rang. He picked it up with a jerk that sent the ashtray skidding over the edge of the desk.

'Inspector Hebburn on the line for you sir.'

'Put him through.'

'Eric? We've got another little problem. Might be a link with Brundish. Can I come over?'

'Any time you like.' Blaines noticed Caragh had picked up the ashtray; it was less satisfactory that he was leaving the cigar butts on the carpet. 'I've nothing on this afternoon.'

He put down the phone and swept Liam Caragh out of the room. The office next door had no windows and no furniture except a chair and a desk; it still seemed overcrowded. On the desk was a telephone, a pad, two pencils and pile of newspapers four feet high.

'*Le Monde*,' Blaines said. 'You speak Frog, don't you? Says so on your CV. Good lad. Well, I've got a problem. Complaints about the quality of our scanning service. So I thought, we'll do an independent experiment. Can't get much more independent than the Irish, can you? There's three months' worth there. You go through and note everything on . . . let's say Ulster, shall we? Put it down in writing just as if it was for circulation. Let my secretary know when you're through and she'll send you another batch. We need the full picture – popular press, magazines, you name it. And when you've done, we'll compare what you've got with what we've got already. Then we'll know if the critics are right or wrong. See? Simple, ain't it? Like all great ideas.'

He glanced at Caragh's face. It showed nothing but polite interest. Perhaps Paddy *liked* reading newspapers.

'You might as well make a start now. We clock off at five-thirty in theory.'

Blaines lumbered back to his office with the sense of a job well done. He put his feet up on the desk.

Hebburn must have been in the building already because he was no more than a moment. He coughed as he came in. His face was built for expressing disapproval. Blaines relit his cigar.

'We've got another one, Eric.'

'Suicide?'

'Not this time. Disappearance. Julian Feniscliffe mean anything to you?'

Hebburn sat down on the edge of the visitor's chair. He looked at the soles of Blaines's shoes and blinked. The blink was a muscular tic. Blaines thought it was a by-product of the unwavering attention that Hebburn directed at things that nobody in their right mind would want to look at.

Another one?

'Academic?' Blaines suddenly saw the connection. 'Vice Chancellor of somewhere?'

'That's the one. Sir Julian. He's at the University of Suffolk. Or that's where he should be. Last seen on Friday. Rang his wife from the office and said he had to go to a meeting. Not to keep dinner for him. A porter saw him leave the university car-park. When he wasn't back by morning, his wife got in touch with the police.'

'What does she say?'

'Usual stuff. It boils down to loss of memory or left-wing grudge. You remember Feniscliffe had that trouble with Third World students who couldn't pay their bills?'

Blaines nodded. It was an open secret that even the Prime Minister found Feniscliffe a little too right-wing for comfort. He had contributed articles to the *Salisbury Review*. He was a biologist who drew unpopular political conclusions from the theory of Natural Selection.

'The local CID reckons there's a third possibility. He might have run off with a woman. Julian's got a bit of a reputation that way. But everyone's too polite to mention that.'

63

'Bank account?'

Hebburn's thin shoulders twitched. 'I was coming to that. I had a word with his bank manager this morning. Over the last two months he's withdrawn about six thousand pounds from a deposit account. In cash. Said he was buying antiques. His wife knew nothing about it.'

Blaines scratched his thigh. 'Secretary?'

'Middle-aged … devoted. Knew nothing about the meeting. Said Sir Julian had been a bit peaky lately, as if he was under strain.'

'They all say that. Afterwards. So it looks like he went of his own accord?'

Hebburn blinked.

'I suppose we can't ignore the coincidence.' Blaines swung his legs off the desk and picked up the phone. 'Rosie? See if his nibs can see me this afternoon.'

'Sir Julian?' Wreningham said pettishly. 'Surely not. I've met him actually. He's a friend of the Sandridges. Well, perhaps not a friend exactly.'

He moved away from the fireplace and tacked across the carpet to the window. He peered at the rain and turned back to his visitor.

'What do Special Branch think?'

Blaines was using his tongue to worry a shred of meat that was jammed between his teeth. He left it for later.

'Hebburn doesn't rule out blackmail. If it is blackmail, it needn't necessarily be about this.'

'But there's no doubt that at one point Feniscliffe was involved with the Communists?'

Blaines sighed. There was always doubt. Wreningham had an unreasonable appetite for certainties.

'Well, sir. He was at Jerusalem College at the same time as Brundish. In their second year they shared rooms. People thought of them as part of the same set. Feniscliffe was never a party member, mark you. Canvassing for the Labour Party was as far as he went. But in '39 he moved right rather suddenly.'

'So did a lot of people. Stalin's pact with Hitler–'

'Feniscliffe joined the Liberals in May. So that won't wash unless Stalin gave him advance warning. Spent most of the war with SIS.'

'Did he have access to anything of importance?' Wreningham had gravitated to the mirror by the door. He picked a strand of hair from his lapel and looked doubtfully at it. 'Was he in a position to–?'

Blaines shook his head. 'Advanced bottle-washing was about his level. He wanted to stay on after the war but they wouldn't have him. So he went back to Cambridge. In the '45 election he stood as a Conservative candidate. Didn't get in. It's the thought that counts.'

'Did he know we had an interest in him?'

'We talked to him in '63. But it was all very tactful. He still had friends in the service. We made out we were checking up on Brundish.'

'I see.' Wreningham sat down behind his desk and steepled his fingers. It was one of his statesman poses, Blaines thought, a companion piece to the one where he stood by the fireplace. 'Well, thank you, Eric. You'd better keep me informed. As I see it, there's nothing concrete here. Just the coincidence. And it may be no more than that.'

Blaines stood up. The chair creaked with relief.

'One thing, Eric. How's Caragh getting on?'

'Early days yet.'

'Perhaps I didn't make myself clear. The Prime Minister is most insistent that we cooperate fully with the Irish. In practical terms that means you take Caragh with you wherever you go. I don't want him to get the impression we're holding anything back or shunting him into a clerical backwater.'

So the little bastard already knew about *Le Monde* and the cubby-hole.

'That's bloody stupid. He'll –'

'Stupid or not, that's an order,' Wreningham snapped. 'Treat him as your . . . apprentice. We may have to – ah – tailor your workload appropriately.'

Got you! Blaines thought. He should have seen it before: Caragh was the thin end of the wedge. Wreningham was a devious bugger. Despite himself Blaines shivered.

'Feeling cold, Eric?'

Just someone walking on my grave.

'I'm fine,' Blaines growled.

'Good, good. I'll let you have that in writing, of course. About Caragh. Keep me posted on Feniscliffe.'

In the corridor outside Wreningham's anteroom one of the drivers was waiting. His cap was on his lap. His jaws were moving.

'Afternoon, sir.' The voice was like thick black sludge from Birmingham.

Blaines stopped. Frank smiled up at him. The driver whom the Pool sent up every time Blaines ordered a car. Another little coincidence?

Someone else on my grave . . .

*

Which was it to be? The Russian Imperial Guards or the Prussian gun team?

'I'll take the Guards.'

'A wise choice, Mr Blaines,' Liss said as he always did. 'I don't think the wheels on the limber are original. The Guards are a much better investment.'

'Paint's chipped.' Blaines pointed at the hem of one of the greatcoats. 'And that one's lost the top of his bayonet. What about a discount?'

Mr Liss squeezed his knuckles until they cracked. 'I wish I could oblige. But Mr Jones is very firm.'

'Five per cent seems reasonable.'

'I'm afraid it's just not possible,' Liss said uncertainly. 'It hasn't been a good month. You know, cash-flow and so forth.'

Blaines stuffed his cheque-book back in his pocket. 'Never mind, cock.'

Liss waited until Blaines had done up his coat. 'Perhaps Mr Jones wouldn't object to a small reduction in the circumstances.' He peered over his shoulder as though fearing Mr Jones would overhear. 'After all, you are a regular customer.'

'Five per cent,' Blaines said indifferently. 'That's a small reduction.'

'Very well; but I really mustn't make a habit of it. Mr Jones –'

Blaines suddenly lost patience with the charade. 'Stuff it, will you? Last time I saw Jones here was 1962.'

'Technically he's retired.' Liss laid the guardsmen in their box. 'But he still comes in. Still keeps an eye on the books.'

From beyond the grave?

Blaines wrote out the cheque. As he was signing it, the shop bell tinkled behind him.

Mr Liss looked up. 'I was just closing, sir–'

'No problem.' The voice was American. 'Eric. What a coincidence, eh?'

Blaines turned round. 'George,' he said without enthusiasm.

Koslove barely came up to Blaines's shoulder. He was hatless and his bald patch gleamed with raindrops. He bounced up and down on the balls of his toes.

'I just happened to be passing,' he said for Liss's benefit. 'Saw you in here and I thought–'

'You two gentlemen know each other.' Liss sounded pleased for them.

'What brought you to Wardour Street?' Blaines said.

'Exercise.' Koslove sounded surprised. 'I try to walk at least three miles a day. And it's a great way to get to know a city.'

Blaines slid the cheque across the counter and picked up the Guards. He nodded to Liss. 'Tell Jonesey I was asking after him.'

Outside the shop Koslove's minder closed in behind them. The Cadillac was parked on double yellow lines round the corner in Brewer Street. Its CD plates kept the wheel-clampers away.

'Let's go for a ride.' Koslove said. 'Tell you what, we'll take you home.'

It was raining. Blaines didn't bother to argue.

The minder sat in front with the driver. The back of the limousine was better appointed than most living-rooms. Blaines accepted a large Scotch. He fumbled for his cigars.

'Would you mind not smoking?' Koslove poured himself a glass of lemon-flavoured Perrier water. 'It goes straight to my sinuses.'

'Of course I mind.' Blaines said. He finished his Scotch and passed his glass to Koslove for a refill. 'But I'm open to bribes.'

'Eric, I'll be frank. I've got a problem. You've got a problem. I'd like us to put our heads together on this one.'

Blaines edged along the seat towards Koslove as though eager to put the suggestion into practice without delay.

'Eric.' Koslove said warningly. 'Feniscliffe. Brundish.'

Blaines put the guardsmen on the parcel shelf underneath the rear window. He took the glass which Koslove held out to him.

'Okay, George,' he said. 'Take your time, old son. You can tell me anything. You got some more names?'

'You know Jon Lackan?'

Blaines shook his head. 'Not personally.' But it was time to show willing, if only to ensure another whisky would eventually come his way. 'Let me see. Assistant to the White House Chief of Staff till last year's shake-up; his dad was Eisenhower's ambassador in . . . Athens, was it? Family owns a respectable chunk of General Motors among other things.'

'Right. Tina Breighton mean anything to you?'

'Never heard of her. Should I?'

Koslove shrugged. 'She's an analyst at Langley. Specializes in the Far East. I've heard it said that one day she might be the first woman director of the CIA. Crock of shit, of course, but it gives you an idea.'

Blaines stared out of the window. Koslove was boring to listen to because he talked so slowly. You got stuck in the spaces between the words. He saw they hadn't even reached Hammersmith Broadway yet. It was all stop-start with more stop than start.

'Breighton resigned last week,' Koslove said. 'Lackan disappeared. He's got a job in State now. Just didn't turn up.'

'Someone knew too much?'

Koslove looked sharply at him. 'I didn't say that.'

'You mentioned Feniscliffe and Brundish. Same difference.'

'Tina Breighton went off the rails in her middle teens. Just a couple of months. There were family problems. She left home, went to California. Sex and drugs and rock'n'roll. Lived in a commune near Laguna with this guy who claimed to be in the Brotherhood of Eternal Love. You know, the hippie mafia. There were links with the Weathermen, Christ knows what.'

'Lot of people in the CIA with that sort of background?' Blaines said blandly.

Koslove shook his head. 'It was only she ran a little wild when she was sixteen. Then she went back home and turned into a model student. A model citizen. Point is, Eric, someone outside the Agency got hold of the story. They put the black on her. She made a mature decision: she reported what was happening, then she resigned. We were very, very supportive. That woman had a great future.'

'You want to find out who's behind it? She's co-operating?'

'She was.' Koslove clicked his tongue against the roof

of his mouth. 'But last night someone put a bullet in her.'

'And where does Lackan come in? Don't tell me, he's really a Black Panther.'

Koslove sighed. 'Eric, this is *serious*.'

'Was he being blackmailed?'

'I don't know. We think so. All the classic symptoms: signs of strain, short of money, drinking too much.'

'Why you telling me?'

'Breighton was first approached in London. She spent a week's leave here in August. Plus, the guy she lived with in the commune was English. Everyone called him Gus. Never knew his surname. Lackan's girlfriend said he had a visitor the night he disappeared. Middle-aged guy with an English accent. Oh yeah, and he had a weekend in London last month. One strange thing: the *New York Times* mentioned Brundish's death last week. Next day, Lackan called an old friend in White House security: wanted to know if he had anything on the Bishop of Rosington.'

'Click, click, click,' Blaines said.

'What?'

'It all adds up. Connections, pointers. What do you want me to do?'

If Blaines didn't cooperate, someone else would.

'You're a great guy, Eric, you know that? First off I need to know if you've got anything on Lackan and Breighton: could the information have come from here?'

'Okay.' Sensing that the moment was ripe. Blaines held out his glass again. 'George . . . in return: can you tell me anything about Brundish or Feniscliffe?'

'Nothing you don't know already.' Koslove looked innocently at him. 'And all it adds up to is two little question marks.' He rubbed his chin, drawing out the moment as long as he could. 'There's maybe one thing I could tell you. You heard the latest on Feniscliffe?'

Blaines shook his head gloomily. He hated the one-up-manship which was endemic in this job. Especially when he found himself underneath.

'He turned up an hour ago,' Koslove said happily. 'In Suffolk and still in his automobile. The automobile was upside down at the bottom of the Deben estuary.'

'Must you get back tonight?' Patricia Claybrook said.

Jessica concealed her surprise. 'There's no urgency. I'd love to stay.'

Nell and John had already left. They had promised to be back at Reading by seven: they were due to relieve Matthew's babysitter. Patricia had refused their invitation to come with them.

Jessica still felt slightly drunk. The drive to London was not an inviting prospect; and it would do Jack good if she didn't go back to the flat tonight. He should have phoned.

Patricia straightened the cushions and emptied the ash-trays. She had changed out of her black dress and was wearing an old tweed skirt and a jersey. She still managed to look elegant.

The black dress would be hanging in the wardrobe. Her mother liked life to be organized. Jessica remembered her teens as a running battle between them over the mess in her room. Nell, of course, had taken pride in the neatness of her bedroom.

'Can I help?'

'I'm not an invalid.' Patricia softened the refusal with

72

a smile. 'Anyway, you look shattered. I'll do supper. Something light.'

It was all so dreadfully familiar. Jessica listened to the sounds from the kitchen. She had heard them a thousand times before. Her father's presence was still in the sitting room – in the armchair that had moulded itself to his shape over the years; in the photograph her mother had taken of him through the kitchen window; in the Chinese figures of health, wealth and wisdom that he had brought back from Hong Kong last year. There were traces of him everywhere she looked.

The evening stretched ahead, a minefield of potential embarrassments. It was years since she had been alone with her mother; they were both out of practice. The quarrels of the past had thrown long shadows into the future. It was odd that you could know and love someone all your life and yet feel awkward in her company.

And guilty. The guilt Jessica felt about her father's death had been transferred to her mother's account. For the first time she understood how parents could feel that their children owed them a debt. Any emotion was a form of investment.

The phone rang. Jessica ran to answer it. She wanted to hear Jack's voice if only to be reminded that she had her own investments.

She lifted the handset. In her hurry she recited the number for the Notting Hill flat.

There was silence on the other end of the line.

'Hullo? This is Halcombe 34429.'

It wasn't silence, Jessica realized; someone was breathing. The hairs stirred on the back of her neck.

She slammed down the phone.

'Who was that?' Patricia called.

Jessica opened the kitchen door. 'A heavy-breather. I think. Someone was there but they wouldn't say anything.'

Patricia frowned. 'How odd.' She shrugged. 'Supper's ready, such as it is.'

They took trays into the sitting room. Neither of them felt like eating much. Even a boiled egg and a slice of toast were hard work.

Afterwards Jessica made the coffee. Patricia turned on the television. Jessica wondered how people managed in the days before television and radio. The evenings of the past must have been scattered with long silences. They couldn't have spent all their time reading aloud and singing ballads to one another.

Patricia watched the news as if she had been starved of information for years. Afterwards there was a dreary situation comedy. Her mother loathed situation comedies. But she didn't change channels or turn off the set. Maybe she was afraid of silences too. It was difficult to imagine her being afraid of anything.

'John said there's a problem about the pension,' Jessica said. The words came out more loudly than she had intended.

Her mother looked away from the screen. 'They're being difficult,' she said vaguely.

'If there's anything I can do –'

'No, thank you.'

'I suppose you could always take up photography again.'

When Jessica and Nell were children and there was

even less money available, their mother had worked semi-professionally as a photographer. Jessica suspected that it hadn't been a lucrative way of spending the time. Patricia had little sympathy with coy brides and bashful bridegrooms; and it showed in the photographs she took.

'Maybe.' Patricia rubbed her long fingers along the arm of the chair. 'Jess, do you mind if we talk about it later? I don't want to think about that sort of thing. Not right now.'

Jessica flushed. 'Of course not.'

'Time for my walk.' Patricia stood up in one easy movement. She switched off the set. 'You weren't watching that, were you?'

'Your walk?'

'I often have a walk before going to bed. Seems to help me sleep. Could you put some milk on while I'm out?'

The request adroitly prevented Jessica from asking if her mother wanted company.

Patricia pulled on a raincoat and Wellington boots. She paused at the back door.

'I just go along the lane. Won't be more than five or ten minutes.'

Jessica washed up while the milk heated. She dried everything very carefully in deference to her mother's kitchen. The ten minutes passed. The milk boiled over. Jessica cleaned up and opened the window, hoping her mother wouldn't notice the smell of burning milk.

Another five minutes had gone by. Jessica put some more milk on the hob and told herself not to be stupid. Why shouldn't her mother stay out a little longer than usual?

Nevertheless she opened the back door and looked out into the garden. The rain had stopped. The air smelled fresh. The sky had cleared; to the west you could see stars. In London you tended to forget the stars were there.

There was no sign of Patricia. The branches of the apple tree near the door swayed in the wind. The back gate creaked to and fro; her mother must have left it open.

'Mum?' Jessica called softly.

On the other side of the house a car came down the road.

Jessica moved down the path, ready to retreat at the sound of her mother's footsteps; her mother had wanted to be alone.

She paused at the gate. The narrow lane was completely dark. On one side it was bounded by the fences and trees of the gardens that backed on to it; on the other was a high, ragged hedge strung out between a row of hawthorn trees.

From past experience she knew the lane would be muddy. It was a place she associated with secrecy. Here she had her first cigarette while Nell looked on disapprovingly; Nell's disapproval provided ninety per cent of the pleasure. Later, when her parents thought she was in bed, she used to meet a boyfriend here for experimental fumbles in the dark.

'Mum? Are you there?'

The night was full of noises: the rustle of leaves, or perhaps small animals scurrying away from her; a car door slamming and its engine firing; the distant chatter from a neighbour's TV; and the soft moan of the wind on the edge of hearing.

She stepped out into the lane, keeping to the grass verge.

'Jess . . .'

Not the wind–

'Mum! Where are you?'

Another moan which wasn't the wind.

Jessica plunged across the lane. Her eyes were adjusting to the darkness. She could see the darker shape beneath the nearest hawthorn. The face was a lighter blur, as formless as a ghost's.

Her mother stirred. Jessica slid an arm under her. She wanted to pour out questions but they would have to wait. Patricia struggled into a sitting position.

'Oh God . . .'

'Do you think you can walk? We'd better get you inside.'

Patricia grunted. 'I. . . I don't know. My head hurts.'

The darkness made everything worse. There was no way to assess the damage. The helplessness and uncertainty in her mother's voice made Jessica's stomach turn over. The roles were reversed. It was time for the investment to pay a dividend.

'Put your arm round my shoulder. That's right. Now, see if you can stand up. If it hurts too much, just say.'

Patricia's weight surprised her. She was a tall woman but she carried no surplus flesh. Maybe it was due to the mysterious difference between a live weight and a dead weight.

'Do you think you can walk?'

'I think so.'

The arm clung to her shoulders. All Patricia's strength seemed to be concentrated in the fingers of her right hand.

Together they stumbled into the garden and up the path. Patricia moved like an old woman: each step was a separate operation.

An oblong of light stretched from the open kitchen door. Jessica glanced up at her mother's face. It was smeared with mud. Blood welled from a cut above one cheekbone.

The milk had boiled over again. Jessica settled Patricia in a chair and threw the offending saucepan in the sink. Her mother gave no sign that she had noticed. She was slumped across the table. Her eyes followed Jessica's movements.

The priorities were warm water and disinfectant. Jessica washed her mother's face and hands. The cut was about an inch long but it wasn't deep. With luck it shouldn't need stitches. The skin around it was beginning to swell into a bruise. The disinfectant made Patricia wince.

The Elastoplast was where it always was: in the cupboard by the door. Her mother's methodical habits had their advantages.

'Where else?' Jessica said.

Her mother tried to smile. 'Such a lot of fuss . . . The left wrist: I think it's sprained.'

Apart from that, the only other damage was a grazed knee and a ruined pair of tights. Jessica put the kettle on.

'Now what happened?' she asked.

Patricia stared at her for a moment. She touched the piece of Elastoplast. 'Someone attacked me – just as I was coming back. They must have been waiting by the gate.'

'More than one person? What did they do?'

78

'I think there were two of them.' She frowned down at her nails. Mud was still encrusted beneath the rims. 'But I'm not sure. It all happened so fast. They hit me then grabbed me and threw me down.' She shook her head in disbelief. 'In *Halcombe*. It doesn't seem possible.'

'Muggings happen everywhere. Did they try and take anything?'

Patricia shook her head. 'Just ran off down the lane. Where are you going?'

'To call a doctor. And the police.'

The front doorbell rang. A white envelope fluttered through the letter slot and fell to the mat beneath.

'What is it?' Patricia's voice was harsh with panic.

Jessica picked up the letter. 'Mrs Patricia Claybrook' was neatly typed on it. There was no address.

'Give it to me,' her mother said. 'It's for me, isn't it?'

It's the shock, Jessica thought; *she doesn't know what she's saying*.

'Shall I open it for you?'

Patricia snatched it from her and ran her finger under the flap. Inside was a single sheet of paper. She glanced through the contents and crumpled it up with a sudden, savage movement.

'Jess, you must lock up. Every window. Every bolt.' She heaved herself to her feet.

'Mum, sit down -'

'Do as I say. Please.'

'Can I see the letter? What are you doing?'

'What does it look like? Using the phone . . . I'm sorry, sweetheart. I have to call someone who used to work with your father.'

*

There was a boil on the back of Frank's neck. Blaines stared at it, willing it to explode.

'Where are we going, sir?' Caragh asked.

Blaines transferred his malevolence to the young Irishman beside him. 'We're going to have breakfast.' He raised his voice for Frank's benefit. 'At the Membury service station.'

'I meant after that.'

'We're going to see a widow,' Blaines said. 'Her husband used to work for us. She's been having a spot of bother.'

'It might help if I knew what it was.'

'First there was a burglary,' Blaines said reluctantly. 'Then last night someone mugged her. There was a letter . . .'

'Not a police matter then?'

'We wouldn't be here if it was.'

Blaines stared out of the window, putting an end to the conversation. They were on the M4. There wasn't much traffic on the westward carriageway. Everyone was flooding east like lemmings to London.

Patricia's phone call last night had upset him more than he cared to admit. Having to cope with Caragh and Frank didn't help; he would have to be careful what he said and did. He had no doubt that everything would get back to Wreningham.

He was getting old: that was the real problem. A few years back he could have handled Wreningham. The pushy little bastard wanted to ease him out. Blaines had every intention of hanging on until he was sixty-five. He would have to retire then. At sixty-five you were officially senile. But even then there would be the possibility of consultative work of some kind. It all depended on how indispensable you could make yourself seem. He wouldn't get any favours from William Wreningham.

Wanky Willy's tactics were so obvious they were laughable. He was using Frank as a watchdog to report on Blaines's movements outside the office. Liam Caragh had provided him with the opportunity for a slightly subtler move. By attaching him to Blaines and insisting, quite legitimately, on full cooperation, Wreningham was following his orders to the letter. It gave him a wonderful reason to make sure Blaines handled nothing remotely sensitive for the next three months.

Three months? There was a whisper that Caragh's appointment might be extended to a year.

A year would do it, Blaines thought. Three months he could perhaps cope with. But a year away from everything that mattered would turn him into one of those fossils Terry Aughrim was always raving about. No one would tell him anything. His caseload would dwindle. He'd seen it happen to other people; he'd even helped it happen. If they couldn't make you retire they made you superfluous instead.

They'd see him shuffling down the corridor: 'That's old Eric,' they'd say to recruits. 'He knows where they keep the stationery. Good man to ask if you want to know what happened in Tehran in '52.'

But it wasn't going to be like that, not if he could help it. He'd survived this sort of thing before.

His eyes left the M4 and returned to Frank's boil. It made him feel better. Wreningham's watchers had their weaknesses just like everyone else.

Koslove owed him. It would be worth increasing the debt.

And Caragh? Used rightly, he could be a two-edged weapon.

Blaines chuckled.

The car pulled off the motorway.

'Here we are, sir.' Frank's mouth was probably watering in anticipation.

'Bacon,' Blaines said dreamily. 'Eggs, sausages, tomato. He jabbed Caragh in the ribs. 'What do you think? Fried bread too?'

Caragh shrugged. 'I'd prefer muesli.'

You would.

Frank found a parking slot near the cafeteria.

Blaines opened the door. 'You'd better stay in the car, Frankie boy. Lot of vandals in these motorway car-parks. Don't want any scratches on government property.'

The widow was a shock.

Liam had been expecting a grey-haired woman in a black dress; he had nerved himself for red eyes, sagging shoulders and perhaps a trembling lower lip. He had never been able to inure himself to other people's sorrow.

But the woman who answered the door was younger than he was. She wore jeans and a T-shirt which proved that her body, though small, was perfectly firm in all the right places. She had black hair and brown eyes. The set of her mouth made it clear she wasn't pleased to see them.

'Well, if it ain't little Jessie,' Blaines said awkwardly. 'You don't recognize me?'

The brown eyes flicked over him and on to Liam.

'Last time I saw you, you had pigtails,' Blaines said. 'And spots.'

'You'd better come in,' she said. 'My mother's in the sitting room.'

The real widow failed to conform to expectations in anything but her age and the colour of her hair. There was a piece of plaster, surrounded by a bruise, just below her right eye.

She welcomed them with casual efficiency and introduced her daughter Jessica. Liam tried to place the voice: New England perhaps, but overlaid with a good deal of old England.

Jessica went to make some coffee. Liam wondered if he should offer to help but the door closed behind her before he could open his mouth.

'You all right?' Blaines said roughly.

Patricia Claybrook nodded. 'More shocked than anything.' She touched her cheek. 'This looks much worse than it is. The wrist was only a slight sprain. It's fine this morning.'

'All the same – have you seen a doctor?'

'No. Don't fuss, Eric.'

Liam glanced at the old man. He was slightly pinker than usual.

'You'll want to see the letter, I imagine.' Mrs Claybrook opened a bureau, took out an envelope and passed it to Blaines.

'This came just after the attack?'

'Yes. They even rang the doorbell.'

Blaines read the letter inside and handed it to Liam. It was typewritten and unsigned.

I wouldn't call the police if I were you. Remember Nell's pregnant. There's Jessica and little Matthew. And remember Greg? He might be surprised if he found out about his father. There's nothing to worry about if you are sensible and give me Claybrook's notes. They are no use to you or anyone else. Will be in touch re arrangements.

'Has Jess seen this?' Blaines said.

'Yes.' Mrs Claybrook glanced at Liam and then back to Blaines. 'She doesn't know who Charles worked for. Not yet. She's always assumed it was the Foreign Office.'

Blaines took back the letter and put it in his pocket. 'We'll check it out.'

The door opened and Jessica came in with a tray. Liam sprang up to help her. She avoided meeting his eyes. Their hands touched as she passed him a cup and saucer. She asked Blaines if she should take a cup outside for the driver.

'No thanks, love. Frank never drinks coffee.'

'Did you tell the police?' Jessica said to him. 'My mother said you would.'

Blaines nodded. 'They're keeping a discreet eye on the house, front and back. Don't you worry.'

'I'm not. I'm just angry.'

Blaines scratched his greasy, grey curls. 'Me too love. And a fat lot of use that is.' He turned back to Mrs Claybrook. 'Pat, I'm going to have to look through Chas's papers. Everything you've got, I'm afraid. And we'll have to search the house.'

'You're welcome. But you won't find anything.'

'I don't know. Surprising what people bring home

84

from the office. And there must be a reason why someone's interested.'

She shrugged her slim shoulders. 'It's all upstairs. He used Nell's old room as a kind of study.'

'They chocolate biscuits on that plate?' Blaines asked Jessica.

She passed them to him. The T-shirt had a loose neck. As Jessica stretched across to Blaines, Liam glimpsed the top of a full breast. He looked away.

Blaines took two biscuits. She offered them to Liam, who shook his head and tried the effect of a smile. Jessica appeared not to notice it.

'Is there a connection with the burglary?' she said to Blaines.

He grunted. 'It's an obvious possibility.' Fragments of biscuit sprayed over the green woollen tie and the faded check shirt. 'Maybe one method failed so they tried another.'

'But why should anyone bother? Dad wasn't anyone important.'

The second biscuit went the way of the first.

'There's a rumour going round the office,' Blaines said carefully, 'to the effect that old Chas had literary ambitions.' He was looking at Patricia Claybrook now. 'A hobby for his retirement. *My Life and Times in the Corridors of Power*, that sort of thing. *Whispers from Whitehall*. He mention that to you?'

Liam sensed the atmosphere in the room had undergone a change. A tension had developed between Blaines and Mrs Claybrook. He glanced at Jessica, who was frowning.

Patricia Claybrook laughed. Blaines's face remained blank and attentive.

'The exposé?' she said. Her long fingers danced in the air, inserting quotation marks around the word. 'Did anyone actually believe that?'

'Quite a lot of people.'

'But it was a joke.' Her voice was tinged with exasperation. 'He just wanted to ruffle a few feathers. Charles couldn't write a book to save his life. You know what his sense of humour was like.'

'A joke?' Blaines said gently. 'Looks like someone didn't think it was a joke.'

After coffee they searched the house. To be more precise. Liam searched while Blaines supervised him.

The Claybrooks stayed in the sitting room. Liam wondered how they felt about two strangers combing through their private lives. The fat man might be ill at ease with Mrs Claybrook but not enough to make him skimp the job.

They rolled back carpets; they pawed through dresses; they read letters; they examined bank statements; they took books from the shelves and flicked through the pages; they peered up chimneys; they investigated the U-bends and cisterns of the lavatories; they disturbed the dust and cobwebs in the loft; they emptied the tea-caddy and delved into the freezer.

Liam worked slowly and thoroughly, following the text-book procedures to the letter; Blaines breathing heavily through his mouth, hovered at Liam's shoulder like an examiner.

Most of the house was orderly and without secrets: everything was neatly catalogued and on display – almost as if Mrs Claybrook had had a good sort-out before the search. She was not a woman who had kept many mementoes from the past.

The only exception to the rule was the photographs. They were everywhere – framed on the walls, filed in drawers and stacked on top of the wardrobe. Most of them seemed to be portraits chiefly of old people and bleak, empty landscapes.

Blaines paused on the landing in front of a photograph of a beach. The tide was out. The timbers of a boat, half-buried in the sand, dominated the foreground like a set of abandoned teeth.

'She was good,' he said. 'Took a photo of me once. I've still got it somewhere.' The fat man sucked his teeth and turned on Liam. 'What you waiting for? We haven't got all day.'

The room Charles Claybrook had used as a study yielded no secrets, official or otherwise. Blaines himself rummaged through the drawers of the little desk.

'Christ,' he said. 'He didn't even nick the office stationery.'

The back bedroom was the last place to be searched. Liam thought that if he were an archaeologist he would be able to distinguish three layers of occupation. The deepest and earliest layer contained traces of a child and adolescent: the three-legged animal – a giraffe? – on the bedspread; the scraps of china (holiday souvenirs perhaps) on the mantelpiece; and the bookcase whose contents stretched from *The Twins at St Clare's* to *The Catcher in the Rye*.

The next layer was the spare-bedroom-cum-boxroom phase, an era that must have begun when Jessica left home. A rich haul of artefacts was available – from the curtains and carpet, both of which looked inexpensive but relatively new, to the armchair with torn upholstery and the empty suitcases stacked in the wardrobe.

The latest layer consisted of the present possessions of the woman downstairs – of the adult Jessica who wouldn't smile at the men from her father's office. Liam was simultaneously curious and ashamed of his curiosity. He sorted through the contents of the scuffed overnight bag and tried to persuade himself that he wasn't prying, just doing his job.

The fact that yesterday she must have worn the black skirt and jacket which were draped over the chair was of purely academic interest.

On the bedside table was a foil and plastic packet containing birth-control pills. Liam's catholicism was of the lapsed variety; its prelapsarian state had ended with the onset of puberty. He had an uncomfortably vivid memory of Emma looking away when he produced the packet of Durex.

In the handbag he found a photograph among the credit cards in the wallet: it was a passport-size shot of an unshaven man with broad shoulders; he wore a leather jacket with a CND badge on the lapel.

'The boyfriend?' Blaines said. 'Bloody pinko by the look of him.'

Liam held up an NUJ card. 'She's a journalist, sir.'

'I know that. Come on, sunshine. You've done enough Sherlocking for one morning.'

Blaines led the way back to the sitting room. The two Claybrooks were sitting in silence on either side of the empty fireplace like patients in a dentist's waiting room.

'Any luck?' Patricia Claybrook said.

Blaines shook his head. 'But we had to go through the motions,' he said brusquely. 'You do understand that?'

In another man's voice the words would have sounded like a plea for forgiveness. Blaines made them sound more like a calculated insult.

'You want to check the garden and the lane?'

'Not particularly. The police have seen to that already.' Blaines stuffed a finger in his ear and twisted it vigorously; they had called it buggerlugging at Liam's school. 'But I do want to see Chas's letters from Turkey.'

Mrs Claybrook lifted her chin. 'What makes you think he sent any?'

'Come off it, love,' Blaines snarled. 'He always wrote to you when he was away.'

For a moment she held his gaze. Then she shrugged.

'If you must.' She opened the handbag that was tucked between her and the arm of the chair. 'There was only one. Postmarked the day he died.'

'Do you enjoy this?' Jessica said quietly to Liam.

He met her eyes. 'What do you think?'

Her chin lifted just as her mother's had done. She looked away.

Blaines took the airmail envelope and glanced through the two sheets of paper inside. His face was as expressive as a priest's in a confessional. He stuffed the letter back in the envelope and returned it to Mrs Claybrook.

'Satisfied?' she said.

'We'll be off now. The local boys will be keeping an eye on you. You can ring me any time, home or office. All right?'

Patricia Claybrook said nothing.

Blaines jammed a cigar in his mouth; he lit it as soon as he was on the front doorstep.

89

Liam nodded goodbye to Mrs Claybrook; Jessica stayed in the sitting room.

Blaines punched him lightly on the shoulder. 'Go wake up Frank.'

As Liam reached the gate he heard Blaines clear his throat.

'Pat,' the old man said. 'How did they know about Greg?'

3

'Two double bourbon mists.'

In Greg's brain the words were clear enough but once they were out of his mouth they sounded slurred.

The bartender hesitated. He had soft brown eyes like a Walt Disney dog. He used them to make a swift assessment of Greg's capacity for drink and his ability to pay.

Gregory Vanderman recognized the expression. He was accustomed to being assessed. People had been measuring him all his life. Life was one long measuring session which gave employment and job satisfaction to bartenders, teachers, women, employers, psychiatrists, servants and, of course, his father. Most of all his father.

This time he had made the grade. The bartender removed the empty glasses and dropped crushed ice into two clean ones. He used a shot glass to measure the whiskey. He took his time. Obviously he was a born measurer who enjoyed his work.

'Honey, I'm *not* an alcoholic.' The blonde, upset by an accusation which nobody but herself had made, dabbed her eyes. She rested her head on Greg's shoulder so he had a good view of the brown roots of her hair. 'I guess you could call me a social drinker. Even a *heavy* social drinker. You want a cigarette?'

Greg shook his head. The bartender put their glasses in front of them. They reached for them simultaneously in a movement that might have been rehearsed as a double-act. In a sense it had been.

'Fifteen,' the woman said. 'Or maybe seventeen. I know it's an odd number.'

Greg had stopped counting a couple of hours ago. After a while arithmetic lost its attraction. He wished he could remember the pseudo-blonde's name; it would have made things more personal.

'My dad used to count them too,' she said dreamily. 'He said that way you knew when you'd reached your limit. He'd come home Friday night and say to Mom: "I had four beers on my way home," and she'd say, "Sweetheart, you deserve them." Kind of cosy. Tonight's Friday, so it's okay. We deserve them. Don't we? Don't we?'

Greg said he guessed they did.

A band was playing country music at the back. You could separate the customers into those who had come for the music and those who had come for the bar. The singer was pretending to be a trucker with a mother named Mary Ellen. He made her rhyme with heaven.

The pseudo-blonde put her elbow on the bar and her chin in her hand. The elbow slipped first. When Greg had helped her back on to the bar-stool she said: 'How about yours?'

'My what?'

'Your folks. Do they have drinks on Friday nights?'

'I don't know. My mother died when I was born.'

The pseudo-blonde frowned. Greg decided he would have one more drink and then go home. Just one more. He was in control. There was an untouched pint of vodka in the apartment in case he changed his mind. The vodka was a smart move: it showed foresight; it proved he was in control.

'Shit,' she said. 'Really? Your dad marry again?'

Greg shook his head. There was always a woman around but never another wife. When he was a kid, Greg thought his father's love for his mother had been so great he couldn't bear to marry again. The theory also explained Warren Vanderman's attitude to his only son. It was a good theory.

'You must be very close to him.'

'We're like Poles,' Greg said. 'He's North and I'm South.'

She laughed so much she fell off the stool again. This time Greg didn't help her up because he wasn't sure that he could. She lay back with one arm behind her head and her knees up; she was still smoking the cigarette.

The bartender kept glancing their way. Greg had a sixth sense about bartenders' expressions. He could tell when they meant 'Same again?' or 'Where's the money?' This guy's face was saying something rather complicated like 'That woman's legless. Why don't you both get the fuck out of here?'

Total control. Greg ran through the options. He could throw his empty glass at the gilt-framed mirror behind the bar. He could punch the bartender. He could put his head down on the bar and wait for the woman to go away. He could leave the woman here and find another bar. He could leave the woman here and go home to the pint of vodka.

He stood up. The stool heeled over and fell on the pseudo-blonde. She laughed. He laid a twenty-dollar bill on the bar-top. The bartender's face softened.

'Come on, sweetheart.' Greg took a firm grip on the bar and reached down his free hand. 'Let's go find a cab.'

Outside it was cold. The wind was coming westwards from the Bay. They were on the wrong side of Market near the Bus Depot. The pseudo-blonde wept noisily. Greg propped her against a lighted window and went through her bag until he found her driver's licence. She lived out in Bay View.

It took them a while to find a cab that was not only free but willing to stop for them. Greg shovelled her into the back, told the driver where to go and paid him. The driver tried to rip him off and Greg let him succeed.

He walked back to the apartment. He walked for several reasons: because it wasn't far; because he wasn't sure he would make it; and because the pint of vodka had to be earned. He had one for the road in a bar on Leavenworth. Just the one – to demonstrate beyond all possible doubt that you didn't need to have two or more in every bar.

The apartment was in an old block on Post and Polk, near Van Ness. It had been designed for midgets. The bed would fold up into the wall. Greg found it was simpler to leave it down all the time. Cockroaches clambered up the garbage chute. There was a nest of transsexuals in the floor above. Most of the transsexuals liked to sing along with Tamla Motown records.

On his way up Greg checked his mailbox. He had two circulars and a postcard. He put them in his pocket for later.

He was very controlled. He put the vodka on a tray with a glass and a carton of orange juice beside it. He kicked off his shoes and got into bed. Then he had the first celebratory drink. The orange juice made it taste healthy.

With the second drink he remembered the mail. Reader's Digest had another wonderful offer for him. Someone thought he should take out life insurance. The postcard was from England. Guardsmen in red tunics stood like dolls outside Buckingham Palace. He flipped it over. The message on the other side was typed and very short.

Ever asked your mother who your father is?

The St Francis Hotel was expecting Greg Vanderman at six-thirty on Saturday morning.

He got up towards midday. He had the rest of the vodka while he was in the bathroom. Shaving was out of the question because his hand shook too much. But he took a shower. Then he was sick. He re-read the postcard and called the airport. He recited the number on one of his credit cards and was told to have a nice day. He had time to stop at a bar.

On the plane he had two Bloody Marys. By the time they reached Los Angeles he was sufficiently in control to be able to shave.

The cab dropped him at the gate. The security guard had never heard of Greg. Greg said that was okay because he'd never heard of the security guard. After a little more light conversation the guard agreed to call the house and see if anyone there had heard of Gregory Vanderman.

While he was on the phone the guard kept his free hand resting suggestively on the .357 Magnum round his waist. He looked at Greg as he talked.

'There's a guy here says he's Mr Vanderman's son. About five-eleven, hundred and ninety pounds, curly hair sort of dirty yellow colour. Looks like someone left him out in the rain. What? Okay.'

The guard slammed down the phone and jerked his head as if something had stung his ear.

'Okay. You can go up.' To be on the safe side he added in a lower voice: 'Mr Vanderman.'

The garden was a wilderness of weeds. Greg picked his way up the rutted drive. The house looked worse than it had done two years ago. It was vaguely Spanish Colonial, with a touch of the Tudors about the gables and chimneys. His father had bought it in the early seventies from an old woman whose brief career as a film star had ground to a halt thirty years before.

Lilian was waiting for him on the cracked paving stones of the terrace. She was a comfortable brunette who had graduated from being her employer's mistress to looking after his house. Greg noticed that she'd stopped trying to conceal her age.

'How're you doing?' She kissed his cheek. 'Warren's down by the pool.'

'Does he know I'm here?'

She nodded. 'Take care. He's . . .' She lifted her shoulders.

'Sore about something? About me? He usually is.'

'Something's been bugging him this last week.'

'What he needs is the love of a good woman,' Greg said. 'Why don't you marry him?'

'I'm not the marrying kind,' she said. 'Why don't you go and get it over with?'

The pool was at the back of the house. The water was

96

brown and matted with rotting vegetation. It smelled as though animals had died there.

Warren Vanderman was sitting on a cast-iron chair which had once been painted white. He was hunched forward, staring at something on the ground beside the pool. His limbs were long and thin and he wore a battered Panama hat. He was very still yet gave the impression of alertness like an old cat about to pounce.

'You know what I like about this place?' Greg said. 'It looks sort of lived in.'

His father picked up the pocket chess set from the ground and closed it with a snap.

'I often wondered why you didn't have it repaired,' Greg went on. 'Hire gardeners and interior decorators. I mean, the only new thing round here is the security system.'

'What do you want?' The old man looked at him at last. 'You're meant to be in San Francisco washing dishes.'

'You know about that?'

'I know you're drinking too much and living with a bunch of faggots. You want to watch yourself. You never heard of AIDS?'

Greg's insides felt as though someone had scraped them raw when he wasn't looking. His body was a mass of protesting nerves. He should have stopped the cab at a liquor store. He should have made Lilian give him a drink.

'Someone sent me a card from England. It said why didn't I ask my mother who my father was.'

'Get out,' Warren Vanderman said. 'Just get the hell out of here and don't come back.'

He stood up slowly. Even now, with his head bent forwards and his shoulders stooped, he was taller than Greg. There was a phone on the diving-board at the end of the pool. On the other end of the phone were the security guards who policed his private world.

'My mother's dead, right?' Greg said quickly. 'Where did she die?'

'You're a failure. Everything you done, you failed. Now you can't see further than the next drink.'

Vanderman hobbled toward the phone. The arthritis had got worse in the last two years.

Greg wanted to push the old man in the pool and hold his head under the filthy water until he stopped struggling.

'Okay,' he said instead. 'I'm going.'

He took a few steps towards the house and paused. His father was staring at him. His face was sour with dislike.

'You know what?' Greg said. 'I think Lilian wants you to marry her. God knows why. But you'll never do that, will you? Once bitten, twice shy.'

'And who's Greg supposed to be?'

'I don't know. My mother clammed up when I asked.'

'Family? She must have relatives. How about an Uncle Greg?'

Jessica shook her head. 'There was some sort of quarrel when she married my father. We've never met any of them. I've never heard of a Greg.'

Jack raked his fingers down her spine. She twisted in his arms.

The nails were sharp and he never seemed to know his own strength.

'Come back,' Jack said. Their heads were side by side on the same pillow.

'I'm cold.'

He pulled the duvet over her. 'I haven't finished with you. Miss me?'

'Sort of.'

His question gave her pleasure. You could infer from it that he had missed her. She had been away for three nights. She wanted him to have been lonely.

She buried her face in the coarse black hair on his chest. It smelled faintly musty like an animal's fur. 'Did you get a story out of it?'

'Students. Load of bloody piss-artists. They had this theory that two of their professors are leaking exam papers. Maybe they're right but there wasn't any evidence. So I wasted two days. Why does someone want your father's papers?'

Jessica wriggled away from him. It would be nice if he could forget he was a journalist, just for a few hours.

'Apparently everyone thought he was going to write his memoirs. But he wasn't – it was just a joke, according to my mother. There aren't any papers. Never have been.'

'I don't get it,'Jack said. 'A burglary; a mugging; attempted blackmail. I thought your dad was just a glorified filing clerk.'

'I think he was something to do with the archives at the FCO. Before that he was at the Home Office. He never talked about it much. He was just a civil servant.'

'And they gave your mum a special number to ring if there was trouble? The police are guarding the house?

99

Blokes come down from London in chauffeur-driven cars? Come off it, he wasn't any old civil servant.'

Jessica stroked the hard muscles on his groin. Watery sunlight came through the half-drawn curtains. It was pleasantly wicked to be in bed in the middle of the afternoon.

Jack brushed away her hand. 'So why all the fuss? He must have been more important than you thought.'

'I don't think so. In that case he'd've earned more money. He'd've felt less bitter about the job. I think he felt he'd missed out on promotion.'

'What were the two men like? Did you get their names?'

'The senior one was Blaines. Mum called him Eric. He knew Dad – quite well, I think.' Jessica frowned. 'In his sixties, I suppose. Overweight and slopping out of his clothes. The odd thing was, I think he was a bit in awe of my mother.'

'Interesting. What about the sidekick?'

'I didn't catch his name. Sounded Irish. He was dark and quite small.'

'Young? Old?'

'Thirtyish. Looked like he meant to go places.' Jessica shook her head vigorously. She remembered the way the Irishman had stared at her. 'He wasn't important. They spent hours searching the house. Must have gone up in the loft – the younger one got his suit all messed up.'

'Find anything?'

'Don't think so. Blaines made my mother show him a letter from Dad. She was furious. Why the interest?'

'Because none of it fits with what you say your dad was.'

Jessica looked at his face. It had the hard, withdrawn expression it always wore when Jack sniffed a story. His mind was a long way from making love again.

She swung her legs out of bed and reached for her dressing-gown. 'You want some tea?'

'Okay. What was your mother's maiden name?'

'Youlgreave. Jack, drop it, will you? We're talking about my parents.'

'You know what I reckon?'

'No, and I don't want to.'

'I reckon your old man was a spy.'

Early on Saturday morning Senator Glendowan's car turned off the road from Dublin, drove a short way up a farm track and stopped. Then someone smashed the back of the Senator's skull with a tyre lever.

Glendowan had been dining with friends. He was driving himself. There were no witnesses. The Jaguar was found by a farm labourer. The car keys were in the ignition. Glendowan was locked in the boot.

The killer – or an accomplice, or both – had taken the rest of Glendowan's keys and driven, presumably in another car, to Stanham Court near Dalkey. The household – Mrs Glendowan and the two servants who lived in – was asleep.

The killer let himself in, emptied the safe and removed the Bellini cup from the study. According to Mrs Glendowan the safe contained a Picasso sketch, her more valuable jewels and important government papers. As he left, the killer reset the burglar alarms and locked the front door behind him.

Later the same morning Major Aughrim collected Liam Caragh from his flat.

'Sorry to ruin your weekend,' he said. 'But there may be a British angle. How's Emma?'

Liam said she was fine.

'I just want you to keep your eyes open. I'll do the talking.'

Stanham Court was a long, white-painted building with a Regency façade and a ground-floor verandah overlooking the sea.

'Fast-food franchises,' Aughrim said as they came up the drive. 'That's the way to get on in life.'

Mrs Glendowan was glad to see them. She took them into the little sitting room next to her bedroom: the rest of the house was still swarming with Gardai.

The widow was in her late thirties, twenty years younger than the Senator had been. She sat in a low armchair and had a disturbing habit of crossing and re-crossing her legs.

'I wish I could help you, Major,' she said; her eyes were on Liam. 'I'll be frank with you – Ian and I weren't on the best of terms. But something like this . . .'

She touched her eyes with a very small handkerchief. Aughrim clucked sympathetically.

'It's horrible to think the killer was in this very house. Just a few feet away.'

'You heard nothing, I gather?' Aughrim said.

'Nothing at all.'

'Did you or the Senator notice anything beforehand – anything at all that was suspicious or even out of the ordinary? Unexplained phone calls? Strangers near the house?'

She shook her head. 'But Ian kept his political and professional life very much to himself. I knew he'd been worried lately but–'

102

'Why?'

'He didn't tell me.'

'How did you know he was worried?'

'He bit his nails when he was worried. Always.' She turned to Liam. 'Such a childish habit, don't you agree, Mr Caragh? But oddly touching in a grown man.'

A maid came in with coffee. Liam could tell that Aughrim approved of it by the way he sat forward in his chair and drank it in a series of little sips. Each sip involved a respectful bob of the head.

'Columbian,' Aughrim said. 'And do I detect the merest hint of Blue Mountain?'

'Possibly,' Mrs Glendowan said. 'I must ask them in the kitchen.'

'Was your husband afraid for his life?'

'Not that I know of,' she said in the same tone she had used before. 'You could ask his secretary.'

'Waste of time,' the Major said when they were in the car, 'except for the coffee.'

'There might be nothing there for us,' Liam said.

Aughrim pursed his little mouth. 'What if the British knew about Glendowan's link with the INLA?'

'All they'd've had to do was make it public,' Liam said. 'Glendowan's career wouldn't have survived.'

Aughrim shrugged. 'Maybe they had no proof. They're chary about making wild accusations. Because people turn round and accuse them of doing a smear job. Damn it, we had nothing you could call proof either.'

'Would they see him as a serious threat?'

'Any Anglo–Irish agreement is a delicate mechanism,' Aughrim said. 'If it's about Ulster it's even more likely to

103

go wrong. The smallest bit of grit in the wheels can do damage. Glendowan had a lot of grit and access to a lot of wheels.'

'Maybe it's not political.'

'Everything's political in this country.'

'It was well-planned' Liam said. 'Slick.'

'Sometimes the British are slick. More by luck than good judgement.' Aughrim stared at his pink fingernails; they appeared to give him pleasure. 'See if you can find out if they knew about Glendowan.'

'It may be difficult –'

'Just keep your ears open. Snap up unconsidered trifles; pick up hints; you know what I mean. Another thing: there's a rumour that they're trying to ease Blaines out. Attaching you to him is possible confirmation, of course. But I want advance warning. You're going back tomorrow afternoon?'

Liam nodded.

'Good. I'll drop you here. You shouldn't be late for your lunch date. My regards to Emma.'

'He even knew I was meeting you for lunch.'

Emma dropped her eyes. 'It shows he's taking an interest, darling. In us. It's good news, really.'

'Did you tell him?'

'Daddy might have mentioned it last night. I think it's *wonderful* that you went with him today. He's grooming you.'

'I'm not a horse. I was going to see my mother this morning.'

'Well, there's no hurry with that, is there? I mean, it's not as if she knows when you come and when you don't.'

'That's not the point.'

Emma's grip tightened on his arm. 'Oh, look at that ring.'

She examined the contents of the jeweller's window. Liam, who was feeling irritable after a lunch that had been richer than he wanted and more expensive than he could afford, tried to make suitable replies. He found it hard to share Emma's passion for window-shopping. He had noticed that she often paused outside jewellers' shops, and suspected that it was a calculated ploy: she wanted a ring for her finger and an invisible ring for his nose. He on the other hand wanted to go to bed with her.

'Shall we go back to the flat for tea?'

Emma drew herself closer to him. It was a generously provocative move in theory; in practice it was also an empty one since it was impossible to make violent love to a woman, however willing, in the middle of Henry Street on a Saturday afternoon.

'Let's have it here,' she whispered huskily. 'We'll go to the flat later.'

'All right.' Later was better than never.

'You haven't forgotten we're eating with my parents this evening?'

Liam shook his head. It had been hanging over him all day. The threat of Mr Lazonby's golfing anecdotes was not easy to forget.

'There's no need to change.' Emma pulled back to look at him better. 'You look fine as you are. We might as well go there directly after tea.'

'They won't mind us leaving after dinner?'

'Of course not. Don't you worry.'

*

The bells were ringing all over Dublin.

'She didn't come back,' Liam said. 'That surprise you, Ma? Aughrim was there so naturally we had to stay. After dinner we played bridge. And they all talked about golf. You have no idea how boring these people can be.' He paused. 'I think she knew Aughrim was coming.'

His mother might not have moved since he last saw her. But it couldn't be the same pillow the same sheets and the same nightdress. The nuns would have fed and washed her. They turned her every hour or two to lessen the risk of chest infections and bedsores.

'It was after midnight by the time Aughrim left. It was too late for us to go out. Emma said it would make it obvious what we wanted to do. What I wanted to do. She wants me to make an honest woman of her.'

He wondered if his mother would have disapproved. She understood better than most people what it was like not to be an honest woman.

In the old days he had never talked to her like this. When the car crash left her brain-damaged and transected her spinal cord, he realized not only how much he loved her but also how much he liked her. His monologues went some way to make up for all the conversations they had never had.

'How's London, that's what you want to know. Well, it's big and dirty and not very friendly, just like the man I'm supposed to work with. I met a woman on Tuesday, in the way of work. She didn't like me. Or maybe she didn't like what I do for a living. I'm not sure I do either.'

Sister Elizabeth bustled into the room. 'Ah, she does look better for seeing you. The priest will be here any minute.'

106

The last rites already?

No, it was Sunday. A regular dose of spiritual intercession was, like the colour television, the private room and the flexible visiting hours, one of the amenities. Liam was almost sure that his mother would have wanted the priest. He would have liked to be certain.

In his teens he had once told her that she clung to religion from habit, not conviction; at that age conviction had seemed to him to be the only reasonable justification for doing anything. She had punctured his pomposity with a grin. 'I'm clinging to the wreckage,' she said. 'It's what survivors have to do.'

'Will you be staying?' Sister Elizabeth said. 'Father Cassidy usually says a prayer or two.'

'I'm afraid I can't.' Liam read reproach on his mother's face and knew he had written it there himself. He bent and kissed her.

'I'll see you next weekend,' he said. 'Or maybe the one after.'

'Eric, thank God you're in,' Wreningham said. 'Look, something's come up.'

'It's Sunday,' Blaines pointed out. He hated Sundays, the emptiest day of the week, and was relieved to have almost any diversion, even a phone call from Wanky Willy. Wreningham was in quite a state about something. He didn't talk: he twittered.

'I know it's Sunday. Stay there and I'll collect you in the car in about twenty minutes. Lord Sandridge wants to see you.'

The phone went dead. Blaines crunched up the last

piece of toast and lit a cigar. He decided not to shave. After all, it was Sunday. Let them think what they wanted.

Wreningham rated a personal Daimler rather than a beat-up Granada from the Pool. He had dispensed with the chauffeur. Blaines immediately realized the gravity of the matter. It had to be serious if Wreningham voluntarily gave up one of his privileges.

He settled himself in the passenger seat and took his time with the seat-belt.

'Where are we going?'

The car jerked away from the kerb and plunged into the stream of traffic. The driver behind flashed his lights; someone else hooted at them.

'We're going to lunch at Macton.'

'And where's that?'

Wreningham's lips tightened. He kept his eyes on the road. 'Macton Hall. It's near Henley. The Sandridges go there most weekends. You might have shaved. If we weren't late already . . .'

Blaines had often found that straightforwardness could be surprisingly productive. 'Why me?'

'God knows,' Wreningham snapped. 'Sandridge insisted. It had to be you and no one else. Have you met him?'

'Once or twice,' Blaines admitted.

'In what context?'

'Years ago. The Vanderman business. Before your time.'

'I don't like it,' Wreningham said. 'It's most irregular.'

There was a short silence. Blaines guessed a battle was in progress: Willy's desire to seem omniscient was fighting a doomed rearguard action against his need for information.

'What was the Vanderman business exactly?' Wreningham asked in an off-hand voice. 'Was Lady Sandridge involved?'

Your problem, mate, is the reverse of mine: I'm an old man who knows too much: and you're a young fool who knows too little.

'It was back in '72,' Blaines said. 'Vanderman tendered for an MoD contract. When he got it, someone made allegations of corruption . . . We investigated, of course.' He glanced sideways at Wreningham and wondered how far he need go. 'As it happened, it was all above board. Sandridge was naturally concerned because he used to be related by marriage to Vanderman. They have shared business interests too. It's in the files.'

That was partly true: some of it was in the files.

'Could there be a connection?'

'God knows.' In Blaines's experience there were almost always connections; and if there weren't you could usually manufacture them.

They drove in silence for the rest of the journey. Macton Hall had once been a pleasant farmhouse with a Georgian façade; a Victorian owner had added a castellated porch to the front door and a west wing which resembled a small medieval monastery. The house did not have a park; it was insulated from the outside world by a large garden enclosed by a formidable brick wall.

A twenty-year-old Bentley stood on the gravel near the front door. A uniformed chauffeur was improving the

109

shining hour with a chamois leather. A Filipino houseman opened the door to them. Both Sandridges were in the hall. Lady Sandridge was in the act of drawing on her gloves.

'William,' she said without enthusiasm.

'My dear Charmian,' Wreningham replied. 'You look enchanting.'

'Don't be ridiculous. I look like an old witch. I'm going out to lunch. Who's this?'

'Colonel Blaines,' Wreningham said apologetically. 'Eric, this is Lady Sandridge.'

'How do?' Blaines said.

'Have we met before?'

Blaines enjoyed the assumption that underlay the question – that he was expected to have remembered her, while she was to be expected not to have remembered him.

'I'm not sure,' he said. 'What do you think?'

For the first time she looked at him directly. She was a tall woman – taller than he was. Age had lined and spotted the face but it still held traces of the beauty he remembered from over thirty years before. He thought she was faintly amused by him. That made it quits.

She kissed her husband goodbye. 'No alcohol, remember.'

It was a tribute to the force of Lady Sandridge's personality that Blaines had registered the presence of her husband without really noticing him. After the door had closed behind his wife, Sandridge's personality emerged, slowly and cautiously like the head of a tortoise from its shell.

'You look older,' he said to Blaines. The voice still had a hint of the man's Canadian origins; false teeth filled it with background whispers. 'Not past it, are you?'

Blaines shook his head. 'You don't look much younger either.'

Wreningham coughed to hide his embarrassment.

'I suppose we'd better have luncheon,' Sandridge said. 'Don't eat much myself. William just picks at his food – worried about his figure, eh?'

'I'm hungry,' Blaines said firmly.

Sandridge led the way into the dining room. He had never been a large man and age had shrunk him. In the country he affected a tweed suit. His face was dappled with purple patches. The nose was immense; Blaines wondered if, when the teeth were out, the tip of the nose would meet the chin; even now the distance between them was no greater than the thickness of a couple of fingers.

Lunch was a disappointment. Rabbit-food to eat and water to drink. A tomato pip lodged itself in Blaines's teeth. The only diversion was offered by Wreningham's attempts to persuade Sandridge to explain why they were here.

After the coffee, which they had at the table, Sandridge pushed back his chair and nodded at Blaines. 'Come and see the garden. It's looking awful at this time of year.'

Wreningham leapt to his feet. 'Shall I get the coats?'

'By all means, William. But don't bother with yours. You've seen the garden before.'

Wreningham flushed. He looked at his watch. 'I have some work to catch up on.'

111

'Sit in the drawing room,' Sandridge advised. 'It's warmer in there. You can watch TV.'

Blaines was pleased Wreningham was to be excluded; but he wished that Sandridge's dispositions had been the other way round. The day was overcast and there was far too much wind for his liking.

In the hall he farted. Wreningham sucked in his breath. Sandridge took no notice. If he always served food like that he was probably inured to flatulent guests.

It was worse outside than Blaines had feared. At least he could smoke here. As far as he could see there were no ashtrays in Macton Hall.

Sandridge, walking with the aid of a stick, led him across a long lawn. Halfway across he stopped and jabbed the stick sharply into the ground.

'See it?'

'What?'

'Another dandelion,' Sandridge said grimly. 'They're clever devils, you know. They keep themselves camouflaged. The roots get deeper and leaves get longer. Even the buds blend in. Then suddenly whoomph! There you are. The whole lawn is littered with those bloody yellow flowers. And they don't just decay, oh no, not like a reasonable flower. They seed more dandelions. They want to take over the world.'

'I can't see any.'

'Come here in May and you'll see what I mean. I got six acres and two gardeners. I spend money and time and energy. And what for? Know what this is? It's a dandelion reservation. We've got varieties here that Kew Gardens have never even heard of.' Sandridge gave the stick a vicious twist, driving it into the lawn. 'I'm being blackmailed.'

Oh Christ. Not another.

'Try the police,' Blaines said.

'No, no. I want it stopped, and I want it done discreetly.'

'I don't see how I can help.'

Sandridge walked on. They passed through a shrubbery and emerged on the banks of a large grey pond. A waterlogged punt floated in the middle of the water. It began to rain.

'You handled that other business very well,' Sandridge said. 'That's why I want you to do this.'

'That was work. Sort of.'

'Whereas I'm just a private citizen, eh? An irritating old man with more money than's good for him?'

Blaines thought about this for a second. 'Yes,' he said.

'I haven't told Wreningham; nor my wife. I don't want them to know. I don't want anyone to know.'

'Then why are you telling me?'

'Because it's got to stop. You don't want to retire, do you?'

A small pit opened in Blaines's stomach. It expanded rapidly. Soon it would be so large he would fall into it and vanish for ever.

'William's trying to get rid of you,' Sandridge said calmly. 'I expect you know that. You're a threat, see? You belong to the old guard.'

Blaines sucked on his cigar.

Sandridge tapped him on the shoulder with the head of the stick. 'You and I, we've seen the politicians come and go. But William doesn't want to go. He wants to use the department as a power base. And people like you get in the way because you're used to being independent.

113

Because you know all the rules of the game, not just some of them.'

Sandridge had a drop on the end of his nose. Blaines scuffed his heel in the mud at the side of the pond and blew cigar smoke into the cold air.

'You want to go on playing,' Sandridge said. It was not a question but Blaines nodded. 'If William wanted to, he could extend your contract past sixty-five. They do it on a yearly basis, don't they? Getting cold, isn't it?'

In single file they retraced their path through the dripping shrubbery. In front of them the lawn stretched up to the house. Someone moved on the other side of a bay window on the ground floor. Wreningham was keeping an eye on them from the drawing room.

Sandridge gestured with his stick towards the window. 'I paid for his house and his car and his flat in town. I pay his club subscriptions. His wife's a cousin of mine. They have what we used to call expectations. And apart from all that, people owe me favours – people who William would like to know; people he needs to please.' He chuckled softly. 'He'd like to be able to tell me to piss off. He needed me at first but now I'm becoming an encumbrance. But he can't do without me. Not yet. What he really wants is to see me safely in my grave.'

'This blackmail.' Blaines said. 'What have they got on you?'

'None of your business.'

'I have to know if I'm to do anything.'

'No, you don't. They left a letter for me at White's. Clever – anywhere else and a secretary would have opened it.'

'What did it say?'

'It asked for a hundred thousand dollars as – I quote – "a token of my willingness to cooperate".'

'Cooperate?'

'Yes.' Sandridge stabbed another dandelion with his stick. 'I thought that was odd too. Almost as if the money wasn't really important to them.'

When he was in Washington for the weekend George Koslove liked to spend the Sunday evening alone. Tonight he was unlucky.

He put down the phone and placed his hand on his heart. There was definitely a pain. He hoped it was psychosomatic: perhaps a lightning response to the news that his evening was ruined.

Psychosomatic pains were nearly always easier to endure than purely physical ones. Koslove's mind was like a client country: it responded predictably to judicious pressure. His body, on the other hand, was a sovereign state whose policies were incomprehensible and whose actions were consequently difficult to forecast.

His heart had stopped beating. The sudden realization drove the moisture from Koslove's mouth. Perhaps he was clinically dead already. Maybe the first stage of death was characterized by the illusion that you were still alive. He recalled stories of patients hovering over the operating tables where their bodies lay on the verge of death.

While these thoughts were flickering through his mind he patted his chest repeatedly. Suddenly he felt the thudding of the internal pump beneath his palm. Reassurance flooded through him. With relief came anger: it was all the fault of that goddamn Ashkirk woman.

When he had stopped hyperventilating he clambered off the exercise bicycle. He patted its saddle affectionately. His gym had never looked more inviting. It was a bitter thought that the health that a two-hour workout would have given him was now lost forever.

The full-length mirror by the door delayed him for a few seconds. He sucked in his belly and hitched up the boxer shorts. For a man of his age he looked pretty good. He flexed his arm muscles and combed his mind for suitable adjectives to describe what he saw.

Compact? Virile? Hard? Fit? Macho?

He padded upstairs to his bedroom where he shaved, showered and dressed. The suit was dark blue and conservatively cut; it should appeal to Mrs Ashkirk. With the right sort of hat he would look rather like a broader-shouldered Humphrey Bogart.

The doorbell rang. The woman was early as usual. He answered it himself since his housekeeper didn't come on Sundays.

Mrs Ashkirk was standing on the porch. 'Sorry to disturb you,' she said. 'I hope I haven't ruined your evening.'

'Not at all.' Koslove was ninety per cent sure that she would prefer Sundays to have a puritan flavour; he thought he might as well ingratiate himself a little further. 'I rarely socialize on Sundays.'

Anastasia Ashkirk was never an impressive sight. She was a dumpy woman, slightly over five feet high, whose clothes looked as if they had been her Sunday best for at least ten years. She contrived to give the impression that a couple of minutes earlier she had been doing the dishes or mending her husband's shirts.

He showed her into the living room and offered her tea; he knew better than to offer her a drink.

She refused. Koslove didn't like the signs. He associated the refusal of hospitality with bad news if not with downright hostility. The Committee meeting was tomorrow; and the assessment of the National Security Council's liaison policy was high on the agenda. Ashkirk commanded the loyalty of a sizeable minority of her fellow members.

'You said on the phone,' he began cautiously, 'that a preliminary briefing might save time tomorrow. I can give you full details on London, of course, but for elsewhere my in-depth knowledge is necessarily limited. But if an overview would be useful –'

'Mr Koslove,' she said abruptly. 'I haven't come to talk about tomorrow.'

Please God, he thought, *don't let her want to seduce me. Anything but that.*

He put the tips of his fingers together and leant forward in his chair. Perhaps that would inject a sense of professional decorum into the meeting.

Mrs Ashkirk took a deep breath. 'I told a lie,' she said. She avoided his eyes as if she expected to find condemnation there. 'You see, what I want to talk about isn't the sort of thing you mention on the phone.' She hesitated. 'You haven't got any . . . bugs here?'

She made them sound like cockroaches or bedbugs: an unpleasant reflection on the personal hygiene of the householder concerned.

Koslove shook his head. 'Clean as a whistle, Mrs Ashkirk. The Agency does a sweep once a week. You can say anything you want.'

117

Her hands twitched on her lap like a pair of plump white spiders. Koslove fixed his eyes on the plain gold wedding ring, the only piece of jewellery that the woman ever wore.

She opened her mouth, closed it and said: 'I don't know if you're aware my husband was English?'

'I – ah – I did hear something to that effect. You lived over there for a while, right?'

'For five years, in the 1960s. Then my husband died and I came back home. I met him on a course at London University.'

Koslove nodded. He knew it all backwards. When Ashkirk was selected for the Committee he'd got the Agency to produce a ten-thousand-word biography on the principle that forewarned was forearmed. It made depressing reading; the subtitle could have been *Virtue Triumphant*.

'We got married and he joined the Civil Service. A while later he was diagnosed as having multiple sclerosis. The doctors gave him six months, maybe a year. But he died before that. There was an accident.'

'Tragic.' Koslove wondered if she really believed Ralph Ashkirk was a simple civil servant. 'You must have been deeply traumatized.'

She gave no sign of having heard him. 'I came back here, got interested in politics – you know the rest. I tried not to think about it too much – about the last months with Ralph and the way he died. And it worked, most of the time.'

Is it possible for sorrow to act as an aphrodisiac on some people? Why else is she doing this?

Mrs Ashkirk was silent for a few seconds. She looked fixedly at him.

118

'Last night I got a call – at home, on my private line. A man said he had proof I killed my husband; he said he'd keep quiet about it in return for fifty thousand dollars.'

'A crank call, Mrs Ashkirk,' Koslove said. 'Nothing to worry about. The police can handle that – it's their job. Happens more often than you'd think. A lady like yourself who's –'

'You don't understand, Mr Koslove.' She was in control again. 'Cranks don't bother me. The reason I'm here is that my caller wasn't a crank.'

'I'm afraid I still don't see –'

'I said he wasn't a crank. It's quite simple. I did kill my husband.'

The darkness was gathering.

The Daimler dropped Blaines outside the entrance to his block of flats. The street-lights were on; curtains were drawn; winter was here already. Blaines hungered for the simple pleasures of hibernation.

Wreningham lowered his window. 'By the way, Eric. I shall want you to brief me on the Vanderman affair next week.'

Blaines nodded. He had expected that.

'As a matter of fact, Vanderman phoned while you were in the garden.' Wreningham drummed his fingers on the steering-wheel. 'From Los Angeles. Curious, eh? I happened to take the call.'

'Leave a message, did he?'

'No. Said he'd call again later. But – interesting?'

'Maybe. Good night.'

The flats were built round three sides of a yard. Concrete paths threaded their way among hummocks of grass and anorexic trees. The estate agent called the area a landscaped garden. The flats themselves were a modern four-storey development. Internally they were arranged in groups of eight; each group was served by its own staircase.

Blaines walked with his head down, thinking of the evening to come: a stiff drink; a jumbo pack of beef-burgers and a large tin of baked beans; another drink or two and perhaps some repair work on the Russian Imperial Guards.

He wondered what Pat was doing to fill the empty evenings since Claybrook's death. Solitude was a skill; you had to work at it.

There were footsteps behind him.

He might even have a battle or at least a skirmish. Some people collected toy soldiers as an investment; some cherished them as miniature works of art; others used them for war games. Blaines's soldiers fulfilled all three functions.

A little carnage would cheer him up. He fumbled for his keys. They were in his trouser pocket and he had to stop in order to get his hand in.

The footsteps behind him stopped as well.

Blaines found the keys and walked on. He heard nothing behind him but that proved nothing. He opened the outer door, which was common to all eight flats and kept unlocked. He didn't turn on the light. Off the hallway was an alcove for the dustbins. Blaines slipped into it and waited.

A moment later a thickset man pushed open the door. He stood there, listening; he was breathing heavily. He wore a heavy overcoat with the collar turned up. His face was in darkness.

'Eric?'

The whisper was unexpectedly loud. It told Blaines several things besides the fact that the man knew him by name. His follower had realized that Blaines knew he was being tailed; and he had guessed that Blaines was waiting for him nearby.

'Turn the light on,' Blaines said. 'The switch is behind you.'

Antanas Markalis stood blinking beneath the unshaded bulb. He had a long, broad nose that, together with the white streaks in his hair, gave him the appearance of a badger. Blaines bared his teeth at him.

'Eric – perhaps we could go to your flat?'

'Perhaps we could. But we won't.'

'It is dangerous–'

'If you want to talk we can have a little stroll outside.'

'I beg of you–'

'Come on, sunshine. Let's get a bit more fresh air.'

They returned to the communal garden. A door slammed in one of the flats; Markalis jumped.

'Nervy tonight?' Blaines said.

Markalis made a sound that was halfway between a sigh and a sob. 'I want to come over to you.'

'Come off it. Tame Lithuanians never defect.'

'Eric. I'm serious. And it must be soon.'

'Anything else you want? A villa in Cannes? A Rolls-Royce? What about a CBE for services rendered?'

'Please. I haven't much time. I think Osroyan already suspects something.'

'That's his job, old son. Don't let it worry you. Anyway. what makes you think we'd want you?'

'I have a great deal of information to offer,' Markalis said stiffly.

121

'I know. Piddling little currency fiddles. Arty-farty gossip. Who's got Rembrandts under the bed. Suppose you tell me what's behind this change of heart.'

A man and a woman were walking arm in arm across the garden from the garages. Markalis went rigid with attention.

Blaines sighed. 'They live in sin in number forty-three. He's a hairdresser and she manages a clothes shop. Now why?'

'Because I can no longer live under a régime which oppresses the individual. Because–'

'You'll have to do better than that.'

'There are personal problems.' Markalis edged closer. Maybe he thought the grass was listening. 'A corruption charge . . . also a sexual matter. And Eric? I do know something worth having. I have many friends at the Embassy. I know a great deal about some of our subsidiaries.'

Blaines shrugged. 'I'll pass on the request. It would help if you could give me something more specific.'

'All right.' Markalis hesitated. 'Osroyan is very worried at present. So are his superiors. And I know why.'

4

'Gregory, dear. How nice.'

He held his breath as he kissed her cheek, hoping that she wouldn't smell the vodka. The leg of her chair caught him unawares: he stumbled and almost fell.

'Sorry . . . jet-lag catching up, I guess.'

'It's a long flight. So tedious.'

'I expect you're wondering why I'm here? I didn't mean to just turn up out of the blue like this. When I called from the airport–'

'Oh, we knew you were coming before that. Your father called us yesterday.'

'He knew?'

'Not for certain. Call it an educated guess. Do sit down – you look like you're still in transit and it's so unsettling for those of us who aren't. Would you like coffee? A drink?'

Greg nodded. It must be nearly lunchtime so a drink was a perfectly reasonable thing to ask for.

'Then ring the bell, would you? By the fireplace.'

He did as she asked. He had the sensation that he was wandering in a dream: the rambling house, the chatelaine whom nothing could surprise, the old furniture, the servants and the bells – they were all familiar yet completely unreal; they belonged in an old movie.

His aunt patted the sofa beside her. He sat down.

'Aunt Charmian –'

'It's been a long time. I think I saw you last in '71. You were still in high school, I remember that. Rather a lot of puppy fat. Your father lent us the beach house. As I recall he lost his temper because you wouldn't go surfing like the other boys.'

'I was the wrong shape for surfing,' Greg said. 'Still am. Besides . . .'

'Very sensible of you not to surf. It's one thing to have weaknesses but it's quite another to flaunt them in public. Your uncle will be sorry to have missed you – he went up to London this morning. But perhaps you'll see him later. You'll be here for a while, I expect. You must treat the house as a hotel. We shan't mind.'

'How is Uncle Tom?' Greg asked.

'Getting old, which makes him bad tempered. Still keeps busy. Nothing wrong with his mind. Not yet.'

The Filipino arrived. Lady Sandridge asked him to bring in the drinks. They both had Scotch.

'Warren,' she said when they were alone again, 'is furious with you.'

'My father usually is. Did he tell you why?'

'I gather you asked him some questions about your mother.'

Greg produced the postcard from his pocket. The old woman's directness made life much easier. As a child he had been afraid of her on the few occasions they had met. Maybe she had improved with age. Or maybe he had.

'Someone in England sent me this,' he said. 'It wasn't you?'

'I never send postcards. Anyone can read them.'

'Do you want to read this?'

'You'll have to read it to me. These days I need a different pair of glasses for almost everything I do.'

'All it says is: *Ever asked your mother who your father is?* I have an apartment in San Francisco; it was sent to me there.' He glanced at her. 'I never really thought about her before. I know the message is crazy but it triggered something – curiosity? I wish I knew who sent it.'

The thin shoulders lifted. 'Your father has a lot of enemies. It sounds like someone's using you to get at him.'

'Maybe. But why was he so angry with me? And why won't he talk about her? That's why I came to you.'

'What do you want me to tell you?'

'About my mother, of course. What she was like, how she got on with my father, what happened to her.'

Lady Sandridge smiled to herself. 'I told Warren to explain it to you. He wouldn't listen. He should have talked to you years ago.'

'And you will?'

'I'll tell you some of it. The parts you could find out for yourself. Warren wanted me not to but I don't see why I should act stupidly just to keep him company.'

His glass was empty. Greg put it down on the sidetable. If he wasn't offered a refill soon, he could always ask to use the bathroom.

'Why all the secrecy?' he asked.

'Warren Vanderman,' she said slowly, 'is what they call a very private man. Thirty years ago there was a scandal. His private life became public property. He blamed your mother for that. Still does; as you know, he doesn't forgive easily.'

She glanced at Greg as if for confirmation. He nodded. It occurred to him that she was enjoying this. Perhaps she appreciated having a captive audience. One of the difficulties of old age must be finding people who were prepared to listen to you.

'He was twenty years older than she was. She married him to get away from home. He married her because she was a Youlgreave and had a little money. Old money. Old money is worth more than new money, have you noticed that? People put a higher value on it for some reason, or at least they used to. Your father was a rich man already – the war saw to that.'

'So they didn't marry for love?'

'I didn't say that. Your mother was very beautiful. Even Warren could be quite appealing if you liked strong, silent men with the knack of making money. There was an element of romance. But there was also a business side to the marriage contract.'

'Why did she want to get away from home?'

'My dear, we all did. My father – your grandfather – was an appalling man. He ran three wives into the grave. Can you remember him at all?'

'Not really. He died when I was about five.'

Lady Sandridge smiled. 'You're lucky. He treated his family as if they were his domestic serfs. And he was a terrible snob too, which was tiresome at times. It's not as if we had anything to be snobbish about. Do you know how the original Youlgreave made his money? Selling horses to both sides during the War of Independence. Then his son consolidated the family fortunes in the slave trade. The rest of us just sat there and spent it. While looking down our aristocratic noses at people

126

who actually had to earn a living. Do you work?'

'I wash dishes in a hotel,' Greg said. 'Or at least I did. They've probably fired me in my absence.'

'How interesting. But surely you don't have to do that? I thought the Trust paid you an income.'

Greg nodded. 'Enough to live on if I wanted to. That's part of the problem.'

She followed his line of thought immediately. 'I can see that. Enough to live on but not enough to do anything with. I imagine it must sap the motivation. Where was I?'

'Your father and why my mother wanted to get away from home.'

'Yes. Another drink? Would you help yourself? Not for me, thank you.'

Greg refilled his glass. The tray was on the table beside the sofa. It was easy to pour himself a proper drink and swallow half of it quickly before he sat down again. As he walked back he noticed the big mirror over the fireplace. His aunt was looking at her lap. But she could have seen him. He would have to be more careful.

'Your mother was the youngest,' she continued. 'Perhaps that made it worse for her. There were three of us altogether. I was the eldest; then there was Gregory – he was killed in Normandy in 1944; your mother was born twelve years after Gregory in '34. All of us had different mothers.'

'What was her childhood like?'

Lady Sandridge smoothed a wrinkle from her skirt; she was frowning. 'Not much fun, I think. To all intents and purposes she was an only child. And as your grandfather was a diplomat they were moving around all the time; she didn't put down any roots. You know what I mean?'

'I know exactly.'

She gave him another of her rapid sideways glances. 'Of course you do. There were a lot of rows. Your mother was an obstinate child with an advanced sense of justice; always a recipe for disaster, don't you think? When she was in her teens she wanted to become a professional photographer – go to college and so on. Father was furious. His daughters weren't supposed to want jobs: we were meant to acquire accomplishments, husbands and children - in that order. Well, Father wouldn't let her, and that was that. He had a London posting then. Warren was over here – you could make a lot of money out of the ruins of Europe; and he did. She met him at an Embassy party and married him more or less on the rebound from a career.'

The whisky made a comforting glow in his stomach. There would probably be wine with lunch. The flask of vodka was waiting as a back-up; and there was more in his suitcase. Nothing to worry about.

'It didn't work out?' Greg said. 'I guessed that years ago. When I was a kid I thought the reason he never talked about her was that he couldn't bear to. Out of grief.'

Lady Sandridge sniffed. 'It was a disaster right from the start. They had absolutely nothing in common. They rented a flat in London – a huge place near Hyde Park. But Warren was always away on business. Your mother entertained a lot. Even then there was a good deal of gossip.'

'Gossip?'

'Well, you know.' Her face became vague. 'In the newspapers. At cocktail parties.'

'But what about? Men?'

'She was very attractive,' Lady Sandridge said. 'People were bound to talk.'

She had side-stepped the question. Greg decided to let it go for the moment. There would be time enough later. If he dug through newspaper files–

'When you were born,' she said quickly, 'your grandfather was delighted. A boy, you see. You had to have the best of everything. The best nanny, the smartest baby carriage, the most expensive paediatricians. Your mother was hardly allowed to see you which I always said was half the trouble. And then the balloon went up. She fell in love. Head over heels. I've never seen anything like it.'

'Who with?'

'A complete nobody. A minor civil servant. No money. No family. I think his parents had a shop somewhere. He wasn't even good-looking. Your grandfather was so angry. After the elopement, his lawyers found a legal loophole and he managed to cut her out of the Trust.'

'An elopement? It sounds – well, old-fashioned I guess.'

'The world well lost for love.' She sniffed. 'Then the papers got hold of it. It was the silly season. Your mother was determined to marry the man. At first Warren wouldn't give her the satisfaction of divorce, purely out of pique I should add. But in the end they came to some sort of an arrangement.'

'About me,' Greg said. Nausea flooded his throat. He swallowed.

His aunt patted his knee. 'Your mother wanted to keep you. But your father made you the price she had to pay for the divorce.'

'So what was the deal? "You can marry the boyfriend if you forget you have a son"?'

'Something like that. But–'

'And where were you in all this? Whose side were you on?'

'I could hear you perfectly well before,' Lady Sandbridge said. 'You needn't shout.'

Greg flushed. 'I'm sorry. It's kind of unsettling.'

'I understand.' She flashed a smile at him. 'I'd've liked to be neutral but that wasn't possible. Tom was in the middle of a deal with Warren; and he couldn't afford to jeopardize it. Your mother called me up to say I was a sanctimonious bitch and perhaps she was right. I tried writing to her but she sent back the letters unopened. I haven't seen or heard from her from that day to this.'

'Wait a minute.' Greg said. 'You mean she's still alive?'

'As far as I know. I thought you realized – I thought that was why you were here. It was part of her arrangement with Warren: as far as you were concerned she was to be dead.'

Christmas is almost upon us. As usual it brings with it a host of unanswerable questions. How can you stand being in the same house as his mother for four whole days? How can you squeeze the turkey in the oven, let alone the potatoes, the sausages, the bacon and the parsnips? When will you find the time to buy the kids their presents? And, worst of all, what on earth are you going to buy the man in your life?

Jessica Claybrook ripped the sheet out of the typewriter and threw it on the floor. She knew exactly what she wanted to buy the man in her life: a cookery book, preferably one which had a substantial appendix on other aspects of domestic economy.

It would include, for example, a pointed paragraph on the importance of occasionally cleaning the loo. There might also be a few tactful hints (addressed to male readers) on how to improve their aim. Jack had been urinating for 36 years; if he were a military strategist you could say he believed in carpet detonations rather than precision bombing.

Maybe she should write the book herself. She could call it *The Liberated Male in an Apron*. It would describe elementary bedmaking, the operation of a vacuum-cleaner, the advantages of washing up and the delights of dusting.

The cookery section would attempt to strike a balance between health and simplicity. The recipes would be tasty but economical. In Jessica's experience males in the kitchen fell into one of two equally unsatisfactory categories: either they relied entirely on a supermarket-packaged diet of mono-sodium glutamate; or they suffered from identity crises and fancied themselves as budding Escoffiers or Afghan peasants. Both categories produced inedible food which cost far more than necessary; both tended to forget about the washing-up; and both were insufferably and unjustifiably smug about their achievements.

But at least it could be said that they tried.

Jack belonged to an inferior breed of liberated male: the sort that considered the kitchen to be an extension of the jungle. It was not a room but a place where they foraged for food and drink. They treated the refrigerator like a predator treats its prey. They did not think of food except when they were hungry; and when they were hungry their only desire was to satisfy that hunger as quickly as possible.

The book would have to wait: the world was not ready for it, and nor was *Tomorrow's Woman*, which wanted fifteen hundred words on Christmas presents for the males in their readers' lives.

Jessica picked up the sheet of paper and fed it back into the typewriter. She flicked through the last thirty pages in her notebook. The contents represented a hard day's trawl round London. She had visited everywhere from Harrods and Selfridges to esoteric little establishments in Covent Garden and the Fulham Road. She was sick of Christmas.

The telephone rang.

Saved by the bell. She pushed back her chair and went to answer it.

'Hi. Am I speaking to Jessica Claybrook?'

Jessica admitted that her caller was. The voice was American and male. She felt a brief spasm of hope, of the kind that afflicts almost anyone who is self-employed when a stranger calls: it might be the lucrative job, the career-building commission or the news that your ship has finally sailed into port.

'My name's Vanderman. Are you related to a Patricia Claybrook?'

'She's my mother. Why?'

'That's a relief. You're the only Claybrook in the London White Pages; and I thought it was worth a try.'

'But why do you want to know?'

'It's kind of difficult to explain on the phone. You could say it's family business. Look, could I take you out

132

to lunch? Any place you like – I don't know London.'

Jessica thought of the article she didn't want to write; she thought of the man in her life who spent every other night drinking with his mates and who never cleaned the loo; she thought of the strange, polite voice on the other end of the phone.

'All right,' she said. 'There's an Italian restaurant near Holland Park tube station. I'll give you directions.'

Vanderman was waiting for her at a table in the back of the restaurant.

As she followed the waiter's pointing finger, she had a few seconds to study him. She saw a stout man in his thirties with curly hair the colour of dirty straw. He was staring at a glass of red wine. His clothes made her wonder if she had made a mistake in suggesting Cavour's. She hoped he could afford the bill.

He looked up as she approached. The waiter must have pantomimed a message to him, for he stood up immediately and held out his hand. The features were heavy and sullen. His smile briefly realigned them into a face that was unexpectedly attractive.

'You must have been here quite a while,' Jessica said as she sat down. She nodded at the half-empty bottle.

'This okay for you? Or would you like something else?'

'I wouldn't mind some white wine. Red's a bit heavy for me at lunchtime.'

He summoned the waiter. She decided to gamble on her host's affluence and ordered a bottle of Orvieto. The waiter also produced menus. Ordering the meal took some time because Vanderman had difficulty in making up his mind. Either that or he was stalling.

When the waiter had left them alone, Vanderman swallowed the rest of his glass of wine and poured himself another.

'I'd get it over with,' Jessica said.

'What?'

'Whatever it is. Soon you'll be fiddling with your bread and talking about the weather and double-decker buses.'

He laughed. Once again his face was briefly transformed.

'You're right,' he said. 'It's just – hell, I don't know how to handle this. Look.'

He pulled out a bundle of documents from an inside pocket. One by one he passed them over the table.

The first was a US passport. It identified him as Gregory Vanderman. The name Gregory leapt at her from the paper.

The second was a copy of a British marriage certificate. Warren George Vanderman, businessman, had married Patricia Emily Youlgreave, spinster, at the Caxton Hall registry office.

The third was a birth certificate. It showed that Gregory Youlgreave Vanderman was the child of the couple who had got married.

Jessica stared at the papers. It must be some dreadful mistake. She read through them again, noticing the dates and places. Her first emotion was anger: her mother should have told her and Nell.

'I thought you might know about this,' Vanderman said gently. 'If it's any consolation I've only just found out myself. I went to St Catherine's House this morning. You know, the General Register Office.'

She nodded, avoiding his eyes.

'You've gone pale. Can I get you something?'

'No. I'm all right. Just a bit of a shock, Mr . . .'

'I guess you'd better get used to calling me Greg.'

'When I paid the check, why did you look at me like that? Kind of surprised.'

She grinned up at him. 'It was your credit card that did it.'

They were walking back to his new sister's flat for coffee. Greg guessed she was slightly drunk – at the carefree stage you never seemed to reach when you were a heavy social drinker. It took him a few seconds to work out what she meant.

'The gold one?' He paused. 'I get it. You thought I was a penniless bum in search of a free meal.'

'Well, I did wonder. When I first saw you.'

'I get an income from the Youlgreave Trust. That aside, your instincts were right: I'm a financial failure.'

'Do you have a job?'

He thought of the St Francis Hotel. 'None worth mentioning.'

He liked her apartment. From her conversation he had gathered she was living with another journalist; but the man had made little impression on the place. The living room wasn't much larger than his studio in San Francisco but it seemed spacious and airy, chiefly because of the view and the scarcity of furniture.

Jessica left him there while she made the coffee. He stared at the view while he had a quick slug from his flask. There was a typewriter on the table. He read the sheet of paper which was in it. There was no problem

135

about what to get the man in your life for Christmas. You got him a bottle. At least one bottle but preferably more, as many as you could afford.

He was a long way from being drunk; since arriving in England he had found less time for alcohol. That's what came of having an interest in life. He took another nip from the flask and joined Jessica in the kitchen.

'Greg, how do you think we should play this?'

'Meeting . . . her?'

She smiled at him. 'Not easy to know what to call her? Maybe I should go and talk to her first. Pave the way. It's hard to tell but she must be pretty fragile at present.'

'I'm sorry about your father.'

'I felt such a fool. Because of that last quarrel.'

She poured boiling water over the coffee grounds. He noticed that tears were going in as well. Without thinking he put an arm around her. She leant against him.

'Hey,' he said awkwardly. 'One quarrel doesn't ruin everything. It's just that – a quarrel. You can bet he felt guilty about it too. It doesn't cancel out what went before.'

The words came stumbling out, as inadequate as a paper handkerchief to a streaming cold. He put the other arm around her. She nuzzled her head against his shirt. He felt the tears soaking through.

'I'm sorry,' she mumbled. 'I thought there was something wrong with me.' She sniffed. 'I haven't cried properly since he died.'

'It's the shock. Delayed reaction. Happens all the time.'

'And what the fuck's going on in here?'

Jessica jerked herself away from him. There was a

man standing in the kitchen doorway. Greg could feel aggression radiating from him like heat from an electric fire.

She held out her hand towards the newcomer. 'Jack–'

Jack threw himself at Greg. There was no warning. One second everyone was still; the next was a confusion of flailing limbs and heavy bodies in a confined space.

Greg's first thought was to wish that Jessica wasn't in the room. His second thought was a purely protective anger on her behalf. Then he stopped thinking. Old reflexes took over. They were slowed by alcohol and disuse but still adequate for the average brawl.

He side-stepped Jack's charge, receiving nothing worse than a blow on his shoulder. The side-step and the blow swung him round. His right hand grabbed Jack's neck. The momentum of the charge carried the pair of them toward the sink. When they got there, Greg banged the front of Jack's skull against the faucet. He seized the left arm and yanked it up towards the small of Jack's back. Someone was shouting. Greg was dimly aware of Jessica trying to break his hold on the neck.

'Okay, okay,' he said softly. 'Let's cool it.'

'Jack,' Jessica said urgently. 'This is Greg. He's my *brother*.'

Jack's muscles relaxed. Greg let go of him and backed cautiously away. He wondered if the instructor at the Academy would classify Jack as an Emotionally Disturbed Person; he certainly behaved like an EDP.

'Get out,' Jack said. His voice was unexpectedly quiet. He turned round. A trickle of blood slid down his forehead.

'You're hurt,' Jessica said. 'Let me–'

137

'Just bugger off, will you?' Jack ignored her completely. All his attention was concentrated on Greg.

Greg glanced at Jessica, then back to Jack. 'I'm going.'

'I'll phone you,' Jessica said. She was looking at Jack.

'I'm at the Westbury,' Greg said. 'Conduit Street.'

'I might have known. Bloody Yanks.'

Greg ignored him. He smiled at Jessica. 'Take care.'

'Civil servant *shit*,' Jack said, an hour later.

'What do you mean?' Jessica said sharply.

They had had the usual reconciliation scene, set in the usual place. But Jessica wasn't feeling quite as reconciled as she usually did. Perhaps it was the physical humiliation that had made Jack more violent. His lovemaking had edged dangerously close to the border that separated the exciting from the frightening.

'I talked to people in the unions. Your dad didn't belong to one. Nor does Blaines.'

'They don't have to belong to a union, do they? Not in the civil service?'

'In their case they weren't allowed to.' Jack hesitated. 'Jess, Blaines is quite well-known. He's in security, a career secret servant. He started out in military intelligence during the war. Then he moved to SIS. He was seconded to MI5 in the sixties. Who he works for now I don't know. No one I talked to knew. It's a bloody maze, the intelligence community. But he's somewhere in there all right. And somewhere near the centre.'

'And my father?'

'Well, what do you think? Use your head. What I'd like to know is how your precious Greg fits in.'

Jessica got out of bed and padded into the bathroom.

She needed a shower. She felt filthy, inside and out.

'You can't run away from it,' Jack called from the bedroom.

She turned on the shower.

'Or wash it away.'

Colonel Blaines spent Tuesday morning talking to Suffolk policemen and people who had known the late Sir Julian Feniscliffe.

The police wanted him to believe it was an accident. Lady Feniscliffe tried to patronize him; he reduced her to tears before he left. Tears of rage. At the university assorted academics showed surprisingly little regret that their Vice Chancellor should have ended his life at the bottom of a river.

It was all frustratingly inconclusive. It was all increasingly disturbing.

Somewhere south of Ipswich Blaines said: 'I want some food. Stop at the next caff.'

Frank nodded. His eyes gleamed in the driver's mirror.

Ten minutes later he swung the Granada off the road and on to the rutted forecourt of a transport café. At least a dozen lorries were parked there already. It was a good omen, Blaines thought; truck-drivers had the right ideas about food.

He opened his door. 'Haven't got time to stop,' he said over his shoulder. 'I'll get us something to eat as we go. Bacon sandwich suit you?'

Frank nodded. 'The more the merrier, sir.'

Blaines stumped into the cafe. A young woman with lank brown hair took his order for one sandwich. He asked for a mug of strong, sweet tea while he waited for the sandwich, and another cup of tea to take out.

He watched approvingly as she laid thick, fatty rashers on the sliced white bread. She topped them with a generous layer of mustard. They did things properly here.

'Where's the toilet?' he asked as he paid.

'That door by the space invaders,' the woman said wearily. 'Next one.'

He spent a couple of minutes in the lavatory before he returned to the car.

'There you go, sunshine,' Blaines said. He handed Frank the sandwich and a plastic beaker full of tea. 'You owe me one pound fifty.'

Frank took a mouthful of sandwich and fumbled for the money.

'You not having one, sir?'

'I changed my mind,' Blaines said. 'Come on, we haven't got all day.'

When he got back to the office, his secretary pounced on him.

'Mr Wreningham's been trying to get hold of you.' Rosie thrust a small sheaf of messages at him. 'I think it's urgent.'

'All right, love.' Blaines patted her bottom. 'Get me a cup of tea and a sandwich. And tell Caragh I want to see him.'

The messages told him nothing except that Wreningham was at home and wanted to speak to him; otherwise they were merely a monument to Rosie's talent for unproductive industry.

Caragh tapped on the door and came in. Blaines lit a cigar and stared at him for a second.

'I want you to go to Curzon Street,' he said. 'Talk to them in Registry. Say the word blackmail and see what the machines spew out: I want a list of known blackmailers and victims covering . . . let's say the last ten years.'

'But that's a clerical job' Liam said. 'You can get it direct from the computer.'

'Maybe. But I'm not going to.' Blaines scowled. Perhaps a little explanation would be diplomatic in the circumstances. 'If you go personally, you can see the up-dates. Who knows, you may have a flash of inspiration. Then you can ask questions on the spot.' He glanced piously at the ceiling. 'Jesus Christ. What do they teach them these days?'

Liam backed away from the smoke that was rolling towards him. 'I don't have authorization for Registry.'

Blaines picked up a pad of memo forms and scribbled rapidly. 'You do now. For this afternoon. In reception you can show them the pass you've got for here. I'll phone them and let them know you're coming. Okay? Is that simple enough for you? Think you'll be able to cope?'

'Yes, sir. By the way, I think your jacket's on fire.'

Blaines threw down the pen and slapped his arm. A fragment from the match head had lodged in the tweed. It was already smouldering. He wondered when Caragh had noticed. The bloody Mick wasn't quite as dumb as he looked.

He dealt with the crisis, finished writing and passed the memo to Caragh. 'Right. Bugger off.'

141

As soon as he was alone, he picked up the phone and dialled a number through the internal switchboard.

'Mike? Eric here. Paddy O'Reilly's on his way . . . Good . . . Yes . . . I'll do the same for you one day. . . And up yours too, mate.'

'That's just what we need, Mr Russell,' Liam said.

'Call me Mike. Everyone else does.'

'I'm Liam. This is everything, I take it?'

Russell rubbed his hands together. 'For England and Wales, yes. That's what Blaines wanted, wasn't it?'

Russell was a small, rotund man, untidily dressed and almost overpoweringly helpful. Liam liked him: it was a pleasant change to find a friendly Englishman.

'That's right.' He took a step towards the door and then turned. 'Oh, one thing. He did say something about the Glendowan file as I was leaving.'

'The Irish senator?' Russell drew his hand across his throat in a graphic but child-like gesture. 'I know the one. I'll have a look.'

He left the office for a few minutes. When he came back he was carrying a file, imaginatively colour-coded in green. He sat down at his desk and leafed through it.

Russell shook his head. 'We haven't come across a blackmail angle. For what that's worth.' He glanced at his watch. 'Would you like a coffee?'

'Please.'

'Won't be a moment.'

He went out of the office, leaving the door ajar. Liam heard him feeding the vending machine in the corridor.

'How do you like it?' he called.

'Black, no sugar,' Liam said. He was already on his

feet, glancing through the abstract below the table of contents at the front of the file. It told him all he wanted to know. He was back in his seat by the time Russell returned with the coffee.

'What's it all about then?' Russell said. 'Blaines thinking of a second career?'

Liam grinned. 'It'd suit him. I don't know what his interest is. I'm just the messenger boy.'

Liam decided to walk back to the office from Curzon Street.

It still amazed him that in one of the largest cities in the world it was possible to walk for miles across grass.

The computer print-out was locked in the black briefcase with the royal monogram. Liam hoped eventually to steal the briefcase as a souvenir of his secondment. Its handle was cuffed to his wrist. In theory he should have called up a car or taken a taxi. Sod it, he thought. He wasn't carrying Irish secrets and for once there was a bit of sun in the sky. In any case he felt like celebrating.

It was in Green Park that he began to suspect he was being followed. The possible tail was a thin man with a bony face and long overcoat. He was clutching what looked like an A-Z map of London. He looked subtly alien – German, perhaps, or Swiss.

The man had waited at the same pedestrian crossing on Piccadilly; and now he was in the park. Liam thought nothing of it until he stopped to watch a group of squabbling sparrows. The man stopped too; he seemed to be consulting his road atlas.

Liam was not alarmed at this stage, merely curious. A hypothesis needed testing; and it would almost certainly be proved wrong. Why should anyone bother to follow him?

He changed direction and walked in a long arc back to Piccadilly. To Liam's surprise the thin man changed his mind too.

On Piccadilly Liam strolled east towards Hatchards. The bookshop had two entrances, several floors, a confusing layout, lifts and a staircase. As he went into the shop he caught a glimpse of the tail weaving slowly along the crowded pavement.

Liam walked through the shop to the smaller door. He was just in time to see the thin man going into the main entrance. Once inside he would have a difficult job finding out if Liam was there or not. Provided he hadn't got a partner.

'Can I help you, sir?'

Liam started. One of the assistants had materialized at his elbow.

'No, thank you,' he said hastily. 'Just browsing.'

So much for fieldcraft. Liam walked quickly down Piccadilly to the tube station at the Circus. He bought a ticket and spent ten minutes proving definitively that the tail had been working alone. He took a tube back to the office and kept a close eye on his fellow passengers.

The episode worried him the more he thought about it. His own ineptitude was only to be expected. He had never scored well in the field tests; and he had had neither the opportunity nor the inclination to improve his skills in Dublin.

But the tail had made himself obvious; and he had apparently been without a back-up. Maybe the thin man's movements had been entirely innocent; maybe his

144

fieldcraft was even worse than Liam's; or maybe getting himself noticed had been the thin man's aim from the start.

A message without words?

Liam realized he was going to have to tell Blaines. And Blaines was going to bawl him out, first for not taking a taxi; second for not phoning in at once so the department could put a trace on the thin man; and third for the abysmal quality of his fieldcraft. If Blaines was as much of a bastard as he seemed, the story might even get back to Aughrim.

A stay of execution waited for him at the office.

'He's gone out,' Blaines's secretary said. 'And it's no use asking me where. He never tells me anything.'

It was the same car, Blaines realized. The lazy buggers hadn't cleared out this morning's cigar butts from the ashtray in the back.

But the driver was different. He was fair and freckled. Judging by the *Guardian*, which was folded open on the front passenger seat to show a completed crossword, his tastes were intellectual rather than gluttonous.

'Eh, Jim,' Blaines said. 'Where's old Frank?'

'I'm Henry, sir,' the driver said. 'Frank was taken ill.'

'Really? Nothing serious, I hope?'

'They think it's food poisoning.'

'Good God. He seemed all right this morning.'

Blaines lit a cigar and opened his briefcase. He hummed quietly to himself. These days you couldn't even trust a transport café.

His destination was thirty miles up the M1, in the suburbs of the overgrown town that Wreningham represented in Parliament. Blaines had never been there before. The address turned out to be a detached redbrick house in an acre of garden. You didn't have to be an estate agent to know it was a desirable residence.

Wreningham opened the door. He was wearing a dressing-gown. Blaines raised his eyebrows.

'I'm not well,' Wreningham said pettishly. 'Leave your coat here and come into the study.'

As he walked, Blaines sniffed. The aroma of whisky was faint but perfectly discernible to the trained nose.

The study was a small room at the back of the house. It overlooked a leaf-strewn lawn. The interior decoration relied heavily on leather. Wreningham sank into the sort of armchair you were supposed to find in gentlemen's clubs. He waved Blaines to the chair on the other side of the fireplace.

Blaines noticed there was a moist ring on the polished surface of the wine table by Wreningham's chair. He wondered where the glass and the bottle had gone. Probably in the fancy cupboard beside the even fancier desk.

Blaines sat down heavily. 'You'll want to hear about Markalis.'

'Markalis?'

Blaines stifled a sigh. 'I mentioned him yesterday but you were in a hurry. Bloke who came to see me on Sunday evening.'

'Oh yes. The Lithuanian.'

'He says he wants to defect.'

Wreningham looked at the ceiling. 'Is he worth having?'

'Maybe. I've known him on and off for years. He keeps popping up in Soviet trade delegations, here and in the States. KGB Captain and won't get any further. He's meant to be an art expert. Lately he's fronted for one or two deals. Toe-in-the-water stuff: Soviets want to exchange some of their loot for Western currency, but only if the price is right. Bit of an old woman. I've heard a rumour that he's queer but I doubt if he'd have the guts.'

'But he has the guts to defect?'

Blaines screwed up his face. 'Surprised me too. I've never had the impression that he likes the West. He said something about a corruption charge and a sexual matter.'

'Sounds like another plant,' Wreningham said. 'A well-publicized defection followed by an even better publicized return to the Motherland. I don't want to risk another one of those.'

'Could be. But if that was the case, they'd usually choose someone who we'd jump at. Not someone we couldn't care less about one way or the other.'

'Turn him down,' Wreningham said waspishly. 'Tell him to try the Americans. I don't care what you do with him as long as we're not involved.'

'I think you're right,' Blaines admitted. He found it faintly unnatural to be in agreement with Wreningham. 'There was one other thing: Markalis said something was worrying his superiors, from Osroyan upwards. And he knew what it was.'

'Well, he would say that. Just trying to make himself interesting.'

'Probably. So I'll tell him to go elsewhere?'

Wreningham nodded.

'I'll need that in writing,' Blaines said.

'All right, Eric. Don't fuss.'

Wreningham passed a hand over his forehead. The great statesman, Blaines thought unkindly, oppressed by cares of state. Wanky Willy looked as though he needed a holiday. Or, better still, permanent retirement.

Blaines hoisted his briefcase on to his lap. 'You want some more on the Vanderman inquiry?'

'Not now, Eric; I've got a splitting headache.'

Blaines frowned. He had assumed the main reason for this meeting was to supply Wreningham with more ammunition for his forthcoming war of independence against Lord Sandridge. Why else the urgency?

'In that case . . .' Blaines set in train the complex sequence of muscular operations that would eventually extract him from the armchair.

'Oh, there's one other thing. That business about Feniscliffe and Brundish. No need to go any further with that.'

'I don't agree,' Blaines said sharply. 'We're not just talking about a pair of poofs in pre-war Cambridge. Koslove says that –'

'It's a police matter,' Wreningham said. 'There have been complaints about undue interference and, speaking personally –' he glared at Blaines '– I can quite see their point of view. Lady Feniscliffe phoned the Home Secretary after your visit. I understand that the Superintendent in charge of the Brundish case is contemplating a formal complaint. Anyway we've no hard evidence that the cases should come under our jurisdiction.'

Blaines cleared his throat so forcefully it sounded as though he were snarling. Wreningham shifted uneasily in his chair.

'Hard evidence?' Blaines said scornfully. 'What's that got to do with it? We're not in a magistrate's court.'

'The point is –'

'The point is, it's becoming increasingly possible that someone's mounting a blackmail campaign against selected targets here and in the States. *Possible*, that's all. We don't know who and we don't know why. Of course we should be investigating.'

Wreningham stood up. 'Eric, with all due respect, sometimes I have to follow my own judgement.' His voice rose in volume and pitch. 'I've made up my mind: this lies outside the department's scope. And it's staying there. Do I make myself clear?'

'You do that all right,' Blaines said. 'But you'll confirm it in writing too, won't you? Just for the record.'

'I think that's all.' Wreningham turned his back to Blaines and stared out of the window. His shoulders were shaking. 'Thank you for coming, Eric.'

Blaines paused by the door, wondering why Willy was in such a state. Maybe the Minister had given him such a bollocking he still hadn't recovered. Maybe he really was ill.

Against his better judgement he made one last effort. 'Why? Why the change of direction?'

'I've already told you.' Wreningham scratched the window-pane with a fingernail. 'Can you find your own way out?'

The internal phone rang.

'Caragh?' Blaines coughed for a few seconds. 'Any luck?'

'No, sir; not really.'

'I'm going home.'

'There was one thing you ought to know.' Liam thought he might as well get it over with. 'I think I had a tail on my way back from Curzon Street.'

He explained briefly what had happened. To his surprise Blains listened without interruption.

'Well, never mind that now,' was all he said when Liam had finished his confession. 'Next time, don't walk. And if you're ever tailed again, ask for help.' His voice was unusually mild, as though his mind was on other things. 'And now there's something else I want you to do. Run down to Halcombe and see Mrs Claybrook. She may have remembered something else about the attack. Besides if you turn up it'll show her we're taking her seriously.'

A trip to Halcombe would ruin most of Liam's evening. But Blaines's unexpected leniency was some compensation.

'And Caragh?'

'Sir?'

'Treat her like she was your favourite aunt. Courtesy and consideration at all times. That's an order.'

'Shit,' said Koslove. 'Shit, shit, shit.'

He scowled through the windows at a passing traffic warden.

'These guys don't understand the meaning of work,' he went on. 'No wonder they lost their empire.' He put down the car phone and wagged a finger at the driver. 'He's gone home. It's hardly four o'clock. Can you believe it?'

The driver shook his head.

Two men were waiting for Blaines at Teddington Station. They were smartly dressed and could have held any nationality but only one job.

The taller one flashed a card at Blaines.

'Mr Koslove's waiting for you in the park.'

'Oh Christ,' Blaines said. 'In this weather?'

'This way Colonel.'

Koslove was jogging up and down under a tree in Bushey Park. It was raining gently so an assistant held an umbrella over him. Three other men were discernible in the gathering gloom. Koslove preferred not to leave his office without a protective screen around him.

'Go away,' Koslove said to his aide. He snatched the umbrella from him. All the while he continued to jog.

'Why don't we go to my flat?' Blaines said. 'It's drier there. And warmer.'

'This is safer. Besides, I need the exercise. Why aren't you in your office?'

Blaines shrugged but said nothing. He edged under the umbrella. Koslove stopped jogging.

'It's amazing,' he said. 'I feel like I'm glowing.'

'I feel cold.'

'Eric, listen. You know I had a Committee meeting yesterday? I ran into a shitstorm over Lackan and Breighton. They're a no-go area. Any personal problems they may have are way outside our frame of reference.'

'Snap,' Blaines said. He rammed a cigar into his mouth. 'Brundish and Feniscliffe are a police matter.'

'They're closing ranks. It stinks.'

'I think I'll get drunk tonight.' Blaines swore as the first match received a direct hit from a raindrop.

'But afterwards I made a few calls, saw a few guys.

The Committee hasn't got a monopoly on clout.'

The second match fizzled and died.

'The conspiracy theory looks very, very persuasive to some of them. And the general feeling is that England is at the centre. They want this followed up, but quietly, you understand.'

'Wish I could help, George. But I can't afford to. Willy's watching.'

'Screw Willy.'

'Trouble is, he can screw me.'

Koslove patted Blaines's shoulder. 'We're all insecure. It's an occupational hazard. Will you do something for me?'

The third match refused even to fizzle.

'I'm going home,' Blaines said. 'Unless you've got a light.'

Koslove sighed. He beckoned the nearest of the watchers and pointed to the limp cigar in Blaines's mouth. The man produced a slim gold lighter. Blaines held the cigar to the flame. Koslove coughed and moved away from him.

'We both want information on this,' Koslove said. 'Right?'

Blaines blew smoke at him.

'You've got better access,' Koslove went on. 'I mean, it's your country. But I've got facilities and money. Deal?'

'No. Willy'd castrate me if he found out. Besides, it's probably treason.'

'Now wait a minute, Eric.' Koslove plunged forward in a desperate attempt to touch his toes with his free hand. The umbrella caught in a branch. 'Shit. Tell me – just as an academic question – how would Wreningham react to a formal complaint about you? From the Agency. Or from us?'

'Don't be stupid,' Blaines said. 'You know me. If I went, you'd have to start all over again with someone else.'

'It wouldn't be my decision. Not my style, you know that.' Koslove's face became mournful. 'I'm just the hired help.'

'Bullshit.'

'It's true. Look at it the other way: if we're right and Willy's wrong, you make yourself a lot of friends in Washington. You need friends, Eric. We all do.'

Rain dripped from the tree. A hundred yards away traffic poured across the Park between Teddington and Hampton. Blaines thought about all the friends he needed and about how Wreningham could use a formal complaint. He tried unsuccessfully to shut his mind to the prospect of retirement.

He stared dreamily at the black leaves above his head. 'If tomorrow was Christmas, you know what I'd want from Santa Claus? Some money. A base – a sort of clearing house for information. Manpower.'

'Money, yes.' The relief in Koslove's voice was obvious. 'Some facilities. But manpower's difficult; and so's a base. This will have to be unofficial.'

And therefore untraceable to George Koslove.

'I could handle the other things if I had money.' Blaines thought about the friend he wanted. Stuff the ones he needed.

'That's your affair.'

'Won't be easy,' Blaines said hurriedly; it was never wise to undervalue your labours. 'For one thing I'll have

153

to find the time. For another I don't know where to start.'

'I may be able to help,' Koslove said. 'I've got another name. Anastasia Ashkirk. She came to see me Sunday night.'

'Mrs Clean? What's her problem?'

'The people of South Carolina. She's afraid they may not want to be represented by a woman who murdered her husband.'

'She murdered Ralph? Balls.'

'I thought you'd remember. He was one of yours, wasn't he? She said it was a mercy killing. He had MS and asked her to help him die. That's what she said.'

'There was an inquest' Blaines said slowly. 'Didn't he go over a cliff? Somewhere in Kent?'

'Uh huh. The verdict was accidental death.'

'No one mentioned suicide?'

Koslove shrugged. 'Would you kill yourself like that?' He shuddered. 'A long drop, and your eyes open all the time? The police asked a lot of questions but they didn't really believe she'd done it. Besides, his doctor testified that he wasn't suicidal about his condition – he was resigned, almost cheerful.'

'And where was Anastasia when it happened?'

'Twenty or thirty yards behind him. A couple of hikers saw them. She told me that her husband wanted her to kill him – partly because he couldn't stand the waiting; but more because he wanted to spare her. They didn't want suicide because it would invalidate his life insurance. He didn't want to know when or how. He just wanted it to happen.'

'Well, how did she do it?'

'When she parked him on the clifftop, she didn't put on the brake. The wheelchair was on a slight incline. Apparently Ralph was asleep. Then she gave him a push, just a gentle one, and ran backwards. That's when she screamed.'

Blaines nodded. 'So the hikers turned round, saw the wheelchair toppling over the edge, saw a woman a good distance away.'

'She told the police that Ralph jerked awake and released the brake, not realizing where he was. She was very distraught, blamed herself. She earned a lot of sympathy. Plenty of people were ready to say what a devoted couple they'd been. No one even mentioned murder.'

'Must be twenty years ago.' Blaines dropped the remains of his cigar. 'I can check our end but I don't think it caused much of a stir at the time. Ralph was off the books by then. Do you believe he wanted her to kill him?'

'Sure I believe her. But does it matter? Either way she's vulnerable. She's built her political career on being whiter than white. Traditional American values. The work ethic. The sanctity of marriage. A smear campaign would probably be enough. The blackmailer wouldn't even need proof for that.'

Koslove paused. By now the rain was coming down in sheets. The watchers were getting soaked. Whisky, Blaines thought; with hot water, sugar and a slice of lemon; and for supper one of those family-sized tinned steak-and-kidney puddings with a regiment of oven chips.

'The blackmailer's source,' he said. 'That's the crucial point. Who knew?'

155

'A guy came to see her after it happened. Colleague of Ralph's. She said he knew or maybe guessed. Didn't want a fuss. In effect he told her to take the money and run – get out of England and stay put. She figured he was worried about scandal – didn't want the press to get on to Ralph's old job.'

'She remember the name?'

'She thought it was double-barrelled. Something like Monder-Stowe. An old guy. Very dapper.'

'Bertrand Monastow,' Blaines said. 'Burlington bloody Bertie.'

'You know him? He's still alive?'

'I don't know. He left the service maybe fifteen years ago. I can find out. But right now I'm going home.'

He stepped away from the tree's shelter and plodded across the sodden grass. Water seeped through his shoes. One of the watchers took a few steps towards him and then stopped. Koslove must have given him the nod.

'Eric?' Koslove's voice was lowered to a whisper. 'We need results fast. I can't block that complaint for ever.'

Blaines turned. 'You know what I like about you, George?' he bellowed through the rain. 'You're so fucking subtle.'

5

'Why?' Jessica said. 'Why couldn't you tell us?'

Patricia Claybrook touched the sleeve of her daughter's jacket. 'Darling, you're soaked through. Go and have a bath. I'll make some tea.'

Jessica nearly stamped her foot. 'You're putting me off.'

'No, I'm not.' Her mother's smile made Jessica feel a child again. 'You've waited so long it won't hurt you to wait ten minutes longer. Besides, you're dripping on the carpet.'

Sweet bloody reason. Her mother was always reasonable. Jessica's body betrayed her by sneezing.

'Go on. I'll put the kettle on.'

Recognizing defeat, Jessica went upstairs. She found an old pair of jeans, a jersey and a shirt in her room. While she ran the bath she looked at her back in the mirror. Jack's nails had left red marks; at one point they had even drawn blood. She shivered and put one foot in the bath.

The water, of course, was too hot. She ran the cold tap and it became unpleasantly chilly. Instead of soothing her, the bath gave her time to catalogue the causes of her anger.

Her parents' double duplicity headed the list. Then came the row with Jack. She had stormed out of the flat only to find that her car had a dead battery. Pride made it impossible to return to Jack so she had taken the tube to Paddington. The through-train to Halcombe was pulling out as she arrived on the concourse. She had nearly an hour's wait before the next one – which took longer and involved a change at Swindon. The train was crowded with schoolchildren and she failed to get a seat. When at last she reached Halcombe, it was pouring with rain and all the taxis had been taken.

Life had not been kind to her today. There was a final psychological refinement to the situation: she had passed the age when it was possible to indulge unselfconsciously in a tantrum.

She heaved herself out of the bath, careless of the water that splashed on the floor. She dried herself quickly and pulled on her clothes. Her face in the mirror looked pale without make-up; her hair was a mess; the jeans were so unfashionable that they were practically an antique; and the sweater looked as though mice had been eating it. What did it matter? She wasn't here to make a good impression.

Patricia Claybrook was waiting in the sitting room with toast and tea. Jessica's suspicion that she had unwittingly regressed to childhood grew; there had been a thousand occasions like this. The ritual seemed unchanged apart from the absence of her father. Maybe that was why her mother clung to it.

But she wasn't a child any more.

'Are you staying the night?'

Jessica shook her head. 'I should get back this evening. I'm in the middle of an article with a deadline.' What to get the man in your life for Christmas. She took a sip of tea and one bite of toast. 'You going to tell me now? Why all the secrecy?'

'There were reasons,' Patricia said calmly. 'Your father didn't want you and Nell to know about his job. He wasn't just being protective – it's what normally happens. Spouses are told but not children. It's better that way.'

'Who for?'

'Everyone concerned.' Her mother looked faintly surprised as though shocked that a child of hers could be so stupid.

'What did he actually do? Peep through keyholes?'

'Nothing so dramatic. Latterly he just looked after records. He was a sort of librarian, that's all.'

'And how about Greg? And you being married before?'

Patricia stared at her hands on her lap. 'I was very young when I married Warren Vanderman. It didn't work out. Then I met your father and we both wanted a new start. We didn't want to remember the past. There's no point in dwelling on old mistakes, is there?'

Jessica's temper slipped away from her. 'Greg was a *mistake*?'

'No, of course not.' Her mother's knuckles whitened. She took a deep breath. 'Warren refused to give me a divorce unless I gave up all rights in Greg. My father was alive then. He and Warren threatened to make life very difficult for your father. Even before we broke up I saw very little of Greg. He had a nanny. He was too young to know what was happening. It seemed kinder to him . . .'

Her voice faded away. She was still staring at her lap. Her defences had cracked at last but Jessica

159

lacked the ruthlessness to maintain the attack.

'Jess – what's he like?'

'Big. Sort of untidy. I liked him. In fact I liked him a lot.'

Patricia Claybrook twisted the wedding ring round her finger.

'He wants to see you,' Jessica said.

'I don't know. I really don't know.'

'I don't think I can remember you not being certain. About anything.'

Her mother forced a smile. 'Weak spots. We've all got them. Perhaps we were wrong, your father and I. But –'

The doorbell rang destroying the moment of intimacy.

'That'll be Mr Caragh. Eric called to say he was coming. Would you answer it? I'll get another cup.'

Jessica's anger flooded back as she went into the hall. Her mother had known there would be an interruption. No wonder she had been so forceful about the bath. Probably she hoped to avoid the confrontation altogether. It was typical of today that the intruder should be that damned Irishman.

She opened the door. 'Yes?'

Liam Caragh smiled at her. 'Hullo. I didn't expect you to be here.'

And you can switch off that charm for a start. Jessica gave him an insultingly artificial smile. 'I wasn't expecting you either.'

He slipped past her into the hall. His hair gleamed with rain. She was suddenly aware of her appearance. In contrast Caragh looked almost elegant. She was looking her worst which was also typical of today. Not that it mattered. It was only Caragh. No doubt he was some sort of spy too. A slimy little secret servant.

'We're in the sitting room.' Social conditioning scored a short-lived victory over her desire to be bloody-minded: 'Can I take your coat?'

As far as Jessica could tell, the visit was entirely un-necessary. Colonel Blaines had sent Caragh to check on Mrs Claybrook's well-being and to question her once again about the evening when she had been attacked. Her mother was fine, and she had nothing to add to her previous account.

Caragh drank two cups of tea while they were talking. He took hardly any notice of Jessica which perversely annoyed her. After the second cup he glanced at his watch.

'Well, that's it. I must be going. I'm sorry to have bothered you, Mrs Claybrook. You know what it's like: check and recheck; and then we have to check all over again.'

'You're going back to London straight away?'

He nodded and turned to Jessica. 'Can I give you a lift?'

'How kind of you,' Patricia Claybrook said. 'It's still raining and it's a long walk to the station. Going by car is much faster, too.'

Jessica wondered if her mother had planned this as well. It was difficult to refuse the offer without making a scene; and in any case a lift did have its convenient side. She thanked Caragh in a way which she hoped would make clear to him that she was grateful for his car not his company.

Mrs Claybrook hastened their departure by finding a

carrier-bag for Jessica's damp clothes; she contrived to create the impression that she knew they were both in a hurry and that she was doing her best to help. It occurred to Jessica that her mother was a clever woman. The realization came almost as a revelation; she had never thought analytically about her mother, she realized – it was simpler to take your parents for granted.

Caragh was driving himself in a white Metro. Jessica was secretly pleased: if it were true that men in organizations used cars to express their position in the hierarchy, then Caragh's position was somewhere near the bottom of the heap.

She was less pleased to discover that he was a good driver – fast, smooth and safe. In her present frame of mind she would have preferred him to be a gear-crunching lunatic.

Neither of them said anything until they were on the dual carriageway leading to the motorway.

'Did I interrupt something back there?' Caragh said without warning.

'Nothing that matters. Just family business.'

'I'm sorry.' His eyes were on the road but she sensed his attention was concentrated on her. 'It must have seemed a pointless interruption, too.'

Jessica shrugged. So he was pretending to be sensitive. Some men used sensitivity as a tactic in preliminary sexual skirmishing.

'It's your job. You know what's pointless.'

'If it's any consolation, I thought it was pointless as well. My boss insisted.'

'Blaines? The fat man?'

He nodded.

Jessica switched to the attack. 'What do you do exactly?'

'I'm just a civil servant,' he said smoothly. 'A member of the Dublin sub-species. I've been seconded here for a few months.'

'You're a secret policeman,' she said scornfully. 'Like Blaines, like my father. Who do you really work for?'

For an instant the headlights of an oncoming car showed the smile on his face.

'You know I can't go into detail,' he said at last. 'What about you?'

'I'm a journalist.' Enraged by the smile, she parodied his voice: 'A member of the freelance sub-species.'

'What are you working on now? Anything interesting?'

'No.'

As she had intended, the conversation died. They reached the motorway. Traffic was scarce. Caragh kept the speed at a steady, sensible 70 m.p.h. Trust him: a visiting secret policeman wouldn't want to get done for speeding. The steady roar of the engine and the slapping of the wiper blades across the windscreen combined to have a soporific effect.

Jessica's eyelids grew heavier. It had been a tiring day. And she had made it worse by behaving like a spoiled brat to her mother – and, if it came to that, to Caragh.

Her mind slid sideways into a waking dream. Jack and Caragh were arguing about something that lay between them on the floor of the room they were in. Jessica tried to make them stop but neither of them would listen to her. Caragh moved aside and she saw what was on the floor. Her brother Greg. She jerked fully awake.

'It's all right' Caragh said quietly. 'We're coming up to Reading. Go back to sleep.'

His voice was unexpectedly reassuring. She was still tired. She bunched the bag of clothes into a makeshift pillow between her head and the window. This time she slept completely.

The next thing she was conscious of was the silence: the car had stopped. She opened her eyes and licked her dry lips. She must be looking awful. They were in the city now. The street lamps filled the interior of the car with a yellow glow. She peered out of the window and saw that they were just north of Hammersmith Broadway.

'Sorry to wake you,' Caragh said. 'I don't know where you live.'

'This is fine. I can get a tube from here.'

'No need. Besides, I need your help. I haven't sorted out the geography here. I was hoping you could point me in the right direction.'

'Where do you want to go?'

'The Embassy's lent me a flat in Bayswater. But what about you?'

'I'm in Notting Hill. Just down the road.'

'There you are. It'll be much easier for both of us if I give you a lift.'

She smiled at him. The sleep had refreshed not only her body but her conscience. She had behaved like a bitch to Caragh. At least he was trying to be kind.

He began to smile back. His eyes widened and slid away from her.

The door behind her swung open so suddenly that Jessica fell sideways. The cold night air invaded the car.

164

An arm went round her neck. Something pressed into her side.

'Nice and easy huh?' an unfamiliar voice said behind her. 'No need to panic.'

The last time Liam had been this scared was in Belfast.

He'd been in his first year at university. He'd come north to see an old schoolfriend who was now doing a course at Queen's. One night he was walking alone across a bridge when three men stopped him. None was much older than he was. They were very polite. They just wanted to know if he was Catholic or Protestant.

Sheep or goat? The question didn't allow for the existence of other species. Later, Liam wondered what would have happened if he'd said he was a Buddhist or a Jew. He certainly couldn't have told them what was then the truth: that, as a lapsed Catholic with a Protestant father, he tended towards the belief that God was a convenient philosophical abstraction which had had an unfortunate effect on history in general and on the Irish in particular.

The three men on the bridge had smelled of whisky and sweat. They were standing very close to him. One of them held the glowing tip of a cigarette close to Liam's cheek.

There was no way of knowing which was the right answer. The wrong answer meant a dip in the river if he was lucky and much worse if he wasn't.

Liam said he was Protestant. It was the right answer. They gave him a drink instead.

He held on to the memory of that fear. Last time it had been all right. Maybe this time it would be the same.

The snatch had been smoothly organized. Liam thought there were at least four men involved. Two of them were now with him in the Metro. The other two had taken Jessica. He assumed he had been the target. Jessica could have nothing to tell them, whoever they were. He hoped they would just let her go. It seemed unlikely. They weren't stupid.

'Stop here,' said the thin man with the bony face. 'On the left.'

It was the man Liam had seen in Green Park a few hours earlier. His English was poor and Liam found him difficult to understand. The man repeated his instructions in a louder voice. Liam pulled over to the kerb.

The street was lined with cars and builders' skips. It was somewhere in north London, Liam thought, a late-Victorian, working-class terrace which, having hit rock-bottom, was beginning to climb again.

'Switch off the engine and don't move.' The thin man leant across the divide between the seats. 'I am going to undo your trousers.'

'You're *what*?'

'Be quiet.' The thin man hit Liam's cheek with the palm of his hand. 'It is necessary for security.' He undid the button at the waistband and tugged down the zip. 'Now. We are going to walk to the van. You see?' He pointed through the rear window at a Transit van twenty yards behind. 'We go there.'

Liam shuffled down the road with his hands in his pockets and the thin man at his elbow. The lesser fear temporarily drove out the greater; it was difficult to concentrate on being afraid when you were trying to prevent your trousers falling down.

The wind drove the rain into his face. The muzzle of a gun was digging into his side. Even if he had the courage to shout for help, there was no one on the street to listen. Behind him he heard the Metro's engine firing. The sidekick must have been told to dump it.

The passenger door of the Transit slid back. Liam tried to read the van's number but the light wasn't good enough. The lettering on the side was no easier to decipher; but the lower line might have ended *and Builder*.

An arm reached out of the van, grabbed his tie and pulled. Simultaneously the thin man pushed. Liam shot into the van. He steadied himself for a second on the back of the seat; but another shove broke his grip and sent him sprawling face downwards behind the seats.

He lifted his head. The van's engine came to life. He was barely inches away from the huddled body of Jessica. Her face was a pale blur but he recognized her smell from the Metro – freshly-washed skin with a touch of perfume. He stretched out his hand. The face was warm. Her breath brushed his skin.

The thin man laughed.

Liam rolled over, suddenly aware that his trousers were round his knees.

'Lie on your front,' the man said.

'What have you done to her?' Liam tried to scramble up. 'She's *hurt*.'

The thin man kicked him in the ribs. 'Lie down.'

The man from the passenger seat turned round to watch. Liam lay down because it was the simplest thing to do. He felt like an unwillingly obedient dog in the grip of a stronger will. Apathy swept over him; there was no point in trying anything because nothing could succeed. Maybe his captors knew about the terrible fatalism that afflicts a victim. That would explain why they hadn't bothered to tie him up. It was difficult to think clearly with two armed men behind you.

It was impossible to guess where they were going. The driver kept to a sedate speed. He slowed considerably at corners to avoid inconveniencing his passengers. There were long pauses at road junctions or traffic lights. The metal floor transmitted the inequalities of London road surfaces with painful accuracy. The other two men talked quietly. They weren't far away but Liam couldn't distinguish the words.

He rubbed his fingers along the floor. Grit? Sand? An island which might be a splash of caked paint? He remembered the importance of contact traces and tried to scrape some of the dirt under his fingernails.

The darkness was rarely complete. Street-lights and passing cars threw brief surges of light into the back of the Transit. At one point Liam could see Jessica's face clearly. The eyes were open and staring at him.

They stopped again. This time the driver got out. A hinge creaked. When they went on, the tyres rustled over gravel. A few seconds later they stopped again. The engine died.

'Okay,' said the thin man. 'Everybody out.'

Liam raised his head. A torch beam hit him full in the eyes. The light slid from him to Jessica. Her eyes were closed.

Outside the rain had stopped. The evening was still dank. All around the sky was yellow with the lights of London. The gravel was slippery with dead leaves.

Liam shivered, partly from fear and partly because his jacket and coat were still in the Metro.

The driver opened the rear doors of the Transit and hauled Jessica on to his shoulder in a fireman's lift. He said something in a language with guttural Arabic vowels. The third man laughed.

The thin man gestured with the torch. 'Inside.'

Wooden steps echoed dully beneath Liam's feet. Some kind of a verandah. The torch played over a door which had once been painted red. The thin man turned the handle – no need to unlock it? – and went inside first. Liam came next, followed by the others.

He had a confused impression of a crowd in a confined space. The door closed behind them. The torch-beam swept the length of what seemed to be a hall. A reproduction of Constable's *Hay Wain*, blotched with damp and slightly askew, was hanging on one wall. There were five interior doors but no sign of a staircase. A bungalow?

Another torch came on. The three men were obviously familiar with the layout. The driver took Jessica into a room on the right of the door. For an instant the light rested on her face; her cheek was streaked with blood.

Liam was hustled into the room opposite by the other two men. A match scraped. The thin man lit two candles on the mantelpiece. The flames grew higher filling the room with soft, gold light.

Once this had been a sitting room. There were two chairs, a sofa and a small sideboard. Heavy curtains covered the window. The carpet was spotted with fallen plaster. Holiday accommodation? Or perhaps the owner had died and his heirs had so far removed only the

169

smaller objects. Maybe they decided it wasn't worth coming back for the rest.

'Sit, please.' The thin man pointed at one of the chairs.

Liam made an immense effort. 'What's happening?' His voice wavered and he tried to steady it. 'What did you do to her? She's bleeding.'

The second man pushed Liam back into the armchair. A broken spring dug into his thigh.

'You were following me this afternoon,' Liam said. 'Why?'

'No, no.' The thin man lowered himself carefully on to the arm of the sofa. He rested the gun on his leg and patted it with a gloved hand. 'We ask the questions, Mr Caragh. Tell us about the blackmail.'

The driver was breathing heavily.

He had dumped her on uncarpeted floorboards. She guessed he was crouching beside her. His hand slipped between her legs and squeezed. She willed herself to relax – to pretend someone was massaging her. Thank God she was wearing jeans.

The hand moved away and then returned to fumble at her breasts. She longed to scratch her face. The blood had contracted as it dried; and it was pulling her skin.

Her head ached fiercely but she thought the cut on her forehead was little more than a graze. It was her own fault. She had made a blind dash for freedom when they transferred her into the other car. One of the men hit her with the butt of a gun. She had blacked out for an unknown length of time. Minutes, perhaps, or even hours. The next thing she knew she was on the floor of the van with Caragh lying uselessly a few feet away.

Judging by the amount of traffic on the road she guessed it was still evening.

The driver found her hair. He stroked it for a few seconds and then gave up. Evidently he preferred his partners to be more active. He stood up and lit a cigarette.

It was very quiet. The only sound was the rise and fall of voices somewhere in the house.

Then Caragh screamed.

Just at the moment when he would have told them everything, they decided to stop.

The thin man conferred with his colleague by the door. The latter was another Arab, judging by his features and the tan. A European and two Arabs? It didn't make sense.

Liam's finger was throbbing. He flexed it gently. It felt twice its usual size and the tip burned with pain. His face was wet with tears and his throat felt as though he had swallowed sandpaper. By now the agony was almost bearable, unlike earlier when they had driven the matchstick beneath the nail. He wondered if a few shreds of wood were still lodged in the flesh.

They knew who he was and who he worked for. It was odd their questions hadn't been more specific. Most of them revolved around blackmail but they were framed in a way which suggested that the questioner had no idea who was blackmailing whom. It was as if the thin man had been told to ask a set of questions without being briefed about what they meant.

The two men turned and came towards him. Liam's stomach muscles contracted. The Arab produced a roll of nylon fishing line from the pocket of his jeans.

'Stand up,' the thin man said. 'Face the wall. Hands behind back.'

Liam did as he was told. His legs were shaking. Again he felt like a performing dog. *But I'm not a hero, I'm just a bureaucrat.* He would have liked to have been a hero, if only for Jessica's sake.

They lashed his wrists behind his back, holding his hands away from his body. In consequence his trousers slid down to his ankles. The nylon bit into his flesh. The Arab bent down to tie his legs.

'Good,' the thin man said. He took Liam by the shoulders and manoeuvred him backwards to the armchair. Liam screamed once more as the tip of his finger was crushed between his body and the back of the chair. He wriggled slightly, ignoring his protesting muscles, and managed to ease the pressure. The thin man smiled and said, 'Okay!'

The Arab – another performing dog? – produced a rag and crammed it into Liam's mouth. It tasted of oil. He gagged. He was suddenly afraid of choking to death on his own vomit.

The thin man put on the torch, blew out the candles and stowed them carefully in a carrier bag. He nodded to the Arab and both men left the room. Liam could hear them talking in the hall. He strained his head so that he could see the line of light beneath the door. It was faint and wavering but nevertheless it was there. That was the important thing. Another door opened and closed.

The light vanished.

For the first time the darkness was complete. It took strength from the silence and pressed upon Liam like a shroud. It would be like this, he thought, if you woke up in your coffin beneath six feet of earth. The familiar panic welled up in him. He was sweating heavily and his pulse was racing. The impossibility of movement made everything worse.

He forced himself to count slowly to twenty. He reached twelve; but then his mind slid into the past.

'Ma, it's smothering me . . .'

As a child he always slept with the curtains open, the door ajar and the landing light on. Even now he never slept in complete darkness. He thought about the things that made nights bearable – street lamps, illuminated clock displays and night-lights.

Just an irrational phobia.

His breathing was uneven. It sounded like someone tearing strips of paper. More air was essential. He worried the gag with his tongue but it refused to budge. He was going to die.

From somewhere in the house came the sound of breaking glass.

When the phone rang, Eric Blaines was lying fully-clothed on the brass bed that had once belonged to his parents. Here he had been conceived; here his mother had given birth to him; and here he hoped to die.

The continuity of occupation gave him an unsentimental pleasure. These days people changed their furniture almost as often as they changed their socks. It was a waste of money. This bed, for example, was strong enough to outlive another generation. Except that there wasn't another generation.

The phone rang on. Blaines allowed his head to roll on

the pillow. The overhead light was still on and everything seemed painfully bright. There were two red phones on the table and two alarm clocks. Both clocks told him it was a quarter to one in the morning – a stupid time to call. Two bottles of Johnny Walker Black Label caught his attention. They were both nearly empty. Pity. Wisps of smoke obscured the clocks.

His eyes dropped lower. He counted two ashtrays with two cigars smouldering beside them on the purple eiderdown. More smoke drifted upwards – in two columns, naturally. It was like the bloody Ark – everything two by two.

Oh Christ! The eiderdown was on fire.

He jerked awake and seized the cigar. The ashtray toppled off the bed. He put the cigar in his mouth and rubbed the black spot on the ciderdown. The phone rang on. There would be an office crisis on the other end and he didn't want to know. The phone call had possibly saved his life.

'Well, don't expect *me* to be grateful,' he said aloud. He swung his legs off the bed and kicked over an empty glass on the floor.

The damned phone wouldn't stop. It showed perseverance if nothing else and that was a quality Blaines admired. It deserved a reward. He picked up the handset.

'Yes?'

'Eric? It's Pat.'

The words brought him fully awake. He was still three-quarters drunk but he was used to handling that. He wondered if he would have recognized her if she hadn't said her name. Her voice was almost shrill.

174

'D'you know the time?' he said with automatic outrage. Simultaneously he wondered if the shrillness was a by-product of hysteria. 'Pat, what's wrong?'

'It's Jess,' she said in a rush, 'someone's got Jess.'

'Now hold on. Take it slowly, love. Tell me what happened from the beginning.'

'Jess . . . came down to Halcombe for the afternoon. Your man Caragh offered her a lift back to London.' She spoke more calmly now as though sorting out the facts was having a tranquillizing effect. 'Then someone called me twenty minutes ago – said she'd been kidnapped. A man. He didn't identify himself. So I phoned her flat. Jack – Jess's boyfriend, you know – said he thought she was with me.'

'And Caragh?'

'I don't know. He wasn't mentioned.'

'Oh Jesus.' Blaines rubbed his forehead. Aughrim would have a field-day if Caragh ran into trouble on British soil through no fault of his own. But there were more important things to think about.

'Eric? You still there?'

'Listen. Bolt your doors and stay by the phone.'

'Yes, but–'

'I'll get things moving this end and phone you back. All right?'

'Okay.'

She put down the phone first. Blaines relit his cigar and went to the living room for his briefcase. He would call Caragh's flat, he thought, and then the duty officer.

As he was crossing the tiny hall, someone hammered on the door. Blaines was tempted to ignore it: the woman in the flat below had a neurotic dislike of noises above her head after midnight.

The hammering continued. If it went on for much longer all the bloody neighbours would hold a protest meeting outside his front door. Blaines peered through the spyhole and received the second shock of the evening.

He was looking at a smile – two rows of teeth crowded with gold fillings and embedded in pink gums. Above the smile was a pair of brown eyes and one of those silly fur hats.

Blaines opened the door. 'And what do you want?'

'Conversation,' Osroyan said. 'Chit-chat. Discourse.'

Blaines noticed the second man waiting at the head of the staircase. There would be more elsewhere. Osroyan was like Koslove in that respect.

'What about?'

Osroyan edged closer. His breath smelled of peppermint. 'This and that. We might begin with Mr Caragh and Miss Claybrook.'

'You'd better come in.' Blaines glanced at the man by the stairs. 'Just you.'

Osroyan shook his head. 'No. I have a car outside. It is safer.'

'Safer?'

'More private.'

Blaines cleaned his left ear with a finger. He thought about the timing of this visit and wondered how much of the evening's events had been heard. Or even seen.

He nodded to Osroyan. 'I'll get my coat.'

It had to be Markalis, he thought. Maybe the Lithuanian knew more than they realized. Osroyan couldn't have heard of Wreningham's decision to turn down his request for asylum.

Blaines yawned as he pulled on his coat. It could be worse. If it was Markalis he had something to bargain with – something he didn't even want.

The car, a black Mercedes limousine, was parked in the slip-road that led to the row of garages serving the flats. Besides Osroyan there were two men in front; the third, the man from the stairs, stayed outside.

Osroyan opened one of the rear doors. He poked his head inside.

'Get out.' He spoke in his American-accented English for the benefit of his guest. 'Have a walk.'

He stood back to allow Blaines to enter first.

Blaines was appalled by his own recklessness. He wondered what Wreningham would say if he learned that Blaines was having a midnight chat with the KGB's Deputy Resident in the latter's car.

'What have you done with them?' he asked brusquely.

'Me?' Osroyan pantomimed outrage. 'We do not do that sort of thing here. Any more than you do in Moscow.'

'I know. We save it for the Third World where the poor buggers can't defend themselves. Who did you get? The Bulgarians?'

Osroyan smiled. 'I want to do you a good turn, Colonel. Let us say that we know where Caragh and Claybrook are. Difficult for you, eh? The Irish won't be pleased and nor will your politicians. Questions in Parliament, perhaps?'

Blaines grunted. 'Why the girl?'

'I imagine she just happened to be there at the time. Such a pity. A shame. Even a tragedy. She's of no importance in herself. But she could be awkward for you. A

177

journalist, I think? And pretty too. The media would enjoy her. It would be especially interesting if her father's occupation became known.'

'And even more interesting if we told the world who kidnapped them.'

'You won't do that.' Osroyan's teeth glittered briefly. 'I'm sure we can make an arrangement. A deal.'

'A swap?' It occurred to Blaines that Osroyan wouldn't be here if they had Markalis still. So poor old Anatanas had slipped his halter. It could be nasty if he was on the loose in the UK. Especially if he talked to the press.

Osroyan shook his head. He was an oddball in KGB terms – not a Slav but a thickset Armenian. He was also widely tipped to be the next Resident in Washington.

'Markalis?' he said slowly. 'You cannot bargain with something which is not yours to give. Besides, Markalis is unimportant. A little piece of straw in a very big wind. Did he tell you he was being blackmailed?'

Blaines shrugged.

'You mean no?'

'I mean we thought it was a possibility.'

'There's a lot of it about, these days. A disease. An epidemic.' Osroyan smiled cheerfully at Blaines. 'A cancer.'

'It's a tool of the trade.' Blaines groped for a handkerchief and blew his nose. He needed time to work this out. But there wasn't any time. 'You've had some problems too?'

'A few. It's all very curious.'

'Why?'

'The scope, my dear Colonel. Here, in Russia, in the States. And who knows where else? Essentially

178

imperialist but unexpectedly efficient. It is too widespread and too concerted to fit into the pattern. I am afraid, my friend. I have this terrible worry that we are only seeing the tip of the iceberg.'

Blaines said he was sorry to hear that.

'So,' Osroyan continued, 'I set my mind to work. The people behind this have long memories and many sources. So I think of a well-established organization. Also they need money – you've noticed that, of course? A self-funding destabilization programme. Perhaps they are setting up a series of networks too. Who would that benefit?' He laid his hands on his chest. 'Not *us*. Nor, I think, the Americans. But the British are another matter. A different kettle of fish. A different ballgame altogether.'

'Oh Christ,' Blaines said. 'Do you have to say everything in at least three different ways?'

Osroyan ignored him. 'Many of the cases have a British link. Some of them go back fifty years or more. You *could* be responsible. The British still have a remarkably wide frame of reference.'

'Don't be so bloody stupid.'

'And you have the motivation, too. Things have gone badly for you since the war. And for your country as well. Little people with big memories. Big memories mean large ambitions, you know that.'

'You're crazy.'

Osroyan looked thoughtfully at him. 'Someone must be doing it. Someone with the capabilities I have mentioned. Oh, I concede that the British may be operating at second-hand. Remote control. At long distance.' He paused. 'More than likely, really.'

179

Blaines put his hand on the door-handle. 'There's no point in going on.'

'Miss Claybrook?' Osroyan said. 'Caragh?'

'What about them?'

'A little lever. A form of pressure.' Osroyan's voice was as bland as baby food.

'There's nothing I can do – about the other matter.'

'No? I disagree. I think you can and you will. Because if this doesn't stop, we'll find skeletons in your cupboards, niggers in your woodpile. And we would take it personally too. For example we could contact Mr Wreningham. You might find retirement came a little earlier than planned.'

Blaines felt the sweat on his forehead. 'I know nothing about it.'

Osroyan shrugged. 'Then I'm sure you can find out. You have three weeks to abort this. To nip it in the bud.'

'Have you got authorization for this?'

'I don't think you need worry about that.' He rolled down the window. His entourage converged on the car. 'Goodnight, Colonel.'

The door opened from the outside. Blaines lowered one foot to the pavement and turned.

'Caragh? Miss Claybrook?'

Osroyan smiled. 'Goodnight. Farewell. Goodbye.'

The night air flowed through the hole in the window.

Jessica positioned her wrists along the ridge of broken glass. The nylon that bound them together was looser than it should have been. The man who had tied her up had been in a hurry. Besides, he had assumed she was still unconscious.

180

The air was cold and damp. It belonged to a graveyard. Slowly she moved her wrists to and fro along the glass. She was terrified of hitting an artery. It was impossible to exert as much pressure as she would have liked because the harder she pressed down on the glass the deeper the nylon line bit into her flesh.

But the effort and the pain had one advantage: they distracted her at least partly from the questions. Had all the men gone? Were they coming back? Where was Caragh? Was he still alive?

It was fortunate that the remaining glass was still held firmly by the frame of the window. It was less fortunate that the only way to get her wrists along the cutting edge was simultaneously to crouch and twist. Twice she was forced to rest leaning up against the wall and trying to ignore the pain in her muscles.

She felt the nylon give. But there was no corresponding sag in the pressure on her wrists. For a moment she was close to panic again. Then she remembered that there was more than one strand. She moved her wrists and arched back her fingers.

The line fell away. Her hands were free. Their first action was to pull out the rag that had been stuffed in her mouth. She bent down to untie her ankles but a wave of giddiness surged over her. Instead she sat down heavily on the floor.

It took much longer to deal with the line round her ankles. Her fingers were cold, which made them far too clumsy to unpick the knot. In the end she had to resort to the glass again. This time she cut herself.

The house was silent. The night sky had the orange tinge she associated with London. So they weren't in the depths of the country. She was tempted to lift the window and run. But what about Caragh? She could hardly leave him here. Or leave without knowing whether he was here or not.

She felt her way across the room to the door. Maybe it was locked, in which case she would be justified in forgetting about Caragh. But the handle turned and the door opened.

The hall was completely dark. The air smelled faintly and sweetly of dry rot. Nothing was moving.

Then she heard the whimpering.

It was low-pitched and irregular. It reminded her of unhappy dogs who were afraid to make their unhappiness too audible. The memory of the scream she had heard made her shiver.

She followed the sound across the hall. The whimpering stopped abruptly as soon as she opened the door. She cleared her throat and had the absurd thought that this would be much easier if she knew Caragh's first name.

'Caragh?' she whispered.

A grunt answered her. He was near at hand. She extended her arms and, sweeping them from side to side, moved into the room. First she found the armchair. Then a shirt with the warmth of a body behind it. The material was damp – with blood or sweat? She ran her hands upwards in a parody of a lover's caress until she found his face.

Caragh didn't move as she fumbled with the gag.

'Are you all right?' she said.

Caragh coughed. 'Draw the curtains.' His voice was hoarse. The Irish accent was more pronounced than before.

'What?'

'Pull them back. Now.'

Jessica shrugged in the darkness. She'd have thought he'd at least be grateful. A word of thanks perhaps. She backed away. The room was on the left of the hall; so the window was probably somewhere on her left now. She stumbled across the carpet with her arms outstretched. More by luck than good judgement her fingertips brushed against loose folds of heavy fabric.

She tugged the curtains apart. One of them screeched as it moved along its rail. The other tore as it moved; the material had rotted. The view from this window was the same as the one from the other room: shades of darkness surmounted by the glow of a city sky at night.

Caragh sighed.

'Thank you,' he said. 'Oh God. We must get out of here.'

It was easier said than done. Jessica fetched her piece of glass from the other room. Caragh seemed to have little control over his limbs. She wanted to shout at him, to make him realize the urgency. She had to haul him out of the armchair before she could reach the nylon which bound his wrists. It was strange to be touching a man like this. She thought of nurses and bedbaths. Maybe you got used to impersonal contact.

At one point he screamed again.

'Sorry,' he muttered. 'My finger . . .'

'Can you walk?'

'I think so.'

Suddenly the problems dropped away. They hobbled together into the hall. There was no need to scramble out of a window because the front door was unlocked. No one prevented them from walking down the gravel path to the gate. Caragh grew stronger with every step. By the gate he let go of her arm.

He glanced back at the bungalow. Fir trees masked it on three sides; here at the front the gate was set in a six-foot-high wooden fence. He ran his hand along the top of the gate. Jessica guessed he was looking for the house's number or name.

On the other side of the gate was an unlit road with bungalows scattered on either side. The bungalows were all in darkness. It must be three or four in the morning. They turned right because the orange glow was stronger in that direction. In a few minutes they were in the well-lit road lined with 1930s semi-detached houses. On the opposite corner was a telephone box.

They crossed the road and squeezed into the box.

'At least we know where we are.' Jessica pointed at the notice above the handset.

'Where?'

She realized abruptly that his knowledge of the environs of London was almost as sketchy as her knowledge of Dublin.

'We're south east. Practically Kent. It's a commuter suburb.'

He picked up the phone and dialled the operator.

'Why not 999?' she asked as the phone rang at the other end.

'This isn't police business.' He gave the operator a Freephone number. Covering the mouthpiece, he said, 'Watch the road, will you. Just in case.'

'You think?'

Caragh gave her the ghost of a smile. 'I don't know. But they did make it easy for us.'

*

184

The duty officer sent two cars.

One went to the bungalow; the other ferried Liam and Jessica back to London. There was an office with strip lighting. A doctor saw to Liam's finger. Someone promised to telephone Patricia Claybrook and Jack.

They were questioned separately and then together. They sat side by side on plastic chairs in front of a table scarred with cigarette burns. Mugs of sweet tea appeared at regular intervals.

The interviews had a dream-like quality. Liam had been up for nearly twenty-four hours. Too much had happened since he woke up. The day's events lay raw and indigestible, in his memory. Most of all he wanted a hot bath and dreamless sleep.

He knew one of the interviewers – a Special Branch inspector called Hebburn who blinked with every question and seemed to disapprove of every answer.

At intervals, Jessica protested. She demanded her solicitor. She wanted to make her own telephone calls. She made several pointed remarks about fascist police methods.

Once, between questioners, they were left alone for a few minutes.

'Just do as they say,' Liam said. 'They're trying to help. It's not worth fighting them.'

She said nothing – which, in a way, was a relief because he knew someone would be monitoring them. He sensed she was on the verge of tears. He would have liked to put his arm around her.

'It won't be long now,' he went on. 'They'll let you go home.'

'They're treating me as if I've done something wrong. You live in a mad world, you know that?'

Liam shrugged.

'What's your name? Your first name?'

His eyes narrowed. 'Liam.'

'You're not much good at your job, are you?'

'What happened tonight isn't my job. Not usually.'

'Why were you so upset? It wasn't just the finger. That business about the curtains.'

'I was afraid.'

She looked curiously at him. 'So was I.'

'Not just that.' He rubbed his bandaged finger and wondered why confession made you feel so relieved. 'It was the dark, you see. The complete dark. It's terrified me since I was a kid.'

6

'An East European.' Blaines said. 'Probably Bulgarian, maybe Czech – who cares? And two or three greasy Arabs. We'll show you some pretty pictures, see if you can put names to faces. Not that it matters.'

'I'm not sure I agree,' Caragh said.

Blaines raked his fingernails up and down his thighs. Caragh was looking peaky today. Pale and interesting. Bags under his eyes and that bloody ridiculous bandage on his finger. The dark stubble helped to make his skin look grey. But he was still fighting. He had some sort of stamina.

'All water under the bridge.' Blaines said. 'These things happen. No lasting damage. Miss Claybrook signed on the dotted line, so *that's* all right. Let bygones be bygones, eh?'

'I shall have to report this to Dublin.'

'Really? I don't think we should bother old Terry with something like this. Storm in a teacup.'

'Not as far as I was concerned.' Caragh paused. 'Or Miss Claybrook.'

Blaines sighed wheezily. It was very quiet in the office. They might have been alone in the building. It was the dead time in the morning: the night staff were on the verge of clocking off; most of the morning shift had yet to arrive. The desk was strewn with papers and with plastic beakers that had once held coffee. His hangover had gone. He felt forty-five again. Or even thirty-five. He was fit enough to cope with any number of young, upwardly-mobile colleagues.

With an effort Caragh straightened himself on the hard chair that faced the desk.

'Major Aughrim –' he began.

'Stuff Aughrim,' Blaines snarled. 'Stuff Dublin. You want them to know what a cock-up you made yesterday? One damn thing after another.'

'If necessary, yes.'

'You sure about that, sunshine? I don't just mean that business in Green Park. Or the high jinks last night.'

'I don't follow you.'

'Yes, you do. I'm talking about Curzon Street. About nice old Mike Russell. About Senator Glendowan's file.' Blaines bared his yellow teeth. 'You made a dog's dinner out of the whole business.'

He sat back and let Caragh work out the consequences of disobedience. Wreningham couldn't overlook a guest who so blatantly took advantage of his hosts' hospitality. Aughrim didn't like his subordinates to make mistakes, particularly when they rebounded on his own head as this one would.

Caragh's face gave little away but Blaines could guess what he was feeling. It was never pleasant to learn that you had been set up.

'Well?'

Caragh shrugged. 'I don't have much choice.'

'Good lad.'

'But one thing I don't understand. Why don't you shop me? The last thing you want's an Irish liaison officer. If you went public on this you'd destroy the whole arrangement.'

The telephone began to ring. Blaines put his hand on it but did not pick it up.

'Don't you worry about that,' he said. 'You'll find out.'

George Koslove was nervous.

He was in a strange car, in a strange country and heading for a strange destination. The office had no idea where he was. He had no protection whatsoever. And the cigar smoke was irritating his sinuses.

'Eric, are you sure this is wise?' As he whispered, he nodded towards Caragh, who was driving.

'No problem.' Blaines leered at him. 'Loyalty guaranteed. Besides, he'll be useful. His nationality gives him more room for manoeuvre. And he's trained.'

Caragh must have heard. His hands tightened on the wheel. He was wearing a stall on one finger. Koslove wondered what Blaines had on him. In the end he decided that he preferred not to know.

Outside the car windows England unrolled itself like a carpet. Koslove hated it. The environment was an unknown quantity; therefore you had to bear in mind the possibility that it was hostile. Anything could happen. Those black and white cows in the next field could stampede on to the road. Even the hedgerows looked out of control.

'What about Mrs Claybrook,' he asked after another mile had gone by. 'Can we be one hundred per cent sure that she's the right choice?'

'We have to have a clearing house, George – we agreed on that. Pat's an outsider so she's clean. But she knows

189

what's what because of Chas. I've known her for years. She's already involved, as one of the victims. She'll be the ideal housekeeper.' Blaines added, apparently as an afterthought: 'And she needs the money.'

'But is she trustworthy?'

Blaines patted Koslove's arm reassuringly. 'I trust her like I trust myself. Like I trust you.'

The tiredness came in waves.

At its worst, it blurred his vision and muffled his hearing; he stumbled when he spoke. Fortunately the other three were doing most of the talking.

Liam found it difficult to follow the conversation. It wasn't just tiredness, he thought: he was in shock as well.

'It's spreading,' Blaines was saying. 'Here, the States and now Russia. Osroyan's worried enough to play silly buggers. He thinks we're behind it.'

'Maybe the British are,' Patricia Claybrook said softly. 'Would you know?'

Blaines looked old and tired; Liam almost felt sorry for him.

'I think I'd know.' The old man's head swayed from side to side above the polished surface of the table. A distorted reflection swayed with it, drawing Liam's eyes. 'But I wish I could be sure.'

Liam's concentration faltered. They were sitting in the dining room of the Claybrooks' house. To an outsider they would have made an oddly domestic picture. Blaines, Liam noticed, still wasn't allowing himself to smoke in Mrs Claybrook's presence.

'. . . attempts at interference and at the highest level,'

Koslove droned on in answer to another question from Mrs Claybrook, 'have forced us, with the greatest of reluctance I may add, to implement this - uh - *sub rosa* investigative strategy . . .'

Koslove spoke so slowly he might have been inventing each word before he said it.

'And you don't even know the reason for the interference,' Patricia Claybrook interrupted. She had a gleam in her eyes which might have been amusement.

'Dirty washing?' Blaines said. 'Maybe. Everyone's had enough of that. Or it could be that someone up there is a victim and wants to limit the damage.'

'Alternatively,' Liam heard himself saying, 'they're behind the blackmail themselves.' He felt himself losing the thread of what he was saying. He gabbled the last sentence before he forgot it entirely: 'Naturally they wouldn't want an investigation.'

'Naturally,' Mrs Claybrook agreed.

Blaines growled to gain their attention. 'We haven't got much time if the Russians mean what they say.'

Koslove frowned. 'In my considered opinion –'

'We can do two things,' Blaines cut in. 'First, work backwards from the victims. How were they approached? What sources could there be for the information? Second, we can work forwards to the blackmailers. Who does all this benefit?'

'Any intelligence agency with an interest – uh – in sowing dissension in the international community. Having said that –'

'You're right, George. But dissension might be just the secondary aim.' Blaines poked an ash-rimmed forefinger in Koslove's direction. 'It's more than likely that we only

191

know a tiny percentage of the victims. Maybe the others have knuckled under.'

'I don't like it, Eric.' Koslove wrinkled his forehead and stabbed the table to emphasize his points. 'We're talking networks here. Agents of influence. International in scope. In government intelligence, the establishment in the widest sense – you name it.'

'It's a bloody nightmare,' Blaines said cheerfully. 'Tell you one thing. I'm going to have to do something about Willy Wreningham before we can even start.'

Koslove waved aside the change of subject. 'In my considered opinion –' he paused, scowling as though daring anyone to interrupt again '– we can deduce the likely source. Not for sure, no; but I'd say maybe eighty-per-cent probability. We just have to ask the right questions. Who has varying degrees of antagonism towards the US, the UK and the USSR? Who is by nature devious and fond of long-term plans? Who has a strong track record in information-gathering? Who is likely in the near future to make significant changes in their international stance?'

Blaines nodded. 'All right, George. It's a possibility. But it wouldn't explain the British angle, would it?'

'Well, who is it?' Mrs Claybrook demanded.

Blaines turned to her. At that moment the front doorbell rang.

At the last moment, Greg's nerve failed him and he stayed in the car.

Jessica understood. She put her hand on his arm. 'She won't eat you. But I'll go and make sure.'

The driver's window was open. Greg listened to the

sound of her heels on the path. He stared at the little houses on either side of the road. Little cars and trucks went by. Two little women, laden with shopping, trudged along the opposite pavement. In this country everything was small to the point of pokiness. He wished he was somewhere else.

It was all happening so quickly: meeting his half-sister yesterday; her calling him at the hotel this morning; the journey in the unfamiliar hire car along unfamiliar roads; and now this.

He wanted a drink. He hadn't even had time for that.

The doorbell rang.

Jessica was angry today, though not with him. She had refused to tell him why. Nevertheless he blamed himself. He had brought his own problems into the lives of complete strangers. It was harder for them than for him. At least he had had the luxury of being able to make a choice. According to Jessica, her mother – *our mother* – had been noncommittal about seeing him.

There were footsteps on the path. Not Jessica's; the stride was longer and slower. Greg scraped his fingers through his hair and opened the car door. He reached the gate at the same time as his mother.

In a way the gate made things easier: it kept them apart during the first few seconds of the meeting. Greg held out his hand. He was looking at the hands, his and hers, not at the woman. His hand was thick and clumsy; it belonged to one of nature's peasants. Hers was thin but strong; the little finger was almost as long as the others.

They shook hands. Greg lifted his eyes. He and the woman were of much the same height but there the resemblance ended. Even at her age, she had the sort of figure that displayed to advantage on a surfboard. For a split second he hoped he had made a mistake: his real mother was dead, as she always had been.

They spoke at the same time and with the same words: 'I'm sorry.'

'Come in,' she said. She backed away and pulled the gate open. 'I'm afraid some friends are here. Oh God.'

Greg grinned apologetically. He cleared his throat. 'I don't know about you but I could use a drink.'

In the hall, Jessica was staring at Liam.

'I just can't get away from you, can I? What's it about this time?'

'Are you all right?' Liam said. 'After last night.'

She shrugged. 'What about your finger?'

'I've known worse.'

Blaines loomed in the doorway of the dining room. 'Well, well. If it's not my little Jess.'

'I'm not your little anyone,' Jessica said. 'Why are you pestering my mother again?'

'Just routine.'

Jessica advanced; Blaines took a step backwards; Liam hovered, his admiration for Jessica struggling with apprehension.

'Are you going to tell me what's happening?' She peered into the room beyond. 'And who's that?'

'Uh.' Koslove struggled to his feet. 'Miss Claybrook. I'm delighted to meet you.'

'His name's George Koslove, love,' Blaines said. 'He's an old friend of your dad's.'

Koslove glanced angrily at Blaines, presumably because he wasn't accustomed to being introduced by his real name.

'That's right, Miss Claybrook.' he said venomously. 'He was an old and valued colleague.'

'And why are you here, love?'

Jessica turned to Blaines. 'I've come with Greg,' she said casually. 'I don't think you know my brother.'

The Ragged Bear was two miles from Halcombe. It was the only pub in a spruce Cotswold village. By the time the three of them arrived, the thin November sun had come out.

The scene was so pretty that you looked instinctively for a stage manager. Ducks picked their way across the village green to the pond. A policeman with a helmet wheeled a black bicycle past the village stores. An elderly clergyman chatted with a large woman in tweeds. Two King Charles spaniels sniffed their shoes.

Liam pulled the Granada into the pub's car-park. He felt that they had arrived in a plump and prosperous England ripe for a barbarian invasion.

'I hope the restaurant caters for vegetarians,' Koslove said.

'There isn't a restaurant,' Blaines said absently; he had hardly spoken during the drive. 'Pat says it's bar snacks only. And you're paying. Don't flash your credit cards around either. We're pretending to be untraceable.'

The bar was nearly empty, which was scarcely surprising for a Tuesday lunchtime on the fringes of winter. Horse brasses twinkled from the walls. The man behind the bar was reading a biography of Proust. He welcomed them effusively. He was thirsty for conversation.

Blaines was thirsty for beer. He cut the man short and ordered pints for himself and Liam and Perrier for

Koslove. They sat at a corner table near the radiator, which provided considerably more heat than the log fire. Koslove studied the bar menu.

'I can't eat this sort of crap.'

'I expect they do peanuts,' Blaines said. 'Monkey food.'

Liam glanced quickly at him. The old man's words were as abrasive as usual but his tone was oddly muted. Perhaps that was understandable enough. Liam sipped his beer cautiously. He wasn't sure what it would do to him. Blaines was already halfway down his first pint.

'It's a disaster,' Koslove said. He wasn't referring to the food.

'Eh?' Blaines paused in the act of lighting a cigar. 'You ready to order? Might as well get in the next round. Caragh will do it, won't you?'

'A green salad,' Koslove said, ignoring the menu. 'Wholemeal bread. And an omelette if they've got free-range eggs.'

Blaines persuaded Koslove to part with the necessary money. As Liam stood at the bar he could hear them talking quietly. The barman tried to pump him about their reason for being here. Liam said they were just passing through and he'd like his steak medium-rare.

He watched Blaines and Koslove in the mirror behind the bar. They looked like a couple of unhappy business-men. It suddenly occurred to him that it was the height of folly to want to be like them. Ambition was blind. It prevented you from noticing the effect that your heart's desire had on other people.

To his surprise the conversation didn't stop when he returned to the table with the second round.

'But it won't work, Eric,' Koslove said with the air

of a man who has said the same thing more than once in the recent past. 'She may be all you say she is but, let's face it, she's got personal problems. I mean, you could cut that atmosphere with a butter knife.'

'Ah, they were just visiting. Nothing to worry about.' Blaines seized the fresh pint from Liam's tray.

'Bullshit. The girl knows too much already. And she's a *journalist* for Christ's sake.'

Liam swallowed a mouthful of beer. There were advantages in belonging to the rank and file: you didn't have to make decisions or contribute to the conversation unless asked; you were free to think of other things. He thought about the way Jessica Claybrook's neck joined her head to her shoulders. He wondered why she had wanted to know his first name. Probably she would have gone when they got back to Halcombe.

Blaines shrugged. 'We're running out of time. Got an alternative? Caragh, what do you think?'

The question was so unexpected that Blaines had to repeat it before Liam took it in.

He covered his confusion with another mouthful of beer. 'One solution might be to bring them into this.' The possibility of daily meetings with Jessica dangled enticingly in his mind. He struggled to find convincing reasons. 'As you say, Miss Claybrook's already involved. Maybe the one way to keep her quiet would be to tell her part of the truth. She won't want to hurt her mother – we can play on that.'

'And young Vanderman?' Koslove said.

'I was coming to that,' Liam improvised. 'The same logic applies. We can use him, not alienate him. Subject to the obvious checks, of course. They'd both need screening.'

'You need your head examined,' Blaines said. 'A couple of amateurs? And the girl's as pink as a baby's bum! Be your age, sunshine.'

'Wait a minute, Eric. Our friend's got a point. Mrs C's their mother, right? The child-parent bond is a very, very powerful thing. It's got far more psychological impact than most political loyalties.'

Koslove's support took Liam by surprise. Was he just trying to get his own back on Blaines? Or maybe the solution actually appealed to him for its own sake.

'Crap.' Blaines turned to Liam. 'And what do you mean by "use him"?'

'Just that. And Miss Claybrook.' The idea gathered momentum the more Liam thought about it. 'We need their silence. Why not have their cooperation too? Perhaps we could use them for some of the legwork. They've got two advantages over us: they've got time and their faces aren't known.'

'Exactly.' Koslove nodded vigorously. 'We need foot soldiers, Eric.'

'You just want a pair of cut-outs,' Blaines snapped. 'Anything but get your own hands dirty.'

'Let's be rational about this, Eric. As I see it we can't afford to play this one by the book. We haven't got time. It's not like we can sit this one out and just wait for retirement.'

There was a moment's silence. Koslove and Blaines were looking at one another. Liam knew that a struggle of some sort was taking place; but he had no idea of the weapons each side was using.

'Did one of you gentlemen order *two* steak-and-kidney pies?'

Koslove knocked over his water. A woman loomed over them with a large tray in her hands. She had the same middle-class vowels as the barman.

'I did, love,' Blaines said. 'With two lots of chips. But where's the ketchup?'

Lord Sandridge hailed a taxi in Parliament Square.

He gave the driver the Wilton Crescent address and clambered into the back. Blaines followed him. He resented this summons but it wasn't worth showing it. At least the backs of taxis were reasonably discreet places.

Sandridge rested his chin on the head of his stick. 'You made any progress yet?'

Blaines leant forward so he could whisper into Sandridge's hearing aid. 'None worth mentioning. I hope to see a man tomorrow, if he's still alive. He may be useful. I wish you'd get Wreningham off my back.'

'You can handle William.' Sandridge turned his head. 'Just watch him,' he said carefully. 'Watch him when he thinks he's alone.'

Blaines lost patience with being subtle. 'Why?'

Sandridge ignored the question. 'April – that's his wife – is taking the children to her parents this weekend. She often does that. He'll be by himself on Saturday night. Catching up on his workload.'

'At the flat?'

'No. He'll be at home. He's got a constituency surgery in the afternoon.' Sandridge hesitated; he was chewing something invisible in his mouth. 'And there's something else you might as well know. Warren Vanderman's over here. And he's got a similar problem to mine.'

'I wish you'd tell me what they've got on you.'

'I'll tell you what they've got on Warren.' Sandridge sniffed. 'You remember the MoD contract? Someone knows something.' He chuckled. 'And Warren thought it might be me. No, to be fair, either me or that son of his. He's getting quite paranoid you know. Getting old.'

'So are we all,' Blaines said brutally. 'I met the son yesterday as a matter of fact. Just briefly. At his mother's.'

'That is interesting.' Sandridge yawned. 'I must remember to mention it to Charmian. He turned up at Macton on Sunday. I wasn't there. Haven't seen him for years. Turned into a bit of a misfit by all accounts.'

Christmas was less than six weeks away.

It was a useful excuse. Wreningham had unwittingly made it more plausible: one of his departmental memos last month had requested senior officers to reconsider and if possible extend their pastoral responsibilities; he singled out those on sick leave and those who had retired as being in particular need of reassurance.

Altruism had nothing to do with it; Wreningham's action sprang from a recent survey which concluded that these two groups of people were the most likely to leak information to outsiders. Blaines also suspected that a copy of the memo would be forwarded to the standing committee which monitored the union's attempts to get a toehold in the department. After all, the memo could be interpreted as demonstrating that the managers cared for their workers. Wreningham believed in using one stone to kill as many birds as possible. It was one of the few things which Blaines liked about him.

Blaines explained to Rosie that, as a result of the

memo, he had decided to send Christmas cards to retired
and still-surviving colleagues who had worked in and
with the department in the last twenty years. He sent her
down to Personnel where the computer would produce
a list of names and addresses if you asked it nicely. Rosie
was delighted. She liked talking to VDUs and she liked
to be reminded that they were really one big happy
family.

At the end of Wednesday afternoon she came back
with the list.

Blaines glanced through it. His eyes ran down the Bs,
noting with superstitious relief that BROWN, H.R. followed on directly from BINYON, C.T. de V.

'Dear God,' he muttered to himself. 'There's hundreds
of them.'

Rosie's face fell. She was a motherly twenty-five-year-
old who had long since given up trying to mother
Blaines.

'Still,' he said quickly. 'We must show them all that we
care.' He found the name he wanted near the middle of
the list. At least the old bastard was still alive and collec-
ting his pension. 'You'd better buy the Christmas cards
tomorrow. Get them off early, eh?'

'And the invoice, sir?'

Blaines looked blankly at her. 'Well, I'm not paying,
love. Staple a copy of that bloody memo to the invoice
and send it to Accounts. Let them sort it out.'

At Victoria he paid cash for the return ticket. When he
reached Brighton he wandered around until he found a
street-map rather than ask someone the way. It was foolish, really – a matter of superstition rather than security.

It was a long walk to Eden Park. The name was misleading, he discovered. Maybe the Eden commemorated the politician not the place. And maybe the housing estate stood on what had once been open parkland.

The estate consisted of four tower blocks, small by London standards but depressing nevertheless, surrounded by an uneven quadrilateral of houses. It was the sort of council estate that made you see the advantages of living in more traditional inner-city slums.

Buffeted by the wind, he struggled across a desert of mud and concrete to the house he wanted. Number eighty-seven had lace curtains in the windows, a neo-Georgian front door and a goldfish pond with its own pump-powered waterfall.

The door was answered by a sharp-featured woman with a disconcertingly large moustache. 'Yes?'

'Is Mr Monastow in?'

'Who's asking?'

'He's a mate of mine. We used to work together.'

'What's your name?'

'Blaines.'

'I'll see.'

She closed the door in his face. Blaines pulled his coat more tightly around him. He heard the woman shout, 'Uncle! You got a caller!'

There were footsteps and a muffled conversation. At last the door opened.

Monastow wore a red silk dressing-gown and a cravat. He was smoking a thin brown cigarette in a meerschaum holder.

'Hello, Bertie,' Blaines said. 'Long time, no see.'

'Eric.' Monastow raised his eyebrows. 'What on earth are you doing here?'

The dressing-gown was threadbare and stained, the relic of palmier days. The voice was the same as ever – it reminded you of BBC newsreaders in dinner jackets on the old Third Programme.

'Who'd you think it was? The bailiffs?'

The door began to close.

Blaines stuck his foot in the doorway. 'Joking apart, old son, I happened to be passing: thought I'd look in, you know, see if I could tempt you out to a spot of lunch. Courtesy of the department, of course.'

It worked, though the cost ran well into three figures. Monastow demanded a taxi and a seafood restaurant in the Lanes; the restaurant had London prices and Monastow had a seemingly limitless thirst for the more expensive white Burgundies on the wine list.

Monastow blossomed in this setting. Outside his home he dressed for his public. His voice became fruitier, his gestures more mannered. Bertrand Monastow, Blaines felt, had returned to his natural element. His long, bony body was draped in a three-piece single-breasted pinstripe suit in immaculate condition; only the size of the lapels betrayed its age. The assemblage was topped by a suitably faded Old Harrovian tie. Blaines appreciated the fading: Monastow had always been good at those little touches of manufactured authenticity.

The conversation stayed with the department and its sister organizations for most of the meal. Monastow was starved of gossip. He had attended none of the reunions since his retirement nearly fifteen years before. The circumstances of his departure had precluded that.

With the fourth bottle and the coffee, Monastow lowered his barriers.

'I wish you'd phoned or written, Eric.'

'Your niece doesn't like visitors?'

Monastow's thin shoulders twitched. 'She needs me to help with the mortgage; I need her because I can't afford anywhere else.'

'You've got your pension . . .'

'It's not that much – as you know, I retired . . . slightly earlier than planned. Besides, one has to have a social life.'

'Brandy?'

'Why not? Do you know, I had a premonition about today. I dreamed I was playing chess last night. Curiously enough that dream almost always brings good fortune the following day.' Monastow looked earnestly at Blaines; his blue eyes were as faded as his tie. 'Do you dream, Eric?'

'Never. Tell me, what would you do if you had more money?'

'I'd winter on the Riviera.' Monastow smiled at the waiter who took the order for brandy. 'There's little to keep me here. A few friends with shared interests – that's all. I don't think I can bear another English winter.' He studied the rear view of the departing waiter. 'My wants are modest enough. A small hotel. Perhaps a view of the sea from the balcony of my room. Two simple meals a day. Nothing more.'

'Perhaps we can help.' Blaines paused while the waiter set the brandies on the table. He ordered two more to follow. There was no point in spoiling the ship for a ha'p'orth of tar.

Monastow's hand, brown-spotted and blue-veined, lay on the tablecloth; it was trembling slightly. Excitement? Parkinson's? Blaines was afraid. Monastow was no more than ten years older than he was. Time was running out for both of them. Death was nothing; but dying, like retirement, was full of fear.

'My dear Eric. That would be perfectly sweet of you. How the department has changed since my day..'

Blaines caught the irony in time; it wouldn't do to patronize the old man.

'All right,' he said abruptly. 'We make a deal. I use your memory. You get your trip to the Riviera. Fair enough?'

'In principle.' Monastow fed a cigarette into the holder. The waiter brought the second round of brandies. 'Thank you so much.'

'I'm interested in the sixties and early seventies, Bertie. When you were seconded to Curzon Street. You remember?'

'I remember perfectly. My little section. My corner in the sun. My moment of glory. They also serve, and so forth. But first we must talk about numbers.'

Blaines realized that Monastow was well on the way to being drunk; so, to be fair, was he. However, he noticed that Monastow still kept his voice lowered.

'Numbers? That would depend. On the time it takes – on the quality of what you can tell me.'

'No, no, no. Not my style. I think we should agree on a deposit. With a sliding scale of further increments. Perhaps a bonus scheme?'

'Five hundred for starters.'

Monastow pursed his lips. 'You disappoint me, Eric. You need me, I know that. And it's all – how can I put it? – a little under the counter? If it wasn't they would have sent a pair of young men in matching raincoats. I know the form. Add another nought and we can begin.'

'We could play this another way, Bertie.'

'But you won't, will you? Who breaks a butterfly on a wheel? Besides, what you really want is a little heart-to-heart. Torture chambers are such public places, aren't they? People tend to notice the screams.'

'Okay.' Blaines could see no point in being careful with Koslove's money. 'But I can't give you it all now. Six hundred now and the balance next week? Plus bonuses, if you earn them?'

'Scout's honour, Eric?'

'You can pretend I'm a bloody Girl Guide if it helps. Wait here. I want to piss.'

Blaines locked himself in the lavatory and counted twelve fifty-pound notes from the roll that Koslove had given him. He had enough left for the meal but not much else. When he got back to the table, he found that Monastow had ordered more coffee and brandy.

Blaines shooed the waiter away and passed the money to Monastow.

'Vanderman,' he said softly. 'The MoD contract. The inquiry was instigated by your section. By you?'

Monastow shook his head. 'My deputy. Chap called Harry Ryal. It was all terribly technical, if I remember rightly. The Ministry had a pile of semi-obsolete SAMs. Then some bright spark had the idea that you could quadruple their long-range efficiency by installing a piece of string and a few microchips – if you wanted the details, you can look them up. The point was, it was going to save about eighty million pounds, so everyone was very excited. Went out to tender in the normal way. The manufacturers sent in their estimates. An American company undercut everyone else and got the contract. Everything seemed quite straightforward until Ryal came across an AO with a taste for heroin.'

'Name?'

Monastow peered suspiciously over the rim of his glass. 'Surely you remember? It was Michael Edgeley.'

'What was the timing?'

'About six months later. There was no connection at first. We had a tip-off from the Yard via Special Branch: they'd arrested a pusher and found Edgeley's name and address in his little black book. Drugs mean potential security risk so Ryal went through the motions – just routine at that stage. Hauled the man in, spun him the line about random vetting. Edgeley cracked, of course, but when he did, something unexpected spilled out. His job included processing tenders. According to Ryal, he admitted taking bribes. Or rather one bribe. He passed on information about the SAMs contract - including the details of the tenders and MoD assessment criteria – to an American. Edgeley described the American to Ryal and it sounded remarkably like Warren Vanderman. Subsequently we discovered that Vanderman had a substantial stake in the company which got the contract.'

Blaines put his elbows on the table. 'According to Ryal.'

'Yes.' Monastow patted the back of his hair. 'That was the unfortunate part of it. It has to be said that Harry Ryal wasn't what you'd call a cuddly interrogator. Efficient, yes. I'd had complaints before. But Edgeley didn't complain. He took an overdose of heroin instead.'

'No supporting evidence? The interviews must have been taped. You saying it all rested on Ryal's word?'

'Oh, stop growling at me, Eric. There was no other evidence because Ryal didn't get beyond the preliminary interview. No tapes. Nothing.' Monastow sipped his brandy and coughed. 'You knew this already. You knew at the time. You can read the file. Why are you asking me?'

'A fresh approach,' Blaines said. 'Last time was like looking for needles in a haystack. This time we're looking for pins. Different technique. We have to start all over again.'

Monastow glanced over his shoulder. By now the restaurant was empty, apart from two waiters by the door. The one who had served them consulted his watch with studied ostentation.

'Really!' Monastow said. 'Most discourteous. I shall think twice about coming here again.'

Blaines pushed back his chair. 'We'll go somewhere else.'

Outside it was still raining. Gusts of wind raced ashore from the English Channel and drove the rain into their faces. Blaines wrapped his raincoat around him and wished it was summer. The alcohol and food were a form of central heating but they wouldn't last long in this weather.

It was too early for tea and far too early for another drink. Monastow said he knew of a little club which was open in the afternoon. Blaines shied away from the idea; he didn't want to meet any of Monastow's friends, particularly those who frequented little clubs.

In desperation Blaines towed his guest towards the

domes and pinnacles of the Royal Pavilion.

Monastow chirruped with pleasure. '*Quite* my favourite place. How did you guess?'

At this time of year the Pavilion was nearly deserted. Blaines bought their tickets and hurried Monastow through the apartments. He closed his ears to the pleas that followed him. 'Eric, just *look* at that dragon. Have you ever seen such *trompe l'oeil*?'

Instinct drove him to the kitchen where Monastow had less to distract him. True, he pointed out the copper-iron palm leaves with proprietorial pride and informed Blaines that the great Carème, the inventor of caramel, had once been chef here; but the mechanics of cooking held less charm for him than the more decorative delights elsewhere.

'So what happened when Edgeley died on you?'

'Not on me,' Monastow corrected him. 'Edgeley was entirely the responsibility of Ryal. Oh, I was kept informed, naturally; but Edgeley was Ryal's baby.'

Blaines sighed. 'When Edgeley killed himself you had two problems instead of one.'

'The section did; not me personally. But you're right: we had to do something about Ryal – it's most unpleasant when an interviewee dies on you; and then we had to see if there was anything in what Edgeley was alleged to have said. That's where you came into it.'

'Skip the MoD investigation. Vanderman was cleared completely. There wasn't a shred of evidence to support what Ryal said.'

Monastow stared at his bulging reflection on the side of a vast copper pan. 'Nor to disprove it. But by that time no one wanted to listen to Ryal. Vanderman had unleashed Sandridge. I almost felt sorry for him – Ryal, I mean. He was such an eager beaver. And then the establishment put its foot down and squashed him.'

'There was a board of inquiry?'

Monastow nodded. 'Triggered by Edgeley's death but its brief was wider than that. They went through Ryal's career pretty thoroughly. Did you know he was once a military policeman? They dressed up the verdict: "Unacceptable working methods" – that sort of thing. Asked to resign. If you want chapter and verse on it, ask Chas Claybrook. He sat in for the section.'

A party of school children came into the kitchen. Blaines and Monastow edged away. Blaines scowled automatically at the woman teacher who was in charge of them.

'Tell me,' he said in a lower voice than before, 'd'you remember Ralph Ashkirk?'

'Dear me, you have been a busy bee.' Monastow ran his finger along the grain of a huge table as though checking for dust. 'Why this sudden interest in the past?'

'Don't stall.'

Monastow pouted. 'I thought that was a purely verbal matter between me and the DG. And Mrs Ashkirk, of course.'

'No one else? You sure about that?'

'Only Harry Ryal. The police notification came through him. But he wasn't involved in the later stages.'

'Any evidence to go with it?'

'I did see a letter,' Monastow admitted. 'Ralph Ashkirk wrote to a colleague just before he died. A former colleague. It mentioned insurance policies. And it implied that an early death would be convenient for everyone concerned.'

'Is the letter on file?'

Monastow looked him straight in the eye. 'I believe the DG shredded it personally.'

'Don't piss me about. You shredded it.'

'You're such a bloodhound, Eric. Anyway, it was shredded. No one wanted any fuss – it was best for all concerned. Nothing was added to Ashkirk's file. Shall we go and find a cup of tea?'

Blaines shook his head. 'I've got a train to catch.'

'But you'll be back?' Suddenly there was an edge of panic to Monastow's voice. 'If you prefer I could come to you.'

'Don't worry. You'll get the balance. I haven't finished with you.' Blaines thought about the Bishop and the Vice Chancellor; they were Monastow's vintage too. 'You on the phone?'

Monastow nodded. 'Yes, but my niece is rather tiresome about –'

'Give me the number.'

Blaines scribbled it on the back of the restaurant bill. A ten-year-old boy jogged his elbow while he was writing. 'Piss off,' Blaines said. All the other children stopped talking. In the succeeding hush Blaines glared indiscriminately at them.

Monastow insisted on walking him to the station.

'Why me?' he asked as they waited to cross a road.

'You know what they say.' Blaines rammed a cigar into his mouth. 'Set a thief to catch a thief.'

'I'm not sure I like that, Eric.'

'By the way, what happened to Ryal when he went private? Did he go freelance?'

'If he did it wasn't for long.' Monastow raised his hat

211

to a passing lady. 'One of our little circle,' he explained parenthetically. 'Totally untrained, but a very gifted medium. I thought you knew: Ryal's dead.'

'I won't allow it,' Patricia Claybrook said.

'You haven't got much choice,' Blaines said. 'Nor've I, for that matter.'

They were sitting in the non-smoking section of the buffet at Paddington Station. The evening rush-hour had passed its peak and they were surrounded by empty tables.

'But it's totally absurd, Eric.'

'Koslove backs the idea. So does Caragh for what it's worth. Neither of them has a track record, that's the charm. Also, it's the only way to keep your precious Jessica from talking.'

'I don't give a damn whether she talks or not. I just don't want her to get hurt. Or Greg. I would have thought you'd understand that.'

Anger drained the colour from her face. Blaines stared at her for an instant before forcing himself to look away. She had phoned him at the office, just after he returned from Brighton, and insisted on a meeting. He wanted to see her but not when she was in this mood.

'Greg can look after himself,' he said. 'According to Caragh, he finished off his education at the Los Angeles Police Academy. Passed out second in his class. And then he chucked it all in. I tell you this, Pat, the only problem that boy has is Warren Vanderman.'

'And Jess?'

'For Christ's sake. She's no fool and I'll keep her in the background. I can't say more than that. We've run out of alternatives.'

212

'And her politics?'

Blaines shrugged. 'Left-wing but not considered subversive. Woolly liberal, basically. Jedborough's another matter. She's agreed not to see him for the duration. We're arranging journalistic cover so she's got a reason for not being at home.' He hesitated a second. 'If you ask me, I think she was glad of the excuse.'

'I didn't.' Patricia closed her handbag with a snap. 'My train will be in. In any case I can't see what use she could be to you.'

Blaines looked at his watch, leaving the implicit question unanswered. He lacked the courage to tell Patricia what Jessica and Caragh would be doing on Saturday. He had planned to persuade her to take a later train and have dinner with him; but his nerve failed him. Why not admit it? She couldn't wait to get away from him. This meeting was strictly business.

'You know what to say to Koslove when he calls?' he asked brusquely.

She nodded. They had been over it twice.

'For God's sake stress the need to keep Monastow sweet. If Koslove pinches the pennies we'll get nowhere.'

Patricia shrugged herself into her coat and picked up the shopping-bags which provided her excuse for coming to London.

'I'll say goodbye, Eric.'

'Wait a minute. One more thing: I want Greg to move in with you.'

'In Halcombe?' Patricia bit her lip. 'Is that wise?'

'After what happened before, you may need protection. And he's the natural choice. If anyone asks you can tell them the truth: your son from America's come to stay.'

'But – Eric, it's the wrong way to get to know him – too much and too quickly. We're strangers to one another.'

'Who's fault is that?' Even Blaines was surprised by the bitterness in his tone. 'It's too late to pull up the drawbridge and keep the world out. We're already inside.'

She stood up. Blaines resolutely remained in his seat, avoiding her eyes. He thought about the long journey home to the flat. He thought about the oven chips in the freezer, the regiments of toy soldiers in the spare bedroom where no one had ever slept and the brass bedstead where he hoped he would die.

As Patricia passed him on the way to the exit, she touched his shoulder: she gave it a swift and gentle squeeze.

It was the sheerest bad luck that they were seen – and seen by one of the few people who would take notice.

On Saturday afternoon Liam picked up Jessica in a rented Ford Escort; the Metro had not been returned to him yet.

Jessica was no longer at the Notting Hill flat. On Thursday evening she had moved to a private hotel in Kensington. It was run by a woman who had worked for Blaines in the Dark Ages; Koslove was footing the bill. A Sunday newspaper whose editor owed Blaines a favour had commissioned her to write a series of articles on the winter face of English seaside towns. From what Liam gathered, Jedborough had swallowed the excuse for her absence from the flat with an insulting lack of fuss.

Liam explained that he had to stop at the embassy on

the way. There was no need to give her the details – that Aughrim insisted on weekly reports delivered either in person or through the diplomatic bag.

He parked on a double yellow line in Grosvenor Place and took the lift to the third floor. His destination was a small room which was grandiosely called 'The Communications Centre'. He dropped in the envelope and, avoiding offers of coffee, tea and conversation, left the building. The door swung shut behind him. It was then that Liam realized his mistake.

Six-foot-three of magnificent Irish manhood stood between him and the Escort. The specimen had red-gold hair, broad shoulders and the air of a conquering hero, as befitted a former army officer. Worst of all, he was staring at Jessica as though she was a potential vassal.

Liam was about to dart back to the shelter of the embassy. Before he could move, the conquering hero turned. Simultaneously Jessica rolled down her window, thereby destroying the last chance of pretending that they were not together.

'There's a traffic warden on her way,' she called.

'Liam!' John Fitzpatrick said with a plausible imitation of pleasure. 'I hoped I might see you around.' He glanced back at the car, quickly assessing the situation. 'You must introduce me.

'What are you doing here?' Liam said before he could stop himself.

Fitzpatrick fired a boyish grin in the direction of Jessica. 'Liaising, of course. Aren't we all?'

'I'm sorry, John, I must go. I'm late already.' Liam hoped he sounded suitably regretful. Fitzpatrick was the nearest thing to an enemy that he had. It was a convention of their rivalry that they should pretend to be the greatest of friends. 'How long will you be here for?'

'Three nights.'

'I'll give you a ring this evening. Maybe we can have dinner.'

'That'd be grand.' Fitzpatrick turned back to the car. 'Why don't we all have dinner together? Maybe a four-some?'

'Why not?' Liam abandoned finesse and climbed into the car. He pulled away with grating gears and a wave to Fitzpatrick.

'Oh *shit*!'

Jessica waited to break the silence until they reached the M1.

'Why don't you talk about it?' she suggested.

He glanced sideways at her. 'Is it that obvious?'

'I suppose you could grind your teeth as well if you wanted to go the whole hog. It's not just security, is it?'

'That's part of it. I should have gone there first, before I picked you up.'

'What's the problem then? Your friend can't know what we're doing. He'll think it's perfectly natural.' Her voice dropped in pitch and acquired a passable imitation of Fitzpatrick's heartiness: 'Old Liam's got a bit of stuff on the side.'

'That's the problem. There's someone in Dublin, you see. And Fitzpatrick isn't my friend; he'll make sure she hears. Just to make matters worse, her dad's a friend of my boss.'

For an instant Jessica wished she hadn't asked. Things had been fine as they were: herself and Liam in a car, on their way to do a job. It was a business arrangement which was proving less distasteful than she had expected; largely because it had no connection with the real world of earning a living, having friends and keeping yourself fed and watered. But when Liam talked about the other part of his life, about people in Dublin, it was no longer possible to keep the compartments separate. One leak led to another: Jack hadn't bothered to kiss her when she left the flat on Thursday; he had been too involved in stripping down the motorbike's carburettor. With an effort she forced herself back to the subject of the predatory John.

'He sounded friendly enough,' she said lightly. 'So did you.'

'He wanted the London posting himself.' Liam grinned unexpectedly. 'I shouldn't be telling you this.'

She smiled back, safe in the knowledge that he couldn't see her face because his eyes were on the road. Her pleasure faded as she remembered the purpose of this journey. She reminded herself she was doing this for her mother, who would suffer if she didn't cooperate. The job itself was unpleasant but essentially no different from investigative reporting. In any case politicians made themselves public property when they stood for election; their lives had no compartments. There were the best of reasons for being where she was. Nevertheless she felt both ashamed and scared.

Liam sensed the change in her mood. 'Nervous?'

'Well, this isn't how I usually spend my weekends.'

'Nor me.' Liam paused. 'Personally, I'm terrified.'

The weather was on their side.

The sky was already darkening. It was one of those

217

premature winter twilights that keep people inside because they have yet to relearn the methods of coping with short, raw days and long, cold nights.

There was little traffic on the road outside Wreningham's house. Even parked cars were relatively rare because the houses in this area had more than their fair share of garages.

The house was called St Mary's Lodge. It stood on a corner site, a squat redbrick pile with Dutch gables and disproportionately large chimney stacks. It was older than its neighbours, separated by the Great War from the other houses in the road. The garden was ringed by a wooden fence. A line of trees gave the Wreninghams further shelter from the outside world.

They drove past without stopping. Liam parked the Escort several streets away. He switched off the engine and cleared his throat.

'It might look better if we walked arm in arm. Would you mind?'

'If you think it would help.'

Her voice gave Liam no clue to her feelings. He rushed on: 'Courting couples are expected to dawdle outside, whatever the weather. No one looks twice at them.'

'Except the prurient.'

The wind hit them as soon as they left the car. Both of them were wearing jeans, several jerseys, gloves and a coat. Liam wished he had brought a hat as well. As they walked along the pavement Jessica's grip tightened on his arm. The street-lights came on. Through an uncurtained window they saw a family having tea by a fire.

First they reconnoitred the roads around St Mary's Lodge. Liam was looking for parked cars with aerials outside and people inside. According to Blaines Wreningham was unlikely to be guarded unless the circumstances were exceptional, though the local police included his house in routine patrols. But there was always the possibility that someone else was watching him. Blaines wasn't omniscient.

Nothing suspicious delayed them. Liam unlatched the tradesman's gate that led into the garden at the side of the house. Jessica let go of his arm. It was then he began to be afraid. He saw himself hauled in front of Aughrim and trying to explain away a complaint from Wreningham.

They moved slowly round the house. Dead leaves rustled under their feet. There was still enough light to see where they were going. Fortunately most of the garden was laid to lawn. At the back of the house they found a cluster of outbuildings grouped round the kitchen door. The double garage contained Wreningham's Daimler.

Most of the windows were dark. But two rooms showed signs of occupation. There was light behind a curtained window on the far side of the garage. By the position it was probably the study that Blaines had mentioned. The old man's information had included the fact that Wreningham should be alone in the house. The Wreninghams had a daily woman but no one who lived in.

At the front of the house they found the uncurtained windows of what was evidently a drawing room; long and high-ceilinged, it looked like a stage set for a Noel Coward production. The lights were on but no one was there. It was Jessica who noticed that one of the two sash-windows was slightly open at the top. Wreningham either had a passion for fresh air or a very good central-heating system.

It was time to choose their positions. Jessica covered the front gate and Liam the tradesman's entrance. As he was settling her in the shrubbery, Wreningham himself came into the drawing room. He was in his shirt sleeves and carrying a glass. He came to the window and stared out for a moment before drawing the curtains. A few seconds later he switched out the light. It was a relief to know the man was actually there.

They had gone over their tactics in the car. Both of them were carrying cameras. If Wreningham came out they were to tail him; if he had a visitor they would tail the visitor. Blaines had seemed certain Wreningham was up to something but had been irritatingly vague about its likely nature: 'What I'd really like is a nice juicy choirboy but Willy's probably hetero. Nothing's perfect in this world.'

Liam waited in the angle between the garage and the utility-room which abutted on the kitchen. From here he could see the gate, the back door and the gravelled path to the side door.

Time stretched as the temperature dropped. He had done nothing like this since he left the Garda. He had for-gotten how appalling the combination of boredom and physical discomfort could be. Seconds grew into minutes and minutes into hours; you had to force yourself not to stare at your watch. Your concentration flagged. Your mind filled with unwelcome thoughts. Surveillance was worst of all when you were outside; you lacked even the minimal comfort of shelter.

A light went on upstairs. Wreningham drew the curtains immediately afterwards. The light stayed on. Maybe the lucky bastard was lying on the bed with his shoes off, watching TV and sipping his drink.

The hours dragged on. Every thirty minutes Liam and Jessica met to compare notes; they took it in turns to come to each other. Jessica had had the forethought to bring a packet of biscuits. Liam fantasized about mugs of steaming coffee. The meetings were oases in the desert of boredom; it was difficult to resist the temptation to prolong them.

No one came to the house. A passing car was an event. Liam wondered if Blaines had got it wrong: Wreningham's private life might be as blameless as it ought to be.

Just after eight o'clock another light came on upstairs. A shadow moved quickly across a window which was shielded by a blind. Perhaps it was a bathroom. Liam waited. The shadow returned. This time it was closer to the window and therefore clearer. As he watched, the shadow changed shape. Liam had a brief glimpse of the unmistakable profile of a well-endowed woman.

So Blaines was right. The woman must have been there all the time. But it was unfortunate that she had arrived so early. The problem was, she might not leave until Sunday afternoon – April Wreningham wasn't due back from her parents until the early evening.

Liam picked his way across the damp grass to Jessica's shrubbery. In a whisper he described what he had seen.

'Maybe we should wait until midnight,' he said. 'If she doesn't come out we could call it off and come back in the morning.'

'We might miss her.' Jessica's voice was shaking with cold. 'Besides, people would notice us in daylight, even if we stayed in the car.'

'I wonder how she got here. The Daimler felt cold.'

'On foot? Or she might have parked in one of the side roads. They'd hardly want to advertise her presence to the neighbours.'

'Damn Blaines,' Liam muttered. 'We haven't got the resources to make a proper job of this.'

'We could phone him. There's a call box in the next road.'

'I don't see how he could help.'

'Then there's only one alternative.'

He could see the way her mind was working. The consequences could be disastrous. 'No,' he said firmly. 'It's too risky.'

'Why?' Jessica sounded amused. 'Anything's better than freezing to death. And he's hardly in a position to call the police.'

The window slid upwards with barely a murmur.

Liam parted the curtains and shone the torch round the drawing room. Its thin beam was his protection against the darkness. He had a spare torch in his pocket as well as a box of matches.

The door to the hall was closed. Jessica prodded him in the small of his back. He eased his leg over the sill and waited. The night remained quiet. There must be some sort of alarm system; but they were gambling on the probability that Wreningham wouldn't switch it on until he locked up and went to bed.

A moment later he was inside the house. For an

222

instant he saw his reflection, eerily lit from below, in one of the pier glasses flanking the door. He had pulled a pair of tights over his head. His features were flattened beyond recognition. His appearance terrified him.

Jessica waited like a ghost outside the window. Liam had agreed to the plan only on condition that he went alone. He edged towards the door. As he opened it, light spilled into the room. He slipped the torch into his pocket.

The hall was carpeted. A broad flight of shallow stairs led upwards. Music was playing softly. After the cold outside the temperature felt tropical. Liam was damp with sweat. He forced himself to go slowly, counting up to five between every step. To his relief, the stairs made no noise; this was the sort of house where creaks were not allowed.

The landing ran round three sides of the stairwell. The music was louder here – Nat King Cole was informing the world that he got no kick from champagne. On the left two adjacent doors were ajar. The only light came from the open doors and from the hall.

Without warning panic set in. It had two sources: the music ended; and simultaneously Liam remembered that he had forgotten to switch on the flash on the camera. The music gave way to a mid-Atlantic voice announcing a song by Ella Fitzgerald. A red light glowed on the camera, indicating that the flash was ready for use.

Liam goaded his legs into action. He tiptoed along the landing. Through the first doorway he saw a basin and the edge of a bath. He heard nothing. They must be in the bedroom.

The music came from the second doorway. His view

223

was partly blocked by a massive Victorian wardrobe with a walnut veneer. Beyond it he saw the end of a double bed covered with a rumpled blue duvet.

He raised the camera. His hands trembled so the picture would probably be blurred. He inched into the room. It smelled over poweringly of perfume.

A woman was sitting on a pink velvet stool at the dressing-table. She had her back to the door. He registered the details automatically: shoulder-length blonde hair, a dark blue dress with a full skirt and patent-leather, high-heeled shoes. The important thing was that she wasn't April Wreningham who, according to the photographs, was slight and dark.

But there was no sign of Wreningham.

The woman was in the middle of applying lipstick. A sound or perhaps a slight movement in the mirror must have alerted her. She raised her head and looked straight at Liam's reflection. Her mouth opened to scream.

Liam recognised the eyes first, then the small, neat features. She was almost a pretty woman. He couldn't believe what he saw.

The woman swung round. Her eyes widened as she saw the camera. The scream turned into a throaty whimper.

'No. No, *please* . . .'

Liam pressed the shutter.

7

Greg Vanderman was getting his hands dirty.

It was a crisp, bright day, cold enough to freeze the water in the birdbath. He had gathered together the leaves from the paths, the flowerbeds and the little lawn. He had dug up a dead peach tree which had succumbed to the rigours of last winter. He had built a bonfire on the tiny patch of rough ground near the shed. It was three o'clock in the afternoon, and he hadn't had a drink for fifteen and a half hours.

The bonfire had got its second wind. It burned fiercely, creating a haze in the air above. It devoured everything that Greg gave it and was hungry for more. Besides the tree and the leaves, six months' worth of woody rubbish was waiting to feed it.

Over the lintel of the shed door someone had laboriously carved a message in drunken capitals: GOD ALMIGHTY FIRST CREATED A GARDEN.

Greg knew why. Gardening kept the hands full, preventing them from doing other things like pouring drinks. Equally important, the activity produced a combination of tedium and pleasure that had a curious effect on the brain: most of the mind seemed to shut down for the duration.

He threw a bundle of cuttings from the apple tree on to the bonfire. A cloud of ashes rose in the air, dispersed and drifted lazily towards the gardens of Patricia Claybrook's neighbours. He stood back and lit a cigarette. As he drank less, he smoked more. Sometimes he thought he was addicted to addiction itself.

His mother knew about the drinking, he was sure of that. She was waiting for him to raise the subject, just as he was waiting for her to tell him who his father was. He suspected that they were both holding back for the same reason: they were living in the eye of the storm and had no wish to subject themselves to the full force of the tornado.

This week they had spent together in Halcombe had been unexpectedly peaceful: they had made no demands on each other and no one from outside had made demands on them. His mother relayed information between Jessica, Blaines, Koslove and Caragh. Once she had gone up to London by herself.

On the Tuesday his half-sister Nell had come over from Reading, bringing her son with her. Nell shook hands with Greg when she arrived and made polite conversation about living in America.

Matthew was five years old; he looked two years younger and sounded two years older. He was listless and withdrawn; his moon-like face and spindly limbs were side-effects of the steroids they gave him.

Greg played two games of backgammon with the boy and made him smile once; he would have liked to have done more for him. Poor, pregnant Nell saw the smile and kissed Greg when she left.

Patricia called him from the house. He turned, expecting to see yet another cup of tea waiting on the window-sill.

226

Instead he saw Warren Vanderman.

Vanderman was standing in the kitchen doorway. His long face was twisted with pain or displeasure. He raised his hand and beckoned. The tornado had reached Halcombe by another route.

The gesture and the expression took Greg back to his childhood. It reminded him of unbearable sessions in his father's den, of being measured and failing to make the grade. He threw his cigarette into the bonfire and walked slowly towards the house.

The second surprise arrived on the heels of the first: Charmian Sandridge appeared beside Vanderman.

'Greg,' his aunt said, 'you look almost like a human being again. Gardening suits you.'

He kissed her cheek. Vanderman didn't offer to shake hands. Patricia was filling the kettle at the sink.

'I've come to apologize to your mother,' his aunt went on. 'It's time we buried this ridiculous feud. We're too old for such things.' Vanderman tried to interrupt but she swept over him: 'And I'm glad to say that we've at least agreed to discuss things.'

'I want to discuss things,' Vanderman succeeded in saying. 'Which one of you is blackmailing me?'

There was a short, embarrassed silence.

'Warren!' Lady Sandridge said. 'Must you drag that up? You promised me –'

'That's why I came over today, isn't it?'

'But it's not why I agreed to come. There's no reason why good shouldn't come out of evil. I'm sure the vicar said something like that on Sunday.'

Patricia Claybrook plugged in the kettle and started to laugh.

227

Vanderman glared at her. 'Well?'

She stared back. 'Why me? And how am I supposed to be doing this?'

'Why you? You want revenge, of course. And you're envious – the poor are always envious, haven't you noticed that? As for the how, I had a break-in in the Los Angeles office last year. Some private files went missing. Claybrook could have arranged that. Just his line.'

'You're being absurd.'

'Am I?' He swung round and peered down at Greg. 'Then maybe it's you. You've got the motive, you know enough about burglary and you mix with the right sort of scum. Come on, you drunken son of a bitch. Is it you?'

Greg shook his head.

The blood drained from Vanderman's face. He screamed at Greg as he used to in the den, all those years ago.

As he paused to draw breath, Patricia Claybrook made herself heard: 'That's enough,' she said in her soft voice. 'Get out.'

'I can have you killed,' he said. 'You stupid bitch.'

Greg's head cleared. The past was over; it affected the present but need not dominate it. He grabbed Vanderman's arms and pushed him into the hall. For a few seconds the old man struggled. Then he allowed Greg to manoeuvre him through the front door. Aunt Charmian followed them down the hall.

The Sandridge Bentley was outside the gate. The chauffeur climbed out.

'Take Mr Vanderman back to Macton,' Lady Sandridge said. 'I'll be coming later.'

'Shall I come back for you, my lady?'

228

She shook her head. 'I'll get a taxi.'

Vanderman climbed into the car. Once again he beckoned Greg. 'You'll never get a penny out of me, I promise you that. It's over. You're no son of mine.'

Greg said, 'Well, that's a relief,' and shut the door.

The Bentley pulled away. In the kitchen Patricia Claybrook was making tea as though nothing had happened. Greg opened the cupboard where the teacups were kept. In a moment, he promised himself, he would have that drink. The bonfire still smouldered; its smell clung to his clothes; but you couldn't spend all your life burning other people's rubbish in a garden.

Charmian Sandridge eased herself into the Windsor chair at the head of the table. She treated her body with care as though she had suddenly realized how fragile it was.

'I'm sorry about the melodrama,' she said. 'He promised he'd be reasonable. I'm afraid he's getting senile. He was always so taciturn in the past.'

'Not always,' Greg said. 'You should have tried living with him.'

'Is he really being blackmailed?' Patricia asked. 'What about?'

Aunt Charmian shrugged. 'God knows. I'm sure he's got any number of dark secrets. But at his time of life why should he care?'

'You know why,' Patricia said. 'He doesn't like scandal. Remember?'

'All right. I'm sorry about that too. It's one thing to realize that you've backed the wrong horse for all these years but quite another to admit it.' She hesitated, picking at her wedding ring with a fingernail. 'I was sorry to hear about Charles. Truly.'

229

Patricia gave her a cup. 'I wish you'd stop saying sorry. Still lemon and no sugar?'

'One sugar nowadays. Who cares anymore? Tom can hardly see me and I stopped looking at myself in mirrors long ago.'

Siblings always talked in shorthand. Something had been settled, Greg realized, though he wasn't sure what; if the hatchet wasn't buried, it was at least removed from sight for the time being.

'I think I'll take my tea outside,' Greg said. 'The bonfire needs attention.'

Aughrim squatted by the fireplace in his office with a long-handled saucepan in his hands. He looked like an alchemist in tweeds.

'Mocha beans,' he said abstractedly, 'are the traditional choice. High acidity, you know. But I suspect geography played a part – Mocha comes from the Yemen, you see. The really important thing is to *pulverize* them properly.'

He put the pan on top of the small electric ring on the tiled hearth. He watched, frowning, until the black syrup came to the boil. When it had, he removed the pan from the heat and stood up.

'I'll just let the grounds settle one more time,' he said. 'How's Emma?'

'I haven't seen her yet.' Liam wondered what Aughrim had heard. 'I'm meeting her this evening.'

'Fitzpatrick said he ran into you last weekend,' Aughrim said with apparent inconsequence. 'And I had your report, of course. Can you amplify what you said about Glendowan?'

230

The truth. Blaines had said. *If he asks, just tell him the truth*.

'I only had time to see the table of contents and the abstract. The Brits were keeping tabs on him, all right. They suspected he was acting as a banker for the INLA but they weren't sure. "Investigation Pending" – that sort of thing. They knew about the Black and Tans shooting his father.'

'But no indication that they might have been behind his death?'

Liam shook his head. 'Quite the reverse. They were hoping to use him to unravel the INLA's finances.'

'Now that's interesting. Pity they didn't kill him, though. I suppose his friends did that.' Aughrim poured a single cup of coffee from the pan. He sniffed it and grimaced. 'It's not quite right.' He took a sip. 'It should have more of a winy flavour. Can you go and see Mrs Glendowan this afternoon? She's been making a nuisance of herself on the telephone.'

Liam had been looking forward to a Saturday afternoon doing nothing. Working for two masters left you with little leisure.

'What do you want me to say to her?'

'Pass the buck,' Aughrim said promptly. 'Tell her that all the indications are that it's a criminal matter. The Garda are handling it. Nothing to do with us. Anyway, the woman's only interested in the insurance.'

'I wonder if she would take it better from someone like Fitzpatrick?'

'Nonsense.' Aughrim sat down behind his desk and sipped his coffee. 'I think the grounds are too coarse. Maybe that's it. When I talked to her yesterday, Mrs

231

Glendowan mentioned you twice. By name. So I said you'd give her a ring this morning and set up a meeting. She'll take it from you, I'm sure.'

Liam said nothing. There was a tiny silence. Even so, it lasted far too long.

'And now,' Aughrim went on, 'tell me about Blaines and Wreningham. Pretend they're horses, eh? Which one would you put money on?'

Liam looked at his watch. 'I must be off, I'm afraid. I'm late for my next appointment.'

'Everyone's passing the buck.' Catherine Glendowan fixed her large, mournful eyes on him; they nailed him to his chair. 'The Garda refer me to you, and you refer me to the Garda. The Department of Justice doesn't want to know. It's like living in a vacuum.'

'I do sympathize.' Liam said.

She eyed him as if assessing the potential extent of his sympathy.

'By the way,' Liam continued, 'last time you said that your husband had been looking worried. Can you remember when that started?'

'Ages ago.' She shrugged in a way that made her breasts rise and fall before him. 'I remember we had a row about him chewing his nails in Hong Kong. It was in a funny little floating restaurant. That would make it May. But it could have started earlier than that. I don't know.'

'Just a thought,' Liam said. To be precise, it had been one of Blaines' thoughts. 'I really must be off.'

'You'll stay for a drink, won't you?'

*

Emma Lazonby wrinkled her nose. 'Have you been drinking?'

'Yes.' Liam wondered whether to explain but decided it wasn't worth the effort.

'Bit early, isn't it? You must be careful. It's an occupational hazard in your job.'

'One gin and tonic in the course of duty,' Liam said wearily. 'Can we talk about something else?'

'Like what?' Her voice was loud enough to draw the attention of the diners at the next table. 'Your social life in London?'

The waiter arrived with pre-dinner drinks, giving Liam a brief but welcome respite. Emma had been twenty minutes late arriving at the restaurant. Usually she made a fetish of punctuality. Instead of the normal kiss on the mouth she presented her cheek to him. But she got close enough to smell Mrs Glendowan's gin.

When they were alone again, he said: 'Fitzpatrick's been talking to you.'

'Is there any reason why he shouldn't? John's an old friend.'

Liam wished she would come straight out with it and ask him if he was having an affair. Her tactics reminded him of those old Westerns where the Indians galloped interminably round and round the wagon-train instead of going in for the kill.

'I had dinner with him, actually,' she said. 'On Thursday night. I'd forgotten how nice he is.'

'I ran into him last weekend. It was at the embassy. I was with someone and Fitzpatrick jumped to the wrong conclusion. I was working.'

'A dark girl, rather pretty. She was sitting in your car and she called you Liam.'

'Pretty?' Liam said mendaciously. 'Is that what Fitz-patrick said?'

Emma's face softened.

'We're looking at the whole family,' Liam continued in a lower voice, appealing to Emma's love of secrets. 'The father died unexpectedly. He was in the business.'

The evening gradually improved. At one point it oc-curred to Liam that Emma might have built up the quar-rel in order to enjoy the pleasure of reconciliation. She liked to be wooed.

Liam fell in with the spirit of the occasion. He wooed with enthusiasm and increasing success. Emma agreed to come back to the flat for coffee. While the coffee was brewing they went to bed.

Afterwards she said, 'What's her name?'

'Whose?'

'You know. That woman.'

'Jessica Claybrook.'

As he said her name, his pleasure in the evening seeped away. Emma was stroking his arm. The scratch of her nails began to irritate him. He swung his legs out of bed.

'I'll get the coffee.'

'Will I make you a cup of tea?' Sister Elizabeth asked. 'And maybe a nice scone?'

Liam managed tactfully to decline both offers. He was on his way back to London after a heavy Sunday lunch with the Lazonbys. The last thing he wanted was food.

'I can't stay long,' he said to his mother when they were alone. 'Emma's taking me to the airport. She's downstairs in the car. She sends her regards.'

Do you mind if I don't come up, darling? I can't bear sick people.

234

The tradescantia on the window-sill had flourished in his absence. Perhaps he should have accepted the tea and given the plant another dose. His mother's breathing was more stertorous than he remembered it. Before the accident she had been a heavy smoker.

'I think I've made a mistake.' He sat on her bed and touched her hand. 'People are pulling at me in all directions and I'm coming apart at the seams. You were right Ma. I should have been a lawyer instead.'

Did the eyelids lift a fraction?

'My father was a lawyer, wasn't he? I often wondered why you wouldn't tell me about him. I don't even know if he's alive. Maybe it's better that way, I don't know.'

The hand was clean and very small. The skin looked softer than before; the nuns must give her hand cream.

'I have to please Aughrim. So I do something for him that I shouldn't. Blaines finds out, and I have to please him as well. Blaines is the man in London, he's as odd as two left feet. And what's it all for? If I'm lucky, it means I can be just like them in twenty years' time. You get a big office and your own secretary and you can make people do what they don't want to do. You can be as eccentric as you please. There's always someone bigger who can lean on you, but at least you can have your revenge on the little folk underneath.'

Why, he wondered, did a naso-gastric tube look like an offence against nature? It sustained a form of life at the cost of violating the body.

'Everyone's vulnerable. There's a politician . . . but you don't want to hear about that. The real enemy isn't the man on the other side of the fence. He's the excuse for the whole thing, just like we're his excuse. No, the one

235

you have to watch out for is your colleague or your boss or your deputy.'

Restlessness drove him to his feet and across to the window. The car park below was crowded. There were two white VW Golfs and one of them was Emma's. This was prime visiting time. Mass in the morning and a visit to the family ghost in the afternoon. He turned back to the bed.

'An Englishwoman called me a secret policeman a little while ago. Her name's Jessica. They're leaning on her too. I don't want her to get hurt.'

If he stopped paying the bills here, his mother would die sooner rather than later. She had given him life and then sustained it. Now the roles were reversed. Then, as now, the recipient had no choice in the matter.

'Don't worry,' he said as she used to say to him. 'It'll be all right in the end.'

The phone rang as the Russian army was advancing through Turkey on Sunday afternoon. The Crimean War had backfired on the Allies. Blaines threw down the dice, wondering how the Anglo-French alliance would cope with a siege of Constantinople.

He picked up the phone. 'Blaines.'

'Hebburn here.'

Blaines switched on the scrambler. 'What's the problem?'

'Not really a problem as such. At least I don't think so. But violent death of former staff is covered in standing orders.'

'Whose?'

'Bertie Monastow. You remember him? He seems to

have had a one-night stand with a psychopath. The body was found this morning. The local CID are keeping it quiet until they hear from me.'

Blaines said nothing.

'Are you still there?' Hebburn asked.

'Where d'you think I am? You'd better come over here and collect me.'

'I didn't think you'd be that interested.'

'We all make mistakes.'

Detective Inspector Ottery was thrilled to see them.

He was young for the job and hadn't yet learned to relish the tranquillity of routine and the pleasures of inactivity. He bounded about his office, finding chairs for his visitors and calling for cups of tea.

'And this is Mr Brown.' Hebburn indicated Blaines. 'From London.'

'Pleased to meet you,' Ottery said, holding out his hand.

Blaines ignored it. 'How do?' He saw the uniformed constable waiting in the doorway with a tray of tea. 'Three sugars in mine.'

Ottery was a fresh-faced man with ginger hair. His neck was sprinkled with shaving cuts.

'We haven't had a proper murder for months,' he told Hebburn cheerfully. 'Nasty business.'

Blaines lowered himself into the chair that looked the least uncomfortable. He lit a cigar, not so much because he wanted one but because Ottery had a no-smoking sign prominently displayed on his desk.

Hebburn blinked at the Inspector. 'You didn't waste much time.'

Ottery sat down behind his desk. 'He was on the Home Office list. Unusual name – rang a bell right away.' He grinned at them, revealing a mouth that was overstuffed with teeth. 'So there's a possible security dimension here?'

'Most unlikely,' Hebburn said. 'But there's no harm in making sure.'

'We've got the scene of the crime cordoned off and a complete news blackout.'

'You've got him on other lists as well.' Hebburn blinked and looked even more disapproving than usual.

The Inspector nodded. 'We get a lot of old queens down here.' He was young enough to be able to take the subject in his stride. 'He's never given us much trouble in that direction. We've had no complaints. Liked them over-age and the same way inclined, thank God.'

'No one regular?'

'Not as far as we know. Some of them are like that: they prefer to keep it casual.'

'You'd better give us the details.'

Ottery rubbed his hands together. 'The body was found at approximately eight-thirty this morning in the outside toilets of the Timworth Arms. The clothes were stuffed down the lavatory and Monastow was sitting on top, propped against the wall. The killer had locked the door from the inside and climbed out over the partition. No prints – he was wearing gloves. We didn't find any of Monastow's prints either. So he might have been killed somewhere else.'

'Where's this pub?'

'A couple of miles out of town, just off the A27. For some reason it's quite popular with homosexuals,

238

especially the older ones. Low-key stuff. You know, silk cravats and pink gins. The loo's on the other side of the car-park from the pub. It's often left unlocked at night.'

'Who found him?'

'The landlord himself. Bloke called Overstone. He owns the place, in fact – used to be an executive in an oil company. Nothing known against him though his wife was done for shop lifting in Selfridges. I gather he's a bit of an old woman. No fruit machines allowed, Radio Three instead of muzak, that sort of thing. Give him his due, he kept his head: locked the door and phoned us straight away.'

'Does he know Monastow? Did he recognize him right away?'

'He'd seen him around before. Not a regular. Didn't remember him being there last night but that might not be significant. The place gets very busy at weekends. People come from Lewes and Brighton – even London. The weekend-cottage crowd turns up. Overstone says he was short-staffed last night. Spent the evening pouring drinks and taking money – didn't really notice who was there.'

Blaines looked round for an ashtray. Finding none, he dropped the cigar butt into the dregs of his tea.

Hebburn frowned. 'Other customers?'

'We've traced twelve so far, mainly regulars. One or two admit to knowing Monastow. No one saw him last night.'

'How did he get there?'

Ottery shrugged. 'He didn't have a car. Someone might have given him a lift. There's a bus service but the driver doesn't remember him. It's even possible that he walked.'

'At his age?'

'He did a lot of walking, or so his niece said. That's Mrs Speedwell of Eden Park. He lived with them. She and her husband said he left the house at about six last night. Said he'd eat out. We don't know if he did yet. Post-mortem's tomorrow morning.'

'What does your surgeon say?'

'He puts the death any time between eight in the evening and two in the morning. Cause of death looks like a blow on the back of the head with a blunt instrument. Probably a hammer. The lacerations were done after death with a small, serrated blade – something like a kitchen knife. No obvious signs of intercourse. You want to see him?'

Hebburn glanced at Blaines, who nodded. Ottery leapt to his feet.

'This way, gentlemen.'

He led them along a windowless corridor and down two flights of stairs. The little mortuary had pale grey tiles on the walls. The attendant was listening to rock music on the radio.

Ottery pulled open one of the drawers.

Monastow's left wrist and left arm were tagged like a newborn baby's. A yellow luggage label had been tied to the big toe of his left foot.

'Mrs Speedwell's done the formal identification.' Ottery cocked his head on one side. 'Skinny old boy, wasn't he?'

The killer had slashed what looked like an inverted capital T on the body of his victim. The crossbar dug deep into Monastow's groin, passing through the pubic hair; at either end of it was a crude shape resembling a semicircle. The upright consisted of two lines, roughly parallel and about four inches apart. Just below the neck the lines petered out. They were linked together by another semicircle, the top of which had exposed the collarbone.

'Not exactly subtle,' Ottery said. 'As these things go.'

The face no longer belonged to anyone. The overhead lights bleached the skin. The nose reared out of the skull, reduced to a ridge of bone. The remaining teeth were stained with nicotine. The thick grey hair had been cut recently; it clung to the head like a wig.

There were traces of talcum powder in the armpits and at the crotch. Blaines counted the ribs and noticed the toenails needed cutting. Monastow had concentrated his efforts on those parts of his anatomy that were on public display.

'We'd like to see his clothes,' Hebburn said, 'and the contents of his pockets.'

'Right you are.' Ottery slid the drawer home. 'They're upstairs. Forensic are still working on the suit and the overcoat.'

Monastow's belongings had been catalogued, sealed in plastic bags and laid out on a trestle table. Ottery was called to the phone so Blaines and Hebburn were able to examine them undisturbed.

'Looks like he was robbed,' Hebburn said. He checked the label on the bag which contained the wallet. 'Driving licence is still there. Library tickets. Credit cards. But no cash.'

Blaines sniffed. 'Someone made a profit.'

He poked the meerschaum cigarette holder with his fore-finger and passed on to an unopened packet of condoms. There were two clean hankerchiefs, a cigarette-case, a lighter, a cheque-book, a wristwatch, a copper bracelet, a handful of loose change, a Yale key and a sheaf of handwritten notes. He ripped open the bag and took out the manuscript. The writing was bad to begin with; a host of corrections made it worse. The title was underlined twice on the first page: *A Forgotten Sussex Fetch*.

'A forgotten what?' Hebburn said.

Ottery put down the phone. 'It's a sort of ghost. I looked it up. The wraith of a living person.'

Blaines rounded on him: 'What ghosts?'

'It's some nineteenth-century story which Monastow found in the back files of the local papers. I asked Mrs Speedwell about it. Apparently he was researching it for the Society of Psychical Research.'

'He believed in that sort of thing?'

'Yes, sir.' Ottery grinned. 'In ghosties and ghoulies and long-legged beasties and things that go bump in the night.'

Blaines frowned and the grin vanished.

'Well, you should see his bedroom,' Ottery said defensively. 'One whole wall's filled with books. All of them deal with the occult in some shape or form. Weird but quite harmless. Do you want to go round to Eden Park?'

'Why not?' Hebburn said.

Blaines shook his head. 'You go.' He turned to Ottery. 'I want to use an office and a phone.'

'I'm sorry, Eric,' Wreningham said, 'but enough is enough. It's evident that you've been acting without any authorization whatsoever. I tried to get hold of you

242

yesterday, only to be told that you'd gone on a jaunt to Brighton without so much as a by-your-leave. I made it quite clear to you that these incidents were to be considered as a police matter.'

Blaines stood in the middle of the room with his head slightly bowed. He guessed that Wreningham was enjoying himself. You could always tell when someone was listening to the sound of his own voice.

'Moreover,' Wreningham continued, 'I confirmed that in writing – at your request, I might add. From what I gather you've dragged Caragh into this as well. An Irish national, for God's sake. It's the height of irresponsibility. We have no means of controlling his actions. The long-term damage to this department may well be irreparable. Flagrant disobedience coupled with astounding folly. I'm surprised at you, Eric, I really am.'

He paused, expecting Blaines to defend himself. Blaines examined the carpet. Wreningham looked away from him and at the bewigged gentleman over the fireplace.

'I'm afraid you leave me with no option. There'll have to be a board of inquiry in the circumstances. You'll be suspended from duty with immediate effect until it meets. On full pay, naturally.'

Blaines raised his head. The time had come to gamble. 'I suppose you used to do it in public. That's how they got on to you.'

'In view of your age, resignation on the grounds of–' Wreningham broke off and frowned. 'What on earth are you muttering about?'

'What have they got? A photo?'

243

Wreningham looked blankly at him. 'I don't know what you mean.'

'Maybe this will jog your memory.'

Blaines fished the photograph out of his top pocket and tossed it on the desk. It was a good print. You could even recognize the framed close-up of April Wreningham on the dressing table.

Wreningham stared at the photograph. He made no move to pick it up. His ears reddened.

'Keep it, if you want,' Blaines said. 'Plenty of others where that came from. You weren't ill, the other week, were you? Just scared.'

'I really must . . . I've no idea . . .'

Blaines sat down uninvited. 'Tell me about it. When did they approach you?'

The silence lasted for five seconds. For Blaines the delay was pleasurable, like the moment in a darkened theatre before the curtain goes up on a lighted stage. Willy was looking for the way out and he wasn't going to find it.

'Three weeks ago.' Wreningham's face glistened with sweat and his breathing was fast and shallow. 'They sent another photograph, addressed to me at the flat. London postmark. Next day there was a letter. Electric typewriter on Croxley Script paper. They wanted five thousand pounds. Otherwise they'd send copies to the Prime Minister and the *News of the World*.'

'Sounds cheap at the price. How?'

'In fifty-pound notes.' Wreningham slid the photograph off the desk and slipped it in his pocket. His voice gathered strength. 'I had to put the money in an envelope and wrap it in an old copy of the *Financial*

Times. I left it in a litter-bin at Baker Street. On the southbound platform of the Bakerloo line.'

'Just the one demand?'

Wreningham nodded.

'Let me know if there's another. Did they want you to do anything else? Like point me in another direction, for instance.'

'No. I promise you, that order came from upstairs. I can't countermand it, even now.'

Blaines glanced up at the ornamental plasterwork of the ceiling. Now there was an interesting possibility. He wondered if Wreningham was telling the truth.

'Do you reckon they've got their claws into him as well?'

Wreningham shuddered. 'Nothing would surprise me any more. He said the Americans had been on to him. It may well be true. It seems to have spread to France. You've heard about that?'

'I heard something,' Blaines admitted.

Yesterday's papers were full of one of the stories: a prominent left-wing politician had been accused of collaborating with the Germans during the war; it promised to turn into one of those scandals that the French do so well. The other story was unlikely to become public knowledge: a senior officer in the *Direction Générale de Sécurité Extérieur* had committed suicide after an interview with officials from the financial section of the *Direction de la Surveillance du Territoire*.

Wreningham poured out everything he knew about the French. Blaines let him speak, though he learned nothing new. He had no illusions about Wreningham's present mood of cooperation. On balance, leaving him

245

in place had more advantages than forcing his resignation. But only just.

The flow of second-hand information petered out.

'What will you do?' Wreningham asked him.

Blaines shrugged. 'Carry on as before.'

'Can you keep me out of it?'

'I can try. If it seems the best thing to do.'

'I'll do everything I can to help. Short of direct involvement, I mean. Think of us as a partnership, Eric.'

Blaines winced at the thought. 'I want to keep Caragh.'

'It's entirely your decision. If you think it's wise.'

'There's one thing you can do: try and soothe Osroyan.'

Wreningham steepled his fingers and leant forward. 'I'll do my best. As a matter of fact I saw him last week. He's threatening all sorts of reprisals in kind if this thing doesn't stop. Know what he calls it? The Blacklist.'

There was a small rectangular card pinned to the gatepost. *Miss Amaryllis Philleigh-Smith, M.A.*, it said. *Consultations by Appointment Only*. A telephone number was printed underneath.

Jessica pushed open the gate. She had found the address by the simple expedient of asking the public library for a list of organizations and individuals connected with psychic matters in the Brighton area. After that it had been a matter of standing in a call box with a pile of change until she found someone who admitted to having known Bertrand Monastow.

It had taken some time. The news of his death had been released yesterday evening. The police were treating it as a straightforward homosexual murder. The location where the body had been found underlined its sordidness. Mrs Speedwell was said to be outraged.

Blaines had been dubious about the wisdom of letting Jessica come to Brighton. She had pointed out that the place would be flooded with journalists by now; one more wouldn't make any difference. Besides, it was a coastal town in winter, so her cover story was ready.

He was also dubious about the value of the exercise. Jessica, on the other hand, felt it might be important. Monastow's life had four main ingredients: his past employment; his homosexuality; his life with the Speed-wells; and his interest in the paranormaI. They knew about the first three; but the fourth was still unexplored.

'If you're right,' she had told him on the phone on Sunday night, 'and Monastow was killed because he'd been talking to you, we've got a possible lead. Someone must have known you'd been in contact. Someone must have gone to Brighton to kill him.'

'You're pig-headed.' Blaines said. 'Just like your dad.'

Later she wondered if he'd worked out the ramifications: to have known about that one meeting someone must have been following Monastow or, more likely, Blaines himself.

Miss Philleigh-Smith's garden path was lined with dustbins and black plastic sacks filled with rubbish. The house was at the end of an early-Victorian terrace. The front door needed a new coat of paint; the fan-light above it could have done with a wash. There were six doorbells. Jessica pressed the bottom one.

The door opened. A large ginger cat stalked out, made

a detour round Jessica and began to investigate the contents of one of the sacks.

A bulky woman, made bulkier by the faded fisherman's smock she wore, stared accusingly at Jessica. 'Well?'

'Miss Philleigh-Smith? I'm Jessica Claybrook. I phoned you earlier.'

'My name's Privitt actually. You'd better come in.'

The narrow hall smelled of cats. Rock music boomed down the stairs. The hall table was almost hidden beneath a pile of unopened circulars.

'Bloody students,' Privitt said. 'Make so much noise.'

'Lodgers?' Jessica asked.

Privitt nodded. 'You need a thumbscrew to get the rent out of them. We used to go in for what the agency called retired gentlefolk. They were even worse. Kept dying on you.'

She led the way downstairs to the basement and showed Jessica into a room at the back. Once a kitchen, it had been converted into a sitting room; french windows opened on to a small but surprisingly tidy garden.

'We keep the rabble out of there,' Privitt said. Her face softened as she looked at the garden. 'Too good for them. You wait here. I'll find Philly.'

The room was crowded with furniture, most of it old and scuffed. Photographs of the dear departed hung on the wall; they stood on tables; they were marshalled in a double line along the top of the upright piano. There were boys in sailor-suits, wedding groups where the men wore frock-coats or regimentals, and big-bosomed women encased in the uncomfortable splendour of Edwardian clothes.

248

Footsteps thundered down the stairs. Privitt surged into the room, towing a small, thin woman in a flowered dress and a brown cardigan.

'My cousin,' she announced.

Miss Philleigh-Smith crept across the carpet. She was in her seventies, Jessica guessed, perhaps ten years older than Privitt. When they shook hands, Miss Philleigh-Smith did not return Jessica's pressure. Her hand was hot and dry. Shaking it was like shaking a small animal, paralysed with fear.

Privitt sat down and put her hands on her knees. 'Better get a few things straight first. Eh, Philly?'

Miss Philleigh-Smith subsided into a chair. 'There's the usual consultation fee . . .'

'Which is ten pounds an hour, in advance,' Privitt said firmly. 'And as we're talking to the press, I think we'd better treble that.' She glared at Jessica. 'We have to make ends meet, you know. After all, you're making use of her professional skills.'

Miss Philleigh-Smith stirred in her chair. 'Yes, dear, but–'

'She's uniquely sensitive to character; she's not just a medium.' Privitt glanced doubtfully at her cousin. 'I daresay we could manage twenty-five, for cash.'

'I was thinking perhaps fifty pounds would be fairer,' Jessica said. 'But it's up to you.'

Privitt nodded. 'We'll throw in a cup of tea for that. But there's one condition. No names, no packdrill. This is off the record. It's an unsavoury business. Won't do Philly's professional reputation any good if her name's linked to it. We want you to sign something to that effect.'

'That's fine. I'm doing a background piece on Mr Monastow's life. I don't need to name sources.'

'Whom are you writing it for?' Miss Philleigh-Smith asked.

'Nobody yet. I'm freelance.'

Privitt ejected herself from the armchair and rummaged in the bureau by the window. She returned with a piece of paper, torn from an exercise book, and a biro. Jessica wrote to her dictation: she promised not to mention to anyone, in conversation or in writing, that she had talked to the cousins about Bertrand Monastow. That done, she produced fifty pounds from her handbag. She wondered what they would do if they found out she had broken her promise. It was difficult to imagine the cousins in court.

'It was such a shock,' Miss Philleigh-Smith said suddenly. 'Not so much that he's dead. But that Bertie Monastow was – well, like *that*.'

'You had no idea he . . .?' Jessica let the sentence trail to a halt. Her brain refused to produce an acceptable euphemism.

'That he was queer?' Privitt asked. 'No, of course not.

'Had you known him long?'

'Six, seven years. We met him at a lecture. Turned out he'd been at Harrow at the same time as Philly's brother. After that he came to one or two of Philly's little sessions and we gradually became friendly. No harm in that.'

'Did he tell you much about his old job?'

'The Foreign Office? To be perfectly frank he never stopped. He was rather miffed they'd never given him an embassy. He liked to tell you anecdotes.' Her voice deepened. ' "When I was in Budapest" "When I was having lunch with

250

Khrushchev" – that sort of thing. If the truth be told, it got a bit boring sometimes.'

Miss Philleigh-Smith twitched. 'At our age, one does tend to go on. One lives in the past.'

Privitt flushed. 'Of course. I only meant–'

'When was the last time you saw him?' Jessica said quickly.

'Wednesday? Thursday?' Privitt chewed her lower lip. 'He dropped in around teatime. Often did that. We used to get the impression that his niece didn't like him under her feet.'

'Thursday,' Miss Philleigh-Smith said with great distinctness. 'He brought a cake. A Black Forest gâteau. Most unlike Bertie.'

Privitt nodded. 'Usually he didn't splash his money around. Hadn't any to splash.'

'He told me,' Miss Philleigh-Smith interrupted, 'that he was going to spend Christmas in Menton. Or was it Nice?'

'I didn't hear him.'

'You were out of the room, dear. Besides, I think he found it easier to talk to me. We were more of an age.'

The cousins glared at one another.

'He couldn't afford it,' Privitt said.

Miss Philleigh-Smith yawned. 'I believe a small investment had unexpectedly matured. But he was worried about the omen.'

Jessica glanced from one cousin to another. Both were nodding their heads.

'I beg your pardon?' she said.

'He had a Sign.' Privitt's emphasis made the initial capital unmistakable. 'A Call from the Other Side.'

'It often happens that way,' Miss Philleigh-Smith said. 'When my aunt was ill, her father came into her room. Didn't say anything – just hovered at the end of the bed for a few seconds. He'd been dead for forty years. She died in her sleep that night.'

'Monastow saw a ghost?'

'You could put it like that.' Miss Philleigh-Smith coughed. 'I prefer to call it a spiritual vibration emanating from the past. So we weren't altogether surprised when we heard the news. It was the manner of his death that was so shocking.'

'Turns your stomach,' Privitt agreed. 'Mark you, I always said he was a bit of an old woman. Remember the fuss he made when he spilled tea on his trousers?'

'Or that time he slipped in the snow. I remember–'

'The ghost, 'Jessica said desperately. 'Did he say who it was?'

'It wasn't family,' Privitt said. 'I distinctly recall him saying it was an old friend.' She dropped her voice to a stage whisper. 'Philly's hearing isn't what it was.'

'No, dear, he said it was a colleague.' Miss Philleigh-Smith hesitated. 'At least I think he said that. In any case, I'm sure he said it was someone he'd been talking about recently. To someone else.'

'Talking?' Jessica said. 'Not thinking?'

'Yes, talking.'

Privitt put a finger to her head and nodded at her cousin. 'Thinking,' she mouthed to Jessica.

'I offered to try to make contact,' Miss Philleigh-Smith went on. 'Bertie wasn't sure it would be wise.'

'He was keen enough at first,' Privitt pointed out. 'He got cold feet after the phone call.'

252

'Someone phoned him?'

'No. He asked if he could use our phone.' Privitt glanced upwards. 'We've got a pay-phone upstairs, for the lodgers. He often used it.'

'He borrowed fifty pence.' Miss Philleigh-Smith paused. 'He wasn't his normal self, you know. It's even possible that he imagined everything. I did wonder if perhaps . . .?'

'What Philly means,' Privitt interrupted, 'is that Bertie smelled like a brewery.'

George Koslove peered into the Three Elephants and shuddered.

He avoided pubs whenever possible. This one was tucked in a side-street east of Grosvenor Square. The single bar was thick with customers. Briefcases and umbrellas were everywhere. The roar of many conversations blended with the thudding of the jukebox. A fog of tobacco smoke obscured the dim lighting still further. Some customers, caught in the rain, were actually steaming. The place was a hotbed of germs.

He pushed his way through the crowd to the bar. A woman trod on his foot. The British, he thought, took their pleasures like animals. You could hardly classify these people as human. Most of them were on their way home from work. It was a bizarre thought that they were here to relax.

Blaines was sitting on a high stool at one end of the bar. He cleared a space for Koslove and shouted for Perrier water and another pint.

'Eric, are you sure this is wise?'

'What's that?'

253

Koslove shouted the question into Blaines' ear.

'Don't worry. You can't get any more private than this.'

'Why the urgency?'

'I need to talk to you.'

'I thought we'd agreed that everything was to be routed through Halcombe.'

Blaines shook his head. 'Not in this case. I want to know about Claybrook's death.'

'You know what happened already.'

'Come off it, George. Don't tell me the Agency hasn't produced a report on it. Four inches thick and with twenty-nine annexes.'

'Why the sudden interest?'

'Because of Monastow. There's a possibility that, just before he snuffed it, he saw someone he used to work with. Someone we talked about. Someone who's meant to be dead.'

Koslove's confidence returned. 'Claybrook's dead. That's one thing we can be sure of.'

'How do we know that?'

'Maddox-Brown saw the body. So did two of our people, both of whom knew Claybrook. If it wasn't him, it was his *doppelgänger*.'

Blaines lit a cigar. 'I hope you're right. Let's pretend you are, for the sake of argument. In that case I want to know how.'

'You know how. They wanted Tonanyev. Claybrook got in the way. The purest accident.'

'Accident my arse. Why was he talking to Tonanyev?'

'I don't know. Ran into him by chance, I guess. Gave our boys a hell of a shock.'

'Another bloody accident. You were watching Tonanyev. You must have investigated how he died. And that means you must have done some work on Claybrook.'

Koslove shrugged. 'It's kind of delicate.'

'Because you forgot to mention it to us? I don't care about that. All I want to know is how Chas died.'

'Non-attributable? Off the record?'

'It always is.'

'Okay. We were watching Tonanyev. Hadn't made up our minds how to handle him – there was a very serious possibility he was a plant, you understand. We'd told London that he was there; you and Wreningham knew, I know, and so did a few others, including Maddox-Brown in Istanbul. But we were keeping it very quiet. So naturally we were interested in how Claybrook knew. You do see that?'

Blaines assured him that he would have felt the same.

'Claybrook hadn't been out there long. So at first we worked on the assumption that someone in London must have talked to him. But that wouldn't work because as far as we could see no one in London talked to Claybrook about anything let alone something as big as this. In Istanbul he didn't do much besides work and go to his hotel. He even ate there.' Koslove paused, relishing the moment of revelation despite the company he was in. 'Only one thing was out of character: the night before he died he went to a disco up in Taksim. We found a book of matches in his pocket.'

'A disco? Chas?'

Koslove grinned. 'Seems kind of shocking, doesn't it? Our people found someone who claimed to remember

255

him.' He licked his lips. 'A male prostitute.'

For once Blaines looked surprised. His face turned an unhealthy shade of purple. 'You saying Chas was queer?'

'Claybrook turned him down.' Koslove paused, wondering how much he need tell Blaines. 'But the boy saw him later that evening with a man in a leather jacket and mirrored sunglasses. A middle-aged guy. He said they were speaking English. And it sounded like English English, not American English. Talking very quietly and earnestly. They left separately.'

'Oh Christ,' Blaines said wearily. 'You think Chas was set up? By a colleague?'

'Well, it's a distinct possibility. A lot of people didn't want him to write his memoirs.'

'He wasn't going to. It was a joke.'

'I hope someone's laughing.'

'The tart. Did you show him any pictures?'

Koslove shook his head. 'Our people can't find him again. Which may or may not be significant.'

Blaines beckoned the barman. 'You want a proper drink?' Koslove shook his head. 'Well, I do. Someone knew what the Sons of Ataturk were going to do to Tonanyev, and when. And you think they fixed it for Chas to be on the spot at the same time?'

'That's the current interpretation. And there's a strong probability that the guy concerned is one of yours.'

'Another pint,' Blaines told the barman. 'And a large Johnny Walker.' He waited until he had been served. 'Don't you tell Pat,' he said quietly.

'Would I do a thing like that?' Koslove sipped his Perrier. 'Why are you so interested in Claybrook? What's the link with Monastow?'

'Nothing concrete. I wish it was. I've second-hand information to the effect that Monastow thought he saw a ghost, just before he died.'

'You're kidding. White sheets and clanking chains?'

'Search me. All I know is, it was probably a former colleague and/or friend, and probably someone we talked about when we met last week. Presumably someone who Monastow knew was dead. That gives us a list of four people. One of them's Chas, who seems to be dead. One of them is a very senior officer who died of stomach cancer ten years ago: I saw him dying and I went to the funeral. Another one's Ralph Ashkirk; you know all about him.'

'And the fourth?'

'Ah, he died fourteen years ago.'

The barman set down Blaines's drinks on the counter. Blaines paid.

'Who's number four?' Koslove said.

'His name was Harry Ryal.'

'Monsieur Ryal?'

'Harry Ryal,' Liam said. 'I have a photograph.'

He placed it on the desk. Taken in 1969, it showed the head and shoulders of a thin-faced man with short, dark hair; he had a narrow moustache and he was staring straight at the camera.

Henri Lombez studied the photograph for a moment.

'It is a legal matter, you say?'

Liam nodded. 'My firm's client died intestate. We are trying to trace everyone who may have a claim on her estate. A considerable sum of money is involved, you understand. Monsieur Ryal is, or was, a first cousin once removed.'

Lombez leant back in his chair. He had a long, thin skull and was going prematurely bald; he looked like an intelligent sheep who needed to shave at least twice a day. For a while he stared at the cracked plaster on the ceiling. Liam wondered if he did this with all his clients. The cracks formed a wavering quadrilateral with a marked resemblance to the coastline of South America.

'And what precisely do you want me to do?' Lombez said at last. He tore his eyes away from South America and peered over his glasses at Liam.

'Monsieur Ryal is believed to have died in or near Biarritz, approximately fourteen years ago. I understand there was a bathing accident. We need a copy of the death certificate and if possible a transcript of the autopsy. We would also like to talk to the investigating officer.'

Lombez rubbed his chin, producing a faint rasping sound like nails being buffed by an emery board. 'You need a lot of detail,' he said drily.

'The more the better. We have been approached by a man who claims to be Ryal.'

'A false claimant?'

'It would appear so. We wish to be absolutely sure.'

'Naturally. A margin of error is not desirable in such cases.'

'One more thing, Monsieur Lombez. There is an element of urgency about this enquiry.'

Lombez inclined his head. 'That is not uncommon. I regret that we are compelled to charge more when undertaking such cases. The demand for our services, you understand, is considerable.'

Liam thought about the layer of dust on the dented

filing cabinet, the pretty young secretary applying her nail-polish in the anteroom and the empty in-tray on Lombez's desk.

'Money,' he said, 'is not a problem.'

To be more precise it was a problem that George Koslove and the United States Treasury between them seemed able to solve with enviable ease.

'Our usual terms are a week in advance,' Lombez said, 'plus a deposit on expenses.'

'A *week*?'

Lombez looked hurt. 'It is customary.'

'Very well.' Liam smiled at him. 'Perhaps I should make it clear that there will also be a bonus, equivalent to another week's salary. This will decrease in inverse proportion to the duration of your enquiries.'

'What a pleasure it is,' Lombez said, 'to do business with an Irishman, Monsieur Caragh. The Irish are so direct. How would you like to pay?'

That night Greg got drunk.

It was the first time he had been properly drunk since he left San Francisco. It was the first time in months that he had enjoyed the process from start to finish.

They began innocuously enough with beer, in a café overlooking the Grand Plage. He and Liam sat there for two hours. The sea was no longer visible but the dull pounding roar of the Atlantic breakers was always there; it lurked beneath the jukebox, the conversations and the traffic outside. After the first hour they switched to wine. Later they moved to a restaurant where they drank more wine in the intervals of pecking at their food.

'Why did he send us both?' Greg said abruptly. The

conversation had reached the point where sudden changes of subject were the rule rather than the exception. 'You speak French, you know what you're doing. I'm just the fifth wheel.'

Liam shrugged. 'I don't think Blaines trusts me. You're his insurance. He trusts you, have you noticed? I sometimes wonder if he's a bit sweet on your mother.'

'Blaines?'

'I know it sounds unlikely.' Liam saw the expression on Greg's face and laughed. 'It's just he sometimes gets flustered when she's around.' He remembered the original question. 'There's another reason why he sent us both: we're not obviously linked with him, not as far as the French are concerned. And here's a third reason: he wants us to watch each other's back.'

'He's scared,' Greg said. He was surprised by his own certainty.

'Maybe.' Liam laid down his fork. 'I tell you one thing: he scares me. If I don't please Blaines I screw up my career in Dublin.'

'You sound like you wonder if it's all worth it.'

'Well, is it? I mean, it's like being a sewage-worker but less useful. Outsiders think you're a necessary evil, by and large. You can't talk about your job to them. So you stay inside, among the other sewage-workers and their families. If you're lucky, you'll maybe get to manage a sewage farm. It's a world within a world. I'm not sure I want to stay there for the rest of my life.'

'So why don't you quit?'

'Commitments.' Liam's face twisted. 'Sounds pompous? It's really my mother. She was in a car accident three years ago.'

'Do something else. There are other ways to pay the bills. Me, I'm going to be a gardener.'

'Now that's a sensible occupation.'

A bottle of Armagnac materialized with the coffee. Neither of them could remember ordering it but it seemed a good idea.

When he was sufficiently drunk, Greg said: 'Does Jessica know? About your mother?'

Liam shook his head.

'I think you should tell her.'

'Let's go back to the hotel,' Liam said. 'I want to get drunk.'

Lombez telephoned the hotel just before lunch the following morning. Liam and Greg were nursing their headaches in the residents' lounge.

'A progress report, Monsieur Caragh. I thought you would appreciate it. An Englishman named Ryal was drowned near St Jean de Luz. Fourteen years ago last July. He was swimming after a heavy meal and seems to have got cramp.'

'What's your source?'

'There was a short report in the local paper. The incident received little publicity, you understand. Not in July. Such things are bad for business.'

'Were there any other details?'

'He was staying at a camping site. His age was given as forty-one and he was described as a businessman from London. The accident was reported by his cousin, a Monsieur Padgate. It was implied they were on holiday together.'

'And now?'

'This afternoon,' Lombez said, 'I shall plunge into the bureaucratic labyrinth.' He chuckled unexpectedly. 'If I can find the way out, I will telephone you at the hotel, about six o'clock. Would that be convenient?'

'That will be fine. I look forward to it.'

But Lombez did not telephone at six o'clock or at any other time. Instead Liam and Greg were visited by two men in dark suits. They came from the *Direction de la Surveillance du Territoire* and they felt that Messieurs Caragh and Vanderman should return to England as soon as possible.

8

Blaines sniffed. 'All that garlic addles their brains.'

Jessica pulled out to overtake a lorry. 'Why were they so unhelpful?'

'They got a whiff of the Blacklist and they don't like the smell.'

Blaines folded his hands across his belly and glanced at Jessica. She was a pretty girl, though completely unlike her mother. It was easy to talk to her, perhaps too easy; usually he found it difficult to hold a conversation with any woman under the age of forty. Her ability to persuade people to talk was the main reason he had brought her with him; she had done unexpectedly well in Brighton.

'French always overreact to a crisis,' he went on. 'Usually they blame us or maybe the Americans. Never themselves, of course. And for a while things are awkward. They take offence if you blow your nose in French airspace. Even so, we were unlucky.'

The road narrowed. Jessica settled down to a steady 20 mph behind a tractor towing a trailer heaped with potatoes. 'Greg thought Lombez must have noticed something.'

'The police file was probably tagged. So Lombez knew the DST had an interest in Ryal. You can't blame him for checking with them – wouldn't want his licence revoked.

The DST knew Ryal had been one of ours. It must have taken them all of five minutes to explode Caragh's cover. Give them their due, they've got dossiers on almost everyone and they're damned efficient at digging out information. They make the connection; they don't know what's happening but they do know that they don't want it happening on French soil. So they send a pair of bouncers to see the intruders off the premises.'

For a while they drove in silence up the Al2. Blaines picked his nose and stared out of the window at cows, leafless trees and huge, lonely churches built of flint. Suffolk was an overrated county with bloody awful roads and too many American air bases. He pulled the briefcase on to his lap and went through the file on Padgate.

The file had been assembled hastily in the last twenty-four hours. Blaines had invoked the power of Wreningham's name at the Inland Revenue, the Passport Office, the Department of Health and Social Security, the Department of Education and Science, the Ministry of Defence and the General Register Office. He had persuaded people to talk to him at the National Westminster Bank and the Leeds Permanent Building Society. With Koslove's cooperation, he had checked the files of four intelligence services. The results of so much effort, imaginative lying and bad temper were disappointingly meagre.

John Miles Padgate had left little documentary evidence of his life. For the last fourteen years he had left none at all.

If he was still alive, he was fifty-four years old. He did not have a criminal record. He had done his national service in the RAF. According to the Inland Revenue, he had spent his working life as a self-employed salesman with a variety of firms. His Tax Returns had been irregular and inconsistent – so much so that the Inland Revenue were contemplating an investigation at the time of his disappearance.

In 1965 he married a teacher. He fathered three children by her. They were divorced in 1972. Mrs Padgate was granted custody of the children.

Padgate was Harry Ryal's only known relative. He was also Ryal's heir, and had inherited nearly £5000 after Ryal's death.

At the time of his disappearance Padgate was living in a rented flat in Dollis Hill, north-west London. In June of that year he applied for a mortgage to buy a flat in the same area. By August, however, he appeared to have changed his mind. He transferred his savings from the Building Society to his current account. He emptied his current account of everything except £800.

It stank all right. The problem was, it didn't necessarily stink of Ryal.

'Why are you interested *now*?' Mrs Padgate said. 'When I reported he was missing to the police, they more or less told me to mind my own business. And that was years ago.'

Blaines rearranged his features into something resembling an apologetic mask. 'To be honest,' he said earnestly, 'circumstances have changed. There's a possibility that your husband – your former husband – was involved in something criminal. Possibly in association with his cousin, Mr Ryal.'

'Harry?' Mary Padgate's square face was devoid of

make up and uncompromisingly bitter. 'I might have known he'd be concerned.'

'You know him then?'

'Of course I do, Inspector. But I haven't seen him for years.' She glanced impatiently at Blaines, her tone reducing him to the position of a backward pupil. 'He was Miles's best man at our wedding. Miles's only relative. Come to that, he was Miles's only friend.' The words came out in short, angry spurts. She added a final burst: 'If friend is the right word.'

The kettle was steaming. Mrs Padgate poured boiling water into the cafetière. Jessica glanced round the kitchen. They were in a modern extension tacked on to the pair of agricultural cottages that now formed a single house. The kitchen was like its owner: it gave an impression of sober efficiency and hard-won comfort.

Jessica's offer to carry the tray was curtly refused. Mrs Padgate took them through the house to the sitting-room. This was a low, narrow room with deep, book-lined alcoves flanking the brick fireplace; the fire itself was laid but unlit. A pile of exercise books stood on the table by the window; one of them was open. The interrupted marking was a tacit and perhaps intentional hint that they were disturbing a busy teacher's weekend.

'Are any of your children at home?' Jessica asked. If they were she could see no sign of them.

Mary Padgate almost smiled. 'My eldest lives in Norwich now; he works in a bookshop. Simon's away at university. Jill's still here but she's staying with a friend this weekend.'

'Presumably they can hardly remember their father?'

'Of course they can't. And I don't want him prancing

266

back into their lives. If you find him, you can tell him from me that he's not wanted. He's given them nothing.'

Blaines was sprawled in an armchair and staring at the ceiling. Jessica assumed he was leaving the questioning to her.

'When did you last see him?'

'When the divorce was settled. He didn't want to visit the kids but he agreed to pay maintenance. He used to pay monthly, by standing order. He didn't keep in touch in any other way. It was only when the money stopped coming I realized something was wrong.'

Blaines stirred. 'And you've heard nothing from him since the bank account ran dry?'

Mrs Padgate nodded. She ignored Blaines and concentrated her attention on Jessica. 'From what I found out afterwards, he did a bunk in August. His landlord tried to make me pay the back-rent on his flat. Miles left just enough money in his current account to keep the standing orders going until December.' She hesitated, her mouth tightening. 'It wasn't a good Christmas.'

'It must have been appalling,' Jessica said angrily. Immediately afterwards she wondered if detective sergeants in the Metropolitan Police were encouraged to show their sympathy quite so openly. But if Blaines insisted on foisting a false identity on her, he would have to take the consequences.

'We managed.' Mary Padgate smiled grimly. 'There were bad times but they used to be ten times worse when Miles was still at home. He made life hell for everyone. I suppose he wasn't particularly happy himself. Thought the world owed him a living but unfortunately the world didn't agree.'

267

'Was Ryal like that too?' Jessica asked.

'The same but more so.' She stared out of the window into the past. 'Miles got it from him. He copied Harry – always had done. You'd think he'd've grown out of it. Not Miles, oh no. Everything had to be just like Harry, just as Harry wanted it. Harry says this and Harry does that. I used to get so sick of hearing his name. Harry smoked a pipe so Miles did too. When Harry bought a pipe with a curly stem Miles had to have one. He even wanted to look like him, for God's sake. Grew the same, revolting little moustache, wore the same sort of clothes. You know what he really liked? For him and Harry to be taken for brothers.'

Mrs Padgate's voice had been rising gradually in volume and pitch as twenty years of accumulated resentment poured out of her. She fell silent abruptly; perhaps she was aware that she had disinterred an old jealousy and displayed it with unseemly venom to a pair of strangers.

Jessica finished her coffee and created a diversion by asking for another cup. Mrs Padgate found it necessary to go to the kitchen for more cream. The jug on the tray was still half-full.

'Keep at it, love,' Blaines said quietly while he and Jessica were alone. 'I want to see some pictures.'

In the kitchen Mrs Padgate blew her nose. A minute later she returned with the cream. Her hands were steady as she poured the coffee.

'What is this about?' she said as she handed Blaines the sugar. 'What are they up to?'

'Hard to know,' he said. 'We had a request for information through Interpol. Suspected evasion of currency

268

regulations in Brazil. We're not even sure it's them.'

'So Harry's not a civil servant any more? He was at the Home Office when I knew him.'

Blaines shook his head.

'At one point he wanted to be a private investigator. Miles and he were going to go into partnership.' She glanced at Jessica, inviting sympathy. 'They were just like children sometimes. Didn't live in the real world. I tried to talk Miles out of it but he wouldn't listen to me. In the end he only changed his mind because Harry did.'

'When did you last see Harry?' Jessica said.

'The night Miles walked out on me. God, it's so long ago. All those years and it feels like last week. Miles walked down the garden path – we were living in Bromley then – and there was Harry waiting for him in the car.' She shivered. 'Harry was smiling.'

'Do you have any photographs of them?'

'No.' Mrs Padgate raised her chin as though preparing to rebut criticism. 'I threw them all out when we moved up here. Everything – even our wedding photographs. Especially those.' Her face changed. 'In fact I do have one. I only kept it because it includes Richard – he's my eldest.'

She got up and crossed the room to one of the alcoves. A row of photograph albums filled most of the bottom shelf of the bookcase. Kneeling down, she selected a volume and flicked through it until she came to the page she wanted.

'There they are,' she said quietly.

Her grey hair hid her face. For a long moment she stared at the photograph. Then she stumbled to her feet and handed the album to Jessica.

269

'Miles looks quite nice there,' she said harshly. 'But believe me, he was a little *shit*.'

Spoken in that controlled voice and in this carefully-organized room, the word was more than out of place: it verged on blasphemy. Jessica bent her head over the photograph.

It was a square, colour snapshot of two men standing on a lawn. A toddler with a plump face stood between them, clinging to their legs and screwing up his eyes. Both the men were slight and dark, with thin moustaches. Harry Ryal was smiling at the camera. Miles Padgate stared at the ground, the curly-stemmed pipe clenched between his teeth.

Jessica passed the album to Blaines.

He glanced at the photograph. 'We'd like to keep this.' His fingers were already peeling back the transparent sheet which held the photographs in place. 'If that's all right with you.'

'If you like,' Mary Padgate said listlessly.

'You'll get it back, of course,' Blaines went on.

She said nothing.

Blaines struggled to his feet. One of his shoelaces had come untied. He patted his pockets, searching for cigars and matches.

'We'd better be going' he said. 'Eh, Sergeant? We'll be in touch if there're any developments. Thanks for the coffee.'

'So they're in Brazil?' Mrs Padgate said suddenly. 'Are they in jail?'

'Not that I know of.'

'What will happen to him?'

'To Padgate?' Blaines didn't bother to look back; he was already at the door. 'Search me.'

But Jessica saw Mrs Padgate's face. She realized with a slight shock that the question had not really been about Miles. Mary Padgate was still far more interested in Harry Ryal.

'George,' Patricia Claybrook said. 'I still don't understand what you're doing here.'

Koslove smiled up at her. 'I was in Bristol last night – thought I'd drop by on the way back. It's not much of a detour. So I picked up the carphone and called you. Simple as that.'

She led him into the sitting room and offered him coffee. Koslove eventually settled for a glass of orange juice.

'I knew you'd be alone,' he said when they were seated. 'Eric and Jessica are in Suffolk. Greg's in London with Caragh, working on the Ryal business. So why not? I thought. Why not cheer up Pat? Maybe she's feeling a little lonesome.'

He glanced swiftly at her, hoping that he had imagined the expression of distaste on her face. He disliked women who towered over him; he preferred them small and cuddly like Mrs Claybrook's daughter.

'I was about to go out,' Patricia said. 'The weekend shopping. Perhaps you could give me a lift into town.'

'Into Halcombe? I wish I could. Unfortunately I left the car up by the shops. Didn't want to have it parked outside your house. The neighbours might talk.'

'You know something, George? You're a terrible liar.'

'But it's true. The question of security –'

'I'm not talking about the car. I mean your reason for coming here.'

Koslove gave her a grin that he hoped was boyish.

'You're right. of course.' He removed the grin and put on his worried face. 'I wanted to talk to you. Alone. I have to tell you this, Pat. I'm very, very worried about this business.'

'I thought we all were. Some more than others, naturally –'

'I've got something on my conscience. Something I told Eric which I don't think he told you. But it's something you should know. About Charles.'

Her reaction disappointed him. He had expected a little natural emotion after that build-up. Instead she merely raised her eyebrows over the rim of her coffee cup and asked if he could be a little more specific. That was New England breeding for you: all brain, no heart. Now was not the moment to remind her that they were fellow Americans in a strange land.

'Charles's death may not have been an accident,' Koslove said desperately. 'Is that specific enough?'

Patricia slowly lowered the cup to the saucer. 'You'd better tell me about it.'

Koslove cleared his throat. 'The received version is that he met Tonanyev by chance and just happened to get in the way of a stray bullet. Now I don't like accidents like that. According to our information, Charles acted out of character the night before he died: he went to a disco and talked to an Englishman there. Next morning he calls the office, says he's sick and goes to the café where Tonanyev just happens to be. It's a fair presumption that we're looking at a cause-and-effect scenario.'

She put the cup and saucer on the table beside her chair. Her eyes never left his face. Her stillness reminded Koslove of stone statues in cathedrals – all those saints who stood or sat in judgement over the unfortunate mortals below them. But Patricia Claybrook wasn't a saint. Just an impoverished widow whose cooperation was temporarily desirable.

'Right!' he said with more emphasis than he had intended. It was time to return to the script he had rehearsed in the car. 'Now someone knew where Tonanyev was and wanted to kill him. The Sons of Ataturk are a tinpot outfit; I can't see them as the principals. They make most of their income out of contract jobs. So who knew about Tonanyev? Us and the Brits. We didn't want him dead – he had too much to tell us. But maybe the Brits did. It figures: before he retired, Tonanyev was the KGB Resident in London and it's more than likely he knew things they didn't want the world to hear. Especially us, maybe? Then some guy comes up with the idea of getting two for the price of one.'

'But why would the British want to kill Charles?'

Koslove bent forward and tapped his knee. 'For the same reason they wanted to kill Tonanyev. Charles was going public: they thought he was writing a book.'

'But that was–'

'I know. Just a joke. But no one knew that.'

'This man in the disco. What was he like?'

'Middle-aged. Sunglasses. Leather jacket. Could have been anyone.' Koslove hesitated. 'There were two details I didn't mention to Eric. Our source thought he heard one of them mention Hong Kong. Does that mean anything to you? Like a colleague who was posted there?'

Patricia shook her head. Koslove noted with satisfaction that her face had lost its colour. He had got through to her at last.

'The other thing was, our friend lit up a pipe as he left. Our source noticed that – it's the sort of place where most people smoke Marlboro Lites. Did Charles know any pipe-smokers?'

She shrugged. 'Not that I know of. I don't believe this, George. If they were that worried about the book, they'd have tried other ways to stop him.'

Koslove nodded. 'Maybe you're right. But maybe there was another reason why they wanted him dead.'

'What do you mean?'

'Remember his job. He knew all about registries and what was in them. He must have known about patterns of use – who wanted what files and when. Suppose he stumbled on the preparations for the Blacklist.'

'No!' Patricia sat up sharply. The shock on her face pleased Koslove. The ice-woman had finally cracked. She added in a lower voice: 'He . . . he would have told me.'

'My guess is that he only put two and two together in Istanbul. One little assumption explains everything. The reason for the Blacklist. Why I had to pressurize Eric into investigating. Why we've found nothing so far. Why that old man in Brighton had to die. Why Eric's holding things back from you - and from me too. Why there's been a British angle right from the start. You must see it. Pat - it's the only theory that fits the facts: the Blacklist is a British invention.'

Lord Sandridge squirted tomato ketchup on to his quarter-pounder with cheese. He replaced the top of the bun and raised it to his mouth. The false teeth struggled to cope with the bun but Sandridge persevered. He masticated the mouthful thoroughly, swallowed it and dabbed his mouth with a paper napkin.

Blaines had already finished his half-pounder. He was crunching his way through a large portion of french fries.

'Charmian,' Sandridge said, 'would raise the roof if she ever found out. Says it's bad for me. But I like this kind of food.'

Blaines grunted. If he were Sandridge, he would rather eat at McDonalds than at Macton Hall. Any day of the week.

They were in the Haymarket branch. The meeting place had been Sandridge's idea. It was Saturday afternoon and there were too many screaming children about for Blaines's taste.

Sandridge fastened his lips around the straw that protruded from his strawberry milkshake. He sucked vigorously; his Adam's apple bobbed up and down as he swallowed.

'Have any luck with William?' he asked.

Blaines nodded. 'A photo. He's eating out of my hand and wondering when it'll be safe to bite it. How did you know?'

'Caught a glimpse of him once. It was at Macton, years ago. At first I thought he'd smuggled in a girl. He didn't see me.' Sandridge captured a spot of ketchup from his upper lip with a lizard-like movement of his tongue. 'Poor William. Takes all sorts, eh? How's it going?'

'We've got a lead.' Blaines said. 'Though it may not get us anywhere. Does the name Ryal ring any bells?'

Sandridge nodded. 'The little muckraker. Motive

enough, I suppose. But I thought someone said he was dead.'

'Maybe. I've a feeling that's just what we were meant to think.'

'He must be working for someone. If it is him.'

'A lot of people use a freelance these days. Especially for this sort of job.'

'Well, whoever it is, it's got to stop.' Sandridge glared across the table. 'As far as I can see, everyone's doing an ostrich on this: head in sand and hoping it goes away. I've decided to tell you what they've got on me.'

'Why?'

'Because circumstances have changed, that's why.' Sandridge addressed himself to his milkshake. There was a spot of colour on each of his cheeks. 'As a matter of fact, they know about my first marriage.'

Blaines pulled the ashtray towards him. 'What's so important about that?'

'My wife – Charmian – doesn't know. Or rather she doesn't know the full story.' Sandridge glanced at him. 'I married Lilian in '32, in Quebec. She's been in a nursing home just outside Montreal for over fifty years. An asylum for the incurably insane. I was raised a Catholic, so was she: so divorce was out of the question.'

'Bigamy?'

'Charmian and I were married in a civil ceremony,' Sandridge said stiffly. 'It doesn't count in the eyes of the Church. Damn it, of course it was bigamy. Technically.'

Blaines said nothing.

'Lilian and I were very young.' Sandridge's voice was defensive. 'I wanted to get into bed with her. I realized I'd made a mistake in the first week. She was committed in

276

'34. I came to England the following year. It was simpler to say I was a bachelor. I felt like one. During the war I met Charmian. I wanted her more than I've ever wanted anything.'

'She never knew about Lilian?'

'I told her Lilian was dead.'

'Who did know?'

'Lilian's mother. She died in '43, before I married Charmian. Lilian had no other family. My parents were dead and my only relatives were in England.'

'April Wreningham,' Blaines said suddenly. 'She's a cousin of yours. Could she have known?'

Sandridge shook his head. 'I never told her parents about Lilian. I didn't even meet them till I came to England.'

'Friends? Someone must have known.'

'You don't understand. In those days I lived in Toronto – used to work on the *Star*. I met Lilian when I was on vacation. Ten days later I married her. It went wrong almost immediately; she stayed in Quebec with her mother when I went back to work. It wasn't something I felt like talking about.'

'Did you keep in contact?'

'I sent them money occasionally. Through my bank in Toronto – they didn't even know I was in England. When the mother died I took over responsibility for the nursing-home bills.'

'So they knew?'

'I'm not a fool.' Sandridge sounded both tired and petulant. 'I put her in another nursing home. Said I was her cousin.'

Blaines lit a cigar. 'If the worst comes to the worst,

does it really matter if the story gets out?'

'You fool. I don't care about the scandal. It's Charmian.'

'Why did you decide to tell me after all?'

'Didn't I say? I had a letter yesterday. Lilian's dead, thank God.'

On Sunday morning they arranged to meet in the buffet at Reading Station. The location had been Patricia's suggestion. She was going to spend the day with the Dallows.

Blaines drove up from Teddington. He wore his best suit, which he had recently had cleaned; the jacket and waistband were uncomfortably tight but none of the buttons was missing. He was early and the train was late. The buffet depressed him and he couldn't sit still. He remembered that other time they had met in a railway buffet, at Paddington Station. Another bloody brief encounter.

The *News of the World* failed to hold his attention. He wanted to see Patricia but he wished she had suggested somewhere more private. Suggested was the wrong word. On the phone last night it had sounded more like an order. The fact that he half-enjoyed obeying her revealed a hitherto unsuspected facet of his character. He preferred not to think about it.

He was waiting on the platform as her train pulled in. She stepped down to the platform and the familiar pain appeared in his chest. Indigestion of the heart. There was no fool like an old fool.

The other passengers scurried away. She stood still, looking for him. He moved towards her, aware he was

278

beaming foolishly but unable to control himself. He realized with a jolt that he was happy.

The happiness lasted no more than a few seconds. She saw him. Her face hardened as if Blaines were a shopkeeper who had tried to overcharge her.

'Why did you lie to me?' she said.

'Eh? What do you mean?'

'About the way Charles died.'

The next half-hour was full of misery. They sat at opposite sides of a table in the buffet. Between them their cups of coffee cooled and a carnation wilted for lack of water in an old Perrier bottle. Trains and travellers came and went. These details were important and Blaines clung to them.

Patricia's anger was cold and fluent; she might have been a prosecuting counsel at a court martial. It seemed to Blaines that he was trapped in an invisible cage, barred from escape by his own emotions. Marital quarrels must be like this: the relationship enclosed the participants like an arena. He wondered if the Claybrooks had fought. Surely not. The perfect couple would live without battles.

He defended himself automatically but clumsily, for he was unused to fighting on the defensive. Koslove, he pointed out, had only told him the details on Wednesday. Naturally he, Blaines, was going to tell her; but he hadn't wanted to upset her unnecessarily. First he wanted to investigate the possibility that Claybrook had been betrayed. No, he had failed to confirm or rebut the idea. He scored a couple of points when it emerged that Koslove had held back information from him.

279

'You sure? A pipe-smoker?' he said, sensing a thaw. 'And Hong Kong was mentioned?'

'Of course I'm sure. But Koslove wasn't. He said the source was unreliable.'

'Ryal smoked a pipe. Probably thought it made him look like an empire-builder.'

She wasn't listening. 'You know, all this rests on Koslove's word. He was trying to recruit me – to turn me against the rest of you.'

Blaines pounced. 'He might have his own reasons for wanting to sabotage the investigation.'

Patricia looked startled. 'You mean he's being blackmailed himself?'

'Maybe. Or he could be behind the Blacklist.'

'You're joking. Why?'

Blaines shrugged. 'You know what they're like on Capitol Hill. They play games with one another all the time. And they treat the world as their playground.' He scratched his ear. 'It would explain Monastow's death. Koslove knew I'd seen him, and he knew I was going again. My bet is that Monastow would have given me more pointers towards Ryal. If Koslove's behind Ryal –'

'Ryal's dead.'

'More likely his cousin died on his behalf.' Blaines told her the results of yesterday's interview with Mrs Padgate. 'Trouble is, I don't see how Ryal or Koslove could have found out about Sandridge.'

'Tom? Has he told you what they've got on him?'

Glad to have diverted her interest to a relatively safe subject, he described his conversation with Sandridge. He nursed a small and sickly hope that the confidence would prove he was being open with her.

'Is that all?' Patricia said. 'I knew about Lilian years ago.'

Blaines blinked at her. 'How?'

'Charmian told me. It was in the days when we saw a lot of each other. Before I married Warren.'

'Charmian *knows*?'

'I wish you wouldn't interrogate me,' she said coldly. 'Charmian was looking through some bank statements and she happened to notice these regular payments to a nursing home. In Montreal, I think – somewhere like that. Naturally she was curious. She phoned the place and managed to get the patient's name out of them. Tom had told her that Lilian was dead.'

'But she said nothing to Sandridge about it.'

'Well, it would have been rather tactless, don't you think? She'd have had to admit she'd – well – pried. Anyway, what was the point? I think in a way she was rather flattered: Tom loved her so much he'd committed bigamy for her.'

Blaines put his head in his hands. He was unnerved by the alarming combination of domestic espionage and conjugal pragmatism. Were all women like this?

'Do you know if she told anyone else?' he managed to say.

'I very much doubt it. It's not the sort of thing you publish.'

'So how did Ryal find out?'

Patricia shrugged. 'You're obsessed by Ryal. You don't even know if he's alive.'

'He's the only lead we've got.' Blaines said obstinately. At least she was still talking to him; at least she hadn't walked out. 'I dug out his file at MoD. Before he joined the service he was in the military police. There was a nasty incident in Aden: suspected terrorist died in his cell after Ryal had talked to him; internal bruising, the PM said; nothing was ever proved. Similar thing happened when he was at Aldershot. Only this time the bloke didn't die.'

'You've wandered off the point,' Patricia said sharply.

The pain twisted in his chest. 'Which is?'

'Who do I trust? You or Koslove?'

On Saturday night the problem had become acute.

Jessica brooded on it at teatime on Sunday. Mrs Inkerman, her landlady, studied her surreptitiously. Jessica avoided conversation by pretending to be absorbed in the *Observer*.

She had been living in the boarding house – or, in Mrs Inkerman's terminology, the private hotel – for more than two weeks. When she had packed she had made two assumptions: that she might have to carry her own bags and that practical clothes would be more appropriate than frivolous ones.

Then on Saturday Liam invited her to the theatre and to supper afterwards. This necessitated an afternoon spending-spree in Kensington High Street. The need for a dress led naturally enough to the need for a pair of shoes; and shoes raised the question of a handbag. Her pleasure in buying clothes was marred by the fact she couldn't afford them; and the knowledge that she had plenty of clothes in the Notting Hill flat made her feel still guiltier.

The flat was off-limits until this was over; Blaines insisted on that. Jack was a security risk and it was possible that she herself might be in danger.

On the other hand, she and Liam had talked of going to see *The Magic Flute* this week. She could hardly go to the opera in jeans. The only alternative was to wear the same dress she had worn last night. There was no rational objection to this scheme; and indeed there were strong arguments in favour of it. But reason was not a reliable guide to how you felt about your appearance.

Suppose she went to the flat while Jack was away? All she needed was a suitcase full of clothes; it wouldn't take a minute. She had to wear something. Blaines could hardly object.

Mrs Inkerman swooped. 'Have you got enough toast, dear? Won't take me a moment to do some more.'

She was a large, untidy woman with a penetrating voice and a habit of making hot-water bottles and cups of cocoa at the slightest provocation. Jessica liked her but had no doubt where her loyalties lay.

'No, I've had enough, thank you.'

'The Colonel likes his toast. You should see him – he has to have marmalade, whatever the time of day. And he cuts his toast into soldiers, just like a little boy. We always have a good laugh about that.'

Mrs Inkerman invariably referred to Blaines as the Colonel. Once she had worked with him in some capacity. Jessica suspected her of nursing a secret passion for him.

Jessica folded the newspaper. 'I think I'll have a walk in Kensington Gardens.'

'Will you be long, dear? In case someone phones.'

'About an hour.'

Mrs lnkerman peered out of the window. 'It'll soon be

dark,' she said doubtfully. 'And there's a *savage* nip in the air. If I were you I'd put on an extra woolly.'

Jessica rang her own number from the phone box at the end of the road. There was no answer. She checked the area in front of the house. Jack kept his motorbike there among the dustbins. The only sign of it was a patch of oil on the concrete.

Her caution made her feel ridiculous. This was where she lived – and it seemed like no man's land. She let herself into the house with her latchkey and climbed the communal stairs. Everything was familiar at first sight; yet she noticed the details with a freshness which robbed them of their familiarity. The tear in the wallpaper on the first half-landing nagged her: had it been there before? She scuttled past the doors of the other flats. The desirability of avoiding neighbours had become as imperative as a taboo.

Last night they had gone back to Liam's flat for coffee. Something he had said came back to her: *That's the trouble with this job: you become a foreigner in your own country. Your home is where you work, not where you live.*

By the time she reached the top of the house she was panting. She was out of training for flights of stairs. She waited for a few seconds on the landing. Jack abhorred silence. When he was at home he usually demanded some form of aural wallpaper – the television, the radio or a tape.

She let herself into the flat. There was a small hexagonal table in the hall. An empty spirits glass lay on its side beside the telephone. Near the glass, a lighted cigarette had been left to extinguish itself; the walnut veneer of the table was now permanently disfigured by a long, brown scar.

The living-room door was open. The cushions from the sofa had been strewn over the carpet. The unsavoury remains of a Chinese takeaway were scattered about the floor. A dozen records had lost their sleeves.

She moved into the room. Bottles and glasses were everywhere. The twelve-year-old malt – which she had left in her wardrobe with the intention of broaching it on a particularly rainy day – had lost both its cap and its contents. The fruit bowl had been used as an ashtray; judging by the number of roaches inside, it had been quite an evening.

Shock anaesthetized her emotions. Jessica knew she was angry but somehow the violation of her flat seemed to have happened to someone else. She was a spectator at her own misery.

A pair of tights were on the carpet. She stooped automatically and picked them up. They were rather a nice colour, she thought – a sort of harebell blue. As she straightened up she noticed that someone had left a dark blue shoe by the sofa. A woman, obviously; her feet were a couple of sizes larger than Jessica's.

At that moment she heard a woman giggle.

Jessica took an immediate dislike to her. The giggle sounded coy to the point of hysteria.

Jessica dropped the tights and followed the trail of discarded clothing. The trail led to her bedroom. In the doorway she stopped. The room smelled of someone else's perfume. The curtains were still drawn across the window but there was enough light to see what was

285

happening. To see two bodies under the duvet – *her* duvet. Jack was on top, raising himself on his arms. The woman was still invisible.

But you could still hear her. Instead of giggling she was moaning.

Jessica crossed the room. She tore back the curtains and opened the window as far as it would go. She turned back to face them. Her legs were shaking so much that she had to lean against the window-sill.

'I want you both out of my flat.' At least her voice was calm. 'And your belongings.'

The woman's frizzy ginger hair was all over the pillow. Jack liked his women to have long hair; it had always been a bone of contention between him and Jessica. This one had a lot of freckles and blue, scared eyes. When she went to bed she had forgotten to remove her outsize earrings.

Jack said nothing. The muscles on his shoulders tensed.

'I'm in a hurry,' Jessica said. 'I'll be in the living room.'

She left the bedroom. The dignity of her exit was marred when she stumbled over the second blue shoe. It was typical of Jack that he had hardly seemed to notice she was there.

In the living room she forced herself to begin tidying up. It gave her something to do. Looking for record sleeves was more productive than looking for solutions.

The doors were still open. It soon became obvious that Jack was finishing what he had begun. The woman protested, to give her her due; but he insisted. That too was typical.

The record which Jessica was holding had a smear of

286

sweet-and-sour sauce on the label. She dropped it in the waste-paper basket. A surge of rage cancelled the anaesthetic.

In the kitchen she emptied the dirty crockery from the washing-up bowl to the floor. She filled the bowl with cold water and carried it carefully into the bedroom.

Jack was still grinding away. The duvet had been kicked on to the floor. The woman was not responding; her head was turned away and her eyes were closed. Jessica felt a twinge of compassion for her. When you were pinned beneath thirteen stone of rampant masculinity, escape could be difficult at the best of times.

Anger swamped the sympathy. Jessica upturned the bowl above them and let go.

The woman shrieked. Jack snarled; raising himself on one arm, he swung blindly at Jessica.

She was already out of reach. By the door she paused. 'I said I was in a hurry.'

In the living room she sat down and put her head in her hands. The trembling wouldn't stop. The scene in the bedroom had left a foul taste in her mouth. It disgusted her – and all the more because the situation was so trite. It was the stuff of a thousand farces: the philandering male discovered with the other woman. In real life it wasn't amusing; it was dreary, sordid and above all painful.

In the other room Jack was swearing, softly and monotonously. The woman said to him, over and over again, 'You should have told me, you should have told me.' There was the sound of a slap.

Jack was the first to emerge. His eyes were bloodshot. He wore jeans and an old sweatshirt. His wet hair was scraped back off his unshaven face.

The woman was close behind him. Like Jack's, her feet were bare. Her dress looked as though she had slept in it.

'I can't find my other shoe,' she said to no one in particular.

'Try under the sofa,' Jessica said coldly. She stood up and pointed. 'Just beside your tights.'

The woman stuffed her feet into her shoes. One of her cheeks was red. She picked up the tights and looked at them uncertainly.

'Jack . . .?' she said.

'Go home, Sally.' He kept his eyes on Jessica. 'I'll call you tonight.'

Sally scuttled into the hall. The front door closed very quietly.

'You are a bastard, Jack,' Jessica said conversationally. 'It wasn't her fault.'

Without warning he hit her. It was a back-handed blow, delivered almost casually. It swept her off her feet and on to the uncushioned sofa.

'It's about time you were honest with me,' he said.

'Get out,' Jessica said. 'Just get out.'

He stood over her. 'Had enough, have you? Decided you don't like rough trade?'

'It's over,' Jessica said. 'We're finished.'

'What have you been doing? Where've you been? I've been hearing some fascinating rumours.'

'I told you about the assignment. Anyway, it's none of your business.'

Not now, she thought. And never again.

'Don't piss around. I've got my sources too. There's a cover-up, isn't there? And you're helping. People are

288

being blackmailed, that's what I hear. What about that old queer in Brighton? Your dad used to know him, so did Blaines. Once upon a time he had a very sensitive job.'

'I don't know what you're talking about.'

'Yes, you do. You've reverted to type. You've had your fun, sown your wild oats; now you've got bored with slumming and you want to be *respectable* again.'

'Don't be so stupid.'

'I've been doing some digging.' He bent down and grabbed her ears, forcing her to look at him. 'You've joined the family firm. Sandridge is your uncle, isn't he? Why didn't you ever mention that? Sandridge, for Christ's sake. And your brother Greg: he's the son of Warren Vanderman. What a coincidence. Vanderman used to be married to your mother. Sandridge and Vanderman do a lot of business together. There was an MoD contract – you hear about that? Vanderman got his hands dirty but Sandridge sorted it out for him. And who helped him? Eric Blaines, your dad's old friend.'

'You're mad,' Jessica said.

He twisted her ears and she screamed.

'Mad, am I? Better than being a fucking traitor. You're going to tell me all about it.' He released the ears, grabbed the collar of Jessica's shirt and tugged. The shirt came apart in his hands. 'But first I want to finish what you interrupted.'

Jessica jerked her left leg into his crotch. Her position reduced the impact of the blow but Jack gasped and doubled up. She wriggled sideways and off the sofa.

Jack's face was dark with blood. 'You bitch.'

She backed away towards the window. He threw a

punch which glanced off her cheekbone. She picked up the typewriter and hurled it at him. It bounced off his chest and smashed to the floor. He shouted with pain. It must have hit one or both of his feet.

Jessica darted round the back of the sofa, into the hall and through the front door.

She ran down the stairs and into the street. She met no one. She could hear no sign of pursuit. Her mouth tasted of blood.

It was nearly dark. The street-lights were on. The air was unpleasantly cold. She realized that she had left her coat and bag upstairs. She had no money.

A car came down the street. It slowed; a man leant out of a window on the passenger side and asked if she wanted to have a bit of fun.

Jessica ran on.

The doorbell rang while Liam was in the shower.

He swore. Five o'clock on a Sunday evening was an odd time for callers. He turned off the water and wrapped a towel around him. He left a trail of wet footprints on the carpet.

The door had two locks and a spyhole. The spyhole revealed a grossly distended version of Emma Lazonby.

'Darling,' she said as he opened the door. 'How lovely to see you.' She pecked him on the cheek and edged past him into the single room of the flat. She was carrying an overnight bag, which she tossed on to an armchair. 'I hope you don't mind me dropping in like this.'

'No, of course not,' Liam said automatically. He wondered if his lack of enthusiasm was as obvious to her as it was to him. 'But – what are you doing in London?'

'There's a reception at the embassy on Tuesday.' She glanced around the room, taking in the unmade bed and the heap of Sunday newspapers on the floor. 'Another Common Market free-for-all. Someone went sick on Saturday and they sent an SOS. They want me to supervise the caterers.'

'I wish you'd let me know.' Aware that he sounded ungracious. Liam added: 'I could have met you at the airport.'

'It was all such a rush.' Emma wandered into the little kitchen. There was a pile of unwashed crockery on the draining-board; it included last night's coffee tray with two cups and two glasses. 'Anyway I thought it'd be nice to surprise you.' She turned and came towards him. Her skirt swirled, giving him a tantalizing glimpse of her legs. 'You are pleased, aren't you, darling?'

'Of course I am.' He was also cold; the draught from the open door had raised goose-pimples on his wet skin. 'Look, would you mind if–?'

She stroked his arm. 'You're dripping all over the carpet. Go and get dressed and I'll tidy up a bit. It's a real bachelor mess, isn't it?'

His body wanted to respond to her touch. Lust was promiscuous, and any reasonably attractive woman would satisfy its demands. He picked up his clothes and retreated into the bathroom.

Once she was out of sight, his mind began to work. She was checking on him, that was clear. It made him furious. He wondered if she was doing it just for herself or for Aughrim as well.

The outlook grew worse the more he thought about it. She would be here until Wednesday morning at least. He

291

had hoped to go to the opera with Jessica on Tuesday night. And what would Blaines say to her arrival? Worst of all, how would Jessica feel?

He turned on the shower again. this time for warmth. Emma's voice drifted in through the open door.

'I got you a bottle of Powers on the plane . . . Where do you keep the washing-up liquid? . . . Looks like you had someone round for coffee . . .'

Liam ignored her. He stepped out of the shower and towelled himself. Maybe Blaines could give him an excuse to leave the flat. It was worth trying. Alternatively he could stop being a coward: he could tell Emma that they weren't suited to one another and escape from her before it was too late.

The doorbell rang again.

'I'll get it,' Emma said.

Liam dropped the towel and pulled on the clean pair of jeans.

'Yes?' he heard Emma say in the voice she usually reserved for waiters and tradesmen.

'Is Liam in?' Jessica said. 'I'm a – colleague of his. Jessica Claybrook.'

'He's having a shower.'

'May I come in and wait? I've had an accident.'

'I'm so sorry,' Emma said. 'I think Liam's mentioned you once or twice. I'm his fiancée, by the way – Emma Lazonby.'

Liam zipped up the jeans and opened the door. Jessica and Emma were standing together in the middle of the room; both of them were looking at him. Emma's smile was almost triumphant. She was tacitly inviting him to make comparisons.

292

It was no contest. Emma had more than the advantage of height; as usual she was dressed to make an impression on the opposite sex; and she was playing the hostess, the role that showed her to the best advantage.

'Do sit down,' she said sweetly to Jessica. 'You look exhausted. Liam, I'm sure Jessica could do with a drink. Or perhaps she'd prefer tea?'

Jessica had her arms folded across her breasts. She was shivering and the collar was partly detached from her shirt. Her face was pale apart from the tip of the nose, which was pink with cold, and a bruise on her cheek. The knees of her jeans were smeared with mud as if she had slipped and fallen.

Liam realized that he no longer had the luxury of time. He had to make a decision now. The easier and more prudent course would be to give Jessica a suitably tepid smile and fetch her a drink.

'Or would you rather have a wash first?' Emma asked; she contrived to imply that her own standards of personal cleanliness were rather higher than Jessica's.

'Jess.' Liam took her gently by the shoulders.

She tried to pull away. She was still trembling. The bones felt small and fragile. Then she fell towards him and there was suddenly no need to make a decision.

'Jess, love,' he said. 'What's happened?'

9

The man on the plane said that Blaines had picked the right time of year.

In December the climate was cool and sunny and the humidity was low. Really the man added with a nervous giggle, one might almost be in England on a summer day. Naturally there were problems – the overcrowding, for example, and the materialism of most of the inhabitants. And of course one should never forget that the long-term political future was uncertain. One couldn't help feeling sorry for the people who would be staying on. But, taken as a whole at the present moment in time, you couldn't ask for a better place for a holiday. Particularly in December.

The man was a middle-aged British passport-holder with a Chinese face. He introduced himself as Mr Chou and pressed Blaines to accept one of his cards. According to the card Mr Charles Chou was in the import-export business, a description that covered a multitude of sins.

Blaines tried a number of ways to make him be quiet. He watched an in-flight movie; he visited the lavatory; he said nothing in reply to questions. In the end he lost patience and told the man to shut up. The method was simple and immediately effective.

Mr Chou spent the rest of the flight engrossed in *Playboy*. He appeared to have taken his dismissal with good grace. After they landed, he caught up with Blaines on the runway.

'If you need anything,' he said, panting, 'just call me. Okay?'

He gave Blaines another beaming smile and darted away.

Kai Tak International Airport soured Blaines's temper still further. The terminal was crowded with people who were under the impression that they were human dodgem cars. Blaines, being larger and heavier than most of them, was at an advantage. After a while he grew accustomed to having someone collide with him every few yards; they bounced off, seeming hardly to notice him; it was like walking through a horde of flies. His only luggage was an attaché case which he had carried with him on the plane. Though small, it had sharp, hard corners which Blaines used to good effect.

Alexander Kyre had sent a limousine to meet him. This was completely unsatisfactory. Blaines had made it clear that he was not an official visitor; his movements were not to be logged. If Kyre wanted a car to meet him, he should have driven it himself.

'Is this your first visit, sir?' the Chinese driver enquired.

'I hope it's my last. Just keep your mouth shut and drive. All right?'

In one respect Kyre had obeyed Wreningham's instructions: he was waiting for Blaines at his flat in Lai Chi Kok, not at the office. The flat was on the fifteenth floor of a block occupied mainly by civil servants.

Kyre himself answered the door. He rubbed his hands together and offered one of them to Blaines.

'Good journey?'

'Bloody awful.'

He showed Blaines into the living room. The video was purring softly, playing back a horse-race without sound on the twenty-four inch television screen. Kyre cherished racing the way that other Scotsmen were meant to cherish their bank balances.

'I sent Jean to the Ladies' Rec,' Kyre said. 'My wife, you know. She spends half her life at that club. Lunch, hair, bridge – she won't be back till this evening. Like a beer?'

Blaines nodded. He sat down in a rattan chair, which creaked under his weight. Kyre returned with two glasses of lager. He turned off the television and the video. He sank down in a chair that faced the blank screen.

'How's London?' he asked.

Blaines shrugged. He swallowed half the beer. It was as bad as he had expected.

Kyre scratched his thinning hair. 'Haven't been home for over three years. Daresay it's changed.'

'Not really home, is it?' Blaines said. 'Not for you.'

Kyre was an old China hand, part of the flotsam of empire. If he had a home, it was here.

'Of course things have changed,' Kyre went on, as if Blaines hadn't spoken. 'They always do. For one thing, you've got Wreningham in the hot seat. Never met him, myself. They say he's a bit of a Young Turk.'

'Any of your lads been through Istanbul lately?' Blaines said suddenly. 'Not necessarily on business.'

'Eh?' Kyre glanced suspiciously at Blaines's glass, perhaps wondering if, against all probability, there was something stronger than lager in it. 'Istanbul? Not that I know of. Rather off the beaten track as far as we're concerned.'

'Ah, well.' Blaines finished his beer.

Kyre took the hint. He fetched two more cans.

'I don't quite know,' he said after an uncomfortable silence, 'what your brief is. Wreningham's signal didn't make that clear.'

There was a note of anxiety in his voice. Kyre had two years to go before retirement and the index-linked pension. Wreningham had already gained a reputation as a new broom who didn't much mind whom he swept under the carpet. In this he was unlike his predecessors who had left the running of the department to those who had been trained to do it. It was said that his mandate for this unwelcome innovation came directly from the Cabinet Office. Kyre had no wish to be a sacrificial lamb on the altar of political accountability.

'There's no need for you to know,' Blaines said. 'I'm an observer if you like. To be afforded every facility. And most of all I want discretion. That means keep your gob shut and maybe you'll be all right.'

'Of course. Anything you like. I only –'

'What I'd like first is a list of private investigation firms which operate here. I'm particularly interested in those which were established in the last twenty years. Or old firms that came under new management. I want to know who owns them. I want lists of personnel, estimates of turnover, major clients, you name it.'

'But that's hardly a job for us.'

'It is now. You can't do it?'

Kyre smiled nervously. 'Well, of *course* we can. A little complicated and rather unusual but–'

'Good. I need it tomorrow. Come to breakfast and bring the stuff with you. I'll be at the Mandarin.'

'It's very short notice. We'll do our best, naturally.'

'I hope you'll do better than that.' Blaines stood up and drank the rest of his lager. He leered down at Kyre, who was rubbing his hands together once again. 'Wreningham has a personal interest in this.'

Kyre scrambled to his feet.

'By the way,' Blaines went on, 'there was something else I wanted to ask you.' He tapped the side of his attaché case. 'Brought some pipe tobacco for a friend of mine at Government House. Some special mixture he used to like – from a place in the Haymarket. Just remembered he gave up smoking.'

'I see,' Kyre said thoughtfully. Feeling that something more was required, he added: 'Shame about that.'

Blaines led the way to the door. 'Any of your people smoke a pipe? They could have it for cost.'

'A pipe?' Kyre frowned in concentration. He looked appraisingly at Blaines. 'No. Not many people smoke a pipe these days.'

They did a full English breakfast at the Mandarin.

Blaines ordered it from room service. By the time he reached the toast and marmalade stage, he felt capable of looking at the *South China Morning Post* which was propped open in front of him. He was reading the latest corruption story when Kyre arrived.

'Well, sit down,' Blaines said. 'Have some coffee if you want.'

Kyre looked as though he needed a stronger stimulant than coffee. His eyes were bloodshot and his skin had a chalky pallor; the lines on his forehead were so deep that the face as a whole seemed on the verge of disintegration.

He slumped into a chair and laid a manila folder on the table. The folder was labelled confidential and bore the colony's arms. Blaines wondered why Kyre hadn't bothered to go the whole hog and stamp it with a red 'Top Secret'. Perhaps he thought it was obvious enough as it was.

Blaines thrust a finger of toast into his mouth. 'Well? What's the overall picture?' he asked indistinctly.

'Forty-two firms. Thirty-three of them fit your guidelines.'

'That many?'

Kyre rubbed his eyes. 'There are five and a half million people here and a lot of them are wealthy. The business houses account for most of the demand. Some of these outfits do security work as well. It's a growth business.'

Blaines opened the folder and pawed through the pile of paper inside. The material was neatly laid out, with a table of contents, an introduction and a separate section for each firm. Someone on Kyre's staff knew how to operate a word processor.

'Some of the entries are rather patchy,' Kyre said. 'Of course we'll try to expand them if you want.'

In the table of contents several firms had asterisks after their names. Blaines smeared a thin coating of marmalade over one of them.

'What's this mean?'

Kyre restrained a yawn. 'Known to do business with the Chinese. On the mainland, I mean.'

'Why did you mark them?'

'I thought you'd be interested. These days that's all

300

London *is* interested in: the Chinese, Peking, the hand-over of sovereignty.'

Blaines glanced quickly at Kyre and decided that the man was probably speaking the truth. He refilled his coffee-cup, lit a cigar and worked his way through the folder.

He was dimly aware that Kyre was breathing heavily. Halfway through the pile he looked up. Kyre, slumped in his chair, was asleep with his mouth open. *Past it*, Blaines thought idly. *Maybe I should get Wreningham to bounce him out*. Retirement wasn't the same if it happened to someone else. Besides, Kyre was looking forward to it. In the sunset years of his life he'd be able to spend all day at the racetrack.

Blaines sorted the sections into two piles as he read. He went through one of the piles a second time, winnowing out a few more firms. He was left with one front-runner and half a dozen possibles.

He kicked Kyre on the shin to bring him back to consciousness.

'I've got another job for you.' Blaines fished out a card from his top pocket and passed it to Kyre. 'See if you've got anything on him. Check with Special Branch and the Criminal Intelligence Bureau too.'

Kyre blinked at the card. 'Charles Chou? Doesn't ring any bells, I'm afraid. Should it?'

Blaines kept a firm grip on his temper. 'That's what I want to know. Phone me here this morning, will you?'

Kyre staggered out of the room. Blaines picked up the phone and dialled an outside number. It was answered on the second ring.

'This is a recorded message on behalf of Peterhouse

International Investigations,' a woman said carefully, 'in English and Cantonese. Owing to a fire at our offices, PII is not accepting new clients at present. Our new offices will be opening shortly. If you wish us to contact you, please leave your name and number after the tone.'

Blaines replaced the handset.

'No record of him,' Kyre said an hour later. 'The phone number's a fake. You want me to check with immigration?'

'Don't bother.' Blaines looked at his watch. 'I'm going out. Stay at the office – I'll phone you later today.'

They made contact sooner than he had expected.

Charles Chou was waiting in the hotel lobby. When he saw Blaines emerging from the lift, he beamed and waved. Still smiling, he thrust his way through the crowd that divided them. A few seconds later he was shaking Blaines's hand with an enthusiasm that was not reciprocated.

'I have a car outside,' he said. 'Mr Liu is waiting.'

Blaines nodded.

Chou said nothing during the drive; he contented himself with the occasional smile. The driver in the front needed no instructions. He drove them out of town to Victoria Gap and then up to the Peak. The higher you lived, the greater your status; Liu's house – and a house was a rare luxury in this overpopulated city – was near the top.

Liu was waiting for them in the small living room. The official representative of the New China News Agency was tall for a Chinese. He shook hands gravely with Blaines and motioned him to a seat.

'What a pleasure this is, Mr Blaines. You would like tea? Or something stronger? Perhaps Johnnie Walker Black Label would be acceptable?'

Blaines agreed that it would. He warmed to Liu. The agency was a front for Peking's Central External Liaison Department, which had a well-deserved reputation for thoroughness. Liu's command of English was remarkably good. Unlike many of his compatriots he managed combined consonants with ease.

Chou brought the whisky and a single glass on a tray. No one asked if he wanted water, ice or soda; they knew he took it neat. Chou beamed, bowed and withdrew.

'I hear that you and your colleagues have a little problem.' Liu said delicately. 'How distasteful you must find it.'

Blaines poured himself a generous glass. 'I was wondering if you might be able to help.'

The skin at the corners of Liu's eyes crinkled momentarily. 'We know very little about that sort of thing.'

'Someone must know.'

'No doubt you're right.' Liu hesitated. 'I gather that you are looking for a firm of private investigators. Have you tried Peterhouse International Investigations? We have used them ourselves, once or twice.'

'I phoned them,' Blaines said. 'They've had a fire and they're not accepting new clients at the moment.'

'How unfortunate. A fire, you say? Mr Quendale must be most upset.'

'You know Mr Quendale personally?'

'By reputation, shall we say. A good man in his way.

303

Very much the Englishman. The military moustache and the pipe. If he has a fault, it is that he sometimes acts on his own initiative.'

'Do you know where I can contact him?'

'Sadly, no. I believe he is in Europe at present. Perhaps his amah could tell you where to find him.'

Liu produced a notebook and a small penknife. With great care he cut out a page and passed it to Blaines. A name and an address had already been printed on it in small, neat capitals.

'You must not let me delay you,' Liu said. 'I'm sure you have other appointments.'

Blaines didn't move. 'You heard the sad news about Tonanyev?'

'Yes, indeed. Though in many quarters it gave pleasure, not sadness. He was involved in a border incident thirty years ago, in Manchuria.'

'One of our men was killed at the same time.'

'Now that was most unfortunate. Someone must have blundered, Mr Blaines.'

Quendale's apartment was at the top of a big high-rise block overlooking Repulse Bay. Blaines talked to the amah on the entryphone. She was unwilling to let him in until he mentioned Liu's name. In some ways, Blaines thought as he rode upwards in the lift, the British had already handed over most of the power that mattered to the Chinese.

Mrs Yip opened the door to his ring but kept it on the chain. She refused to let him in until she had seen his passport. Her English was fluent but full of subtly disturbing inaccuracies of stress, pronunciation and meaning;

304

Kyre would have called it Chinglish. She referred to her guest as Mr Brains.

She talked to Blaines in the hall. On the wall was a map of the world: it showed the British Empire as it had been in Blaines's childhood. While she talked she held on to the handle of a Hoover that wasn't much smaller than herself.

Despite the power of Liu's name, it took ten minutes and a hundred-dollar note to persuade her to part with an address. She wrote it on the back of an old envelope, apparently from memory.

Blaines frowned at it. 'The Scuola Pencombe? Are you sure?'

She shrugged in reply, as if to remind him that the vagaries of her employer were none of her business.

'What does he want with a school?'

Mrs Yip said nothing. She stared up at him with small, blank eyes. Blaines held up another hundred-dollar note.

She snatched it from his fingers. 'Not for Mr Quendale,' she said. 'For Missee Susan.'

On Thursday they had the first snowfall of the year.

Liam drove down to Gatwick early in the morning. There was little traffic yet. He was ten minutes late but in the event the weather delayed the plane by over an hour.

Blaines came through the arrival lounge with his shoulders hunched and his head down. He carried nothing but his little attachée case and a bag from the duty-free shop at Kai Tak.

He glared at Liam. 'Bloody hell. If we're not careful we're going to have a white Christmas.'

He said nothing else until they were in the car. As

Liam drove, he kept hitting Blaines's leg with the gear stick. In a few moments the little car was thick with cigar smoke. Blaines insisted on keeping the windows closed and the heating on full.

'Any news?' he said, once they were on the M23.

Liam thought of Jessica and shook his head. 'Nothing you should know.'

'Peterhouse International Investigations,' Blaines said. 'Founded 1938 by Arnold Peterhouse. Originally they called themselves Oriental not International. His son got into difficulties – he was on the verge of bankruptcy when he sold the business in 1974. To a bloke named J. Adam Quendale who had just arrived from the UK. Quendale changed the emphasis of the firm as well as the name: got into commercial intelligence, handled company security; that sort of thing. There's a well-founded rumour that he regularly fronts for the New China News Agency.'

'Why would they use a European?'

'Because sometimes they don't want to advertise their race, let alone their nationality. You can't hide a Chinese face. PII claims to have links with a lot of firms in Europe and the States. They say that Quendale uses freelance talent and some of it is pretty dubious. A lot of contract work which doesn't go down in the books. I've also heard that the firm's finances are shaky. I talked with a Chink who more or less admitted that they'd hired Quendale to kill Tonanyev. Tonanyev was directly responsible for the deaths of nearly two hundred Chinese civilians in Manchuria, way back in the fifties. The Chinese had a long wait but they got their revenge in the end.'

306

'And Claybrook?'

'As far as Peking's concerned, his death was an unwelcome accident. If they employed Quendale to arrange Tonanyev's death, they wouldn't like it if he went beyond his brief. Maybe that's the reason why they're giving him the push.'

'Or he's outlived his usefulness in another way.'

'Meaning the Chinese are behind the Blacklist and he was their agent? It's possible. They certainly know about it – they had a man beside me on the flight out. They want to move into the world league. They like Western currency. They need influential friends in the West, if friends is the right word. And they've got tidy minds, too. Either way would explain why they're willing to give us Quendale. Let us do the dirty work.'

'So Quendale's Ryal.'

'Quendale smokes a pipe,' Blaines said. 'He's the right age, roughly the right appearance and he turned up in the right job at the right time. The only problem is, he's not in Hong Kong now.'

'You're taking a lot for granted.'

'Well, what the fuck do you expect me to do? We've been chasing our own shadows for the last few weeks.'

By now they had left the motorway. The traffic grew heavier as the road narrowed and they approached London. The sun was up and the snow was disappearing quickly. The tarmac glistened. Brown slush was heaped in gutters. Pedestrians trudged to work in a variety of outlandish boots.

'Any sign of Koslove?' Blaines said.

'He phoned Rosie yesterday, asking where you were. He wants to see you urgently. So does Wreningham.'

'Everything's urgent with them. If Koslove contacts you, tell him the minimum you can get away with. I don't want an open breach, not yet.'

'A breach? I don't understand.'

Blaines sniffed, intimating that it wasn't Liam's job to try to understand. 'What does Willy want?'

'I don't know,' Liam said stiffly. 'He saw Osroyan on Tuesday afternoon.'

'I've got some jobs for you today. You and little Jessie.' Blaines dug him in the ribs. 'You'll enjoy that, eh?'

'Talking of Jessica,' Liam said, 'there may be a problem with Jedborough. They had a row on Sunday and–'

'She shouldn't have seen him at all. What the hell's she playing at?'

'It's just as well she did. Jedborough thinks he's on to something. He's linked her with Vanderman and the Sandridges; he knows about you and he's heard something about the blackmail; he even mentioned Monastow's death.'

'Don't tell me. Establishment cover-up conspiracy. Corruption in the highest places. Socialist democracy under threat. Intrepid boy-reporter reveals all. Jesus Christ. Don't they ever grow up?'

The bitterness in Blaines's voice surprised Liam.

'In a way you can't blame him,' he said mildly. 'Not for that. He's only doing his job.'

Blaines was overtaken by a fit of coughing. When it was over he said: 'Has he got anything concrete?'

'Not as far as we know.'

'I'll talk to Hebburn about him. What with Osroyan and Jedborough, we're running out of time. Maybe you'd better make the bookings for this evening.'

'What bookings?'

Blaines chuckled, his good humour mysteriously restored. 'We're going to Italy. Didn't I tell you?'

'Show her in,' Aughrim told the intercom on his desk.

He swallowed the rest of his coffee and stood up. He smiled at his reflection in the mirror. He looked a good ten years younger than he was. Some women preferred older men. He smoothed a wrinkle from his Trinity tie. A position of authority, he had read somewhere, had the side-effect of increasing a man's sex appeal. Success in one field bred success in another.

Emma Lazonby came into the room with a rustle of silk. He liked a woman who took trouble with her appearance. Caragh was luckier than he deserved. Aughrim ushered her to one of the armchairs by the fire.

'How was London?' he asked. 'You got back this morning?'

She nodded. 'I'm sorry to burst in like this.'

'Not at all.' Aughrim tried the smile on her. 'If I'd known, we could have had lunch together. You saw Caragh, of course?'

The red hair swung like a curtain across her face. Aughrim would have liked to stroke it.

'That's what I wanted to talk to you about.' Her voice was muffled. 'It's . . . it's not just a personal problem.'

Aughrim frowned. 'What do you mean, my dear? Have you quarrelled?'

'He's got someone else, Terry.' It was the first time she had used his Christian name. 'She's a journalist. An English journalist.'

'Are you sure? Is this serious?'

'I'm afraid it is.' She glanced at him; he could see that her eyes were filled with tears. 'She turned up at Liam's flat just after I got there. He made it quite clear where I stood. So did she.'

The tears spilled over. The next few seconds were confused. When Aughrim came to his senses he found that he was kneeling beside Emma's chair with his arm around her shoulders; she was wiping her eyes with the handkerchief from his breast-pocket while he murmured comforting monosyllables into her hair; he wondered whether it was touching her or the sight of the tears that was arousing him sexually.

He pulled away but left his arm around her shoulders. 'He's behaved appallingly. John Fitzpatrick mentioned something the other day but I had no idea that it was like this. The man's a fool. It's the only explanation.'

'Terry, he pretended she was a colleague of his. It was obvious that she knew what he does. God knows how much he's told her. That's why I had to see you.'

'You did quite right.' Aughrim stroked her hair absent-mindedly; she did not seem to find this distasteful – indeed she moved a fraction closer to him. 'There might be a security angle to this. Unlike Caragh, we can't afford to take chances. No wonder he's lying low.'

'What do you mean?' Emma said sharply.

'I gather some hospital was trying to reach him just after lunch. Something about his mother. Eventually they got through to us. My secretary tried to contact him on their behalf. But he wasn't at the department or his flat. Apparently the British were most unhelpful. The embassy hasn't seen him for days.'

'His mother? What's happened to her?'

Trust a woman to seize on the one inessential, Aughrim thought tolerantly. 'She's had a relapse or something,' he said. 'Or was it a chest infection? Anyway, they think she's dying.'

The cemetery was still sprinkled with patches of frozen snow.

The sky had clouded over during the morning. By now it was a dark, uniform grey, heavy with the promise of more snow. The temperature had dropped and there was enough wind to make it seem even colder than it was.

Jessica held on to Liam's arm as they walked along the gravel path. The memory of her father's funeral refused to leave her alone. It would have been easier to bear if the graves showed signs of being cared for. The dead were forgotten. Death had regained its sting.

They were almost alone at the cemetery. They passed an elderly black woman kneeling bare-legged on the ground; she was feeding gaily-coloured plastic flowers into a concrete vase. She did not look up as they passed.

'It should be somewhere round here,' Liam said, glancing down at her. 'Are you okay?'

She nodded, not trusting herself to speak.

His grip tightened on her arm. 'When this is over, we'll go somewhere warm. Everything will be different, I promise.'

'Everything?'

'Everything that matters.'

She wanted to say, 'Stay with me tonight'; but the words refused to come. She had a premonition that they would never make love – that one of them would

311

die. In this place death was the only certainty.

They took a side-path and began to study the inscriptions. Many of them were obscured by weeds or erosion. They had to push aside or pull up clumps of grass. Soon their gloves were soaked. Jessica felt her hands would never get warm again.

Then she saw the name. It was at the top of a small stone marker. The base of the stone was surrounded by a mass of rotting leaves from the elder tree which had sprouted beside the grave. If the leaves had drifted much higher the marker would have been entirely covered.

'You found it?' Liam said.

She had said nothing and he was several yards away. She had noticed before that they sometimes seemed able to communicate without words; perhaps a change in her posture had alerted him.

'Well, thank God for that.' He grinned at her and kicked aside the leaves. 'Typical Blaines. If you ask me this is completely unnecessary.'

The leaves slithered away, exposing the whole inscription. *John Adam Quendale. 28 June - 10 September 1933. Not dead. Only sleeping.*

Liam stripped off his sodden gloves and focused the camera with difficulty. He took three shots.

Jessica bit her lip.

He lowered the camera. 'What's up?'

She nodded at the gravestone. 'I was thinking of the parents.'

'Who was it?' Greg said.

He was washing up after an early lunch. The telephone had rung just as he was wondering how to tell his mother that he was going down to the pub on the main road. The problem was finding the right form of words; it had to sound casual; and the phrasing should suggest that there was no significant difference in his mind between going and not going.

'It was Eric.' Patricia automatically picked up a plate and began to dry it. 'He wants us to go to Italy this evening. All of us except Koslove. The only other thing is that Koslove isn't to know.'

'Why?'

'He wouldn't say.'

Greg rinsed a handful of cutlery. 'He's not exactly one of the world's great communicators.' His voice was bitter; he didn't want to be dragged away from Halcome again; the more he thought about it, the angrier he became. 'He never lets any of us see the whole picture,' he burst out. 'He's the only one who's allowed to know what's really happening. Why Italy? Where in Italy? Why all of us?'

His mother shrugged.

'He wouldn't say,' Greg went on, aware that he was sounding petulant. 'Of course he wouldn't. Who does he think he is?'

Patricia examined the cutlery and returned a fork to the washing-up bowl. 'Will you go into Cheltenham for me this afternoon?'

'Sure.' He could drive down to the pub and go on from there. 'What do you want?'

'Several things. There's some dry-cleaning to collect. And you could get some food for the freezer – God knows when we'll be back. I'll give you a list. We're to be at Heathrow by six-thirty. Liam's getting the tickets.'

Greg attacked a saucepan with a scourer. Liam was another of Blaines's victims. Greg forced his mind on to another level: why did he dislike Blaines so much? He had never attempted to manipulate Greg in the way he did other people.

'Don't use the scourer,' his mother said. 'That's a non-stick pan. There's something you'd better know. Maybe I should have told you before. Eric Blaines is your father.'

It had happened long before she met Charles Claybrook.

She had been barely out of her teens. Her marriage to Warren was a little more than a year old. It had been clear to her from the first month that by marrying Vanderman she had merely exchanged one form of domestic tyranny for another. At least Vanderman's tyranny, unlike her father's, was interrupted by his business trips; he was away from home so much that it was hardly like being married at all.

Nevertheless her life was circumscribed. In a moment of openness she had told Vanderman about her desire to be a photographer. He had taken it as a slur on himself; no wife of his should have to work; Patricia insulted him by wanting a job. It had led to their first overt quarrel, which culminated in him smashing her cameras. He opened them one by one, laid them on the tiled floor of the kitchen and stamped on them. It was the first time she had seen what anger could do to him. She still dreamed of that incident more than thirty years afterwards.

She never dreamed of making love with him. The sexual side of their marriage was better forgotten. Warren was a forceful lover – he was forceful in almost everything he did – but he was neither skilful nor unselfish. In the first few weeks at least he showed a sort of rough passion when he came to her. Later they made love less frequently and their coupling became mechanical. Patricia thought of it as a necessary evil like going to the dentist.

There was nothing to do. The servants took care of the housework, even if she had wanted to do it. In the eyes of the world she was a wealthy woman but her ability to spend money was severely hampered by Warren's insistence that all the bills came through him. She came to dread those monthly sessions when he did the household accounts; he discussed every penny she had spent and produced the bills as a prosecuting counsel produces evidence.

Ironically enough it was Warren who encouraged her to go to parties. It pleased him to see his wife's name in the gossip columns, providing that no malicious comments were made about her. It was useful that she should know the wives of the men with whom he did business. And of course a beautiful wife was a wonderful advertisement for a successful but still ambitious businessman.

They were well placed. In those years the British and the Americans were almost as close as they had been during the war. Through the Youlgreaves Patricia had a wide range of contacts – the sort of contacts of whom Warren approved. She moved in the embassy crowd, which naturally overlapped with the Foreign Office on one side and the business world on the other. There were many parties.

And what do you do at parties except drink and flirt? Of the two, Patricia found flirting much more exciting if

315

only because the results were less predictable. Besides, it annoyed Warren more. There was even some consolation in the knowledge that other men found her desirable.

There were affairs. These were like flirtations but even more exciting because of the risks involved. Most were short; and some were more discreet than others.

Wilbur Cunningham was one of the embassy crowd. Everyone was supposed not to know what he did. Occasionally he threw a party. At one of them Patricia met Eric Blaines.

To give him his due, Eric was different. At that time it was not yet fashionable to be working-class. Everyone else she knew was pretending to be a gentleman; Eric made no bones about being a slob – indeed he seemed to revel in it. He had no pretensions and very few manners. He was fat, ungainly and usually rude to people he didn't like; the majority of the human race fell into this category.

After that party he contrived to take her home. He did not attempt to touch her in the taxi.

Instead he said: 'I want to go to bed with you. I think I'm in love with you.'

And she laughed at him and told him not to be so stupid.

He wore down her resistance over the next two months. He was patient with her and ruthless with his rivals. Once she asked him why he was wasting so much time and effort.

'Don't ask me. D'you think I'd be doing this if I could help it?'

One Saturday a group of them drove out to a hotel in

Buckingham. It was a dinner-dance in aid of a charity. Patricia drank far more than she usually did, partly because she was hot and partly because Warren was threatening to send her to a clinic if she went on the way she was going.

She avoided going down to supper with the rest of their party. She went out on to the balcony and tried to persuade herself that it was fun to be alone.

Eric came after her. 'You're as pissed as a newt. Why don't you go home?'

'We'll have to wait till Stephen's ready. It's his car.'

'Sod that. Come on.'

He took her arm and steered her through the ballroom and down the stairs. While she collected her coat from the cloakroom he bribed the car-park attendant to fetch the car.

She found a flask of brandy in the glove compartment. They shared the contents on the way to London. On the journey she amused herself by stroking the back of his neck. She could feel him shivering. It gave her a sense of mastery which she was drunk enough to enjoy. Sexually these affairs were usually disappointing. The real thrill lay in the power they gave her. All her life it seemed that she had lived under the dominion of men: first her father, then Warren; the reversal of roles intoxicated her, however brief and incomplete it was.

Eric was driving appallingly either because he was drunk or because she was touching him. At Hyde Park Corner he nearly rammed a taxi. He pulled up outside the block of flats with a jerk that flung her towards the windscreen.

'You're a bloody cock-teaser, you know that?'

The anger in his voice did not conceal the misery behind it. She was not drunk enough to have smothered her conscience.

'Do you want to come up for a nightcap?' she said as though he hadn't spoken. 'Warren's away.'

'I don't want a nightcap.'

'I don't want a nightcap either.'

The words were out before she knew what she was going to say. She patted his leg absent-mindedly and thought, *why not*? What did one more matter? Eric was no more unattractive than some of the others. She felt sorry for his ugliness and above all for the hopelessness of his desire. At least he paid her the compliment of caring.

He swallowed noisily. 'You mean that? Really?'

'Come on.' She opened the car door. 'I'll show you what I do mean.'

Afterwards she told Eric that it wouldn't work and that she didn't want to see him again.

Ten weeks later she discovered that she was pregnant. It was good news because it gave her something to think about. Having a baby was a novel way of occupying her time. She didn't tell Eric – there was no point; it wasn't as though she wanted to marry him; she had never loved him and now she didn't even like him. Besides, Warren was statistically likely to be the father.

But someone must have told Eric. After Greg was born he came to see her in the nursing home. He stood at the foot of the bed, looking down at the red-faced bundle in the crib.

'He's mine, isn't he? Why didn't you tell me?'

'Go away, Eric,' she said sleepily. 'If he's anybody's, he's mine.'

*

Jack needed to get the woman on her own.

There were obvious psychological and physical advantages to having Greg Vanderman out of the way. Jack had no wish to repeat the humiliation of their first meeting; and he doubted if Greg could tell him anything useful even if he could be persuaded to talk.

The old woman, on the other hand, could be the key to the whole business, though probably she didn't know it. She was the point where all the lines of approach intersected. She was the mother of Jessica and Greg. Vanderman was her former husband. Her second husband was a colleague of Blaines. Sandridge was her brother-in-law.

He had considered bringing a friend with him, partly as a witness and partly as a safeguard against Greg. In the end he decided against it: this was his story and no one else's.

On Thursday morning he drove down to Halcombe in the elderly Ford Capri he had traded for his motorbike. A red Datsun was parked outside the Claybrooks' house. A sticker in the rear window identified it as a hire car. Jack guessed it was Greg's.

He spent the next two hours patrolling the neighbourhood. He had a couple of pints and a sandwich in a pub on the main road. Just before two o'clock his caution was rewarded.

Greg came out of the house and drove noisily away in the Datsun. He looked flushed and angry. Maybe he and his mother had been quarrelling. With luck that could make her emotionally vulnerable.

Jack rang the doorbell.

'Yes?'

319

'Mrs Claybrook?' He recognized her face at once from photographs that Jessica had. 'I'm Jack Jedborough.'

The door began to close. He put his foot in the narrowing gap between it and the jamb.

'I'd like to talk to you, Mrs Claybrook.'

'There's no point. Will you take your foot away? Jessica tells me –'

'This isn't about Jess.'

'If you don't go away I shall call the police.'

'I don't think you'll do that. I might tell them why I'm here. About Colonel Blaines and Tom Sandridge. About Warren Vanderman. And of course about your husband.'

'What an earth are you talking about?'

'Ask me in and I'll tell you. If you don't, you can read about it in the papers in the next few days.'

Patricia Claybrook opened the door. 'You can come in if you want to. I see my daughter made a wise decision.'

Jack shrugged. 'I'd say she made a foolish one.' He glanced round the little hall. 'Aren't you going to ask me to sit down? After all, I might have been your son-in-law.'

'I can't stop you sitting down.'

He wandered into the sitting room, draped his scarf over the back of a chair and sat down. She remained on her feet by the door. Her calm surprised him. He had expected anger or fear but not this controlled hostility.

'Well, Mr Jedborough?'

'Jack, please. Don't stand on ceremony, Mrs Claybrook.' He hesitated, realizing at the last moment that a change of tactics would be useful. 'Look, I'm sorry to barge in like this. Believe it or not I want to help you – and help myself at the same time.'

'I don't see how that could be possible.'

'Let's stop playing games. You didn't want to call the police and I know why.'

She said nothing.

'You're involved in a cover-up,' Jack went on. 'So are several influential people. Even Jess has been dragged in. One man's died already. My guess is that it's connected with an MoD contract to refurbish some surface-to-air missiles back in 1972.'

'You're talking nonsense, Mr Jedborough.'

Jack sighed. 'Wish I was.'

'Do you have any evidence?'

'Some. I'd like more but it's not essential. You see, Mrs Claybrook it's not a question of *whether* this story will break. You can't stop that. The only question is how.'

She took a step towards him. 'I don't follow you.'

'If necessary I'll find a continental newspaper.' Jack smiled at her. 'I realize I don't have all the details but that doesn't matter too much. Once someone starts asking questions, everyone else will. Sooner or later the answers tumble out. Set a rumour going and in the end it flushes out the truth. There's always a way if you look hard enough.'

'Then why have you bothered to come here? Just for the pleasure of pestering me?'

'Because I'd rather do it another way. This is my story and I'd like it to stay like that.'

'You feel possessive about it?'

He nodded. He was allowing her to ask too many questions. 'I'm offering you a deal, Mrs Claybrook. I want to get chapter and verse on this and I think you can help me. In return I promise I'd keep the Claybrooks out of it. All of you – your husband, Jess, even Greg.'

She twisted the wedding-ring on her finger.

'I don't want to involve you,' he continued. 'You're the minnows; I want the sharks. You do see that?'

'Oh yes. I understand that perfectly.'

Mrs Claybrook came nearer and picked up the poker. Jack tensed himself. For an instant he feared she was going to be stupid. Instead she poked the fire vigorously. A shower of sparks swept up the chimney.

'You're very sure of yourself,' she said.

He grinned at her. 'You didn't ring the police. Have we got a deal?'

She stood the poker on the hearth. It slipped on the tiles and fell with a crash. Both of them ignored it.

'I need time to think it over,' she said.

Jack sensed that victory was almost within his grasp. 'We don't have much time.'

'Just a few hours.'

'Don't try anything stupid. Remember Nell and What-sisname. You know, your grandson.'

'What do you mean?'

'They'll be very vulnerable if you try to double-cross me.' He paused to give her time to realize that they were very vulnerable whatever happened. 'I tell you what: I'll give you till this evening to decide. Seven o'clock.'

'Okay. How will I let you know?'

'Will Greg be around?'

She nodded.

'Then I'll phone you. Not a word to anyone, including him. Remember Nell.'

He left the house. The Capri was parked in a side-street fifty yards away. He had not wanted to advertise the fact that he was visiting her. He had just reached the car when he heard his name. His good humour vanished when he realized that she had followed him.

'Here.' She held out his scarf. 'It was on the chair.'

He thanked her ungraciously. She left without another word. Jack walked on to the pub on the main road; he needed some cigarettes.

Inside, the first thing he saw was the profile of Greg Vanderman. Jack ducked out of the bar. There was no point in hanging around Halcombe: it was too risky. He might as well drive back to London.

He had moved into Sally's house in Battersea on Sunday. Jessica wanted him out of Holland Park and at present he hadn't time to fight her; probably she had come back on the Sunday evening with a posse of heavies and a new lock. Maybe he would change her mind once this was all over. Or maybe the bitch didn't deserve it. Damn Jessica. He didn't want to think about her.

Living at Sally's had one big advantage: no one knew where he was. Sally herself was the one big drawback. She had convinced herself that she had stolen him from Jessica. She failed to understand that he was nobody's property. Other people's guilt was always boring. Sally luxuriated in it and wanted Jack to join her.

He drove down to the motorway, observing speed limits and being uncharacteristically courteous to other drivers. The Capri was neither taxed nor insured.

As the miles passed his mood improved. He sensed that he was on the verge of cracking this story. Its political effect would be considerable; and there would be an agreeable bonus for him personally – if everything went well, a scoop of this magnitude could set him up for life.

He was reasonably confident that Patricia Claybrook would cooperate. Her unwillingness to call the police was a step in the right direction; it showed how vulnerable she had already become. If she tried to stall him, he would have to use Nell Dallow and her son to put the pressure on her; Jack had already found the husband in *Crockford's Clerical Directory* and made a note of their address in Reading.

Reading, it occurred to him, was almost on his way. It might be worth making a diversion and finding out where the Dallow's vicarage was. He would prefer not to have to hurt them; but sometimes little preferences like that were luxuries you couldn't afford.

You could always get to a woman through her family. As a sex they found it difficult to grasp the larger issues. Whether or not he would be able to keep his side of the bargain with Mrs Claybrook was another matter. He wasn't sure if he wanted to. The Claybrooks would make good copy and Jessica was too photogenic to be wasted. In any case he owed her something for what she had done to him on Sunday.

By the time he reached the motorway the desire for a cigarette was becoming insistent. A few miles east of Swindon he turned into a service station.

The car-park wasn't crowded. The sky was heavy with clouds; it looked like more snow was on the way. Jack ran across to the main building. He brought some cigarettes and had a cup of coffee in the cafeteria. For once everything was going right. He was humming 'Over the Rainbow' as he returned to the car. Jessica had told him that he always hummed 'Over the Rainbow' when he was feeling cheerful. Damn Jessica.

In his absence a black Opel Manta had drawn up beside the Capri. He had a fleeting glimpse of a man in the driver's seat, his head bent over something on his lap.

Jack unlocked the door of the Capri. As he opened the door he heard the man getting out of the Opel behind him. Jack slid into the car and reached for the door. As he did so he realized that the man was in the way. All he could see of him was a thick, charcoal-grey overcoat. It irritated Jack: couldn't the man look where he was going?

'Jack Jedborough?'

He turned his head. 'What?'

Then all he had left was a series of impressions. Each one was distinct like a still photograph but they changed from one to the next with bewildering speed. A hand in a black leather glove. A small gun in the hand – a .22 pistol? The distant sound of laughter and revving engines. A cloud that was the same colour as the man's overcoat. A crow with ragged feathers perched on a litter-bin. The forefinger tightening on the trigger.

He never heard the shot itself.

10

'My father believed in education in the broadest possible sense,' Mrs Eskworthy said. 'Our curriculum does not concern itself solely with the single-minded pursuit of narrow academic qualifications. We have a wider mission.'

'My daughter's not particularly academic,' Jessica said.

Mrs Eskworthy looked relieved. 'We encourage the study of Italian, of course. Our prime objective, however, is to teach our girls to appreciate their environment. We are situated in one of the cultural capitals of the world. Regular outings to museums, concerts, art galleries and so forth take place every week. We have a large pool of visiting lecturers to supplement our resident staff.'

'How interesting,' Jessica said weakly.

'Nor do we neglect more practical subjects. Our girls receive a solid grounding in English, French, German, maths, the sciences and of course domestic economy.' Mrs Eskworthy paused briefly. She was a large-boned, elegant woman in her forties. Her eyes were disconcertingly shrewd. 'Finally we encourage self-expression. We are particularly proud of our art department.'

Jessica allowed her eyes to wander round the room. Part sitting room, part office, it was decorated in shades of pale green: the curtains were half-drawn, which helped to soften the outlines of the furniture. Jessica felt as though she were immersed in an over-furnished aquarium.

The room was dominated by an oil painting which hung over the marble fireplace. It was a portrait of a stout, middle-aged man in a chair; he wore a broad-brimmed straw hat and an immense bow tie; on his lap was a Persian cat.

Mrs Eskworthy followed the direction of her glance. 'My late father. He and my mother founded the Scuola Pencombe in 1929. I like to think we have changed with the times while remaining true to his philosophy. Education, he used to say, is not so much a matter of instruction as osmosis.'

No doubt the educators found it a convenient philosophy since the onus was on the students and the results were difficult to quantify. Jessica found it difficult to concentrate on the professional credo of the late Mr Pencombe. It was time to get down to details. Time was slipping away. The very English grandfather clock by the door had a soft, relentless tick, measuring the minutes that Mrs Eskworthy filled with quotations from her own prospectus. What had Blaines said on the flight last night? 'We haven't time to make sure. If we had time we wouldn't be here. If we had time we'd find a better way to flush him out.'

'Then do you have a vacancy for next term?' Jessica interrupted.

Mrs Eskworthy paused in mid-flow. She responded smoothly to the change of subject. 'I think we might be able to fit her in. How old did you say Nell was? Twelve?'

Jessica nodded.

'In that case we could manage it.' Mrs Eskworthy opened the prospectus and showed Jessica a photograph of a small room. 'The students share study-bedrooms in couples. We like to match the ages and if possible the nationalities. Nell could go in with Dawn Foster. She's Canadian; coming up to thirteen if I remember rightly . . .'

A fleet of mopeds passed up the road on the other side of the big window in the principal's office. The whine of their engines made it impossible to hear what Mrs Eskworthy was saying.

'. . . Such a sweet girl.' Mrs Eskworthy seemed unconscious of the interruption. 'Perhaps you would like to meet her?'

Jessica said she would love to. She hoped she did not sound too enthusiastic. 'In fact, it would be very helpful if I could look round and talk to some of your students. Just to get a feel of the place.'

'Naturally. I'll show you round myself.' Mrs Eskworthy glanced at the application form that Jessica had completed in the secretary's office half an hour earlier. 'We're particularly proud of our new indoor games room for senior students,' she added absently. 'How long did you say you'll be in Tunis?'

'It's a two-year contract initially but it may be renewed. My husband's a structural engineer, you see. He's working on a new tourist complex.'

'I see. Most of our girls stay with us until they are about eighteen. My father used to say that they needed at least five years to extract the maximum benefit from what we have to offer.' Mrs Eskworthy hesitated and

329

changed tack. 'So many of their parents lead peripatetic lives. The Scuola Pencombe gives the girls the emotional stability of a home from home.'

'That's one reason why we're looking at schools – to give Nell some sort of continuity of background. My husband's work takes him all over the world.'

'We pride ourselves on being able to cope with that situation.' The phone on the desk began to ring. Mrs Eskworthy rose. 'Would you excuse me?'

Jessica looked at the late Mr Pencombe while Mrs Eskworthy answered the phone. He had unusually fleshy lips. She wondered if he had founded a girls' school in Florence solely for financial and educational reasons. You could imagine a leer on that face.

She eavesdropped on Mrs Eskworthy's side of the conversation. 'Again? Have you phoned for a doctor? . . . In two minutes . . . What did the girl say? I see. Wait for me.'

Mrs Eskworthy put down the phone and turned back to Jessica. 'A small domestic crisis, I'm afraid. I'll take you along to the staff room.' She picked up a timetable and scanned it quickly. 'Anthony Pinner-Jones is free – he'll show you round. A charming man – teaches the history of art.'

Still talking, she swept Jessica out of the room and down a corridor that ran the length of the first floor. The staff room was a cramped and ill-proportioned box; the plastic upholstery of the armchairs and the scuffed metal lockers contrasted with the relative luxury of Mrs Eskworthy's office.

A plump young man was standing by the open window, trying to conceal the fact that he was holding a lighted cigarette. He had a pointed chin; round, gold-rimmed glasses; and coarse, springy hair.

A frown travelled rapidly across Mrs Eskworthy's face but she decided to ignore the cigarette for the time being. She introduced Jessica and asked if Pinner-Jones could spare the time to show her round the school; the sarcasm in her voice was obvious even to Jessica.

When they were alone, Pinner-Jones caught Jessica's eye and gave her a rueful smile. 'Wonderful woman,' he said. He sucked hungrily on his cigarette and threw it out of the window. 'She runs a very tight ship.'

He chatted easily as he showed her round the school. The building, she gathered, had once been a hotel. At present there were fifty students, mainly English and American but with a sprinkling of other nationalities. Mrs Eskworthy wanted to expand the numbers but this would involve moving to another building; the present site was conveniently central but there was no room to extend the accommodation.

Anthony Pinner-Jones was a groper by nature; only the circumstances of their meeting restrained him from being offensive. His arm brushed Jessica's shoulder as he held open the library door for her. He stood as close as possible to her in the lift that took them up to inspect the study bedrooms. He ushered her into a classroom with a hand placed lightly on the small of her back.

Jessica was introduced to Dawn Foster, a small, freckled child in blue dungarees. But the presence of Pinner-Jones made it impossible for Jessica to question her about Susan Quendale.

When the tour was over Pinner-Jones strolled back with her to the secretary's office.

'I hear you have a lot of cultural excursions,' Jessica said.

'We thrive on them,' Pinner-Jones said cheerfully. 'Bit of a nightmare between you and me. The younger girls get bored and the older ones try and slip off when you're not looking; whatever old Pencombe used to say they're far more interested in boys and shops than renaissance art.' He grinned and nudged her arm. 'Can't say I blame them.' He glanced at Jessica and realized that he might be making a tactical error by being so frank to the mother of a prospective student. 'Don't get me wrong, the kids love it, really. We're careful not to overload them with high art. Plenty of ice-creams in between. I'm taking the juniors to the Baptistery of San Giovanni tomorrow afternoon – you can come and see for yourself.'

Jessica said that she might take him up on that.

'Perhaps we could have coffee together afterwards?' Pinner-Jones suggested. 'What – er – what made you choose the Scuola Pencombe?'

She seized gratefully on the opportunity. 'A business acquaintance of my husband mentioned it. I think his daughter is here, or used to be. Her name's Susan Quendale.'

'Susie?' Pinner-Jones added in a voice that had suddenly become cautious. 'Nice child. Do you know her father well?'

Jessica shook her head. 'I've never met him.'

'He keeps sending her most unsuitable presents. A video. Jewellery, even. Ridiculous for a girl of that age and it causes a lot of jealousy.'

'Among the other girls?'

Pinner-Jones nodded. 'Some of them call her the

Yellow Peril, but that's mainly because of her face.'

Jessica looked blankly at him. 'Why?'

'Didn't you know? No reason why you should, I suppose, if Mr Quendale didn't mention it. Susie's mother was Chinese.'

The villa stood at the head of a narrow valley with terraced sides, a few miles north of Prato. The house was built of whitewashed concrete that the weather had stained with patches of beige. It sat on the ridge of the hill in much the same way as Noah's Ark sat on Ararat.

'It was built nearly twenty years ago,' the agent told Liam, as if that explained any incongruity. 'A magnificent setting.'

He changed gear and swung the Lancia into a narrow drive. It wound bumpily upwards through a dense plantation of damp conifers. The house was hidden. The sky was grey with rain and the trees tried to make a green tunnel around the car.

'The owner is German,' the agent went on. 'He planned to retire here but he changed his mind after six months. So he lets it out instead. People come here for their vacations, over and over again. Also we have businessmen.' He remembered Patricia Claybrook in the back of the car and added, 'And business women too. It is very popular for conferences.'

The drive widened and became a gravelled forecourt enclosed by the two arms of the L-shaped house. The building consisted of three linked cubes, each on a different level. The design was bastard Bauhaus at its least appealing.

'You see?' The agent gestured through the mud-streaked windscreen. 'On a clear day you can see Prato.'

The three of them got out of the car. The agent put up an umbrella and gallantly tried to shelter Mrs Claybrook. She was several inches taller than he was; and he was further hampered by his efforts to extract the keys from his trouser-pocket.

The front door was solid hardwood and the damp had warped it in its frame. The agent struggled ineffectually to open it while holding the umbrella at the same time. In the end Liam took the umbrella. The agent abandoned finesse and forced the door open with his shoulder.

The air inside was cooler and danker than outside; moreover it smelled of very old cheese.

'You cannot imagine,' the agent said with perfect truth, 'how welcoming it is when the central heating is on.'

Blaines wondered idly if he was having a nervous breakdown.

People were always having them these days. They tended to be vague about the symptoms so it was possible that he was in the middle of one without knowing it. It was almost a relief to worry about nervous breakdowns. Compared with the other fears in his mind, a mere breakdown was almost something to be welcomed.

He spent most of the morning in his room at the Majestic. The five of them were distributed among three hotels near the railway station. Last night Patricia Claybrook slept in the room next to his; but for all the use that was she might as well have been in Peking.

During the morning he made several phone calls to England. They made matters worse. He did not have the

334

temperament of a gambler. Recently he had been tempted to let everything slide; to let them sort out their own mess for themselves; and to let retirement devour him sooner rather than later. What did it matter if he drank himself to death a little earlier than intended? He was tired of being a rock of certainty in other people's lives.

Just before lunchtime there was a tap on his door. Greg came into the room. Blaines eyed him warily.

'You got the cars?'

Greg nodded. 'A Fiat and Mercedes. They're in the hotel car park.'

Blaines looked sharply at him, alerted by a tone of voice that might have been his own. 'What's up with you?'

'Everything. Jesus, you can't even prove that Ryal's involved.'

'Proof's a luxury we can't afford.'

'Even if he is, how d'you know he'll bite?'

'According to the amah, Quendale's a doting father. We haven't had a glimpse of any other weakness.'

'And that's not the only thing,' Greg went on. 'This whole plan. It's not just risky, it's immoral. And you've dragged in my mother and my sister.'

'There's no other way to do it, not in the time we have. If you didn't want to get muck on your hands you should have stayed at home.' Blaines hesitated for a second. 'And talking of muck I phoned a man in London just now. Jedborough's dead. Did you kill him?'

Greg sat down in the armchair opposite Blaines. 'Of course I didn't.'

'There's no "of course" about it. Someone caught up with him on his way back to London yesterday afternoon. In the car park of the Membury service station on the M4. They put a .22 bullet in his head.'

There was a moment's silence. Blaines remembered the disapproval in Hebburn's voice as he reported the murder. Did he sound more disapproving than usual? Did he suspect that Blaines already knew that Jedborough was dead?

'I left the house before he came,' Greg said in a rush. 'I spent an hour in a pub in Halcombe; they'd probably remember me. Then I went to Cheltenham. I got back about four.'

'So probably you're in the clear. If the alibi holds up.'

'It's the truth.'

'Is it?' Blaines said.

'My mother called you after Jedborough left?'

Blaines grunted.

'So you could have done it. You had as much of a motive as I did. More, maybe. Jedborough could have wrecked everything.'

'You're right,' Blaines said. 'Only snag is, I spent most of the afternoon with Willy Wreningham. I was on my way to his office when your mother's call came through.'

'So? You got someone else to do it.'

'How did I trace him then?'

'God knows.' Greg lit a cigarette. 'Don't ask me. You're the expert. Maybe you put a tail on him after he had that row with Jess.'

'Motives.' Blaines yawned. 'You can give almost anyone a motive. Koslove, Osroyan, Wreningham. Even Ryal. Or Ryal's principal.'

'But how could Ryal hear about Jedborough?'

'I don't know. But he's got good sources, or at least his principal has. We do know that.'

Blaines looked ostentatiously at his watch, hoping that Greg would take the hint. The boy's company made him uncomfortable. But he wasn't a boy. He was a thirty-year-old mistake made flesh.

Greg stretched out his legs. 'There's something else.'

'Well, spit it out,' Blaines said. 'I haven't got all day.'

'Okay. Did my mother tell you?'

'Don't piss around.' Blaines felt a trickle of sweat working its way down the back of his neck. 'Tell me what?'

'That she told me you're my father.'

The words were out. Blaines wished they had remained unsaid for ever.

'You believe that?' he said brusquely.

'Oh, come on. She thinks you are. She said you believed it once. I even look like you. What more do you want? Blood tests or something?'

Blaines shrugged.

'I don't want anything from you,' Greg continued. 'Don't worry. I just wanted to get the facts straight. It won't change anything.'

Blaines levered himself up. 'Don't be a fool. I'm going to have some lunch. You coming?'

'It's funny,' Blaines said, 'how the past can give you a kick in the arse.'

Patricia Claybrook smiled at him across the restaurant table. 'Not unlike the Blacklist. Worried?'

'Yes.'

They were dining at the Lume di Candela in the Via delle Terme. The food was supposed to be excellent, according to the barman at the Majestic who had recommended the place to Blaines. Personally he thought it too fancy for his taste but it didn't really matter; for once his appetite had deserted him.

'Greg can take care of himself,' she said.

'He drinks too much.'

'So do you.'

'It's not the same. You know that.'

Patricia rubbed a piece of bread into a pellet. 'You never stop worrying about children. It doesn't matter how old they get. Or how old you get.' She dropped the pellet on her plate. 'Sometimes I think they're the only thing that's really important.'

'Not for me. It's too late to learn how to be a father. Anyway, Greg doesn't want one.'

'I don't think it's something you learn.'

She swallowed another mouthful of chicken. Blaines threw down his fork and wished he could smoke. He topped up their glasses instead.

'He wants to be a gardener,' Patricia said. 'Maybe in England.'

'Nothing's stopping him. He's got the Trust money to live on.'

'He's talking about making over his income to Nell. He wanted to give it to me but I wouldn't let him. But Nell's another matter. It could mean all the difference for Matthew.'

'Bloody fool,' Blaines muttered.

'You don't mean that, do you?'

Unwillingly Blaines shook his head.

'You'll just have to accept it, Eric.'

Blaines stared into his glass. As a young man he had built a career on the assumption that he could control

338

events. As an old man he knew that events were controlling him. Events had moulded him into a selfish, self-sufficient bachelor; he was quite content with that. Now they were trying to modify the design. He told himself without conviction that he was too old to change.

'Something I didn't tell the others,' he said. 'I talked to Rosie on the phone this morning. Aughrim's been trying to get in touch with Caragh. He wants him back in Dublin.'

'Trouble? That Lazonby woman?'

'That may be part of the reason. But there's something else: his mother's dead.'

The girls flooded out of the Baptistery like a swarm of butterflies.

For an instant it seemed to Liam that the Piazza San Giovanni was seething with brightly coloured females on the fringes of puberty. Beside their vitality, the Baptistery with its marbled façade, its cupola and its bronze doors was inert and unappealing. The nearer pigeons scrambled to escape, transmitting their panic to their neighbours.

There were perhaps twenty girls, ranging in age from ten to fourteen. Two adults brought up the rear of the party. One was a tubby man, presumably Pinner-Jones; the other was a pale young woman with lank fair hair trailing over the collar of her coat.

The children had half an hour of relative freedom. According to Pinner-Jones, they were protected by a host of regulations: they had to remain in groups of at least three; they were allowed only in certain shops and cafés; and there were severe penalties for being late back.

The girl with a Chinese face was one of the last to emerge. Susan Quendale was small for her age. Her features were still blurred by the chubbiness of childhood. She was wearing blue jeans and a quilted jacket.

She tagged on to a foursome which veered away from the Duomo. They passed quite close to Liam. An animated conversation was in progress. He caught the words 'café' and 'Pepsi'.

He followed them into the Via dei Martelli. The square bulk of the Palazzo Medici-Riccardi lay ahead, on the corner of the Via Cavour. Patricia Claybrook turned away from the shop window and fell into step behind them. If she was nervous, she showed no trace of it.

The party swung into a café. Mrs Claybrook darted forward. Liam increased his pace so that he was a few yards behind them.

Patricia touched Susan Quendale's arm. 'Susan?' he heard her say. The other girls were already in the café. 'Mr Pinner-Jones wants you. At once.'

'Why?'

The girl's face gave nothing away.

'He has a message for you. From Mrs Eskworthy.'

The Fiat pulled into the kerb. Mrs Claybrook took firm hold of Susan's arm and pulled her across the crowded pavement. The child did not struggle. None of the passers-by gave them a second glance.

'Look.' Patricia pointed across the road with her free hand. 'There he is.'

Susan stared over the roof of the Fiat at the opposite side of the road. 'Where? I can't see him.' She had a thin, clear voice, more American than English.

The nearside rear door of the car swung open. Patricia scooped the girl inside. Liam had a glimpse of Blaines's arms outstretched to receive her.

'If you're going to be naughty,' Patricia said angrily in Italian, 'we'll go straight home.'

The final remark had been rehearsed for the benefit of curious bystanders. But in the event no one was interested enough to interfere in a squabble between an anonymous woman and a child.

As Liam watched, the Fiat pulled into the stream of traffic. He had not thought it would be so easy. But Blaines had been right. In a city of strangers everyone was alone.

The traffic was heavy but at least Greg knew the route. He had spent yesterday afternoon and most of this morning driving through the city. The pick-up point had been the weak link in the plan; they all knew that. It all depended on how Susan Quendale used her thirty minutes of freedom. They had been luckier than they deserved.

Once or twice Greg glimpsed the girl's face in the rear mirror.

She sat very straight in the middle of the seat, her arms folded across her chest. Her face was pale but it was possible the pallor was her normal complexion; it was accentuated by the lank black hair that hung like a pair of curtains down to her shoulders. Beside Blaines and his mother she seemed tiny and oddly lifeless, like a Chinese doll intended as a child's birthday present. He was surprised that she hadn't struggled or protested.

'I hope I didn't hurt you back there,' his mother said;

341

she sounded genuinely concerned but not excessively so; it was the sort of apology you make when you bump into someone in the street.

Susan shrugged but said nothing.

Blaines's eyes met Greg's in the mirror. Greg looked away.

Jessica's hands were damp with sweat.

It was important that the others shouldn't notice. As she drove, she wiped her hands surreptitiously – on the steering-wheel cover, on her jeans and on a paper hand-kerchief – but the dampness would not go away. It oozed mysteriously like liquid nervousness from her pores.

They had given her the easiest job of all and she supposed she should be grateful. She had waited in the Mercedes in the Piazza Beccaria car-park. Liam had been the first to arrive. The rest of the party came in the Fiat a few minutes later. No one seemed to notice them transferring themselves from one car to the other. The girl caused no trouble when they bundled her in the boot. Greg drove away in the Fiat; he would be rejoining them later.

It was going too well. Jack must have thought things were going well for him just before he died. Then someone put a bullet in his head. His death had shocked her but not saddened her; this had the effect of making her feel like an accessory to his murder. She was ripe for punishment.

The route was familiar. Blaines had made her do it several times in both directions in the last twenty-four hours. She drove in a wide arc through the north of the city and followed the signs to the Autostrada del Mare. They would soon be at the villa.

She was careful not to take the corners too fast. The boot was padded with cushions but it was still a metal prison.

Liam stirred in the seat beside her. 'Maybe she's afraid.'

'Of course she's afraid.'

'Yes, I know. I meant afraid of the dark.'

Liam pushed open the door. The child hesitated on the threshold.

The bedroom was at the top of the house. It was a small room with a narrow single bed, a built-in wardrobe and a chair. The window overlooked the belt of pines that masked the drive.

'There's a new toothbrush on the basin,' Jessica said. 'I bought a few magazines and books. I hope you'll be warm enough.'

Liam thought she sounded like an inexperienced hostess, nervous but doing her best to cope with a difficult guest.

Susan advanced cautiously into the room. Her hands were deep in the pockets of her coat.

'Do you want a drink?' Liam asked. 'Something to eat?'

The child turned and looked at him, as though memorizing his features. Her self-possession chilled him; it belonged to an older person. It was difficult to imagine her laughing or even smiling.

'Is it money you want,' she said suddenly, 'or just my father?'

'Why do you say that?'

Susan transferred her attention to Jessica. 'You're not

Italian. It was me you wanted, not anyone else. The other woman knew my name. My father's not super-rich so it's probably not money. You don't look drunk and you don't act like perverts. So I guess you want to get at him. It figures.'

'But why?' Jessica said.

'He makes enemies, that's why.'

She slouched over to the window and peered outside. Liam and Jessica glanced at one another. The girl ran her finger along the sill and stared dispassionately at the dust that collected on the tip.

'Do you know where he is?' Liam said.

She ignored the question. 'What did he do to you?' There was a faint stress on the last word.

'We don't want to harm you.' Liam stopped and looked helplessly at Jessica.

'We want to have a talk with your father,' Jessica said. 'He's hard to get hold off. So we had to come to you. The school will let him know you've disappeared and –'

'That'll take days,' Susan interrupted. 'They've just got an accommodation address for him. But I know where he is. He gave me a phone number for emergencies.'

'You going to tell us?' Liam said.

'I'll do a deal with you.' She turned away from the window and stared up at his face. Her small, steady eyes reduced him to the level of an intellectual problem – difficult but ultimately solvable. 'I'll give you the phone number if you promise to do something for me.'

'And what's that?'

'Kill him.'

*

At first Blaines thought the living room was empty.

It was a huge room which occupied the whole of the southern end of the ground floor. French windows opened on to a broad terrace. There wasn't much furniture; and what there was seemed to have been designed primarily as an exercise in solid geometry.

Dusk had settled over the room since he was last there. The chrome was a pale shimmer in the gloom; the glass top of the coffee table was invisible; and the black leather sofa was a long, dark shadow. Another, more welcome change was the warmth: Greg had persuaded the central-heating system to work.

Blaines fumbled for the light switch, swearing when he failed to find it.

Something stirred in the shadows.

'Who is it?' he snapped.

'It's me. Jessica.'

His fingers brushed against the switch. A spotlight came on. It was angled to illuminate the chimney-breast, a triangle of undressed stone that was better left in darkness. Jessica was curled up in an armchair on the left of the fireplace.

'What's wrong with you?' Blaines demanded.

'Nothing. Did you get through?'

'To an answering machine. I left a message.'

'The school must have called the police.'

Blaines shrugged. 'We're safe enough. All they've got to go on is your face. Pity you mentioned Quendale to Pinner-Jones. Still, can't be helped. At least it was only you.'

Patting his pockets, he advanced into the room. The iron log-basket was flecked with rust. A cobweb stretched across one corner. A sprinkling of soot lay in the grate. It would be nice to have an open fire. He lit a cigar and pitched the dead match on to the cobweb. A spider scurried to the corner of the web.

'Jack was right about you,' Jessica said in a small, tight voice.

He stared down at her, wishing he could change her mind. Aloud he said: 'Even a fool gets it right sometimes. Is Caragh with her now?'

She nodded. 'They're playing Monopoly. Susan's winning.'

'Did you have any luck?' he said. 'What's the girl got against Quendale?'

'Something about her mother.' Jessica avoided his eyes. 'He never married her. By the sound of it, she was one of those women that men love to beat. Some men, anyway.'

Blaines wondered if she was thinking of Jack.

'Did you know she killed herself?' Her voice was dreamy and almost relaxed, as though she were under hypnosis. 'Jumped off a balcony at their flat. I think Susan blames her father for that.'

'Poor sod,' Blaines said, surprising even himself. 'Ryal, I mean. Greg's making a meal. Do you want a drink?'

She shook her head. 'Are you going to kill Ryal?'

'I don't want to kill anyone.'

'No one ever does, do they? Not in your world. You don't want to kill people. It's just more convenient if they're not alive. My father. That old man in Brighton. Jack. They get in the way and they have to go. It's all so bloody *impersonal*.'

*

346

They were running out of time.

Jessica pulled open her door. In the last few hours her eyes had grown accustomed to the darkness. She thought it was about three o'clock in the morning. Her watch was on the bedside table but she had no wish to turn on the light and look at it. It was better not to know. The time could only be later than she wanted.

The air on the landing was colder than in her room. A draught ran over her arms and around her bare feet. She had forgotten to pack her dressing-gown and slippers. Her nightdress was made of thin cotton. She resisted the temptation to go back for a jersey for a number of reasons which ranged from simple vanity to the fear she would change her mind.

Faint but regular moans rose and fell behind one of the closed doors. After a few seconds she identified the moans as snores. She guessed they came from Blaines.

The landing window had been left uncurtained. The rectangle of lighter darkness gave her something to navigate by – and also an excuse not to turn on the light. She padded down the landing and turned right. A flight of stairs led to the next floor. As she climbed she noticed that the carpet beneath the soles of her feet had changed its texture: it was rough, corded stuff without a pile.

A line of light ran along the bottom of one of the doors. The sight of it constricted her throat. She forgot to think where she was going and in consequence missed the top step; she stumbled and fell to one knee.

For an instant she knelt there, waiting for the thudding of her heart to subside. Susan's room was opposite the head of the stairs. The door was locked. Jessica tiptoed towards it and listened.

She heard nothing. The relief made it hard to breathe. She had been convinced that Susan would be crying.

Behind her a doorknob rattled. Light flooded across the landing.

'Jess?'

She was turning before he whispered her name. Liam stood in the doorway. He was draped in towels, which implied that his packing had been less than efficient too.

'I came to listen,' she said. 'I can't sleep.'

He came nearer but did not touch her. 'I've been doing that as well. She's probably sleeping better than any of us.'

She leant forward until her head rested on his shoulder. 'That wasn't the only reason I couldn't sleep.'

He slid an arm round her shoulders. Neither of them spoke for a moment. Jessica felt his breath on her hair. She slipped a hand under the towel and rested it on his chest.

'You're cold,' he said.

She burrowed closer to him. His other arm came round her.

'This is silly,' she murmured, pushing him towards the lighted room. He moved backwards like a dancer.

She closed the door behind them and climbed into the bed. It was still warm from his body.

Liam said: 'You're sure, now? I didn't want–'

There was no need for him to go on; she thought he saw that in her face. Jessica guessed what the words might have been: *I didn't want to rush you or force you because that's what Jack did. And now Jack's dead, you might not want me, not in that way.*

She held up one corner of the duvet. 'Come on. I kept thinking of the cemetery.'

348

'The cemetery?' Liam tugged the towel from his shoulders. 'Where we found the real Quendale?'

'I thought then we might never have a chance to make love. That something would stop us.'

He pulled the other towel from his waist. It slithered to the floor. Jessica forgot about the cemetery. Time was still running out but now a different urgency possessed her.

Naked, Liam was another person. Clothes belittled his body. The knowledge gave her a shock of pleasure. She clung to it like a shared secret.

She forced herself to stare primly at him. 'You look as if you don't want to wait either.' Her voice betrayed her: it shook with excitement.

He grinned swiftly. 'You always had that effect on me, right from the start.' He bent and stroked her forehead; his face was suddenly serious. 'You'll marry me, Jess?'

'Of course.' She seemed to have decided that long ago. 'Liam . . . It made her so happy to say his name that she repeated it: 'Liam, come to bed.'

Blaines switched off the radio. 'No news is good news.'

Liam sipped his coffee. 'But the police must know.'

The two of them were in the kitchen. Pale sunshine came through the east-facing window, making the world outside look warmer than it was. Liam was finding it difficult to concentrate. Tiredness, euphoria and worry cast a welcome haze of unreality over Sunday morning.

'Of course they know,' Blaines said grumpily. 'Mrs Eskworthy must have phoned them. Probably about an hour afterwards. Can't you hurry up?'

'But not a kidnapping? Just a missing person?'

Blaines nodded. 'Unless we were unlucky and someone saw something.'

'They might have had a news black-out.'

'Unlikely in a missing-person case. No, I think we're okay. Quendale's playing ball.' He looked at his watch. 'Come on. Pat'll be waiting.'

Liam ignored the pressure. 'What exactly did you say in your message?'

'I told him to tell the school that Susan was with him. He'd run into her by chance.'

'Bit tacky, isn't it?'

'Ah, shut up,' Blaines said. 'It's good enough for Mrs E. Ryal's to go to the school this morning to confirm it. Sudden change of plan. Unexpected chance of an early Christmas holiday. That sort of thing.'

'Maybe he won't cooperate.'

'Of course he will. He's not going to go to the police is he? Haven't you had enough toast?'

'No,' Liam said.

As he ate, he was aware Blaines was studying him. The old man was no fool: he must realize that his hold over Liam was slipping. Now that Liam had decided to leave his job, it didn't matter what Aughrim heard about him. If it wasn't for Jess he would catch the next flight back to London. But Jess was staying. She owed it to her mother and to Greg.

He met Blaines's eyes. 'And now what?'

'Eh?' Cigar smoke dribbled from the old man's mouth.

'What if you're wrong? Quendale's Ryal, I accept that; but it doesn't necessarily mean he's connected with the Blacklist. And if he is . . .'

'What?'

350

'Well, he may guess that we took Susan. And if Koslove's his principal, he'll be damn near certain.'

'It doesn't matter if he's got it in writing from the Recording Angel. As long as we've got Susan.'

Liam abandoned the toast. Suddenly he was no longer hungry. 'If Jess gets hurt,' he said, 'I'll –'

Greg flung open the kitchen door. 'My mother wants to know if you're ready.'

'I'm ready,' Blaines said. 'I'm just waiting for this little ray of sunshine to digest his breakfast.'

Liam pushed back his chair. 'Jess is with Susan?'

Greg nodded. His face was puffy this morning and the eyes were bloodshot. Without warning he swung round to Blaines. 'Does Liam know?'

Blaines shook his head. He edged round the table, keeping away from Greg, and sidled out of the room.

Liam waited until the door had closed. 'I never thought I'd see him look embarrassed. Know what?'

Greg rubbed his eyes. '*Ever asked your mother who your father is?*'

For an instant Liam thought the question was addressed to him.

'My postcard from London,' Greg said in a flat voice. 'My mother told me, the day we flew out. My father's just left us.'

'*Blaines?*'

'Yeah.' Greg rolled an unlighted cigarette between his fingers. A thin stream of tobacco cascaded to the floor. 'He doesn't want me for a son. And I sure don't want him for a father. God damn it.'

'God damn what?'

'God damn biology. God damn sex. God damn one-night stands. And God damn Blaines.'

'I'm sorry.' Liam wondered if it was better to have a father you didn't want than not to know who your father was. Unless his mother miraculously recovered, he would never know. He wasn't sure that he wanted to.

'I'm meant to be outside,' Greg said. He threw the remains of the cigarette in the bin.

In the hall they separated. Liam climbed the stairs. It was one of Blaines's rules that in the daytime there should always be two of them with Susan.

Mrs Claybrook was waiting for him at the head of the stairs. He glanced at her, trying without success to imagine her with Blaines; it was beauty with the beast. There was a flash of amusement in her eyes. He would have been prepared to bet that she had guessed what was in his mind.

All she said was: 'Eric's ready?'

'He's waiting in the car.' Liam hesitated. 'Take care.'

'Oh, I will.' As she passed him she said, in a lower voice, 'And you take care of Jess.'

11

Harry Ryal's never smiled
Harry's riled. Ryal's vile
Ryal's one big piece of shit –
Watch out you don't step in it.

On bad days, even now, the jingle resurfaced. It formed a background to his thoughts, like continuous static behind a radio broadcast. In time the words broke down to meaningless units of sound arranged in a monotonously rhythmic pattern: *Ha*-ree-*rye*-ul-*ner*-vah-*smy*-ulled . . .

Once, he supposed, it must really have happened. Maybe more than once. In his mind he could see the grey asphalt of a playground and a pair of scarred knees poking from a pair of short grey trousers; around him was a ring of feet in scuffed shoes; and if he raised his eyes he knew he would see the faces, blank with hatred.

But his memory was not reliable. He might have invented that scene and subsequently remembered the invention as if it had not really happened. However, he was sure he had not imagined the hatred or the jingle that expressed it.

Even then he had sensed it was nothing personal. He was the new boy who had joined halfway through the term after everyone else had settled into groups. He was bright for his age and had been well-taught in his last school; as a result he was among boys who were at least a year older than him. The last school had left him another unfortunate legacy; an accent that was a few degrees more cultivated than those of most of his classmates.

With hindsight he realized that he had been a natural victim, an irresistible gift from providence. The cruelty of the herd had to find an outlet. It so happened that his qualifications were better than anyone else's.

He didn't even bear a grudge. On other occasions and in other places he had run with the herd himself. He understood the herd's excitement – the sheer thrill of being cruel in a group to someone who had no means of redress. Acting as a group was essential to the pleasure; the possession of consciences was restricted to individuals.

But understanding did not lead to forgiveness. They never forgave him so why should he forgive them? The playground changed its shape and became a room in Aldershot, crowded with dummies in khaki. He had survived the court matrial with a reprimand but he knew what they were thinking about him.

> *Harry Ryal's never smiled*
> *Harry's riled, Ryal's vile*

And again at the inquiry, where the nominal accusers wore dark suits like undertakers'; but the real accusers, the Sandridges and the Vandermans, stayed away and whispered the jingle in private. But it was still the same as it had been in the playground, real or imagined. The only difference was that the violence they offered him was no longer merely physical.

Among the herd at the inquiry was Bertie Monastow, the one man who should have backed him up: *Ryal's an enthusiastic officer but sometimes his enthusiasm has led him to overreach himself . . . a tendency to act without authorization . . . Mr Edgeley's death is deeply regrettable.*

Monastow was really saying that Ryal didn't belong in the herd. He didn't fit in. He was a liability.

Monastow wasn't giving evidence; he was chanting.

> *Ryal's one big piece of shit –*
> *Watch out you don't step in it.*

Ryal had plenty of time to think.

His flight reached Pisa in the early hours of Sunday morning. The voice on the recorded message belonged to Colonel Blaines, he was sure of that. He found a hotel in Florence and made a few phone calls. At nine o'clock he presented himself at the Scuola Pencombe.

Mrs Eskworthy was waiting for him in her office. He could guess what was in her mind.

'I must apologize,' Ryal began as they were shaking hands. 'I ran into Susie quite by chance.'

'She's your daughter, Mr Quendale,' Mrs Eskworthy said stiffly. 'You were perfectly within your rights.'

'It was appallingly selfish of me, though. You must have been very worried.'

'But were you intending . . .?'

'No, of course not. I'd just arrived in Florence. A

friend of mine's lent me a villa in the Alps and I wanted to take Susie – your term ends next week and I thought a few days wouldn't matter. Then quite by chance I met her in the street. We went to a café and started talking . . . I had no idea that time had passed so quickly.'

'Two and a half hours, Mr Quendale?'

Ryal spread his hands in apology. 'We had a lot to talk about. It's been a long time.'

'And what do you propose to do now?'

'Well, I'd like to take Susie to the villa. Not much point in bringing her back here, just a couple of days.'

'And will she be coming back next term?'

'Of course. My dear Mrs Eskworthy, I had no idea . . . Look, while I'm here you must let me give you a cheque for next term.'

'That would be convenient.'

Mrs Eskworthy's eyes were like large blue marbles, a fact that reminded Ryal of the playground. The mention of money softened them slightly. It was a pity she wasn't altogether a fool.

Ryal cleared his throat. 'Perhaps I could pick up Susie's things while I'm here. Just a few clothes, I mean. Everything else might as well stay here.'

'I'll ask one of the maids. Excuse me a moment.'

She left him alone in the big green room with the picture of the old goat on the wall. He pulled out his cheque-book. Suddenly sadness overwhelmed him. Neither Blaines nor Mrs Eskworthy knew how absurd the story was.

It was a joyful ficton: father and daughter spending two and a half hours talking in a café – so delighted to be together that time meant nothing to them.

He held on to the fiction. Maybe after this was over – and it would be over – the fiction would become truth. After all, Susie was just going through one of the emotional storms of early adolescence. Perhaps this experience would teach her how to value what she had.

In a sense Blaines might be doing him a good turn.

Mrs Eskworthy returned. 'Your taxi's here, Mr Quendale.'

'My taxi?'

'Yes,' she said with a touch of exasperatiron. 'The driver said he was to meet you here.'

'Of course.' Ryal glanced at her and realized it would be wiser to provide an explanation. 'I walked from the hotel, you see. But I thought I'd need a taxi on the way back. For Susie's cases.'

The driver was a nondescript Italian in early middle age.

He said something in Italian as Ryal got in. It meant nothing to Ryal but he nodded nevertheless. It seemed to satisfy the driver.

He drove with one hand on the wheel while the other tapped in time with the pop music on the radio. Ryal thought the man wasn't involved in this; he looked too bored; it was difficult to fake boredom convincingly.

Their route took them north-west across the city. The blue Alfa was still behind them but not too close; Luciano and Paolo knew their job. The trouble was, Ryal thought, he was no longer sure that he knew his. Worrying about Susie made it difficult to think clearly.

The plan should work. He didn't like it but it was the only one available. For once he had to rely on someone else. And so did Susie.

The taxi dropped him outside the main entrance of the botanical garden in Via Micheli. The Alfa cruised past; no doubt it would stop when it was out of sight.

Blaines was waiting on the pavement. The old man looked tired and rumpled, as though he'd spent the night in the rain.

'Hello, Harry,' he said.

'How's Susie?'

'She's fine. Come on. It's too cold to hang around.'

Blaines led the way past a row of glasshouses to a lawn that was sprinkled with conifers. Ryal had never been here before and he didn't want to come here again. They were walking briskly. It was obvious what Blaines was doing: in one door and out of the other. It was childishly simple and almost certain to work.

'Sorry about this,' Blaines wheezed. 'We'll just get rid of your mates in the Alfa and then we'll be off.'

They came to another gate. Ryal glanced back. There was no sign of Luciano or Paolo. Even if there had been, it would have been too late.

'Here we are,' Blaines said. 'We'll go in the back, shall we?'

The engine was running. Patricia Claybrook half turned her head as they climbed into the Mercedes. Her eyes met Ryal's for an instant. She put the car in gear and pulled away.

'Now don't take this personally, Harry. I want to search you.'

Ryal shrugged. Blaines pawed him efficiently, whistling tunelessly under his breath. He seemed entirely relaxed. He found nothing because there was nothing to find. Ryal could have killed him with a single blow.

'Who was in the Alfa?' Blaines asked.

'Local muscle. They worked for a security firm in Pisa.'

'What did you tell them?'

'Just to stay close. Minders, that's all.'

'I hope you're right, Harry. Really I do.'

They drove in silence for a mile or so. By now they were on the autostrada. Ryal could bear it no longer.

'What does Susie know?' he said suddenly.

'That we want to talk to you. That's all.'

'What'll happen?'

'That depends on you, Harry. No one wants a fuss.'

'How did you find Susie?'

'I paid a few calls in Hong Kong.' Blaines grinned at him almost with affection. 'You know what this reminds me of? Shakespeare. That bit about children being hostages to fate. We had to learn it at school.'

'Not Shakespeare,' Patricia Claybrook said quietly. 'Bacon. "He that hath wife and children hath given hostages to fortune; for they are impediments to great enterprises; either of virtue or mischief." '

'Bacon, Shakespeare – what's the difference?' Blaines sniffed. 'The point is, you –'

'I know what the point is.' Ryal's eyes met Mrs Claybrook's in the rear mirror. 'I'll talk, don't worry. But not till I've seen Susie.'

Susie was sitting on her bed playing knock-out whist with Liam.

They were playing for money. She had already collected IOUs worth over fifty thousand lira. Her face was fierce with concentration. When she won, she smiled.

Jessica heard the car first. Liam looked up. She got up and peered out of the window. The forecourt was invisible from here. Car doors slammed.

Liam and Susie continued playing.

There were footsteps on the stairs. What if something had gone wrong? The footsteps paused outside the door. There was a knock.

'Damn,' Susie said. 'Trumps are hearts. You will remember?'

'Open Sesame,' Blaines said on the other side of the door.

Jessica turned the key. The little room was full of people – her mother, Blaines, Greg and a slight, neat stranger.

'Here's your dad, Susie,' Blaines said cheerfully.

'Susie?' Ryal said. 'You're okay, darling?'

She looked up at her father and nodded. Then she glanced at her hand and put down a ten of spades.

'Come on,' she said to Liam. 'It's your go.'

'She's in shock,' Ryal said. 'Naturally.'

Greg looked curiously at him. Ryal seemed such an inoffensive man. He looked like a bureaucrat or a bank clerk; you could imagine him taking the subway home each evening at precisely the same time; you could almost hear him asking his wife what the kids have been doing today.

'Poor kid,' Ryal went on. 'She's had a tough time since her mother died. No wonder she's wary with people. She's even wary with me, you know. But she'll get over it.'

The door opened. Patricia Claybrook came into the sitting room with a tray of coffee. Blaines scrambled to his feet and blundered towards her. She side-stepped his attempt to help and laid the tray on the glass-topped table.

'Cream or sugar, Mr Ryal?'

'Just cream, thanks.'

Ryal pulled out a pipe and began to fill it. His hands were steady. Patricia handed round the cups. There were only four of them since Liam and Jessica had stayed upstairs with Susie.

'Let me put our cards on the table,' Blaines said. 'You've got something we want; we've got something you want. So we do a deal. Nice and simple, eh? No hidden clauses, no hanky-panky. Straightforward trading.'

'Okay.' Ryal hesitated. 'Has Susie been eating properly? Somehow she looked thinner.'

'She's fine,' Patricia said.

'On our side,' Blaines said, 'we want chapter and verse on the Blacklist.'

'The Blacklist?' Ryal said. 'What's that?'

Blaines overrode the interruption as though it wasn't there. 'We want it stopped. We want to be able to prevent it happening again. And on your side, you want Susie back; and security, of course. Shouldn't be difficult. We can help you disappear. A new life, just the two of you. No one's going to be petty. What's done is done.'

Ryal paused in the act of lighting his pipe. 'Forgive and forget?'

'Just that. It'll take time. And you'll have to be frank with us.'

Patricia Claybrook started to say something but stopped.

'I don't believe you.' Ryal blew out a cloud of smoke.

'You have to, Harry. Susie stays with us until we're satisfied. So do you. If you cooperate, you'll be together again. If you don't . . .'

'What will you do?'

'Put you inside for Bertie Monastow. Or maybe for Jedborough. That's one option.'

Greg watched Ryal's face, half-obscured by a cloud of sweet-smelling smoke. Momentarily the cloud cleared. Ryal was frowning and his soft, brown eyes were out of focus.

'You can't prove anything,' he said; for the first time he was admitting that there was something to prove.

'Then I'll frame you. Either way you won't see Susie. She'd probably end up in a home. An orphanage somewhere. As I said, that's just one option. We've got plenty of others, unlike you.'

'You're bluffing,' Ryal said. 'You're out on a limb. You've got no authorization.'

'Tell you what I have got, Harry. Susie. You want me to bring her down? Tell her about her dad? *I* don't mind. It's all the same to me.'

Blaines pursed his lips as he waited for an answer.

For an instant Greg thought Ryal was going to be sick. He was hunched in his chair. The colour fled from his face until his skin looked like candle wax.

'Begin at the beginning,' Blaines said. 'From Biarritz.'

'Are you cheating?' Susie said. 'That's your second ace. How will you kill him?'

Liam pulled the trick towards him and put down a ten of spades. 'It's not up to me.'

362

'Then who? That fat man, the old one?'

He nodded. 'He makes the decisions round here.'

She studied the remaining cards in her hand. Finally she selected a jack of spades.

'I'll go back to Hong Kong,' she said 'To my Uncle. I hate Europe. It's so cold, like the people.'

'It may not be as simple as that.'

'Why not?'

'Because we can't always do what we want.'

'I didn't kill Miles,' Ryal said angrily. 'What d'you take me for? It was an accident.'

'Convenient sort of accident,' Blaines said.

'Okay, I know it looks bad. But I *liked* Miles, can't you understand that? Probably not. But once he was dead, I could get some mileage out of it. He wouldn't have minded.'

'And you wanted a new start?'

Ryal shrugged. 'There wasn't much left in England for me. Not as Ryal. With a bit of money and a new name I could go anywhere. It was like being reborn. No one could point a finger at John Adam Quendale because of his past. Because he didn't have one.' The pipe had gone out. He laid it gently in the ashtray. 'What's the use? You'd never understand in a million years.'

'Why Hong Kong.'

'It's the other side of the world from England. There's money there. They live in the present tense. No one's interested in what you were. I bought up Peterhouse Oriental Investigations for peanuts, changed the name and that was it. I had a new life. Then Susie came along and I had a daughter.'

363

No mention of the mother, Greg thought. How had Ryal seen her? As a sexual safety-valve? As a breeding machine? As someone to hurt?

'Who employed you?'

'Mainly the Hongs, the big business houses. That's where the money was. They always need someone to do their dirty work.'

'So did the Chinese.'

'Well, why not?' Ryal said defiantly. 'You expect me to be a patriot or something? After what they did to me?'

Blaines scratched his head. 'In the hall of your flat, you've got a map. The British Empire, 1920s vintage. Half a billion people. A quarter of the world's land.'

'That was sixty years ago.' Ryal flushed. 'It's got nothing to do with this.'

'Hasn't it? I wonder. Bit like keeping a photo of your ex-wife on your bedside table. Chinese pay well?'

'Adequately.'

'You on a commission basis?'

'How d'you mean?'

'The Blacklist brings in a fair amount. What do you do with it? Fifty-fifty?'

Ryal stared at Blaines. Something had gone wrong, Greg thought: Ryal was smiling. The smile grew broader and broader until he began to laugh.

Susie bit into the sandwich. Mayonnaise and peanut butter dribbled out. She chewed with her mouth open. Jessica looked away.

'You just want to talk to my dad,' Susie said indistinctly. 'That's all?'

'Yes,' Jessica said.

Liam tossed the pack of cards on the bed. 'Why do you ask?'

'I was wondering.' Susie swallowed the mouthful and reached for the glass of milk. A moment later she added: 'I don't mind if you don't kill him. You don't have to.'

'You've had a change of heart?' Jessica said.

'Sort of. I mean, it's the kind of thing that might come back and haunt me. If you killed him for my sake, it'd be like I killed him. A friend of mine – her name's Dawn – says that maybe one day I won't hate him so much. I don't know.'

Jessica poured herself some milk. 'Dawn could be right. Time changes things.'

Susie nodded. 'You'll tell the fat man, then? Tell him that he doesn't have to kill Dad?'

Greg had never seen Blaines look both angry and shocked. There was something unnatural about it. It was like seeing a saucy smile on the face of the Statue of Liberty.

'You expect me to believe that?' Blaines roared.

'I knew it,' Ryal said. 'You see everything in terms of your own little world. Tunnel vision. Blinkers. You're all the same – the Brits, the Chinese, the Russians – everyone.'

Patricia stared at Ryal. Her mouth was slightly open. As Greg watched, her lips formed a single, silent word: *No*.

Blaines lit a cigar. It was the first time that Greg had seen him smoke in front of Patricia. For a few seconds he smoked in silence.

'You're saying this was your idea? No prompting?'

Ryal nodded. 'I took a lot of material from the

section's files. Photocopies, stuff like that. I knew you were going to sack me and I was dammed if I was going to take it lying down. It was an insurance policy, if you like.'

'Balls,' Blaines said calmly. 'Some of the victims weren't on file. Not in London. Some of them were after your time. That CIA woman, for instance. Tina Whatsername. In any case, you must have needed a small army to run the Blacklist.'

Ryal was still smiling. 'I've not been idle in the last fourteen years. A scrap here, a scrap there, it all adds up. As for manpower, that's easy enough. Peterhouse was international, remember. There's freelance talent in every city if you know where to look. Someone to make a phone call. Someone to post a letter. That's all I needed.'

'Okay, that's the cover-story. How about the truth?'

'It is the truth. It's so bloody simple you can't see it.' Ryal leant forward in his chair. 'Look. Business has been bad and I needed money. Had to burn down the office for the insurance, that's how bad it was. And to be honest I wanted revenge as well. You chewed me up, sucked the goodness out and then spat me out. You owed me something for that. I had the means – a little stockpile of information. You all thought I was dead so I couldn't be suspected. And then I had a flash of inspiration about the method. Sick think.'

'What?'

'It's built into the way you operate. If you work in a sewer, everything smells of shit. You see?'

'I see,' Patricia said suddenly. 'It's so obvious it's transparent.'

Before he could stop himself, Greg snorted with laughter.

Blaines frowned at him.

Ryal glanced round the room like an entertainer assessing his effect on the audience.

'You'd better go on,' Blaines said.

'I've got no reason to lie,' Ryal reminded him. 'Not now. You've got me and Susie.'

'All right. Try me.'

'Anyone who spends a life in an intelligence agency ends up interpreting everything in terms of the trade. At first you can't afford not to; finally it becomes automatic. You have a wet summer and you wonder if the Soviets are tinkering with the weather. And so on. Now, I wanted money, pure and simple. All I had to do was hint that the money was insignificant, just a token of cooperation. And you did the rest. You looked at it from your angle, and what did you see? Networks of agents of influence. Sleepers waking up. A programme to destabilize the intelligence community. Moles to the right, moles to the left. You were like a load of puppets. I just had to pull the strings. Christ, you make me laugh. Sometimes I -'

'Shut up,' Greg said. 'There's someone outside.'

What's that?' Jessica said.

Liam was already by the window. 'Trees are in the way. It sounds like a car on the drive. Maybe two.'

'I'd better tell them downstairs.' Jessica twisted the key in the lock and opened the door. 'You'll stay here?'

He nodded, appreciating her effort to appear casual. The door closed behind her. He turned back to the bed.

'Do you want another game of –'

But Susie was no longer sitting on the bed. She was crouching in front of him, only inches away. She pivoted on her heel and drove the point of her elbow into his crotch.

He screamed. The pain fogged his vision. He was dimly aware of a blur of movements. It sounded like someone was hammering nails downstairs.

The door slammed and he was alone in the room.

They were all on their feet.

Blaines sidled over to Ryal and draped an arm round his neck. 'I didn't think you'd be so stupid,' he said softly.

Greg was at the window that overlooked the gravel sweep. He stood to one side and twitched the curtains so he could see the head of the drive.

'Two cars,' he said quietly.

Behind him, his mother sucked in her breath.

The first car, a VW Passat, surged across the open space to the front door. The second, a big Renault with tinted windows, stopped at the bottom of the drive, blocking it like a cork in a bottle.

'Susie?' Ryal said.

Patricia Claybrook darted to the door.

'Stay here!' Blaines snapped.

Greg swore and followed her.

Someone was running down the stairs. The front door creaked. It wasn't even locked, Greg remembered, but the warped wood held it in its frame.

He looked up and there was Jessica flying down the stairs three at a time. More footsteps followed hers. Susie appeared round the bend of the stairs.

'Get back!' Greg roared. He knew with dreadful certainty what was going to happen.

The shot came immediately afterwards. They blew the lock off the front door. The lock that wasn't even locked.

It was a textbook operation.

George Koslove had insisted on retaining full control. John Smith, the Rome Head of Station, hadn't liked that, any more than he had liked Koslove's determination to keep the Italians out of it.

Koslove directed operations from the back of the second car. He had bottled them up. All of them. His daring astonished him. No one could say he was just a deskman who didn't understand the problems in the field; not now.

The bastards shouldn't have double-crossed him. They were meant to be a team, for Christ's sake. The big question was, had they ever been a team?

He dabbed at the sweat on his forehead, leaning back so the driver couldn't see him. The man was a marine from the Rome embassy; Smith said he was a killing machine with the brains of a worm. Together with the bullet-proof glass of the Renault, the marine was Koslove's insurance against something going wrong. His hand moved across the seat and touched the cold metal. There was his last resort. A Walther from the Station armoury.

The window was down – just half an inch; enough to be able to hear what was going on. There was a good deal of noise but only one shot; and that was when they shot the lock off the front door. Koslove hoped that no one would get hurt. Even other people's pain upset him. With luck they would all be sensible. Not that they didn't deserve a little pain, after all he'd done for them. He looked at his watch. Thirty seconds since they went in. The hand crawled on. Forty-five seconds. A full minute. What in God's name were they doing?

The marine grunted.

Smith was standing in the doorway. He was a burly man with cropped, iron-grey hair. He gave Koslove a thumbs-up sign with his free hand. The other hand was holding a gun.

Koslove climbed out of the car. At the last moment he remembered the pistol. He picked it up gingerly. With the marine towering beside him he walked slowly to the villa. There was an unpleasantly acrid smell round the front door.

Smith waited in the hall. He waved at the marine, moving him out of earshot.

'I don't like this,' he said softly. 'They're unarmed. Seven people. One with a US passport, five Brits and one Irish national. One of them's a little girl. And one of the Brits is Blaines. He's God damn furious.'

'I'm not surprised,' Koslove said primly.

'Are you crazy? They're not going to keep quiet about this. And if the Italians get to know –'

'I'll handle this. Where are they?'

'In the big room over there.'

'I'll talk to them. Alone.'

Smith shrugged. 'If you say so.'

He led the way into the sitting room. Koslove followed, with the gun in his right hand. His thumb was against the safety-catch; it was so long since he'd fired one of these damn things that he wasn't sure if the catch was off or on.

Smith's men were ranged around the walls. Koslove could not help smiling when he saw the others. They were all sitting down: Blaines and Patricia on one sofa; Jessica and Caragh on another; young Vanderman in an armchair; and, near the fireplace, a thin, dark man with a little Chinese girl perched on the arm of his chair.

Ryal? The man who was meant to be dead?

'Next time,' Blaines said, 'just ring the bell. Or even walk in. There's no need to be so fucking formal.'

Smith beckoned his four men. They filed out of the room. Koslove closed the door and leant on it.

'So I was right.' His eyes flickered over them, lingering on Patricia Claybrook. 'It was the British after all. And you're Ryal? The guy who did the dirty work? Like setting up Chas Claybrook.'

Divide and rule, Koslove thought: set the remaining Claybrooks against Blaines.

'No!' Ryal levered himself out of his chair. 'It's not true,' he said to Mrs Claybrook. 'He's lying –'

'How did you know where we were?' Blaines said.

'I had you followed. Not you personally because you skipped the country. Your trip to Hong Kong, remember? But Caragh was easy enough to trace.' He moved into the room. 'You've had a good run for your money. But the game's over now. You tried to be too clever.'

The little girl scrambled off the chair. Her mouth was working and her face was white.

'Daddy, I need to go to the bathroom.'

'It can wait,' Koslove said. He turned back to Blaines. 'How you had the nerve –'

But the girl was running across the room. She whimpered something. Her hand was on the doorknob. A diversion, Koslove thought; one last piece of trickery. He shouted for Smith.

The shout ended in a gasp as Ryal jostled against him. Koslove, caught off balance, stumbled to one side. His leg jarred against a glass-topped coffee table. He fell across it. His arms flailed. The Walther's barrel snagged on the seat of the sofa. The impact jerked the gun from his hand and sent it skidding across the parquet flooring.

Everyone was moving towards the door. The girl had it open. She was in the hall. It was all happening so quickly. Koslove wriggled like a snake between the sofa and the table.

'Get her!' he yelled.

Suddenly he was merely a spectator. The doorway into the hall was like a television screen dividing the observer from the observed.

The hall was full of movement and noise. The big marine nodded at him. The man had a pink, round face and he was raising the Hechler and Koch machine pistol.

Get her? Oh Christ –

Greg Vanderman blocked his view. Damn the man. Seen from the rear, Vanderman's heavy shoulders, broad neck and curly hair were oddly familiar, as though Koslove had seen them on someone else.

A killing machine with the brains of a worm?

It looked like Vanderman was trying to hug the marine. Where was Smith? Why wasn't he sorting out this mess?

The gun clattered on the floor. Two hands, with fingers like pink bananas, tightened round Vanderman's neck. Smith was hanging on to the marine's arm, shouting. The fingers tightened, forcing the blood to Vanderman's head.

The little girl was lying on the floor near their feet. Ryal, partly visible among a forest of legs, crouched beside her, trying to shield her with his body.

And, Jesus, someone else had a gun and they were pointing it at Ryal's head. A Walther, just like the one he'd dropped. A wedding-ring glinted on the hand around the butt.

Vanderman dropped to the floor.

'At last,' she whispered. 'For Charles.'

No, please God, no. It needn't be over. There was still so much to be salvaged. And Susie –

> *Ryal's one big piece of shit –*
> *Watch out you don't step in it.*

EPILOGUE

The black Daimler rolled through Halcombe, turned right just after the derestriction signs and drew up outside the house. Henry switched off the engine and glanced over his shoulder.

'Wait a minute,' Blaines said.

'We haven't got much time, Eric,' Wreningham said. 'It's still quite a way to Cheltenham.'

There were clumps of primroses in the front garden. Green spikes poked out of the earth. The grass looked ragged. The garden needed a gardener.

A thin trail of smoke ascended from the chimney. There was a black and white cat on the front doorstep; it was washing its face and keeping a wary eye on the car. Resident or visitor?

Wreningham cleared his throat. 'The meeting starts at three, I believe.'

One of the sitting-room curtains twitched. After all, Blaines thought, he was expected. He must have been expected for months.

Henry's eyes drifted downwards. The newspaper on the front passenger seat would be folded open at the crossword. One across and twelve down were like the toy soldiers that refought Waterloo and Omdurman, Saratoga and Balaclava: ways of filling the empty corners of the mind.

The mind?

The familiar pain snaked through Blaines's chest. Indigestion of the heart.

'If you could possibly manage to keep it short,' Wreningham laid. The sentence trailed prematurely to a halt.

Blaines nodded. If necessary he could use the bloody meeting as an excuse. That was one reason why he had chosen to come today.

He got out of the car and walked up the familiar path. The cat slipped off the step and disappeared round the side of the house. The front door still needed a coat of paint; after this winter it needed it even more. Now that was odd. But maybe she no longer cared about such things.

The door opened before he reached it. She smiled at him.

Time was overrated as a healer.

'Eric. I'm so glad.'

She inclined her cheek. He brushed it awkwardly with his lips.

'You've got a new car.'

'It's Willy Wreningham's.'

'He's with you?'

'Why not?'

She led him into the sitting room. 'I'll make some tea. Or would you prefer something stronger?'

'Don't bother; not for me.'

He sat down heavily in the armchair moulded by Charles Claybrook's body.

'I hoped you'd come,' she said. 'I expected you sooner.'

Blaines mumbled something about work.

'Of course you've been busy. All those loose ends.'

It was over three months since he had seen her. Not since the day they buried Greg in the Anglican cemetery in Florence.

'Jessica and Liam were married two weeks ago,' she said.

'I know. They sent me an invitation.'

He hadn't gone because Pat would be there. He sent them a cheque as a wedding present, together with a pink card with a champagne bottle on it. Rosie chose the card.

'He's studying to be a solicitor – did you know? There's a course at one of the London polytechnics. They're living in Jess's flat. Now his mother's dead, Liam feels there's no point in him staying in Ireland. He's hoping to get some sort of a night job.'

'Aughrim still isn't talking to me.'

'Nell wasn't there either.' Patricia glanced at the side table where the family photographs were displayed like icons. 'She's in Boston with Matthew and the baby. They've found a possible kidney donor. Whether it works or not is another matter.'

'You gave them the money?' Blaines said in a neutral voice.

'Me? I wish I could. If Greg had lived, he was going to pay. But the Trust income died with him. No, Tom and Charmian offered. I've seen quite a lot of them lately.' She hesitated. 'How did you manage it in the end?'

'What?'

'You know. The villa. And everything else.'

Everything else? What did that include? Two dead men, one of whom was their son while the other had died officially fourteen years earlier. The bullet holes in the

377

hall and a little girl crying over her father's body. The two-hundred-pound marine who hadn't meant to hurt anyone and who didn't know his own strength. The worried Head of Station who really was called John Smith. The Italian authorities.

'Convincing George Koslove was the hardest part,' Blaines said. 'After that, he took care of it. Damn it, most of it was his fault.'

But the only part which really mattered was Greg.

'And George is okay now,' he went on. 'Sitting pretty as the man who defused the Blacklist.'

'You let him share the credit?'

'Why not? It keeps him happy.'

'And Susie?'

'Back in Hong Kong with her uncle and aunt.'

Patricia ran her finger down a pleat in her skirt. 'What about Ryal?'

'We traced him eventually through the phone number. The phone was in a flat near King's Cross. He didn't live there, of course – he'd rented a house in Islington. Everything was there – files, clothes, even the gun he used to kill Jedborough. But don't worry, Pat.'

She frowned. 'Why should I worry?'

'Nothing incriminated you.'

The silence stretched between them like a desert. Then she brushed the hair away from her face.

'Are you crazy?'

For a moment Blaines didn't answer. He lit a cigar with deliberation and pitched the match into the fire.

'Eric?'

'Whose idea was it? Not Ryal's; he was an imitator, a follower. It might have been Chas but I doubt it. His job was providing the raw material and doing the detailed planning.' Blaines was speaking too quickly, like a child reciting a poem before the grown-ups. He tried to slow himself down. 'No, I reckon you thought of it. That horse-thieving Youlgreave blood of yours. It was a brilliant idea, I give you that; far too good for Ryal. How did he put it? *In a sewage farm everything smells of shit.*'

'I think you'd better go.' She stared into the fire. 'There's nothing to say. You're mad.'

Blaines ignored her. 'It went like this. Chas was bitter and so were you. Your family had pushed you out of the nest. They'd taken Greg away from you. They'd made damn sure that Chas never got anywhere. He hated that job, in any case. He was an oddball, like Ryal, and they made him feel it, every day of his working life. They wouldn't even give him a proper pension.'

Outside a car hooted. It sounded like the Daimler. Wreningham must be desperate to do that. His minister was to be at the meeting too.

'And you needed money,' Blaines said. 'Not just for yourselves and your children, but for Matthew. I doubt if you'd have done it, if it hadn't been for him. To give him a chance to live, eh? That was the important thing. So you did it for the three best reasons in the world. For revenge. For gain. And most of all for love.'

'Eric, I find this offensive. I'm sorry but–'

'You two were always so damned self-contained; everyone knew that. A world within a world, a world with your own laws. Chas was in an ideal position to gather material. But you needed someone else – someone to do the work. You needed Ryal.'

379

A piece of coal fell on to the hearth. Patricia picked it up with the tongs and returned it to the grate.

'I don't know how you recruited him,' Blaines said. 'But Chas was in Hong Kong a year or two ago. Could have run into him in the street – who cares? Chas knew Ryal through the Vanderman business. He was sorry for him – felt he'd been made the scapegoat. They were two of a kind, weren't they? Ryal wanted money and revenge too. And he had an organization which you could use; he had contacts all over the place. You were very clever – you even arranged for yourselves to be blackmailed. All that crap about Chas's book. Well?'

The horn sounded again. This time the blast was longer. Wreningham's urgency infected Blaines. Except that his urgency had nothing to do with meetings and ministers.

'Is that your car?' Patricia said. 'Don't let me keep you.'

'It can wait.'

She smiled at him. 'I'd like to think this was some kind of a joke. It's a bizarre theory. It's also tasteless – and unsupported.'

'Then Ryal tried to be too clever. He had a habit of overreaching himself, you remember – Aden, Aldershot, Edgeley. Maybe he felt he deserved a larger share of the proceeds. *Thought the world owed him a living*: that's what Mary Padgate said. The Chinese had already hired him to deal with Tonanyev, and he'd contracted it out to the Sons of Ataturk. All he had to do was arrange for Chas to be there too. If anyone was blamed, it'd be the British. Of course that made you feel even more bitter.'

Tears were sliding down Patricia's cheek. She made no

380

attempt to wipe them away. She wept silently, which was a rare talent.

'He fooled you at first, like everyone else. The fake attack went ahead to make it clear you were whiter than white; that's why you asked Jess to stay the night – to have a witness. And it worked out even better than you'd expected. I not only fell for it, I recruited you to help. I thought you needed the money. God help me. Maybe that saved your life. Ryal would have killed you in the end. Just as soon as you'd outlived your use as an early-warning system.'

She shook her head. He waited in vain for her to say something.

'I think you kept in touch with Ryal by letter. Maybe you phoned in, if the message was urgent. It must have been urgent when Monastow rang you. The phone call he made from the house where the medium lived. You remember? The call we never traced. I'd given him your number. Who else would he ring if he thought he'd seen the ghost of Harry Ryal? You killed that silly old man.'

The loathing in his voice shocked him. He watched her face. Now he had reached this point, he knew he should not have come. For his sake, not for hers.

'No. No, Eric– I called Ryal to *warn* him. I didn't know . . .'

'That Harry was a killer? I think you guessed. And the second time you must have known what would happen. Jack Jedborough?'

She had a spot of colour on each cheekbone. 'He was different. You know that, Eric. He was going to hurt Nell and Matthew.'

Blaines shrugged away the defence. Too many people

381

had died. 'But you must have been lucky too.'

'I was meeting Ryal that afternoon. I phoned his hotel when Jack left. I'd seen Jack's car and I knew he'd probably go back to London.'

'And last of all you killed Ryal. He was relying on you to get him and Susie off the hook. Touching, eh? When Koslove dropped his gun you took the chance. It almost paid off. Everyone thought: *Poor old Pat, shooting the man who killed her husband. It doesn't count as murder.* But it was murder, all the same. You killed him to stop him opening his mouth. And maybe you wanted his share of the money, just as he wanted yours.'

'That's not true.' Patricia's face suddenly tightened. 'I killed him for Charles.'

'You expect me to believe that?'

'Well, it wasn't for the money.' She laughed. 'No one's got that.'

'What do you mean?'

'Charles and Harry Ryal set up the money side. Anything we got went to Guernsey or Liechtenstein. They'd set up a series of trust funds and bought some Liberian companies off the peg. But nothing stayed in one place for long. It was all siphoned off to Austria and ended up in a single account. They said it was safer than Switzerland, nowadays. Ryal couldn't touch that account without one of our signatures, and we couldn't touch it without his. So the money will just stay there. For ever.'

The doorbell rang. Henry looking sheepish? Willy Wreningham himself, hopping from one foot to the other?

Blaines threw the cigar into the grate. He had left a pile

382

of ash on the arm of the chair. He thought she was telling the truth now. It explained why Ryal hadn't exposed her. Ryal knew she couldn't get the money without him; therefore, he assumed, she had to help him escape. And maybe she would have done – if he hadn't killed Charles Claybrook; and if Koslove hadn't arrived.

'It all went wrong,' she said in a low voice. 'Charles dying. Jess being involved. And then Greg.'

'Greg? What's he got to do with it?' Blaines said harshly. 'You gave him away to be with Chas. Don't you remember?'

He stood up and walked carefully across the room to the door. She didn't speak until his hand was on the doorknob.

'What will you do?'

'Me? Nothing.'

'Why not?'

'It wouldn't help anything. Not now. It would just hurt people. Jess. Nell. Me.'

'Will you come back?'

Blaines opened the door. She was standing now. You could read anything into those huge grey eyes. Anything from entreaty to hatred. From fear to love.

'Please, Eric. Will you come back?'

'That's a strange question,' he said.

He walked quickly down the hall and out of the front door. Henry, waiting on the pavement, gave him an apologetic shrug and opened the nearside rear door of the Daimler. Blaines did not look back as he climbed into the car. Once inside, he ignored what Wreningham was saying and stared at the council houses on the other side of the road.

He knew she was waiting in the doorway. Waiting for a look or a wave or even a word of farewell through the open window.

Waiting for an answer.